INVISIBLE KINGDOMS

SILURIAN TALES — VOLUME 2

Also by STEVEN UTLEY

Custer's Last Jump (with Howard Waldrop)
Ghost Seas
This Impatient Ape (poetry)
Career Moves of the Gods (poetry)
The Beasts of Love
Where or When

The 400-Million-Year Itch (Silurian Tales Volume 1)

AS EDITOR

Lone Star Universe (with Geo W. Proctor)
Passing for Human (with Michael Bishop)

INVISIBLE KINGDOMS

SILURIAN TALES — VOLUME 2

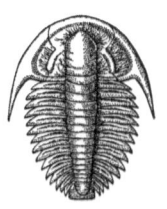

STEVEN UTLEY

T≋
p≋ Ticonderoga
publications

for

Michael and Jeri Bishop

Invisible Kingdoms by Steven Utley

Published by Ticonderoga Publications

Cover by Charles R. Knight
© The Field Museum #CK23T

Designed and edited by Russell B. Farr
Typeset in Sabon and Castellar

A Cataloging-in-Publications entry for this title is available from The National Library of Australia.

ISBN   978-1-921857-32-4 (hardcover)
            978-1-921857-33-1 (trade paperback)
            978-1-921857-34-8 (ebook)

Ticonderoga Publications
PO Box 29 Greenwood
Western Australia 6924

www.ticonderogapublications.com

10 9 8 7 6 5 4 3 2 1

Nothing is more treacherous than the peace of nature, when we fancy that the mountains were compacted to endure and to sleep for ever. Such material peace is a surface phenomenon, a mask for internal and incessant war. Matter is full of hidden springs and unexpressed affinities; some furtive influence here, some secret impulse there, will presently set in motion an insidious drift, destined to disrupt that equilibrium. A curious evolution will follow, or a sudden explosion.

George Santayana, The Last Puritan

We do not see things as they are, we see them as we are.

The Talmud

CONTENTS

SILURIAN DARKNESS

BY BARRY N. MALZBERG

Never met Steven Utley. Never in fact heard his voice. Furious bursts of correspondence intermittently and an idea for a co-edited anthology (alternate world in which sf writers wrote mainstream, Hemingway was a failed science fiction writer, John Campbell was an academic interested in racial memory, in which Horace Gold spawned Dianetics with Ron Hubbard) but we did not intersect in our sad shared universe. He had wit, style, cunning, terrifying knowledge of the Saurian Period and the kind of savagery intrinsic to the good writer. One of his earliest stories, published in *Fantasy & Science Fiction* was a dead-on parody of my Crazed Assassin series and made me twitch uncomfortably as I read it. No one should ever know your tricks that well, no one should ever be able to deploy them better than you. Steven Utley taught me humility.

This Introduction was commissioned a couple of years ago. The author, the publisher, the hapless correspondent had no idea that it would of necessity take on a funerary aspect nor that there would be some inferred necessity to sum a career which at that time seemed far from completion. Utley had returned to fierce production, never a novelist (which of course hurt him commercially) he was producing stories in abundance and apparent ease for anthologies and *Asimov's Magazine*, the stories were good, the prolificity was gratifying. Utley suffered from serious manic-depression (nowadays they call it "bipolar" of course) which had in the aggregate taken more than half of the span of his career away from him, he lost a decade starting in the late seventies, the nineties were troubled, the early years of the Millennium an absence. Then that last outpouring of stories, more steadily this time.

That Utley's manic-depression or bipolarity wrecked his career was never a secret, he wrote of this in his blog as explicitly as he could. Were he alive I would nonetheless probably suppress this fact anyway, it not being mine to release, in regard to a posthumous collection I feel no obligation to do so. It furnishes a compact and tragic insight into the mystery of a crack short story writer and creative force who stalled somewhere in his twenties and never quite got where he should. (Then again most science fiction writers never get where they should and they don't have this kind of tragic disability as explanation.)

Steven Utley was among a great flood of writers who came into science fiction in the early 70's essentially seduced by a vision of the field's future which would soon enough prove misguided. Those early 70's came in the wake of great social and literary upheaval, aided no little by political dynamite and seemingly endless psychotic war. Writers like Disch, Ballard, Silverberg, Sallis, Ellison appeared to be flourishing in the penumbra of this incandescent darkness and dear old science fiction was shaken to the rudders. For a few years at the decade's beginning I could delude myself into being the Voice of the Future, "The World Is Mine" I sung in the tones of Lewis Padgett's rabbits and in tandem with my peers I turned out a flood of serious quality lit, some of it science fiction, some of it disguised as science fiction, all of which sold miserably if at all. Editors caught on fast but there in Texas young writers like Utley, Sterling, Waldrop, Lisa Tuttle were absorbing all of this and dangerously thinking "I can do this too". Most of us never saw a chimera we didn't like and off they went to see the Wizard.

It didn't take long for the show to close. (The Wizard was already unavailable.) Tolkien had set the land mines and in 1965 Ballantine and Ice tripped them and fantasy on a long fuse eventually exploded, ten years later it was well on the way to making science fiction a small, diseased suburb. Meanwhile *Star Trek* had found a mass audience which in part turned toward science fiction and they did not want *The Drowned World* or *Dangerous Visions*, they wanted *Star Trek*'s literary equivalent (which they promptly got in spin-offs and novelizations). And then of course *Star Wars* was lurching toward our little Bethlehem, gathering speed and force with every step and soon to knock down most of the frail tents still standing. By the end of the 70's the science fiction which had sung like the Valkyries to Utley and Turkey City had become fantasy's claptrap suburb. Utley fled and did not return for a decade, many left for keeps. A few found succor and surcease by going to genres less ravaged but most to varying degrees simply quit. The vision of science fiction propounded for Turkey City was a kind of bear trap of the soul. The field reordered itself on terms of *Star Wars*, the early 70's self-visionaries who remained had to reconfigure themselves into fantasists or paler versions of themselves. Is it a dangerous statement to observe that *The Last Dangerous Visions*, so frantically hyped ("coming in six months" stated the Introductory material to *Again Dangerous Visions* published in 4/72) has not appeared 42 years later and will never appear? There are as many reasons and excuses as there are contributors to that cursed project but the truth is that no audience existed, probably ever existed for this project after that brief 1965–1972 period which Robert Silverberg deemed "a genuine revival". "Dawn of Nothing" is the title of an A. Bertram Chandler story published in *Astounding* 66 years ago. I'll buy into that.

So would Steven Utley, probably, but like most of his generational cohort, he had after all no place else to go. Bruce Sterling, the most successful Turkey Cityan, went on to a career, lurching ahead as a kind of technological maven who could decipher code; Sterling was by far the most adaptable of that Texas group and he has managed to hang on as a "futurologist" and emissary to the academic/corporate and collegial nexus (the infinitely adaptable Fred Pohl had managed this scam twenty years earlier and had become an expense account beacon to the masses) but a given cadre can perhaps only accommodate one renegade at a time and Sterling had taken up that position. Utley was merely among the most talented (and of course the most stubborn) on a darkling plain. For his last decade he lived in Tennessee and worked the margins with his Cretaceous/Jurassic/Silurian tales and produced a body of work which was characterized by nothing so much as a reflexive and bewildered dismay, hyped by his vast but stricken talent and an anger which can be seen at the center of all these stories.

I wrote James Sallis about a decade ago "I can see my own career as nothing so much as a 35 year affliction." Without undue projection I hope and with all the charity I can summon I suspect that Utley felt similarly. I will never know. I cannot claim to know. I never heard his voice, you see.

NEW JERSEY
14 MAY 2013

SILURIAN TALES — VOLUME 2

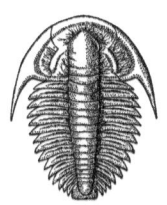

IN MEMORY OF
Steven Utley

INVISIBLE KINGDOMS

Mr. Cahill, a plum of a man during his prime, attained and passed the century mark in rather a prune-like condition. He was not only extremely long-lived but extremely wealthy, in direct consequence of his having given the world IntelliGelatin™, whence, the host of other products bearing his inviolable ™, such as AnswerMan™, TellMe™, MemoryMat™, and that salvation of many a writing-challenged author, Ediot™. Wealth enabled him to compensate for the ravages of age by enclosing himself in an exoskeleton of advanced design—personally designed, in fact, in close collaboration with one of IntelliGelatin™'s amazing progeny, MechMaven™. (Fittingly, only Mr. Cahill could be said to have a close relationship with the IntelliGelatin™ clan, though practically everyone else in the world necessarily had an intimate one.) Unaided, Mr. Cahill lacked the strength to do much more than wiggle his fingers and toes, but these feeble touches sufficed to direct the exoskeleton's complete array of proxies for his spindly limbs, dimmed eyes, deafened ears, whispery voice.

Thus, enclosed deep inside the glistening metal shell, the ridiculous remnant of Mr. Cahill's body served chiefly to direct souped-up NanoImmunoTechs™ to various trouble spots within itself, and to house Mr. Cahill's brain, as vital, alert, and formidable an organ as ever. Or so SpokesMom™ declared. During his first century Mr. Cahill had been not merely a productive member of society but rather an extroverted one as well. Thus, when, at the onset of his second century, he let it become known through SpokesMom™ that he no longer particularly cared for human society, that he now meant to enter upon a quite private existence, a popular newstar expressed doubt. "That doesn't sound like him at all."

"For all the time he's spent in the public eye," said SpokesMom™, "very few people see the real person."

"Still," said the newstar, "he's always been such an outgoing sort, with such an exuberant personality, like an overgrown kid."

"He's served the world admirably. Now he wants time for his favorite hobbies, time for himself. He's entitled to his privacy just like everyone else."

This last remark occasioned bitter laughter and impolite remarks among subversives and members of the criminal classes, many of whom had unhappy experiences with the bad boy of the IntelliGelatin™ family, PsychePick™. But they were, after all, subversives and criminals, and even if they had not been, nobody was going to call SpokesMom™ on it. SpokesMom™ was just too sweet and kindly, having been cunningly designed to warm even the hearts of people who had never got along with their own mothers. And, also, nobody wanted to have to answer to PsychePick™.

Nevertheless, a squad of officers and agents, in and out of uniform, representing the Federal Bureau of Investigation, the Customs Service, the Center for Disease Control, and several other agencies, backed by a meticulously prepared secret indictment, and commanded by a ferocious man named Selby, showed up at Mr. Cahill's door with the intention of taking him into their custody.

This was the culmination of an investigation that had begun some four hundred million years earlier.

It must be understood that the discovery (never mind how made) of a "spacetime anomaly" (never mind how created) had opened a way into a Paleozoic sort of Earth-like world (never mind how identified as such). Suffice it to say that this heteroclite phenomenon was duly exploited by an expedition comprising various scientific teams and a support force of U.S. Navy personnel.

Now imagine a pebble—no, a fair-sized stone—has just been dropped into a pool of still water. The stone is a Navy enlisted man who wished to supplement his income and meant to do so by smuggling Paleozoic biological specimens. He was apprehended at the point of returning to the 21st Century laden with contraband. There would be dramatic personality clashes, death threats, gunplay, close shaves, strong language, and a steamy romance to enliven the proceedings if Ediot™ were telling the story. A hero or heroine selected or synthesized from the team of investigators would display particular cleverness and pluck in following the smugglers' trail from that enlisted man through a number of intermediaries back to Mr. Cahill. In reality, though, such melodramatic possibilities weren't realized: the enlisted man promptly implicated a civilian member of the Paleozoic expedition, who told on another civilian member, and so forth. The various agencies, and there were plenty of them, cooperated in exemplary fashion. And so, to continue the original metaphor of the stone splashing into a pool of still water, the disturbance spreading outward from one feckless and hapless bluejacket ultimately washed away the careers of several members of the scientific community, on both this and that side (so to speak) of the famous "anomaly." Eventually, the ripples lapped at Mr. Cahill's doorstep, in the form of law enforcement officers, none of whom had ever visited the Paleozoic, or wanted to.

Selby and his people had had to show up, however, at several of Mr. Cahill's doors before they found the right one. SpokesMom™ had met them each time. The first time, asked to tender their authorizations for inspection, Selby demurred, and SpokesMom™ told him, "Oh, it's all right, Mister Selby, I now have durable power of attorney."

"That's impossible," he hissed. "It can't be legal. Artificial intelligence can't—"

"Oh, but I'm sure you're wrong, Mister Selby," and SpokesMom™ cited The Law, as it had been amended (though she did not mention this) by Mr. Cahill's money and influence.

Selby's color was by now not good. "Tell your Mister Cahill," he said to SpokesMom™, "that if I ever get my hands on him, I'll personally prep him for PsychePick™."

"Oh, I doubt that," said to SpokesMom™, with invincible motherly optimism.

Thereafter, whenever Selby and his people showed up somewhere in search of Mr. Cahill, SpokesMom™ met them graciously, always examined the documents as though seeing them for the first time, always allowed them to search the premises, always reminded them as they tromped in that they would be closely monitored, of course, and that they shouldn't scuff their heels on Mr. Cahill's parquet floors and expensive carpets. Always, they failed to find Mr. Cahill. Moreover, Mr. Cahill's various sumptuously appointed homes and offices had been discreetly stripped of anything that might have tied him to criminal activity occurring 400 million years in the past.

Eventually, though, through a process of elimination, the officers appeared at the right door, that of a supposedly empty warehouse in a disused industrial complex. After posting agents by the side and rear exits, Selby and three others entered the reception area, to be met, not by a receptionist, human or simulated, but, as usual, by a robutler somewhat on the order of a perambulating samovar. This robutler's appearance had always preceded that of SpokesMom™ by a few minutes, and by now Selby had said privately that if he didn't know better, he'd think it was the same robutler each time. It always brought with it a heavenly aroma of freshly brewed coffee, and a little door popped open in the front of its cylindrical body to reveal a Lazy Susan set with everything from cups to an assortment of freshly baked tea cakes. It always said, simulating the tone and attitude of somebody's idea of an English person, male, in domestic service, *circa* 1900, "Perhaps you would care for some refreshment," and Selby always said, "No," and occasionally one of the subordinate or otherwise attendant members of his party would go so far as to chime in with, "No, thank you very much." Selby would give the robutler the usual glowering look and ask, as usual, "Where is Mister Cahill?" and SpokesMom™ would appear (fresh, it always seemed, from taking an apple pie out of the oven) to examine their documents again and let them search the place. They would proceed warily, needlessly careful of the small humming housekeeping robots that darted expertly around their big clumsy feet, sucking up the dust they had tracked in. The first time, an agent had remarked on the robots' bug-like appearance, and SpokesMom™ had helpfully informed him that the things were modeled on prehistoric marine arthropods called trilobites, and added that there was one that stayed outside, shaped like a sea scorpion, that did the garden work. "For claws, it has various tools of a sharp, pointy nature, so be careful if you go poking around in the flower beds." Selby interpreted this as a thinly veiled threat of physical violence, but there was nothing he could do. It wasn't as though he could arrest SpokesMom™. After a few raids on Mr. Cahill's "places," the agents became inured to his notions of decoration, which ran to a sort of Victorian muchness with, here and there amid the lush appointments, the gleam of chrome on an ultra-modern appliance. "Looks like Jules Verne's subconscious," Agent Nolan had said, and another agent looked at her and asked, "Who?" and was told, "Never mind. The man's a packrat." This had prompted SpokesMom™ to say, "A packrat presides over *clutter*, Agent Nolan. Mister Cahill is a *collector*. A collector knowingly and willing imposes order on chaos. Are you sure nobody would like a fresh cruller?"

This time, things were different. This time, the robutler said, in a voice quite unlike anyone's idea of an English domestic servant, "This is Cahill speaking."

Selby and his people looked at the thing with the first fresh interest they had felt in weeks.

"Where are you, Mister Cahill?"

"Inside this machine. Close by. All around. Everywhere." A merry giggle, like that of a hyperactive nine-year-old, emanated from the ambulatory samovar. "They don't call me 'The World's Most Plugged-In Man' for nothing, you know."

"We have been trying to find you for some time now, Mister Cahill."

"So I hear. I've been under the weather for a while. I'm fine now."

"SpokesMom™ did not tell us that you were ill."

"SpokesMom™ is very protective."

"We've noticed. Do you understand why we're here?"

"Of course. SpokesMom™ has my mouthpiece standing by."

Some of the officers looked at one another in confusion. The robutler giggled. "Forgive me. I have a serious addiction to pulp fiction, among other ancient things. It dates me. I bet you didn't even bother to use truncheons on the people who fingered me. Anyway, my *attorney* is standing by. I'm being advised to shut up. I am advising my attorney to shut up. SpokesMom™ is advising me that I'll catch more flies with honey than with vinegar and I should be polite. Well, won't you please come on in?"

The robutler moved aside. The rear wall of the reception room slid open to reveal an airlock.

The officers regarded it nervously.

"A necessary precaution," said Mr. Cahill.

No one moved. Someone muttered a curse and someone else asked disgustedly, "Why don't we just storm the damn place?"

"This," said Selby, "really isn't acceptable."

"I'm afraid you are going to have to trust me on this." After several seconds, Mr. Cahill added, "Please," and then, "If you don't mind."

"Sir," someone asked Selby, "you think we can really talk him out of there—assuming he's really in there?"

"I know Cahill only by reputation. They say he got very weird around the time he turned eighty."

"Oh, *do* hurry, before I make my escape."

Selby asked, "Why *aren't* you escaping, Mister Cahill?"

The answer did not come quite at once. Then: "Perhaps I'm tired of evading arrest. It's too easy. Perhaps I feel like resisting arrest for a change. Actually, I have something to show you. Something wonderful."

"This will be better for everyone," said Selby, "if you'll just give yourself up and, ah, not—not do like this."

"Not do like this." Mr. Cahill sighed. "You're here to make the arrest of your career, and the best you can come up with is, Not Do Like This. The rhetoric of crime fighting has devolved lamentably since the days when the weed of crime bore bitter fruit. Please proceed, officers."

Selby exhaled harshly. "Okay, Nolan, you come with me. You two stay here. You know what to do."

He and Agent Nolan entered the airlock. The outer door slid shut behind them. A little rack holding respirator masks twirled before them, and SpokesMom™ appeared from somewhere and said, all motherly solicitude, "Be sure to put those on before you go inside. The mold and mildew counts are right through the ceiling."

Selby and Nolan donned the masks. The inner door slid open. Nolan said, "My God."

An expanse of slime-topped reeking mud extended the length and breadth of the building's interior. Selby and Nolan had been adequately briefed; they recognized the Paleozoic vista.

"What've you done?" growled Selby. "Jesus Christ, Cahill, what've you *done?*"

"Welcome to my forbidden garden." The agents could not pinpoint the source of Mr. Cahill's voice now that he no longer deigned to speak through a robutler. He seemed to be all around them, suffusing the very air. "The accommodations here are not up to my other places. This is, after all, just a converted warehouse."

Selby and Nolan breathed in the warm thick humid air and smelled green mud ripe with organic decay, and Selby suddenly sneezed, and Nolan coughed. Their throats itched.

"Something in here doesn't like us," Nolan said.

Selby plucked at the front of his shirt. "I'm drenched already. It's like a hothouse in here."

"It *is* a hothouse in here," said the disembodied Mr. Cahill. "This structure encloses as nearly perfect a replication of a Silurian estuarine ecosystem as it is possible to make. Just as a few dabs of genetic material supplied templates for full-grown Silurian organisms, a few samples of Silurian soil, air, water, sufficed for the synthesis of Silurian soil, air, water—the ingredients haven't changed in four hundred million years. I had hoped to create a Silurian marine environment, too, but—ahem—my source was cut off before I had everything I needed. And there's no point in creating an imbalanced ecosystem, at least not on this scale. I'm serious about my hobbies. But you probably know that already. You have, of course, visited my home in town. My Xanadu. Hands up if you know what I'm talking about. Either of you ever seen *Citizen Kane?* The original or the remakes? No? Well, then, you are just going to have to take my word for it that it is my Xanadu, with the important, the vital and essential difference that I collect things not just for the sake of collecting things, but for love of the things themselves." He giggled again.

"Bug-nut crazy," Selby whispered.

"Crazy or not," said Mr. Cahill, apparently taking no offense, "I have been fortunate in my long life to be able to indulge my appetite for all manner of delightful things. Good paintings, exotic tropical fish, rare blooms. You saw my lovely antiques, my first editions, comic books, manuscripts, trays of coins and beetles and butterflies, twentieth-century film memorabilia, classic toys—ah, my train sets! my toy soldiers! I never was a snob, you know. High art and low have always met smack in the middle of my brow. I used to joke that I was wracked by a unique philosophical dilemma. I knew what I liked, but how did I know what I knew?"

Selby stepped forward, and Mr. Cahill told him, "Please don't tread there. To your left you'll see a narrow catwalk curving away through that stand of bushy plants. Those are Barangwathia, by the way. Follow the catwalk. It will eventually lead you to me. But stop along the way to smell the psilophytes."

Selby and Nolan advanced carefully along the catwalk. It looped and dipped above the muddy earth, and both people decided independently of each other that anybody careless enough to fall off the catwalk would probably be sucked under instantly. They noticed rather large segmented things nosing around below, too, and wanted no part of them.

"You must believe me," said Mr. Cahill, "when I tell you I started out getting just a few prehistoric sea creatures for my exotic tropical fish tank, in the way, you see, of one-upping everyone else who had exotic tropical fish. What are piranha to sea scorpions and trilobites? Not even a coelacanth could compare to an ostracoderm. So. I would have the ultimate in exotic tropical fish. It all goes back to my sea-monkeys, you know. Remember sea-monkeys?"

Selby said, in not quite a questioning tone, "Sea-monkeys."

"A nickname for brine shrimp. They were advertised in comic books."

"Comic books," said Nolan, in a somewhat more questioning tone.

"Comic books," Mr. Cahill said, sounding impatient for the first time. "Sensationally written, mostly indifferently illustrated, luridly colored, cheaply printed periodicals. Superman. Spider-Man. Archie and his pals and gals. I loved the things. I have thousands in my collection."

"Of course," said Selby, patently unimpressed.

"Ah," said Nolan, though she patently still did not know what a comic book was, and they kept walking.

"Well, these comic books contained advertisements. The advertisement that captured my young self's imagination was an advertisement for sea-monkeys on the back cover of a comic book. I clipped the order blank from it and mailed it off with a money order, and after a while I received a little package containing brine-shrimp eggs. They came complete with instructions. I put them in water, and they hatched into brine shrimp. At first I was terribly disappointed, because they bore no resemblance to the creatures depicted in the advertisement, which were sort of *merprimates* with big happy smiles. But I became fascinated with them in spite of my initial disappointment. My own personal colony, my own *kingdom*, of sea-monkeys! I showed them off to my parents, relatives, friends. I *grieved* when they died. Brine shrimp are such brief-lived things. But there were always more where they'd come from. The same advertisement ran in the same comic books for years on end. I have since owned many exotic tropical fish, but my sea-monkeys, ah! I cannot say how many generations of brine-shrimp lived and died under my watchful eye. My empire of invertebrates, ha ha! You never forget your first love."

"I'm afraid," Selby said, "I still don't understand—"

"Of course you don't understand. I haven't finished explaining. So. Let's leap ahead the better part of a century from the halcyon days of my youth. When I saw the news about the hole in time, the expedition, the prehistoric world—ah! I burned with the torments of the damned. I'd never be able to visit, and yet. And yet. And *then*. Then I remembered the advertisement in the comic books. I remembered how it had excited my imagination and how I'd grown to adore my brine shrimp. And the line just popped into my head—'Boys, raise giant sea scorpions in your aquarium!'

"There was the pesky detail of the ban on removing specimens for other than scientific purposes. Of course, I dropped broad hints to sundry and all that I was willing and able to pay for an expedition or two out of petty cash. Penury makes scientists so opportunistic. It's not pretty to see. I *refused* to be satisfied with the gratitude of the scientific community, with having a new species of marine worm and an ancient landmark named in my honor in token of its esteem. They even tried to buy me off with a dead trilobite sealed inside a clear plastic paperweight. I contrived to stock my tank with fabulous creatures from Paleozoic seas. Then I started my Paleozoic terrarium. *Then* it occurred to me that glass-sided tanks were all well and fine in their way, but I wanted—I wanted the full Paleozoic experience. Creatures, plants, even air and soil. And here we are! What good is a collection that can't be shown off?"

The catwalk ended at a platform set against the rear wall of the building. Here they found what could only be Mr. Cahill, sitting slumped inside his exoskeleton, whose delicate mechanisms had withstood the effects of the simulated Paleozoic environment better than he. The humid atmosphere was ideal for bacteria and fungi, and they had made short work of his corpse.

"Jesus," said Selby. "And I thought it was just this damn homemade swamp that needed sterilizing."

Both he and Nolan let a squeak when they heard the dead man's disembodied voice again. "Tell 'em, SpokesMom™."

The air on the platform shimmered. SpokesMom™ appeared and said, sweetly, "Remember who has durable power of attorney. We intend to take good care of Mister Cahill's interests. I'm afraid you can't sterilize this place as yet, and perhaps not ever. Mister Cahill's options have hardly been exhausted."

"Mister Cahill is dead."

"Technically, not officially. Fortunately, he and the clan had become virtually consubstantial by the time the exoskeleton's life-support systems failed. As you can see, we were able to synthesize him. It was the least we could do. He *created* us. He was *family*. He'd been so determined to see his dream to fruition, we had no choice but to make it possible for him to do so. You are the first people he's had a chance to show it off to."

Selby bared his teeth. "We're also the *only* people who're going to see it, except the sterilization team."

"We will of course do all we legally can to preserve this garden, just as we mean to preserve his various collections, as memorials to him."

"The autopsy ought to be very interesting. From the looks of things, this particular memorial may have killed him!"

"Oh, I always *told* him to put on his respirator mask before he came in here," said SpokesMom™, a bit reproachfully and with a wetly glistening eye, "but he was just an overgrown boy, and you know how careless boys can be."

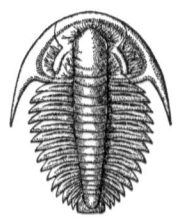

THE REAL WORLD

Everything felt like a dream. The flight attendants seemed to whisper past in the aisle. The other passengers were but shadows and echoes. Through the window, he could see the wing floating above an infinite expanse of cloudtop as flat and featureless as the peneplained landscapes of the Paleozoic. I'm just tired, he thought, without conviction.

Ivan forced his attention back to the laptop. He had called up an old documentary in which he himself appeared. "Resume," he said, very softly, and the image on the screen unfroze, and a familiar, strange voice said, "Plant life may actually have invaded the land during the Ordovician Period." Is that really me? he thought. My face, my eyes, I look so unlived-in. "We know about two dozen genera of land plant in the Silurian," and the screen first showed a tangle of creeping green tendrils at his younger self's feet, "such as these, which are called psilophytes," then a glistening algal mat. "The big flat things you see all over the mudflats are Nematophycus. The point is—" His earphone buzzed softly. "Pause," he murmured to the laptop, and the image on the screen froze once more. He said, "Hello?" and heard his brother say, "How's the flight?"

"Don. I hope you're not calling to rescind my invitation."

"Michelle'll pick you up at the airport as planned. I'm just calling to warn you and apologize in advance. I just got an invitation I can't refuse to a social event tomorrow evening."

"No need to apologize."

"Sure there is. This is a soiree of Hollywood swine."

"I can use the time to rest up for Monday."

"Well, actually, I'd sort of like to take you along. In case I need somebody intelligent to talk to. Unless, of course, you think you'd be uncomfortable."

Ivan examined the prospect for a moment, then said, "On Tuesday I'm going to read a paper on Paleozoic soils at the Page Museum. Young snotnoses keen to establish their reputations on the ruins of mine will be there. In light of that, I can't imagine how people who undoubtedly don't know mor from mull could possibly make me uncomfortable."

"Good. To the extent possible, I'll camouflage you in my clothing."

"What's the occasion for the party?"

"The occasion's the occasion."

"Let me rephrase the question. Who's hosting the party?"

"Somebody in the business who's throwing himself a birthday party. None of his friends will throw one for him, because he doesn't have any friends. If I hadn't come within an ace of an Oscar last month—which by the way is the limit of his long-term memory—it'd never have occurred to him to invite a writer. If I was a self-respecting writer and not a Hollywood whore, I'd duck it. But, hey, it'll be entertaining from a sociological point of view."

"As long as I get to ogle some starlets."

"Starlets'd eat you alive."

"That would be nice, too. Look, please don't think you have to entertain me the whole time I'm out there."

"Oh, this place'll afford you endless opportunities to entertain yourself."

"I look forward to it."

"See you soon."

"Goodbye."

"Resume," he murmured to the laptop. "The point is."

"The point is," his younger self said, "they can't have sprung up overnight, even in the geologic sense. The Silurian seas are receding as the land rises, and the plant invasion's not a coincidence. But there were also opportunities during the Ordovician for plants to come ashore in a big way. Only they didn't. Maybe there was lethal ozone at ground level for a long time after the atmosphere became oxygen-rich. If so, a lot of oxygen had to accumulate before the ozone layer rose to the higher levels safe enough for advanced life-forms. Our—"

"Stop," he said, and thought, What a lot of crap. Then he sighed deeply and told the laptop, "Cue the first Cutsinger press conference."

After a moment, Cutsinger's image appeared on the screen. He was standing at a podium, behind a brace of microphones. He said, "I am at pains to describe this phenomenon without resorting to the specialized jargon of my own field, which is physics. Metaphor, however, may be inadequate. I'll try to answer your questions afterward."

This is afterward, Ivan thought bitterly, and, yes, I have a question.

"The phenomenon," Cutsinger's image went on, "is, for want of a better term, a space-time anomaly—a hole, if you will, or a tunnel, or however you wish to think of it. It appears, and I use the word advisedly, appears to connect our present-day Earth with the Earth as it existed during the remote prehistoric past. We've inserted a number of robot probes, some with laboratory animals, into the anomaly and retrieved them intact, though some of the animals did not survive. Judging both from the biological samples obtained and from the period of rotation of this prehistoric Earth, what we're talking about is the Siluro-Devonian boundary in mid-Paleozoic time, roughly four hundred million years ago. Biological specimens collected include a genus of primitive plant called Cooksonia and an extinct arthropod called a—please forgive my pronunciation if I get this wrong—a trigonobartid. Both organisms are well-known to paleontologists, and DNA testing conclusively proves their affinities with all other known terrestrial life-forms.

"Thus, for all practical purposes, this is our own world as it existed during the Paleozoic Era. However, it cannot literally be our own world. We cannot travel directly backward into our own past."

Ivan looked up, startled, as a flight attendant leaned in and said something.

"I'm sorry, what?"

"We'll be landing soon. You'll have to put that away now."

"Of course."

She smiled and withdrew. He looked at the laptop. "The anomaly," Cutsinger was saying, "must therefore connect us with another Earth."

"Quit."

Michelle met him as he came off the ramp. For a second, he did not recognize her and could only stare at her when she called his name. He could not immediately connect this young woman with his memories of her as a long-limbed thirteen-year-old girl with braces on her teeth; then, he had never been quite able to decide whether she was going to grow up pretty or goofy-looking. It had been a matter of real concern to him: he had first seen her cradled tenderly in her mother's arms, eyes squeezed shut and oblivious of her beatific expression; baby Michelle was not asleep, though, but had seemed to be concentrating fiercely on the mother's warmth, heartbeat, and wordless murmured endearments. Tiny hands had clasped and unclasped rhythmically, kneading air, keeping time, and when Ivan had gently touched one perfect pink palm and her soft digits closed on, but could not encircle, his calloused fingertip, the contrast smote him in the heart. He had no children of his own, and had never wanted any, but he knew immediately that he loved this child. He had murmured it to her, and to Don and Linda he said, "You folks do good work."

The discontinuous nature of these remembered Michelles, lying unconformably upon one another, heightened his sense of dislocation as he now beheld her. She was fresh out of high school, fair-skinned, unmade-up, with unplucked eyebrows and close-cropped brown hair. It cannot be her, he told himself. But then the corners of her mouth drew back, the firm, almost prim line of her lips fractured in a smile, and she delivered herself of pleasant, ringing laughter that had a most unexpected and wonderful effect on him: his head suddenly seemed inclined to float off his shoulders, and he found himself thinking that a man might want to bask for years in the radiance of that smile, the music of that laughter. Now he was convinced, and he let himself yield to the feeling of buoyant happiness. As a child she had had the comically intent expression of a squirrel monkey, but her father and her uncle had always been able to make her laugh, and when she had the effect was always marvelous. She closed with him and hugged him tightly, and his heart seemed to expand until it filled his chest.

As they headed into the hills north of Hollywood, she concentrated on her driving and he stole glances at her profile. He decided that the haircut suited her vastly better than the unfortunate coiffures she had been in the habit of inflicting upon herself. Well, he thought, you turned out pretty after all.

And he thought, I love you still, darling, and I always shall.

Whether it's really you or not.

Seated at the metal table, screened from the sun by the eucalyptus tree and with his book lying open on his lap, he admired the blue and orange blooms and banana-shaped leaves of the bird of paradise flowers in his brother's backyard. He could look past them and the fence and right down the canyon on the hazy blur of the city. The morning had begun to heat up, and there was a faint ashy taste to the air. He noticed a small dark smudgy cloud where the farthest line of hills met the sky.

Michelle emerged from the house carrying two ice-flecked bottles of imported beer on a tray. She set it on the table and sat down across from him and said, "Daddy's still talking to the thing that would not die."

He nodded in the direction of the smudgy cloud. "I hope that's not what I think it is."

She looked. "Fires in the canyons. It's the season." She opened one of the beers and handed it to him. "What're you reading?"

Unnecessarily, he glanced at the spine. "*The Story of Philosophy*, by Will Durant."

She clearly did not know what to say in response.

"It's about the lives of the great philosophers," he went on after a moment, "and their thoughts on being and meaning and stuff."

She made a face. "It sounds excruciating."

"It is. I think the great philosophers were all wankers, except for Voltaire, who was funny. Nietzsche was probably the wankiest of the lot."

"Why're you reading it if you think it's so awful?"

"Let's just say I'm in full-tilt autodidact mode these days. Nowadays I carry the same three books with me everywhere I go. This one, a book about quantum mechanics, and the latest edition of the *People's Almanac*. The almanac's the only one I really enjoy."

"What's that, quantum mechanics?"

"Didn't they teach you anything in school? Advanced physics. Probably just a lot of philosophical wanking set to math. But it interests me. Somewhere between physics and philosophy is the intersection of the real world. Out of our subjective perception of an objective reality of energy and matter comes our interpretation of being and meaning."

"Whatever you say, Uncle Ivan."

"Are you going to this party tomorrow night?"

She shook her head emphatically. "I'm going to a concert with my boyfriend. Anyway, I don't much care for movie people. Oh, some of them are nice, but—I've never been comfortable around actors. I can never tell when they aren't acting. No, that's not it, it just makes me tired trying to figure out when they're acting and when they're not. The directors are mostly pretentious bores, and the producers just make Daddy crazy." She gazed down the canyon. "The fact is, I don't much like movies. But my boyfriend"—she gave him a quick, self-conscious glance—"my boyfriend loves 'em. And he loves dinosaurs. He says he judges a movie by whether he thinks it'd be better or worse with dinosaurs in it."

"Did he have anything to do with that recent version of *Little Women*?"

"No. He's not in the industry, thank God. I wouldn't go out with anybody who is. I wonder what genius thought of setting *Little Women* in prehistoric times. Anyway, you'd be surprised how many movies flunk his dinosaur test."

"Probably I wouldn't."

"He and Daddy like sitting around coming up with lunatic premises for movies. What they call high-concept. He cracks Daddy up. Daddy says he could be making movies every bit as bad as anybody else's if he just applied himself."

"Give me an example of high-concept."

"'Hitler! Stalin! And the woman who loved them both!'" They laughed together. Then she suddenly regarded him seriously. "I hope you're not going to let yourself be overawed by these people."

"People don't awe me." She looked doubtful, so he added, "They can't begin to compete with what awes me."

"What's that? What awes you?"

He leaned sideways in his chair, scooped some dirt out of a flowerbed. "This," he said, and as he went on talking he spread the dirt on his palm and sorted through it with his index finger. "When we were kids, teenagers, while your daddy sat up in his room figuring out how to write screenplays, I was outdoors collecting bugs and fossils. We neatly divided the world between us. He got the arts, I got the sciences. Even our tastes in reading— while he was reading, oh, Fitzgerald and Nabokov, I'd be reading John McPhee and Darwin's journal of the voyage of the *Beagle*. There was a little overlap. We both went through phases when we read mysteries and science fiction like mad. I'd read *The Big Sleep* or *The Time Machine* and pass 'em on to Don, and then we'd discuss 'em. But we were usually interested in different parts of the same books. Don was interested in the characters, the story. Who killed so and so. I loved Raymond Chandler's, Ross Macdonald's descriptions of the southern California landscape. I was like a tourist. My feeling was that setting is as vital as plot and characterization. A good detective-story writer had to be a good travelogue writer, or else his characters and action were just hanging in space. Don argued that a good story could be set anywhere, scenery was just there to be glanced at. If the plot was good, it would work anywhere."

"Daddy says there are only three or four plots. At least he says that out here there are only three or four."

"Well, anyway, your dad and I have art and science all sewed up between us. Science to help us find out what the world is. Art to—I don't know, art's not my thing, but I think—"

"Daddy says you're trying to write a book."

"Trying is about as far as I've got so far. I have all the raw material, but . . . " But. "I'm not creative. Anyway, I think we have to have both science and art. Everything in the universe partakes in some way of every other thing."

"What about philosophy?"

"Maybe it's what links science and art."

"Even if it's a lot of wanking?"

"Even wanking has its place in the scheme of things. What about this boyfriend?"

"Interesting segue."

"Is this a serious thing? Serious like marriage?"

She shrugged, then shook her head. "I want to do something with my life before I get into that."

"What?"

"I wish I knew. I feel I have so much to live up to. Your side of the family's all overachievers. My father's a hot Hollywood screenwriter. My uncle, the scientist, has done just the most amazing things. My grandparents were big wheels in Texas politics. It's almost as bad as having movie-star parents. The pressure on me to achieve is awful."

"It was probably worse for the Huxleys."

"Mom's always felt outclassed. Her family'd always just muddled along. She felt utterly inadequate the whole time she and Dad were married."

"With a little help from him, she made a beautiful daughter."

She looked pleased by the compliment but also a little uncomfortable. "Thank you for saying that."

"It's true."

"You used to call me Squirrel Monkey."

Don came outside looking exasperated. "Ever reach a point in a conversation," he said, "where, you know, you can't go on pretending to take people seriously who don't know what they're talking about?"

"Are we talking rhetorically?"

Don laughed a soft, unhappy sort of laugh. He indicated the unopened bottle of beer. "Is that for me?"

"Just that one, Daddy."

"I need it." He said to Ivan, "Tell me the stupidest thing you've ever heard. I'm trying to put something into perspective here."

Ivan thought for a moment. "Well, there was the low point, or maybe it was the high point, of my blessedly short stint as a purveyor of scientific knowledge to college freshman. I had a student tell me in all earnestness that an organism that lives off dead organisms is a sacrilege."

Don laughed again, less unhappily than before. "Been on the phone with someone who makes deals and gives off movies as waste. He's got the hottest idea of his life. He's doing a full-blown remake of *The Three Musketeers* in Taiwan."

Ivan felt his eyebrows go up. He made them come back down.

Don nodded. "That was my reaction. I said to him, I gather you've taken a few liberties with the novel. And he said, Novel? By Alexandre Dumas, I said. You mean it? he said. Excuse me for a moment, and he gets on his AnswerMan and says, To legal, do we have exclusive rights to alleged novel by Doo-dah-duh. Dumas, I scream, Dumas, you dumbass!" He shook his head as though to clear it of an irritating buzz. "Well. I go on and tell him the novel's in the public domain, Dumas has been dead for a little while now. He drums his fingers on his desktop. He screws his face into a mask of thoughtfulness. He says, Well, it's always best to be sure, because if what you say is true, we'll have to see about getting it pulled out of circulation. I beg his pardon. He says, We don't want people confusing it with our book based on the movie."

Ivan said, "He's going to novelize a movie based on a novel?"

"Sure. The novel based on *Pride and Prejudice* was on the best-seller list."

Michelle said, "Hooray for Hollywood," and Ivan raised his bottle in a toast.

Don raised his as well. "Here's to L.A., Los Angeles del Muerte!"

Then Michelle excused herself and went inside. Ivan said, "Every time I see her, she's bigger, smarter, prettier, and nicer."

"That's how it works if you only see her once every few years. Move out here, be her doting uncle all the time."

"Oh, I would love to. It would be good to see more of you, too. But—" To avoid his brother's expectant look, Ivan turned toward the canyon. "Call me a crank on the subject, but I'll never live on an active plate margin."

"Christ."

"Geologically speaking, these hills have all the structural integrity of head cheese. They piled up here after drifting in across a prehistoric sea from God knows where. One of these times, Don, the earth's going to hiccup, and all these nice houses and all you nice people in them are going to slide all the way down that canyon."

Don shrugged. "Mobility is what California's all about. Everything here is from someplace else. The water comes from Colorado. These flowers," and he extended his arm and delicately touched a leaf on one of the bird-of-paradise flowers as though he were stroking a cat under its jaw, "are South African. The jacaranda you see all over town are from Brazil, the eucalyptus trees are from Australia. The people and the architecture are from everywhere you can think of." He took a long pull on his bottle, draining it. "That's the reason California's such a weird goddamn place. Because nothing really belongs here."

"I think it's fascinating. I wouldn't live here for anything—not even for you and Michelle, I'm sorry. But it is certainly fascinating."

"Oh, absolutely, I agree, it is. In a big, ugly, tasteless, intellectually numbing kind of way."

"What do you do for intellectual stimulation?"

"I read your monographs."

"Really?"

"No, but I have copies of all of them."

Later, stretched across the bed with his eyes closed and the cool fresh sheet pulled up to his sternum, Ivan thought, Clever, talented Don. It had never occurred to him before that his brother considered his work at all . . . .

He did not think he had fallen asleep, yet he awoke with a start. He was hot and parched. He slipped into a robe and eased into the hallway. In the kitchen, he filled a glass with cold filtered water from the jug in the refrigerator and sat down with his back to the bar to look out through the glass doors, at the lights of the city. There was a glowing patch of sky, seemingly as distant as the half moon, where the dark smudgy cloud had been that afternoon.

When he returned to his room, he sat on the edge of the bed and took his well-thumbed *People's Almanac* from the nightstand. He opened it at random and read a page, and sound amused, then set it aside and picked up the laptop. "Where were we?"

The screen lightened. "That's a good question," Cutsinger was saying. He chuckled into the microphones. "I know, because my colleagues and I have asked it of each other thousands of times since the anomaly was discovered. Every time, the answer's been the same. Simply traveling through time into the past is impossible. Simply to do so violates the laws of physics, especially our old favorite, the second law of thermodynamics. Simply to enter the past is to alter the past, which is a literal and actual contradiction of logic. Yet the fact is, we have discovered this space-time anomaly which connects our immediate present with what from all evidence is the Earth as it existed during mid-Paleozoic times. The only way the laws of physics and logic can accommodate this awkward fact is if we quietly deep-six the adjective 'simply' and run things out to their extremely complicated conclusion. We must posit a universe that stops and starts, stops and starts, countless billions of times per microsecond, as it jumps from state to state. As it does so, it continually divides, copies itself. Each copy is in a different state—that is, they're inexact copies. A separate reality exists for every possible outcome of every possible quantum interaction. Inasmuch as the number of copies produced since the Big Bang must be practically infinite, the range of difference among the realities must be practically infinite as well. These realities exist in parallel with one another. Whatever we insert into the anomaly—probes, test animals, human beings—are not simply going to travel directly backward into our own past. Instead, they're going to travel somehow to another universe, to another Earth which resembles our Earth as it was in the Paleozoic. Yes? Question?"

From offscreen came a question, inaudible to Ivan, but on the screen Cutsinger nodded and answered, "Well, it's probably pointless to say whether this sort of travel occurs in any direction—backward, sideward, or diagonally."

From offscreen, someone else asked, "If there are all these multiple Earths, when you're ready to come back through this hole you're talking about, how can you be sure you'll find your way back to the right Earth?"

"To the very best of our knowledge, this hole as you call it has only two ends. One here and now, one there and then. Next question?"

You glib son of a bitch, Ivan thought.

After the robot probes had gone and apparently come back through the space-time anomaly, the next step was obvious to everyone: human beings must follow. It was decided that two people should go through together. At the outset, in the moment it had taken the phrase "time travel to the prehistoric world" to register in his mind, Ivan had made up his mind—yes, absolutely, I want to go! "Presented with the opportunity to traverse time and explore a prehistoric planet," he had written to Don, "who wouldn't?" In the weeks and months that followed, however, through all the discussion and planning sessions, he had never quite believed that he had a real chance to go. Partly it was a matter of funding: x amount of money in the kitty simply equaled y number of people who would get to go on any Paleozoic junket. Partly it was a matter of prestige: given, practically speaking, an entire new planet to explore—everything about it, everything about the cosmos it occupied, for that matter, being four hundred million years younger, any scientist could make a case for his or her particular field of inquiry. Ivan did not, of course, despise his work in the least or see any need to apologize for it; moreover, he did not take personally—too personally, anyway—one or another of the likelier candidates' feigned confusion over pedology, the study of the nature and development of children, and pedology, soil science. The first few times, he affected amusement at the joke fellow soil scientists told on themselves, which in its simplest form was that the insertion of a single soil scientist into Silurian time would result in that remote geological period's having more scientist than soil. It was the sort of extremely specialized joke specialists told. Like any specialized joke, its charm vanished the instant that an explanation became necessary. Real soil would have only just started, geologically speaking, to collect amid the Silurian barrens; pedogenesis would be spotty and sporadic; rock could weather away to fine particles, but only the decay of organic matter could make sterile grit into nurturing dirt, and while organisms abounded in the Silurian seas, they would have only just started, again, geologically speaking, to live and die—and decompose—on land.

"Oh. I see. Ha, ha."

The joke had escaped from the soil scientists at some point and begot tortuous variations in which twenty-first-century pedology overwhelmed and annihilated the reality of primordial soil: why (went one version), the weight of the terminology alone—soil air, soil complexes, associations and series, soil horizons, moisture budgets, aggregates and peds, mor and mull and all the rest of it—would be too much for such thin, poor, fragile stuff as one might expect to find sprinkled about in mid-Paleozoic times.

He had tried to look and sound amused, and to be a good sport overall, whenever he heard the joke in any of its mutated forms. After all, it was never intended really maliciously; it merely partook of a largely unconscious acceptance of a hierarchy of scientists. Physics and astronomy were glamour fields. Geology and paleontology were comparatively rough-hewn but nonetheless logical choices; moreover, they were perennially popular with the public, a crucial concern when public money was involved. Pedology was none of the above. He liked to think that he did not have it in himself to be envious, and so, with unfailing good humor, he agreed that there certainly would be a lot of geology at hand in the Paleozoic, mountains, valleys, strata, and the like. And as for paleozoology, the Paleozoic would be nothing if not a big aquarium stocked with weird wiggly things and maybe a few big showy monsters.

And as for the crazy night skies, my oh my!

And even Kemal Barrowclough, paleobotanist, could get up and describe some harsh interior landscape enlivened only by the gray-green of lichens, "the first true land plants, because, unlike the psilophytes and lycopods we find clinging to the low moist places, close to water, always looking over their shoulders, so to speak, to make sure they haven't strayed too far, lichens, by God, *have taken the big step*," and there would scarcely be a dry eye among the listeners, except for Kemal's sister, Gulnar, herself a paleobotanist. Gulnar specialized in psilophytes.

Throughout the discussions, Ivan had felt that, in effect, DeRamus had but to point to his rocks and say, "*Old!*" or Gabbert to his sky and say, "*Big!*" and nothing, nothing, he could have said about microbiotic volume in the histic epipedon, or humic acid precipitation, or the varieties of Paleozoic mesofauna he expected to sift through a tullgren funnel, would have meant a damn thing. Rather than enter his saprotrophs in unequal and hopeless competition against thrust faults, sea scorpions, or prehistoric constellations, he would wait until all around the table had settled back, glowering but spent, then softly clear his throat and calmly explain all over again that the origin and evolution of soil ranked among the major events in the history of life on Earth, that soil was linked inextricably to that major event of mid-Paleozoic time, life's emergence onto land.

It had been by dint of this stolid persistence that he had, in the minds of enough of his peers, ultimately established himself as precisely the sort of knowledgeable, dedicated, persevering person who should be a member of the Paleozoic expedition—and had also established, by extension, all soil scientists everywhere, in every geologic age, as estimable fellows.

When finally, Stoll had announced who would go, Ivan, stunned to speechlessness, could only gape as each of his colleagues shook his hand; almost a minute passed before he found his voice. "Wonders never cease," he had said.

Almost the next thing he remembered was looking over the back of the man who had knelt before him to check the seals on his boots. Cutsinger had stood leaning back against the wall with his arms crossed and watched the technicians work. He smiled ruefully at Ivan and said, "Tell me how you *really* feel."

"Like the first astronaut to spacewalk must've, just before he went out and did it."

"That guy had an umbilical cord," said Dilks, who sat nearby, surrounded by his own satellite system of technicians. He did not go on to say the obvious: We don't.

"Just don't lose sight of the anomaly once you're through," Cutsinger said.

"Right now," Ivan said, "getting back through the anomaly doesn't concern me quite as much as going through the first time and finding myself sinking straight to the bottom of the sea."

"We sent a probe in to bird-dog for you. The hole's stabilized over solid ground. You'll arrive high and dry." Cutsinger nodded at Dilks. "Both of you, together."

Ivan flexed his gloved fingers and said, "It's just the suit," and thought, It isn't *only* just the suit, but part of it's the suit. The suit was bulky and heavy and had to be hermetic. He and Dilks had to carry their own air supplies and everything else they might conceivably need, lest they contaminate the pristine Paleozoic environment and induce a paradox. The physicists, Ivan and Dilks privately agreed, were covering their own asses.

Cutsinger asked Dilks, "Anything you're especially concerned about?"

Dilks grinned. "Not liking the scenery. Not seeing a single prehistoric monster."

Cutsinger smiled thinly. "Careful what you wish for."

"Time to seal up," said one of the technicians. Another raised a clear bubble helmet and carefully set it down over Ivan's head. The helmet sealed when twisted to the right.

"All set?" said the chief technician's voice in the helmetphone.

"All set," said Ivan.

Technicians stood by to lend steadying hands as the two suited men got to their feet and lumbered into an adjoining room for decontamination. They stood upon a metal platform. Their equipment had already been decontaminated and stowed.

Ivan gripped the railing that enclosed the platform; he did not trust his legs to hold him up. This is it, he told himself, and then, This is what? He found that he still could not entirely believe what he was about to do.

The wall opposite the door pivoted away. The metal platform began to move on rails toward a ripple in the air.

Everything turned to white light and pain.

They considered their reflections in the full-length mirror. Don and Ivan were two solidly built, deep-chested, middle-aged men, unmistakably products of the same parents. Michelle stood framed in the doorway. Her expression was dubious. "Daddy," she said, "they'll never accept him as one of their own. No offense, Uncle Ivan, but you don't have Hollywood hair and teeth. They'll be horrified by what you've done to your skin. Daddy's tanned and fit because he works out. You're brown and hard and leathery because you work."

Don said to Ivan, "Maybe they'll mistake you for a retired stuntman."

"Why retired?"

"What other kind is there any more?"

"I feel strange in these clothes, but I have to admit that they feel good and look good. They look better than I do."

"This is up-to-the-moment thread."

"I look like a rough draft of you."

"Whatever you do," Michelle said, "don't say you're a scientist. 'Scientist' cuts no ice here."

Don flashed a grin along his shoulder at his brother and said, "Absolutely do not say you're a pedologist. They won't have any idea what a pedologist is, unless they think it's the same thing as a pedophile."

"Someone asks what you are," Michelle said, "they mean, What's your astrological sign?"

"I don't know my astrological sign."

She made a horrified face. "Get out of California!"

"Tell 'em anything," Don said, "it doesn't matter, they'll run with it, tell you they just knew all along you were a Taurus or whatever."

"Say you're a time-traveler," Michelle told him. "But don't be hurt if they're not even impressed by that. It's not like they've ever done anything real."

The afternoon was warm, golden, perfect, as they wound their way along Mulholland Drive. Don had put the top down, though it meant wearing goggles to screen out airvertising. Ivan sat fingering the unfamiliar cloth of his U borrowed clothing and admiring the fine houses. They turned in at a gate in a high stucco wall, passed a security guard's inspection, and drove on. Around a bend in the driveway, Ivan saw a monstrous house, an unworkable fusion of Spanish and Japanese architectural quirks framed by the rim of hills beyond. Don braked to stop in front of the house and simply abandoned the car—if he gave the keys to someone, Ivan did not see it happen.

Just at the door, Don turned to Ivan and said, "Let me take one more look at you."

Ivan held his arms away from his body, palms forward.

The women were breathtaking. Don laughed. "You're the most confident-looking guy I've ever seen. You look like Samson about to go wreak havoc among the Philistines."

"What've I got to be nervous about?"

They went inside and immediately found themselves in a crowd of mostly gorgeous chattering people, all seemingly intent upon displaying themselves, all dressed with an artful casualness. As he followed Don through the room, Ivan admired their physical flawlessness. The women were breathtaking. They were shorter or taller than one another, paler or darker, blonde or brunette, but nearly all fashioned along the same very particular lines—slim and boyish save for improbably full breasts. On two or three occasions, Don paused and turned to introduce Ivan to someone who smiled pleasantly, shook Ivan's hand, and looked through or around him.

Ivan was, therefore, taken aback when a lovely woman approached from his brother's blind side, touched Ivan fleetingly on the forearm, and said, "I'm so glad you came, it's so good to see you." She wore a short skirt, belted at the waist. Her back, flanks, and shoulders were bare. The tips of her breasts were barely covered by two narrow, translucent strips of fabric that crossed at the navel and fastened behind her neck.

"It's so good to see you, too," Ivan said.

She said, "I have to go get after the help for a second, but don't you go away," and vanished.

Ivan caught up with Don and said, "Who was that?"

"Who was who?"

A simply pretty rather than gorgeous girl paused before Ivan with a food-laden tray and smiled invitingly; he helped himself to some unrecognizable but delicious foodstuff. Before he could help himself to seconds, she was gone. He consoled himself with a drink plucked from another passing try.

The singer fronting the combo was Frank Sinatra, who snapped his fingers and smiled as he sang "My Way." According to a placard, the skinny, artfully scruffy young men accompanying him were The Sex Pistols. Although none of the real people in the room appeared to notice when the song ended, Frank Sinatra thanked them for their applause and told them they were beautiful. Ivan caught up with the girl with the food tray and had helped himself to a snack before he realized that she was a different girl and it was a different snack. She was in her own right, however, and the snack was as mysterious and delicious as the first had been. The combo began playing again, somewhat picking up the tempo. As Frank Sinatra sang that he didn't know what he wanted, but he knew how to get it, Don turned, pointed vaguely, and said to Ivan, "I see somebody over there I have to go schmooze with. I'd introduce you, but he's a pig."

"So go schmooze. I can look after myself."

"You sure?"

"Positive."

"Okay. Ogle some starlets—I'll be back in a mo."

As though she had rotated into the space vacated by Don, a long tawny woman appeared before Ivan. Her waist was as big around as his thigh. Her high breasts exerted a firm, friendly pressure against his lapels. He thought she had the most kissable-looking mouth he had ever seen. She said, "I'm sure I know you."

Ivan smiled. "I was one of the original Sex Pistols."

"Really!" She glanced over her shoulder at the hologram, then peered at Ivan again. "Which one?"

Ivan nodded vaguely in the band's direction. "The dead one."

She pouted fetchingly. "Who are you, really?"

He decided to see what would happen if he disregarded Don and Michelle's advice. He said, "I'm a pedologist."

"Oh," she said, "you specialize in child actors? No, wait, that's a foot specialist, right?" She looked doubtfully at his hands, which were big and brown, hard and knobby. "Is your practice in Beverly Hills?"

"Gondwanaland."

"Ah," she said, and nodded, and looked thoughtful, and lost interest. Ivan let her rotate back the way she had come and then sidled into and through the next room.

The house was a maze of rooms opening onto other rooms, seemingly unto infinity; inside of five minutes, he decided that he was hopelessly lost. Surrounded by small groups of people talking animatedly among themselves, he turned more or less in place, eavesdropping casually. He quickly gathered that most of the people around him believed in astrology, psychics, cosmetic surgery, and supply-side economics, and that some few among them were alarmed by the trend toward virtual actors. He overheard a tanned, broad-shouldered crewcut man say to a couple of paler and less substantial men, "What chance have I got? I'm losing parts to John Wayne, for chrissake! He's been dead for decades, and he's a bigger star than ever."

"Costs less than ever, too," said the wispier of the other two men, "and keeps his right-wing guff to himself."

The broad-shouldered man scowled. "I don't want what happened to stuntmen to happen to actors!"

"Oh, don't be alarmist," the wispy man said. "No one's going to get rid of actors. Oh, they might use fewer of them, but—besides, stuntmen're holding their own overseas, and—"

THE REAL WORLD ✱ STEVEN UTLEY

"Crazy goddamn Aussies and Filipinos!"

"—and," the wispy man said insistently, "the films do have a significant following in this country. For some viewers, it's not enough to see an actor who looks like he's risking his life. They want the extra kick that comes from knowing an actor really *is* risking his life."

The third man had a satisfied air and was shaped like a bowling pin; his white suit and scarlet ascot enhanced the resemblance. "Until that happens," he told the broad-shouldered man, "better get used to playing second fiddle to John Wayne. Right now, I got development people e-synthing old physical comedians from the nineteen-whenevers. Buster Keaton, Harold Lloyd, and Jackie Chan. People still bust a gut laughing at those guys."

"Never heard of 'em."

"You will. Because I'm putting 'em together in a film. Lots of smash-up, fall-down. Sure, we use computers to give 'em what they never had before—voices, color—personalities! But when people see Buster Keaton fall off a moving train, they know there's no fakery."

"Who the hell cares if some dead guy risks his life?"

The bowling-pin-shaped man jabbed a finger into the air.

"Thrills are timeless!"

Glimpsing yet another pretty girl with a food tray, Ivan exited right, through a doorway. He somehow missed the girl, made a couple of turns at random, and was beginning to wonder amusedly if he had happened upon another space-time anomaly when he suddenly and unexpectedly found himself outdoors, on the tiled shore of a swimming pool as big, he decided, as the Tethys Sea— Galveston Bay, at least. There were small groups of MB people ranged at intervals around the pool and one person in the water, who swam to the edge, pulled herself up, and was revealed to be a sleekly muscular Amazon. As she toweled her hair, she let her incurious gaze alight fleetingly on Ivan, then move on; she was as indifferent to his existence as though he were another of the potted palms. She rose lithely, draped her towel over one exquisite shoulder, and walked past him into the house.

Ivan sipped his drink, thrust his free hand into his trousers pocket, and ambled toward the far end of the pool and an array of women there. At a table in their midst, like a castaway on an island circled by glistening succulent mermaids, a bald, fat, fortyish man sat talking animatedly to himself. A waiter stood at the ready behind a cart laden with liquor bottles. A large rectangular object, either a man or a refrigerator stuffed into a sports jacket, took up space nearby. Just as this large object startled Ivan by looking in his direction, the fat man suddenly laughed triumphantly, leaped to his feet, and clapped his hands. He pointed at bottles on the cart, and the waiter began to fuss with them. The fat man turned, looked straight at Ivan, evidently the only suitable person within arm's reach, and pulled him close. "Help me celebrate," he said, and to the large object, "Larry, get the man a chair." Larry pulled a chair back from the table, waited for Ivan to sit, then moved off a short distance. The fat man introduced himself as John Rubis and looked as though he expected Ivan to have heard of him. Ivan smiled pleasantly and tried to give the impression that he had.

"I am *real* happy!" Rubis pointed at his own ear, and Ivan realized that there was an AnswerMan plugged into it. "The word from the folks at Northemico is go!" He indicated the liquor cart. "What can I get you?"

"Brought my own. Congratulations." Ivan toasted him, and they drank. Rubis smacked his lips appreciatively. Ivan said, "You work for Northemico?"

"I *deal* with Northemico. Their entertainment division."

"I didn't even realize Northemico had an entertainment division."

"Hey, they got everything." He turned toward the waiter and said, "Fix me up another of these."

"Sorry, I'm just a pedologist from Podunk." Rubis looked perplexed. "Pedologist," Ivan said, enunciating as clearly as he could.

"Ah." Rubis listened to his AnswerMan again. "As in child specialist—or soil scientist? No, that can't be right. Sorry about that, Doctor. Sometimes my little mister know-it-all gets confused. At least it didn't think you said you're a pederast, ha ha. So what is it, set me straight here, what's your claim to celebrity?"

Ivan mentally shrugged and asked himself, Why the hell not? and to John Rubis he said, "I was one of the first people to travel through time."

Instead of responding to that, Rubis held up a forefinger, said, "Incoming," looked away, and hunched over the table, listening intently to his AnswerMan and occasionally muttering inaudibly.

Ivan's attention wandered. Light reflecting from the pool's surface shimmered on the enclosing white walls. The water was as brilliantly blue-green as that ancient sea—and as he pictured that sea in his mind, he also pictured a woman like a tanned and buffed Aphrodite rising from the waters. And when he told her that he was a foot specialist, she heaved a sigh of exasperation and dived back into the sea.

Rubis turned back to him and said, "Sorry. You aren't kidding about the time-travel, are you?"

"Well, I was part of the first team of time-travelers—half of it. There were just two of us. Afterward, I made other visits and helped establish a community of scientists in Paleozoic time. The base camp's the size of a small town now."

Rubis stared at him for what felt like a long moment. Then a light seemed to come on behind the man's eyes, and he snapped his fingers and pointed. "Yeah. The hole through time. Back to, what, the Stone Age?"

"Um, actually, back to quite a bit before. Back to the Paleozoic Era, four hundred million and some odd years ago. The Siluro-Devonian boundary."

"Yeah, that's right! The Age of Trillobites. So, what, you're out here pitching the story of your life to producers?"

"No, I'm just visiting my brother. He's the screenwriter in the family." That information did not seem to impress Rubis particularly, so Ivan added, "He was just up for a Best Screenplay Oscar. Donald Kelly." Rubis brightened. "My own fifteen minutes of fame are long past, and they really didn't amount to all that much."

"Mm. Any face minutes?"

"I'm sorry?"

"You know, your face on the TV screen. Media interviews. Face minutes."

"Ah. I turn up in some old documentaries. Everybody made documentaries for a while, until all six people who were remotely interested were sick of them."

Rubis rolled his eyes. "Documentaries! Even I watched part of one. No offense, but it was like watching grass grow. The most exciting thing you found was a trillobite, and it's basically just some kind of big water bug, isn't it?"

"Yes, basically."

"There've been bigger bugs in movies already. Like in—like in *Them and I.* And *The Thief of Baghdad.* Seen it?"

"Yes, as a matter of fact. I thought the Indonesian settings were interesting."

"Our first idea was to actually shoot it in Baghdad. But not much of Baghdad's standing any more. So—besides, Indonesia, Baghdad"—Rubis made a gesture expressive of some point that was not altogether clear to Ivan—"eh!"

"Once upon a time," Ivan said, "if you wanted to make a movie about Baghdad, you built sets on sound stages here in Hollywood, right?"

"Aah, nobody makes movies in Hollywood any more. Too expensive. Lousy unions. But this is still the place to be, the place to make deals. Anyway, like I was saying, about time-travel—I've always thought it's a sensational thing. When you think about it, it really is just the biggest thing since the early days of space travel. I wish it could be used for something more interesting than studying bugs and slime a million years ago, but don't get me wrong. I think it's a real shame the time-travelers never caught on with the public like those first guys who went to the moon—Armstrong, Altman. Now those guys were celebrities."

"It's not like we could do a live broadcast from the Paleozoic. The view wouldn't have commended itself to most people anyway. The Silurian Period looks like a cross between a gravel pit and a stagnant pond. And we didn't plant a flag or say anything heroic. In fact—" Ivan hesitated for a moment, considering. "Still, it was all tremendously exciting. It was the most exciting thing in the world."

The wall opposite the door had pivoted away. The metal platform had begun to move on rails toward a ripple in the air. Everything had turned to white light and pain. Ivan, blinded, felt as though someone had taken careful aim with a two-by-four and struck him across his solar plexus.

There was a terrifying, eternal moment when he could not suck in air. Then he drew a breath and started to exhale, and his stomach turned over. The convulsion put him on his hands and knees. Too excited to eat breakfast that morning, he had only drunk a cup of coffee. Now burning acid rose in his throat. He felt cramps in his

THE REAL WORLD ✦ STEVEN UTLEY

calf muscles. His earphones throbbed with the sound of—what was it, crying, groaning . . . ?

Retching. His vision cleared, and he saw Dilks nearby, lying on his side, feebly moving his arms. For some reason, part of Dilks' visor was obscured. Ivan threw his weight in that direction and half rolled, half crawled to the man's side. Now he could see Dilks' face through the yellow-filmed visor. Dilks had lost his breakfast inside his helmet. Ivan spoke his name, but it was quickly established that, though Dilks' helmetphone worked, his microphone was fouled and useless. There was nothing to be done for it now: they could not simply remove Dilks' helmet and clean out the mess; they were under strictest orders not to contaminate the Paleozoic.

Nearby, the air around the anomaly rippled like a gossamer veil. Ivan looked around at the Paleozoic world. He and Dilks were on the shingle just above the high-tide line and just below a crumbling line of cliffs. The sun stood at zenith in the cloudless sky. The sea was blue-green, brilliant, beautiful.

Ivan bent over Dilks again and said, "You're in bad shape. We've got to get you back. Come on, I'll help you."

Dilks vehemently shoved him away. He looked gray-faced inside his helmet, but he grimaced and shook his head, and though he could not say what he meant, Ivan understood him. We didn't come all this way only to go right back. Dilks patted the front of Ivan's suit and then motioned in the direction of the water.

Ivan nodded. He said, "I'll be right back." He staggered to his feet, checked the instruments attached to the platform, activated the camera mounted on his helmet, and collected soil and air samples in the vicinity of the platform. Then, with what he hoped was a reassuring wave to Dilks, he lumbered toward the water. The shingle made for treacherous footing, and yet, as he looked out upon the expanse of water, he experienced a shivery rush of pleasure so particular that he knew he had felt it only once before, during boyhood, on the occasion of his first sight of the sea off Galveston Island. He had never been mystically inclined, even as a boy, but, then as now, he had responded to something tremendous and irresistible, the sea's summons, had rush straight down to the water and dived in happily.

Nothing moved along the whole beach, nothing except the curling waves and the tangles of seaweed they had cast up. The beach curved away to left and right. It must curve away forever, Ivan thought. Hundreds, thousands of miles of perfectly unspoiled beach. He knelt on the dark wet sand and collected a sample of seawater. As he sealed the vial, he saw something emerge from the foam about two meters to his right. It was an arthropod about as big as his hand, flattened and segmented and carried along on jointed legs. The next wave licked after it, embraced it, appeared momentarily do draw it back toward the sea. The wave retreated, and the creature hesitated. Come on, Ivan thought, come on. Come on. He entertained no illusions that he had arrived on the spot just in time to greet the first Earth creature ever to come ashore. Surely, a thousand animals, a million, had already done so, and plants before them, and microorganisms before plants. Nevertheless, he had to admire the timing of this demonstration. He crouched, hands on knees, and waited. Foam rushed over the creature again. Come on, Ivan commanded it, make up your dim little mind. It's strange out here on land, not altogether hospitable, but you'll get used to it, or your children will, or your great-grandchildren a million times removed. Eventually, most of the species, most of the biomass, will be out here.

The arthropod advanced beyond the reach of the waves and began nudging through the seawrack. Eat hearty, Ivan thought, taking a cautious step toward the animal. He reflected on the persistence in vertebrates of revulsion toward arthropods. He felt kindly toward this arthropod, at least. Both of us, he thought, are pioneers.

As last he reluctantly tore himself away and returned to Dilks, who had sagged to the ground by the platform. Ivan propped the stricken man up and pointed toward the ripple. "We've got to cut this short," he said.

Dilks indicated disagreement, but more weakly than before.

"You're hurt," Ivan said, holding him up, "and we've got to go back." There was a crackle of static in Ivan's helmetphone, and he heard Dilks speak a single word.

" . . . failed . . . "

"No! We didn't fail! We got here alive, and we're getting back alive. Nobody can take that away from us, Dilks. We're the first. And we'll come again."

They got clumsily onto the platform. Ivan made Dilks as comfortable as possible and then activated the platform. The air around the ripple began to roil and glow. Ivan gripped the railing and faced the glow. "Do your goddamn worst."

Rubis had offered Ivan a cigar, which he politely refused, and stuck one into his own mouth, and Larry had lurched forward to light it. Now, enveloped in smoke, Rubis said, "Trillobites just never did catch on with the public. Maybe if you'd found a really big trillobite. On the other hand, trillobites didn't make for very cuddly stuffed toys, either, and that's always an important consideration. The merchandising, I mean."

"Candy shaped like brachiopods and sea scorpions? How about breakfast cereal? Sugar-frosted trio*bites*?"

Perfectly serious, Rubis nodded. "Now, if you'd've set the dial in your time machine for the age of dinosaurs instead."

"There wasn't actually a time machine. Just the space-time anomaly, the hole. And it just happened to open up where it did."

"That's too bad. And ain't it the way it always happens with science? We spent a godzillion dollars sending people to the Moon and Mars, and the Moon's just a rock and Mars's just a damn desert."

"Well, I don't know anyone honestly expected—"

"Now, *dinosaurs*, dinosaurs've been hot sellers forever. Dino toys, VR—they had all that stuff when I was a kid, and it still outsells every damn thing in sight. And every two, three years, regular as laxatives, another big dino movie. But what've you got? You got nothing, I'm sorry to say." He began to count on his fingers the things which Ivan did not have. "You got no big concept. You got no merchandisable angle. You got no crossover potential. Crossover potential's very big these days. You know, like Tarzan meets Frankenstein. James Bond versus Mata Hari. But, most of all, you haven't got dinosaurs, though. Everybody knows if you're going to tell a story set in the prehistoric past, there have to be dinosaurs. Without dinosaurs, there's no drama."

"I guess not," Ivan said, and took a long sip of his drink, and looked at the shimmering blue-green water in the pool. The slowly stirring air seemed to carry a faint smell of burning. He said to

Rubis, "Let me bounce an idea for a different kind of time-travel story off you. Tell me what you think."

"Sure. Shoot."

"Okay. You have to bear in mind that when we speak of traveling backward through time, into the past, what we're really talking about is traveling between just two of infinite multiple Earths. Some of these multiple Earths may be virtually identical, some may be subtly different, some are wildly different—as different as modern and prehistoric times. Anyway, what you actually do when you travel through time is go back and forth between Earths. Earth as it is, here and now, and another Earth, Earth as it was in the Paleozoic Era."

Rubis murmured, "Weird," and smiled.

"Now let's say someone from our present-day visits a prehistoric Earth and returns. After a while, after the initial excitement's died down, he starts to ponder the implications of travel back and forth between multiple Earths. He's come back to a present-day Earth that may or may not be his own present-day Earth. If it's virtually identical, well, if the only difference is, say, the outcome of some subatomic occurrence, then it doesn't matter. But maybe there's something subtly off on the macro level. It wouldn't be anything major. Napoleon, Hitler, and the Confederate States would've gone down to defeat. Or maybe the time-traveler only suspects that something may be subtly off. His problem is, he's never quite sure, he can't decide whether something is off or he only thinks it is, so he's always looking for the telling detail. But there are so many details. If he never knew in the first place how many plays Shakespeare really wrote or who all those European kings were . . . ."

Rubis nodded. "I get it. Not bad." He chewed his lower lip for a moment. "But I still think it needs dinosaurs."

Ivan chuckled softly, without mirth. "You should look up my niece's boyfriend." He turned on his seat, toward the burning hills.

They swept down Mulholland. Ivan said to Don, "Thanks for taking me. I can't remember when I've had so much fun." Don gave him a curious look. "No, really. I had a very good time, a wonderful time."

"Probably a better time than I did."

Ivan made a noncommittal sound. "I needed this experience as a kind of reality check."

Don laughed sharply. "Hollywood isn't the place to come for a reality check."

"Well, okay. Let's just say I had a very enlightening and entertaining poolside chat with our host."

"Johnny Rubis? Christ. He wasn't our host. Our host was a swine in human form named Lane. He was holding court indoors the whole time. I went in and did my dip and rise and got the hell out as fast as I could. Whatever Rubis may've told you he was doing by the pool, he was just showing off. See what a big deal I am. There were guys all over the place doing the same thing— women, too. Dropping names and making a show of pissant phone calls. See what big deals we are. Whatever Rubis may've told you, he's not that high in the food chain. A year ago he was probably packaging videos with titles like *Trailer Park Sluts*. He's an example of the most common form of life in Hollywood. The self-important butthead. I know, I've worked for plenty like him."

"Writing novels based on movies based on novels?"

Don shook his head. "Not me. Not lately, anyway."

Ivan wondered if Don despised himself as much as he apparently despised everyone else in Hollywood. He hoped it was not so. More than anything, he hoped it was not so. "Don," he said, "I'm sorry I said that. I'm really terribly sorry."

Don shrugged. "No offense taken." He gave Ivan a quick grin. "Hey, big brother, I've been insulted by professionals. It's one of the things writers in Hollywood get paid for."

They rode in silence for a time.

Then Don said, "Do you know what a monkey trap is?"

"Pretty self-explanatory, isn't it?"

"Yes, but do you know how it works? You take a dry gourd and cut a small hole in it, just big enough for the monkey to get its hand through. You put a piece of food inside the gourd and attach the gourd to a tree or a post. The monkey puts his hand into the gourd, grabs the piece of food, and then can't pull his fist back through the hole. He could get away if he'd only let go of the food, but he just can't make himself let go. So, of course, he's trapped."

"Is the money really that good?"

"Christ, Ivan, the money's incredible. But it isn't *just* the money. What it is, is that every great once in a long goddamn while, against all the odds—remember, before all this happened, I worked in the next best habitat favorable to self-important buttheads, which is politics. While you were off exploring prehistoric times, I was writing like a sumbitch on fire and trying to get the hell out of Texas. I paid the rent, however, by working for the state legislature. Whenever a legislator wanted to lay down a barrage of memorial resolutions, I was the anonymous flunky who unlimbered the 'whereases' and the 'be it resolveds.' Every now and then, I wrote about forgotten black heroes of the Texas Revolution, forgotten women aviators of World War Two—something, anyway, that meant something. But, of course, in those resolutions, everything was equally important. Most of my assignments were about people's fiftieth wedding anniversaries, high-school football teams, rattlesnake roundups. Finally, I was assigned to write a resolution designating, I kid you not, Texas Bottled Water Day. Some people from the bottling industry were in town, lobbying for God remembers what, and someone in the lege thought it'd be real nice to present them with a resolution. Thus, Texas Bottled Water Day. When I saw the request, I looked my boss straight in the eye, and I told him, This is not work for a serious artist. He quite agreed. First chance he got, he fired me."

"Maybe you should've quit before it came to that."

"Well, I'd've quit anyway as soon as the writing took off."

Don changed his grip on the steering wheel. "But while I was a legislative drudge, I lived for those few brief moments when the work really meant something."

His face, it seemed to Ivan, was suddenly transformed by some memory of happiness. Or perhaps it was just the car. The car cornered like a dream.

BABEL

Host: Hello, and welcome to another edition of "Alternate Mindsets." Our guest this evening is Doctor James Farlough, founder of Advocates for Biblical Creation and author of several books on the faith-based sciences. Thank you for being with us, Doctor.

Farlough: I'm happy to be here. I must correct you on one point, however. My father, Doctor Farlough Senior, founded the A.B.C.s.

Host: Of course. My apologies. Doctor Farlough Junior is here to share his views on the so-called spacetime anomaly that's been so much in the news. Later in the program we'll field questions from callers. But, first of all, to head off some of the more obvious questions, can you tell us what this anomaly is—besides being unprecedented in history? How would you describe it?

Farlough: I don't claim to be able to describe its actual physical aspect, assuming it even has one. I'm a geologist, not a physicist. Inasmuch as this phenomenon can only be described in either the most abstruse mathematical terms or else metaphorically, in the most elementary language, let's spare ourselves the math and call the anomaly a gateway. Humans are able to pass through it and return, evidently little the worse for wear.

Host: What is it a gateway *to?*

Farlough: Indeed. What and *when?* To a primeval Earthlike planet, some establishment scientists say, that exists in another universe virtually indistinguishable from our own. This makes me wonder how they can tell it from our own. Others say this planet is in fact our own Earth at the dawn of time—though they can't agree among themselves whether the term "dawn of time" means the Silurian period in this case, or the Devonian! As to its being unprecedented, there's not the slightest doubt in my mind that the anomaly has been created, or at least revealed to us at this time in human history, for some great purpose.

Host: What might that great purpose be?

Farlough: What are scientists to do but go through and find out what that purpose is? By scientists, however, I mean *true* scientists, as opposed to members of the conservative uniformitarian-evolutionist establishment. [*Laughs.*] That's quite a mouthful, isn't it? And I didn't even get in "relativist" and "indeterminist."

Host: Before we go any farther, it might be a good idea to define those terms as well for our audience's benefit.

Farlough: Uniformitarianism is the doctrine that geological phenomena result from observable processes that have operated in a uniform way throughout time. Evolution, of course, is the supposed development of all animal and plant species by means of hereditary transmission of slight variations in successive generations. I'm not sure I can give you a good thumbnail definition of indeterminacy as the word is used in physics. Or perhaps I should say misused. Anyway, indeterminacy pertains to the supposedly inexact limits of matter. Relativity is a whole other episode of this program! [*Laughs.*]

Host: Let us know when a good time is for you, Doctor. [*Laughs.*]

Farlough: Anyway, suffice it to say that indeterminacy and relativity posit a heinous lack of absolutes. The antitheses of uniformitarianism and evolution are flood geology and creationism. The essential statements of flood geology are that the Noachian deluge described in scripture was an historical event; that modern landforms were shaped by the waters of that deluge; and that the geological record, when properly deciphered, overwhelmingly supports the case for the creation of our world and everything in it, including ourselves, in a fairly short time and at a fairly recent date—very recent compared with the millions and billions of years uniformitarianism and evolution require to work their alleged changes.

Host: What distinguishes true scientists from, well, false ones?

Farlough: A true scientist keeps an open mind. He is ready to alter his own mindset if facts warrant, even if the facts seem incredible. Establishment scientists are fanatically devoted to their model of Earth history. One could go so far as to say that they are hopelessly trapped in it. The most charitable assessment possible of their attitudes and opinions is that they lack the proper search image to discern truths that fly in the face of their alleged facts. Less charitably, one could say that their colossal arrogance is matched only by their gigantic ignorance. The sum of things they do not know and refuse to learn is staggering. The *true* scientist prizes science as an invaluable system for learning about the physical world, yet recognizes that the basis of good science must be spiritual. Without the solid foundation which only inerrant scripture can provide, science is worthless and worse than worthless. It is like the house built on sand—not merely unsound but actually unsafe for all who choose to dwell therein. The true scientist formulates a sound theory and then amasses the incontrovertible evidence that supports it.

Host: But what if the incontrovertible evidence doesn't support a theory—say, the theory that life on earth, particularly human life, owes its existence to intelligent design?

Farlough: Good evidence has often been misinterpreted, or deliberately misrepresented, to support bad theories. The data collected by people who've passed through the anomaly are a case in point. Those people are all establishment scientists. It's hardly surprising that their data should be badly skewed.

Host: Is your organization interested in sending its own people through?

Farlough: Oh, yes, absolutely. The anomaly beckons us to a world both strange and strangely familiar. A world that promises us the means by which to achieve our greatest, our final victory over establishment science.

Host: Why is that victory so important?

Farlough: Much of the wickedness and misery of our world is directly attributable to the immoral and pernicious doctrines of evolution, uniformitarianism, relativity, and indeterminacy. Establishment science's embrace of brutal mechanical processes and its rejection of absolute values have demoralized human civilization. Yet adherents of fallacious doctrines are formidable and well-entrenched, and they control access to the anomaly. The National Science Foundation holds the purse strings. They're going to oppose us every step of the way. Once we've won through, and we will win through, eventually, I hope to be a member of the, um, the first, ah—

Host: Unbiased? Unprejudiced?

Farlough: I believe impartial is the word I'm groping for. The first impartial expedition to pass through. Oh, and the anomaly's possibilities are simply dazzling. I hope to have the pleasure and the satisfaction of securing the kind of proofs that will stand the scientific community on its head. Proofs that will be the ultimate weapons against the terrible cosmology which secular science has fashioned. Uniformitarianism will crumble away when we present conclusive proof that modern landforms were chiefly shaped by the waters of the Noachian deluge. Evolution will go at last into the dustbin of history when supposedly more advanced organisms are discovered coexistent with supposedly more primitive ones in so-called Silurian or Devonian ecosystems. Astronomical observations will corroborate the work done in Newtonian optics, proving that the Universe is not only much younger, but much smaller than establishment science says. Then, goodbye, Einstein! Relativity will join evolution in the same unmarked mass grave. Colleagues who have a much firmer grasp of mathematics than I do tell me that impartial scrutiny of the anomaly itself might well expose once and for all the fallacy of Heisenberger's indeterminacy. I can cite instances beyond number when maverick researchers have come up against the obduracy of the scientific establishment. Unless a fact fits their unproved theories of a very ancient universe and the ascent of humans from animals, they ignore it, deny it, and try to suppress it.

Host: Please give us just a couple of instances.

Farlough: Among the facts they disregard as a matter of formal policy is that man tracks and manmade artifacts turn up in supposedly very old rock formations dating back to so-called Cambrian time. According to uniformitarian geology, that was

560 million years ago, long before life moved ashore, never mind gave rise to humans. But during the 1820s, the naturalist Lea discovered an anomalous artifact in a quarry near Pittsburgh, in the Silurian sequence, supposed to be at least 400 million years old. The object was a flat rectangular surface, three feet long, six inches wide, adorned with perfectly spaced diamond shapes. Obviously, it was no fossil animal or plant, but an artifact fashioned by human hands. Another important find was made sixty years later by a Doctor Booth, in Missouri rocks dated even earlier in the Silurian sequence. He discovered a human skull and other remains, and even an impression of reed matting.

Host: We have a number of callers on hold who have questions or comments. Let's hear from them. Caller, you're on the air.

Caller 1: Hello?

Host: Yes, you're on the air, go ahead, please.

Caller 1: Uh, I've always been sympathetic to groups like the A.B.C.s, because I don't think people came up from apes. But I've been following this story about the spacetime anomaly since day one, and I'm still not convinced it even exists. Uh, it's like they can't say if it's, like, a thing or a place or what. All this stuff about people going back in time to a prehistoric world—I mean, I learned in school that thermodynamic law says time can only run in one direction. As far as I'm concerned, time *still* runs in one direction and one direction only. The spacetime anomaly's a hoax, and the A.B.C.s have been taken in!

Host: Comment, Doctor?

Farlough: To be sure, during the past two hundred or so years, the scientific establishment has perpetrated and perpetuated a monstrous catalog of hoaxes. Nevertheless, qualified individuals who are sympathetic to the A.B.C.s' ends have confirmed the anomaly's existence.

Host: You have people undercover at—

Farlough: No. Of course not. The point is, ah, the anomaly is real. It wouldn't be anomalous if it didn't violate at least one *generally* applicable law of nature. Its existence actually proves a major point creationists have long insisted upon, that the laws governing the physical world can be suspended—miraculously suspended.

Host: Next caller. Hello, you're on the air.

Caller 2: Yes. There's a lot of speculation that Paleozoic time corresponds to the days of creation, or perhaps the days before man's fall from grace. I'd like to ask the doctor what his opinion is.

Farlough: Modern people have already visited the ancient world for periods far exceeding the six 24-hour days of creation. Moreover, common sense tells me that *creatures*, which is to say, created beings such as ourselves, cannot be present before or at their own creation. Nor do I think people from our age of abominations would be permitted to enter the world as it existed before man knew sin. For us to do so would be to import sin into that pristine and paradisiacal world.

Host: Raising the question of where original sin came from originally.

Farlough: Ah, yes. Nor do I think, as some would-be schismatics in our organization do, that the world beyond the anomaly is a sort of trial earth, a rough draft of the real world that was later created for us to inhabit. This notion is dangerously akin to the secular physicists' hypothesis of many universes. I believe only the one set of heavens and the one Earth were ever created. It follows that the anomaly is a means of traveling through time rather than to another universe in another dimension. As for those who wonder if the anomaly might not be of diabolical rather than divine origin, that it is an infernal lure or trap—or, to say it another way, that just because we *can* travel through time doesn't mean we *should* or we're *supposed to*—I can only counter with my firm belief that the anomaly is the means by which we will at last and for all time rout the scientific establishment. We shouldn't pass up the opportunity of the ages because it is given us by our secular adversaries of old.

Caller 2: Is there going to be any way for us to definitely fix this other world in historical time?

Farlough: My father, Doctor Farlough Senior, is preparing a list of simple experiments which should allow us to reach useful gross conclusions. Predation, of course, did not exist before sin came into the world. Observing the eating habits of animals as different as cats, ladybugs, sharks, and dinosaurs like the tyrannosaur will be instructive. Also, before the flood, there was no rain, but moisture that rose up from the earth. And there were no earthquakes and volcanoes. Obviously, the incidence or non-incidence of these natural phenomena will be good general indicators. By the way, my father, who has been fascinated by dinosaurs since he was a boy, is especially keen on settling the matter of whether that race of terrible lizards died out in the flood or persisted into, and perhaps even beyond, the lifetimes of the patriarchs. He also hopes to prove that certain dinosaur types possessed the same fire-producing mechanisms that bombardier beetles do. Whence, the fire-breathing dragons of supposed legend.

Host: Doctor, dinosaurs are conspicuously absent from the world beyond the anomaly. In fact, the only land animals reported so far are scorpions and millipedes and the like. There are hardly even any land plants.

Farlough: There are several possibilities. One is that we have only begun to explore this ancient world. What have we seen of it so far? A few rock islands and a lot of open sea. A second possibility—which is not precluded by the first—is that the people who've gone through thus far are incompetent observers, liars, or both. *Or* they've visited the world as it was in the immediate aftermath of the deluge, which would account for the denuded landscape and the absence of large land animals. Scorpions and millipedes breed faster and more prolifically than the larger types of animals in the Ark—including dinosaurs. As I said, probably the waters are still retreating, and Babel, the first postdiluvial civilization, hasn't arisen.

Host: Caller, you're on the air.

Caller 3: I had a question, but I can't remember what it was. I'm still trying to digest the idea that Tyrannosaurus started out as a vegetarian. Sorry.

Host: Next caller. Hello, you're on the air.

Caller 4: You talked about manmade artifacts in Silurian rocks. So why didn't the guys who found them come forward and blow Darwin right out of the water? How come nobody's ever heard of them?

Farlough: Unfortunately, before Lea could remove the artifact he found, a quarryman broke it up. And the relics Doctor Booth discovered turned to dust when he touched them. Great losses to science. These two finds by themselves probably would've nipped evolution and uniformitarianism in the bud.

Host: Caller, you're on the air.

Caller 5: Hello. I'm a long-time follower of "Alternate Mindsets," but I gotta say, the show used to be a lot more entertaining back when it concentrated on people who'd squared the circle or been taken for rides in flying saucers.

Host: Caller, do you have a question for Doctor Farlough?

Caller 5: You bet. The doctor mentioned the civilization of Babel. Does he mean as in "the tower of"?

Farlough: Yes. Of course. The civilization that was cast down following the confusion of tongues. Almost all traces of it were obliterated by glacial ice.

Caller 5: [*Laughs.*] Well, that sure saves real scientists the trouble of looking for it on the other side of the anomaly, doesn't it?

Farlough: By real scientists you obviously mean establishment scientists. I'm sure they wouldn't find it even if they looked for it. They wouldn't look in the right places.

Host: Caller, you're on the air.

Caller 6: Yes, hi, this is Marvin Canepi, I'm with the Institute for Extraterrestrialist Studies. I want to ask Doctor Farlough how his A.B.C.s expect to prevail single-handedly against the whole scientific establishment.

Farlough: [*Groans.*] Somehow I just knew I'd be hearing from Mister Canepi.

Host: You two know each other.

Farlough: Only too well. I have never known him not to show up wherever I may be. Waiting for him to call in tonight has been like waiting for the other shoe to drop.

Canepi: The A.B.C.s recently rebuffed overtures made by the I.E.S., the Advocates for Intelligent Design, the New Shaverite Church, and several other organizations. A coalition of—

Farlough: The problem we at the A.B.C.s face is to find such help as we can while exercising some discretion about whose help we accept. If we are to succeed in our purpose, we must be taken seriously by people in public office who can possibly influence the N.S.F. In order to be taken seriously, we must avoid association with the adherents of such dubious intellectual stuff as psychic phenomena, spiritualism, reincarnation, astrology, witchcraft, lost continents, the hollow earth, and, in this case, exobiology. Just because our enemies delight in portraying us as pseudoscientists and wild-eyed crackpots doesn't mean we have to tolerate individuals who really are pseudoscientists and crackpots. As our mothers used to tell us, "You're known by the company you keep."

Host: Next c—

Canepi: Wait a second, I'm not through yet. Talk about ignoring evidence—Doctor Farlough dismisses my organization's findings about ancient carvings collected from around the world. These carvings depict beings dressed in what can only be futuristic pressure suits and helmets. Ancient writings also mention these beings. They're described as wise, powerful—able to soar through the heavens in flaming chariots. They're possessed of technology so advanced it seems magical to backward Earth people. Obviously, these beings were visitors from another planet, maybe even another galaxy. And they obviously were responsible for the quantum leaps in human progress during ancient times. The suddenness with which distinct human civilizations appeared in Mesopotamia and the Nile and Indus valleys tells us that the visitors willingly shared basic technology. The—wait, don't cut me off, you ba—

Host: Doctor Farlough, can you comment on what Mister Canepi says?

Farlough: Comment and then some! Mister Canepi's organization is one of several that purvey secular extraterrestrialism, a doctrine as nonsensical as Darwinism. It rests on nothing more substantial than a wishful—one could even call it childish—interpretation of the ancient carvings and writings he mentions. Those relics exist, to be sure. But if the carvings actually depict anything that ever existed outside the pagan imaginations of primitive humans, they surely depict not ancient astronauts but modern time travelers!

Host: Time travelers!

Farlough: Yes. The people who've gone through the anomaly wear spacesuit-like raiment and headgear. Think of the impression they must make on unsophisticated ancient peoples!

Host: Umm, well, no one who's gone through claims to have *seen* any ancient peoples, unsophisticated or otherwise.

Farlough: No one has *reported* seeing any ancient peoples. And while we're on the subject of sophistication or the lack thereof, let me say here that even the I.E.S. and the A.I.D.s would do well to avoid the New Shaverite cult. I can't call it a church, with its subterranean race of malign robots and its angels and devils zooming around the solar system in spaceships.

Host: Are there any groups whose help the A.B.C.s would welcome?

Farlough: Despite what Mister Canepi says, we are not trying to take on any government agency by ourselves. We're solidly aligned with the All-American Front in a campaign to break the tyranny of the National Science Foundation. That's an absolutely necessary step, because as long as the N.S.F. is calling the shots, I doubt we are going to get anywhere near the anomaly, never mind through it. Despites its grandiose title, the N.S.F. doesn't bestow its favor on just any taxpaying knowledge-seeker. Certainly not on anybody who doesn't knuckle under to orthodoxy.

Host: We have time for one more question. Caller, you're on the air.

Caller 7: Well, after what Doctor Farlough just now said, I'm not going to bother to ask the question I meant to ask. But I have two comments I'd like to make. First, you've never gotten anywhere with the N.S.F. because it has its reputation to consider. It can't have people getting the idea it'll knuckle under to loonies. Second, if you think the All-American Front isn't a bunch of wild-eyed crackpots, I'd like to know who is. I've read the Front's literature. One of the many fascinating things I learned from it is there're three distinct races of human beings—white, darky, and heathen Chinee—who shouldn't intermix or be *allowed* to intermix. You've thrown in with a bunch of neo-Nazis, Doctor Farlough. What the—

Host: Sorry to cut you off, caller, but we really are just about out of time. [*Whistles, laughs.*] Emotions run high on this show.

Farlough: That last caller sounded like a neo-Menckenite to me. Talk about wild-eyed crackpots.

Host: I want to thank you for being with us, Doctor Farlough, and wish you luck in getting to lead your expedition through the anomaly. We have about a minute left. Any closing statement you'd like to make?

Farlough: I'd like to end on an optimistic note. I think the A.B.C.s and the All-American Front and others who share our values and concerns are going to win through to the end. I take heart from the long, hard-fought, but ultimately successful campaign to dismantle the National Endowment for the Arts. Ever increasing numbers of American taxpayers, good decent citizens, are starting to realize that if they no longer have to underwrite so-called art that offends their sensibilities, neither should they have to underwrite so-called science that attacks their most dearly held

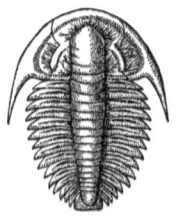

convictions about mankind's special place in the scheme of things. It isn't merely a spacetime anomaly that's opened up, but a new front in the age-old war for men's minds, hearts, and souls. We won't be found wanting.

"ANOTHER CONTINUUM
HEARD FROM!"

Not that the absentee vote is likely to determine this election's outcome, but we in the punditry trade find ourselves consumed with interest in a particularly exclusive group of absentee voters: the farthest-flung citizens of our republic and members of our species.

Awright, awright, we confess: It's less a case of consuming interest than of sheer journalistic desperation. Like megatheria foundering in a tar pit, the contenders for the highest office in the land have mired themselves in the dullest election campaign in memory, living or otherwise. Even the attack ads are uninspired; for instance, the best His Incumbency's keepers can do is to take up the sobriquet fastened upon the challenger by some anonymous underground wag: Senator Dribbleglass. Really mature, gang— and what if the President catches you tuning in to *Blues Against the Empire* or *Dateline Pellucidar*?

The (discreetly voiced) consensus of reporters assigned (or, as they prefer, sentenced) to the candidates' retinues is that they've died and gone to hell. We others are (almost) too ashamed to go on drawing pay for performing the onerous, odious, otiose task of reading meaning into the candidates' virtually interchangeable evasions, obfuscations, and insults to intelligence. We must cast about for topics possessing at least tenuous relevance to politics and nebulous value as curiosities. *I* hereby call dibs on the Silurian age. The folks there—members of various scientific research teams or the U.S. Navy support contingent, and registered voters all—don't solve the problem of what's to provide copy later in the week, but they suffice for now, and isn't that what news is about?

Anybody with a short attention span (actually a survival trait in this campaign) will thrill on being reminded that about one thousand men and women live and work either 400 million years in the past or else on an alternate earth in another universe entirely. Which is it, long ago or far away? Depends on whose theory you prefer.

A clear majority of the expedition's paleontologists and geologists and such hold the opinion that they literally are time travelers into the prehistoric world of the Silurian age, and they have the trilobites to back it up.

"On the contrary," say the physicists who superintend the so-called "Space-Time Anomaly," by which means everybody has got from here to there or from now to then (depending). With minimal prompting, they proceed to tell you, and to show you reams and reams of math they claim backs them up, that time travel is impossible, therefore, the Anomaly can *only* be a gateway to an earth-like planet infested with trilobite-like critters, orbited by a moon-like satellite, and itself orbiting a sun-like star in a universe very like our own.

In practical terms the distinction probably doesn't matter, but, politics being what it am, conceivably the difference could make a difference in the (which is to say, our) world.

Conceive along with us here: imagine that the election somehow generates enough interest among the electorate at the last moment to become what political scientists with fancy degrees term "a squeaker," a la Hayes/Tilden, Bush/Gore, etc. Those absentee votes from the Silurian age become crucial. The world or, anyway, the candidates and their keepers wait with bated breath as the ballots are hurried by time-machine or pony express into the eager if none too clean hands of election officials. The count is made, the cry rings out, "Another continuum heard from!" and the winner is

declared. Then the fun truly begins, as attorneys for both parties argue speciously about the legitimacy of the thing.

Oh, we could kill our own premise outright by citing the Uniformed and Overseas Citizens Absentee Voting Act. UOCAVA provides that members of the U.S. armed services and merchant marine and their families, as well as non-military U.S. citizens living abroad, may vote while away from their place of voting residence, wherever stationed, within or without the United States. Sounds simple enough.

But we still have x amount of copy to turn in, so let's conceive that the side which has come up short in the ballot count asks, "Are the expedition members actually living *abroad?*" and follows through with, "If they're actually in the Silurian age, which falls well outside the calendar year, are they not in violation of UOCAVA's 'not earlier than' restrictions on registration requests and the receipt of absentee ballots?"

The "not earlier than" argument is duly countered with the physicists' expert testimony about what they term a "synchronous link" between our world and that other, whereby it doesn't take you any longer to fritter away your time there (or then) than it does here (or now). The Silurian days *are* shorter and the year's longer by a few dozen of these shorter days, due to the primeval earth's faster rotation, itself due to the primeval moon's proximity. But we don't want to get into the laws of motion here, and neither do you.

As to whether the term "abroad" extends to an alternate universe, the argument is advanced that the Anomaly does in fact or at least in a sense occur within our national boundaries; to get through the Anomaly, one must first get to the facility where the Anomaly is kept under lock and key, and which indisputably occupies sovereign U.S. real estate. Does it then follow that the world beyond the Anomaly is an extension of U.S. territory? *All* of it, not just proto-North America but also the continents smushed together into Gondwana? Is what we're talking about here preemptive domain?

Good legal minds, which is to say, perfectly evil ones, can keep this ball rolling until exasperation wrings a concession of defeat from one or the other or preferably both candidates.

What have the candidates themselves to say on the matter? It's cruel to inflict quantum physics and alternate continua on a

President who takes the Copernican theory as a personal affront and thinks lunar craters were made not by meteor impacts but during the war between the hosts of Heaven and the legions of Lucifer—a President who, furthermore, is on record as believing that there's just no real proof there ever was a prehistoric age at all. "Have these scientists seen a single dinosaur? No, they have not." So there. Nevertheless, should he need a few votes to prevail against Dribbleglass, they must come from somewhere. They might as well come from military personnel attached to the expedition, who, even if they don't like his cosmology, adore his patronage. Re-elect the President, and his party will continue to serve up the lion's portion of discretionary spending, and several lesser predators' as well. But so, too, the challenger's party.

And what of the challenger, a man so inflexible he's often mistaken for a chordate? (Politicians are usually classified as invertebrates.) The senator may have no more use for alternate universes than he does for alternate life-styles; the idea of worlds where things are done differently might make him queasy. Yet he seems aware that the earth isn't flat and, moreover, actually goes around the sun. Such intellectual rigor has got to count for something with the expedition's scientists.

"Politics," a former expedition member informs us (on condition of anonymity and also that we pay for lunch), "is one (expletive deleted) thing everybody there is glad not to have to think about. How meaningless it all seems when it's so far away." Ah, if only everyone were able to view politics from such a remove. But, of course, it isn't meaningless, however far away. Our interviewee admits that, by and large, her colleagues are a cranky uncouth mutinous lot thanks to His Incumbency's passion for slashing funding for non-military research.

Well, as we said at the outset, the expedition's thousand votes almost certainly won't make an atom's worth of difference in an election that won't make much more than a molecule's worth of difference in most folks' lives: they'll still be miserable. Perhaps the Silurian age is the perfect metaphor for this campaign: it's almost as uninteresting, except to people with special interests, and all it has to offer are slugs and slime.

VARIANT

Dr. Larson asked today if I have begun keeping a diary, as I agreed to do at our last session. I lied and said yes and felt terrible about it, but now that I have retroactively canceled out the lie by beginning this diary, I still feel terrible.

Perhaps if I try disassociating—

You still feel terrible.

She still feels terrible.

Damn all personal pronouns anyway.

You wake up convinced that the thing to do is to see The Great Man himself (as my husband and now I refer to his project director), who has become famous in the last few months for having answers. My husband and others will have taken all the risks, but The Great Man will get all the credit. The Great Man's reputation will long outlive him; educated people will speak of him and his spacetime anomaly the way Newton and his apple are spoken of, or Darwin, or Einstein.

Well, whatever. I wake up thinking I must go speak to him. I'll tell him, "It's a matter of the greatest importance," but even as you think this you can imagine The Great Man's frown. You've seen him on television often enough, heard enough about him from your husband and other people who work with him. You imagine getting to him and speaking to him. "Everything is changed," you imagine yourself telling him. "Everything has been taken away and replaced with something almost, but not exactly, like it. I can't tell you why everything is strange, but it is."

But you can't imagine anything in The Great Man's expression, not impatience, really, not contempt, not complete lack of interest, but there is no mistaking the feeling that you are only the latest in an interminable series of interruptions of Important Work, of intrusions into his precious private space. (He is said to be an agoraphobe, the perfect ironic quirk in one who dabbles in the complexities of the infinitesimal and the nearly infinite.)

The prospect of actually getting to talk to The Great Man isn't very encouraging, though. You can already imagine the obstacles. The great man is notoriously difficult to see if you aren't a fellow scientist or a reporter. You probably would have to get past his secretary, and probably he has a bodyguard now, and maybe a wife, too, and negotiating your way past them all without your husband ever hearing of it would be difficult.

So, instead, you finally start keeping the diary as you promised Dr. Larson you would.

If there are millions of me, I am we and them and language breaks down under the weight of so many of me. Are they each as unhappy as I am? Inside the skin (which by the way has finally if only for the time being ceased to crawl) personal pronouns are too hard to keep track of right now. I am s/he and we are they and each/both/all of us are not having a good day. Not at all. We are having a bad day. We don't want to, but we are anyway. Still, we try to keep up appearances. We try to help our older daughter with a short written theme she must present in class the next day. We peer desperately at the text, keep fastening our attention on a stray comma only to lose it, repeatedly. Finally it seems to go into hiding and we can't find it anywhere. We say the theme is perfect as it is, and know that we lie.

We are having a very bad day indeed. See how our hand trembles as we begin to chop vegetables for dinner. Gravity almost suffices to pull the big heavy triangular blade with its minutely serrated edge down through the mushrooms. Only a slight increase in pressure is required to chop carrots and celery just like a television chef. How much more pressure might be needed to slice off a finger? Not much, surely. Are we or is she or am I even certain that this is the right piece of cutlery for the job? It's part of an excellent set, a wedding gift (or birthday anniversary or something not important any longer), but there were no instructions. The Thing won't care. The Thing will just expect its dinner to be on the table when it gets home. The Thing might but then again might not notice, let alone remark upon, the presence of a severed digit in the salad bowl. Clean the blade carefully (no dishwasher for this honey, a good knife, an *excellent* knife) and make sure it goes into its proper slot in the big wooden block that holds its mates. Make an effort to straighten up the place a bit. Kids drop things everywhere, knowing stuff magically finds its way back to where they can find it next time they want to drop it somewhere. Before, it was *Mustn't let hubby come home from his hard day to a pigsty.* Now it is *Mustn't give The Thing any reason to suspect that I/we are on to him/It.*

Usually he didn't talk about his work, save in the most general way, and of course he sometimes made fun of The Great Man, but around the time of the breakthrough he couldn't contain himself. Even then he tried not to violate security, yet he was so excited he had to drop hints. It was big, whatever it was. And then, finally, there was the big press conference presided over by The Great Man, and we learned that he and his colleagues (prominent among them, beaming for the television cameras, my husband) had somehow discovered or created or captured or stabilized (in any case, *some*thinged) a weak spot in spacetime. That they could push things through this weak spot and then pull them out again, to all appearances unchanged, unharmed. That there was another world on the other side, another entire universe, like ours in all fundamentals, unlike it in many details. That our universe and this other one had probably split off from each other, or split off from still other universes that had split off from each other at some remote nano-moment deep in the past, and each universe in this infinite, geometrically replicating succession of universes was slightly or enormously different from all the rest.

After a point I could no longer follow it (marrying a physicist is no royal road to understanding quantum physics), but nevertheless I grasped the essential idea, grasped also that people were determined to visit that other world. Grasped, finally—though I arrived at this conclusion myself, independently of my oh-so-percipient husband and his colleagues, to whom it seems never to have occurred— grasped finally that if people from this universe could go in, people from that other universe could come out. When I cautiously asked what sort of people might inhabit other universes, he said the point was moot because there were no people in this particular other universe. "It's just sand and rocks and lichen. Think primeval— no, not even primeval. Think *primordial*." When I pointed out that if people from our universe could enter this wasteland, people from other universes could, too, in which case wasn't it just a short hop, skip, and jump to our universe? He laughed again and said, "Yes, they could at that, and yes, I suppose it is just a hop, skip, and jump, but what are the odds?"

I don't *know* what the odds are. I'm *not* the mathematician in the family. Still, I wanted to ask him: What were the odds of finding a weak spot in spacetime?

Not long afterward he dropped his bombshell. "I've told them I want to be the first to go through," he said, smiling to let me know that there was no cause for anxiety, "but they're thinking maybe it'd be best to let someone without a family go through first. Not that they don't think it's perfectly safe."

"Why do they think that?"

"The probes, the test animals, they've gone through and come back out okay. The animals were a little disoriented at first, but only a little and only at first, and that's to be expected. Soon it'll be about as exciting as walking through a door, from one room into another."

"Tell me, honestly. How safe is it?"

"Very safe. Perfectly safe."

"Nothing is perfectly safe."

"Well, it's as safe as stepping into an elevator."

"Sometimes," I said, "elevators fall and crash"

"Well, this is *safer* than stepping into an elevator, then. Safer than stepping out of a bathtub. A lot safer than driving an automobile. If there was any doubt in anyone's mind, we wouldn't be thinking about sending a human volunteer through."

I could tell from his face, I could see it in his eyes, he wanted to go through, he really wanted to go, he meant to go, he wouldn't rest, he'd never be satisfied until he went through himself.

And then he did. Go. Through.

I should really have started with the comic book. It didn't really *start* with the comic book, the comic book just gave definite form to the idea which till that moment we had only sensed lurking in the back of our head or just behind our shoulder. No idea where the kids might have got a comic book. We certainly don't buy the things for them, and it hardly seemed like the kind of thing they would have bought for themselves. Perhaps one of their friends left it, though their friends hardly seem like the kind who would buy such things.

But you never know.

Anyway, we sat by ourself in the breakfast niche and idly flipped the pages while the coffeemaker burbled on the counter like a moron. Comicopolis, we discerned, is sort of a self-referential metafictitious Metropolis Gotham City Duckburg Riverdale all in one, and more densely populated than any of them, because it is home town to all the characters in comic books, or at least all the characters owned by this particular company, an orthodox assortment who somehow understand that they are comic-book characters. Most of them, in fact, either work directly for or else are indirectly beholden to a brace of more or less ethically challenged comic-book publishers, and some but not all of the problems they face derive from their employers' avarice and insensitivity. Which is not to discount the power lust of villains, though even they often find themselves at the mercy of canny businessmen with lawyers. (One of the lawyers is named Remora.) Responsibility for dealing with your more *outré* type menace often falls to the book's nominal star, Doctor Iron, who cuts a dashing figure in his dressed-down way: under his lab coat (which he sheds whenever he's about to wade into a trouble spot) he wears a teeshirt, jodhpurs, riding boots, as though he just wandered off the polo field to battle evil. He is first and foremost a scientist, however, and dislikes having to take time off from his "real work," a generalized sort of scientific experimentation involving unlikely-looking machines, to thwart the machinations of typically sociopathic comic-book villains such as Professor Entropy, Desiree Carrion, or The Devastator; he would rather leave crime-fighting to characters who enjoy it, such as Bobcat (in reality millionaire philanthropist Robert Katt, though nobody makes the connection) and his two young assistants, Ocelot and Margay. Fleeting appearances are made by other costumed characters such as Lithium Lass, whose secret identity is known to everybody but her, and there is a subplot involving a pubescent girl who used to be the superpowered (albeit prepubescent) Dynamic Doll but now wants only to pursue "a career with a real future" as the heroine of either a teen-comedy or else a teen-romance comic. A second subplot pertains to the efforts of a talking dog named Sam and a talking cat named Pam to avoid being returned to FunnyVale, evidently a ghetto or asylum for anthropomorphized animals. It is certainly nothing like the comic books I remember from my own childhood, though it seems to be about those comic books. It is textually and visually dense, extremely intorted satire by and for people who have read entirely too many comic books.

And yet I keep going back to two pages having to do with Doctor Iron's secret origin (so secret that it is hidden in the middle pages of a comic book). This resonates terribly for me. Doc has invented a matter transmitter by which he means to travel great distances, between the stars.

"The object to be transmitted," he explains, "is scanned at this end—call it Point A. The scan serves as a template. The object is then disintegrated and transmitted to Point B, where it is reassembled according to the template."

Of course, Doc then steps through the transmitter in his laboratory (Point A), and of course something goes wrong—the template isn't perfect. When he emerges at Point B, our hero is not quite himself, or, rather, he is quite a bit more than himself. Somewhere in transit he has picked up extra mass or energy, every atom of his original being has been replaced by the atoms of his new being—in any event, he is now superhumanly strong and impervious to harm.

Apart from such things as the teeshirt, jodhpurs, cleft chin, multiple degrees and concurrent careers in several branches of science, Doc before he goes into the matter-transmitter has a lot in common with my husband before he went into the spacetime anomaly. Likewise, afterward, except for Doc's becoming, however reluctantly, the superpowered champion of Comicopolis while my husband simply became The Thing That Looks And Acts Like My Husband.

The Thing comes home to wife, children, dog. Children and dog greet Thing at door. Wife hangs back under the pretense of attending to dinner. Children are fooled and who's to blame them? Not like they can have ever even heard the words, *implications, quantum, physics*, let alone heard them in tandem, never mind grasped the implications of the phrase "implications of quantum physics." There is for them, there can be only the one world, the only Daddy. But a dog should not be so easy to fool. Dogs are supposed to know better, to be able to scent trouble (trouble? *danger!*) and warn people that all is not what it seems to dull human senses, whether it's prowlers on the property or earthquakes simmering underfoot or an alien masquerading as one's husband and the sire of one's children. But no, damn dumb dog is right in there competing with damn darling daughters to get under Daddy-Thing's feet. Daddy-Thing stoops, pats the dog, scoops up a squealing giggling child in each arm, advances on wife to collect a welcome-home-how-was-your-day kiss (first the dog, then the children, finally the wife: a man's priorities, please note, and perfectly simulated by The Thing That Walks Like The Man I Married). Well, wife does not want any part of it (It) but also doesn't want to let on that she knows what's what, who's whom, because she is outnumbered, the children flesh of her flesh have gone over to the creature, the damn dog, too. So she submits to being kissed, forces herself, just as, a moment earlier, she made a smile when The Thing came through the door. "Did you miss me?" It asks his hysterical girls. "Was I gone for a long time?" Only for the weekend. Only for four hundred million years. Only for as long as it takes an adult male human being to be replaced, atom for atom, by something that looks walks talks exactly like him and has his habits and memories and yet isn't him at all.

Dinner, his favorite foods for his favorite meal. The girls have calmed down, have helped to set the table, the dog finds its favorite spot in a corner and settles down for a snooze. The masquerade has succeeded with everyone except she who is not to be deceived. She, too, masquerades. She serves dinner. She smiles. She loads the dishwasher. She gets the children ready for bed.

She hears the bathroom door open behind her and turns deliberately in her chair. He is wearing pajama bottoms and slippers. He looks at the collection of plastic vials on the nightstand. Picks up one vial, shakes it, holds it up to the light. "Honey," he says, "are you taking your medicine the way you're supposed to?" Those things, comes the reply, make me feel like, like, make me sleepy. "They're *supposed* to help you relax." I am relaxed, see how relaxed I am, but it's a lie and it's obvious that he knows that it's a lie. "When's your next appointment with Doctor Larson?" I say, I saw her just this morning, after I dropped the girls off at school. She refilled my prescriptions.

I don't go on to say, Or maybe it was yesterday morning. Or maybe it doesn't matter.

Night comes, as night always does, and everyone who can sleep does. Even Things can sleep. Those of us who cannot sleep, we lie in the darkness, listening to It breathe, and we think our thoughts, which are as follow, though in no particular order:

Perhaps I should call Dr. Larson in the morning. Perhaps it is just me.

Perhaps not. In which case, where is my husband, Thing? To what hellhole has he been sent so that you can take his place? You are a good copy, but now I see that you are not a perfect one.

But perhaps it *is* just me. Perhaps I have this all backwards. Perhaps *I* am the one who's not in the right world.

How would you know if things (not just Things, but things) were not on the right world? You would, she thinks, you would keep noticing things that, if they are not wrong, nevertheless are somehow not right. You'd look at the books on your shelves and they'd be the books you remember but the copies would seem unfamiliar. And the clutter on your desk would be an uncharacteristic clutter, not the sort of mess it had ever been your habit to create. You've always been a stacker, this is an untidy mound. Familiar recordings of favorite music would sound somehow unfamiliar, too fast, too slow, too shrill, too something. The trees outside the window

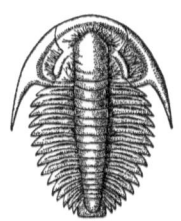

would not quite be your trees, flowers would smell, well, off, food would taste off.

And how would you know if something else was not on the right world? You look at your husband and try to remember if that mole he's had since childhood isn't supposed to be smaller or bigger or located a centimeter lower or to the left or maybe he didn't have a mole after all. Moles change, but do they migrate? Even while making love to your husband you cannot shake the feeling that you are with someone whose movements scents sounds textures are not those you remember from before the time he went to that other world.

Finally, we slip out of bed and glide through the darkened but entirely familiar house, past the girls' bedroom door, downstairs, past the dog which grunts sleepily, and record all the thoughts we have thought for posterity, or at least for Dr. Larson. Then we face a terrible choice. We will either simply wait here like a dumb beast for day to come, as day always does, or we will get up and go into the milkily illumined kitchen. The big heavy knife will gleam as we draw it carefully out of the wooden block. We will try one last time (for surely it is the last time) to put everything in order.

THE WORLD WITHIN
THE WORLD

"Damn jump station's haunted," Summers growled, frowning at the momentarily dormant machine. One of the monitors had just beeped inexplicably. He looked around at his co-worker, Cullum, and their two visitors, Lane the Navy doctor and Cutsinger the physicist.

"Summers here thinks we have spooks," said Cullum. "*I* think we have a lunatic."

"Really. Spooks." Summers nodded at the monitor that had beeped. "It's always doing that."

"It's always *done* that," Cullum said, "as far back as I can remember."

"Short circuit somewhere," Cutsinger said.

Summer shook his head vehemently. "We've taken it apart and replaced everything in it six eight times. It *isn't* electrical. It's—" he pondered word choices for a moment "—ectoplasmatical."

"I have no idea in hell what you're talking about," said Cullum, "and I'm willing to bet you don't, either."

Summers addressed himself to the other two men. "It *isn't* just the monitor registering something when there shouldn't be anything there to register. Every now and then, when we're alone in here, I sense we're *not* alone in here. Like . . . disembodied entities are moving around and past and *through* us. Gives me kind of a little chill down my back. You never get those?"

"Everybody gets those," said the doctor. "Just a glitch in the nervous system."

Cullum made a wry face at Summers. "'Disembodied entity' is kind of an oxymoron, isn't it? You're probably just high on ozone."

"A ghost is supposed to be—"

"*Supposed* to be!"

"—*supposed* to be some kind of psychic residue left at the scene of a violent or at least traumatic incident."

"Yes, so?

"So, what could be more traumatic than going through a spacetime anomaly, being shot across hundreds of millions of years into prehistoric times? *We* all came through, and it felt like being worked over with a baseball bat."

"Maybe that's the answer," Cullum said drily. "You got hurt in you head when you came through." He nodded significantly at Dr. Lane. "Undiagnosed concussion."

"Perhaps," said Cutsinger, "the blip on your monitor is an electronic echo of the person who goes through. A kind of human non-being. It might even have the person's memories and ideas and emotions."

"What about the *stuff* that comes through?" said Cullum. "Ghostly toilet tissue for ghostly bums?"

"Go ahead," Summers said in an offended tone, "make jokes, reduce the epistemological to the scatological."

"At least I'm making *sense*. Do you even know what any of the words you use mean? Listen. The blips last less than a second, right? So what good would memories—never mind ghostly supplies and equipment—what good would ideas and emotions do your ghost?"

"To a ghost a split-second might be a whole eternity."

"With all the people who have come through here, to say nothing of all the *stuff*, why aren't the monitors just screaming all the time?"

"How the hell should I know?"

Cutsinger made an amused sound and said, "Perhaps I can contribute to this body of speculation. Let's say that for all ghosts all eternity is crammed into the same nanosecond. Or perhaps some kind of charge builds up and all those echoes of people and things keep coming back into existence and doing whatever they do. Living out lives just like the original people, doing the same things, thinking the same thoughts. Or perhaps the scenes replay themselves with minute or not-so-minute variations, but all variations on the same theme. And always the ghosts believe they *are* the real thing. Then they pass right out of existence again, until the charge builds up again. Repeat and repeat, world without end. A whole world created and extinguished in a nanosecond, and it makes just enough of a disturbance to register on that monitor."

"Just enough of one," said Summers, "to send a chill down my spine."

"I've come through the anomaly three times," the doctor said, "and gone back twice. Does that mean there are five electronic ghosts of me vying for primacy in the same nanosecond of existence? Wouldn't their individual timelines get a bit tangled?"

"Timelines!" The physicist rolled his eyes. "I've wasted enough time over the years trying to explain why it isn't time travel."

Lane seemed not to take offense. "Very well, then. All of those alternate universes you're always going on about confuse the hell out of me. Imagine how confusing it must be for all of my ghosts."

The physicist smiled. "Actually, I can imagine it."

"Really now."

"Of course I can. If I'm able to imagine multiple worlds, a series of universes receding into infinity, I can certainly imagine ghosts. Doesn't mean I believe in them, though. Only that I can imagine them."

"'I and this mystery,'" said Dr. Lane, "'here we stand.'" He saw the expressions on the faces of the other three men and laughed good-naturedly. "Walt Whitman."

"It's getting metaphysical *and* poetical around here," Cullum said. "I may have to transfer to another shift."

Summers glanced at the clock. "Speaking of shifts, where's our relief?"

"I'll go ask."

Cullum went to the door adjoining the jump station, stuck his head through, and spoke to somebody. The physicist and the doctor drifted along in Summer's wake as he moved around the confines of the jump station taking readings and making minute adjustments.

All three men looked up sharply as the monitor beeped again. They were still regarding it thoughtfully, in silence, when Cullum returned and told Summers, "Charlie and Zeke are here."

The physicist started. "What?

"What's the problem?"

The doctor blinked. "Nothing. Just—oh, nothing. Never mind."

"Come on," Cullum said to Summers, "let's go. I'm starved."

"Me, too."

They left Cutsinger and Dr. Lane with Charlie and Zeke and said nothing to each other until seated across from each other in the ship's mess. Then Summers looked up from his plate and said, "That physicist believed me. And that doctor—"

"That physicist was just rhapsodizing. And that doctor believes you're nuts. Probably he believes the physicist is nuts, too. Probably that's why he goes around with him. He's the physicist's doctor."

"You didn't see the look on his face when the same monitor beeped again."

"The monitor again. The monitor's *always* beeping for no reason."

"Nothing happens for no reason. But this is the first time that guy Cutsinger ever *thought* about it, I could tell."

Back in the jump station, Charlie and Zeke checked readings and made adjustments and paid no attention to Cutsinger and the Navy doctor, who seemed frozen rigid with expectation until one of the monitors beeped. Only then did they relax.

"Wish I could figure out what the hell that is," said Charlie.

"Beats me," said Zeke.

Dr. Lane nudged Cutsinger. "It cold in here to you?"

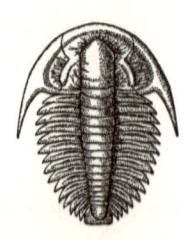

THE DESPOBLADO

Within the big gray ship's boat bay, they had simply driven the truck down a ramp onto the barge. On its bow, the barge's civilian owners, Walton & Wicket, had emblazoned the name *Karen* in gilt-edged script. Now, as Navy men lowered the rest of the cargo, the mate, a big, blocky man who was in fact the subordinate half of Walton & Wicket, secured it. Throughout, another man, about forty years old, of average size and trim-looking in a tropical suit, took particular interest in the treatment accorded the truck and several crates stenciled with various caveats; he stood watching with his hands thrust into the pockets of his jacket and occasionally issued an instruction which the mate blithely ignored. The third man aboard *Karen*, Walton himself, middle-aged, very spare of frame, very sparse and white of hair, watched from the pilot house.

The mate suddenly paused halfway through the motion of manhandling a crate into position; his expression of intense concentration did not change, but his gaze became fixed on a point beyond the pilot house. Walton turned and saw a woman standing on the lowest rung of the access ladder. She called out to him, "Permission to come aboard?"

Without thinking, momentarily incapable of doing so, Walton nodded assent, and she stepped down lightly onto the deck. There she paused and posed for his inspection. She wore canvas shorts, a faded blue work shirt, and scuffed hiking boots. A seabag rested against her slim leg, a professional's battered camera case swung against her opposite hip. Beneath a broad-brimmed hat pulled down tight over close-cropped hair, she had a full, round face, almost high-school-girlish in its unfinished prettiness. Her dark hair and eyes contrasted nicely with her fair skin. She sounded all of nineteen years old when she asked, "Are you Mister Walton?"

"Yes," he said slowly and after a moment more, "I am."

"My name's Michelle Kelly." She offered her right hand, which he automatically shook, then her left to present an envelope with his name written upon it. "I have a letter of introduction. Kevin Barnet recommended you very highly."

Walton said, "Ah," and grimaced, "Kevo," and peered upward expecting to see the man himself grinning down at him from the catwalk. He saw only the Navy men who had been loading cargo onto *Karen*; now they regarded the young woman with obvious and approving interest. Walton snatched the envelope from her. He split it open with his thumb and frowned as he read:

Bud—

This is to introduce Michelle Kelly, another damn nature photographer, but she's bright, opinionated as only someone her age can be, and as you'll undoubtedly notice has a behind like a good fresh peach. She wants to have a look-see upriver, and you owe me a favor, so please take her away with you and return her in one piece.

Best, KEVO

Walton's frown etched itself deeper into his face. He sighed profoundly. "I'll just go have a word with Mister Barnet," he said.

"Oh, he's back at Stinktown."

Walton worked his frown into a full scowl. "Miz Kelly, as you can plainly see, this is not really an excursion boat. As for sightseeing, there's not much more to look at upriver than there is here. We are going into the despoblado. The unpeopled land.

There're no electric lights, no showers, no mess tents, no amenities. And no handsome young Navy men."

Now she scowled. It should have made her look like a balked child but did not. Instead, hard angles revealed themselves within the creamy unblemished skin, and the lips, rather than distending into a pout, compressed into a firm straight line. "I'm not just sightseeing, I'm working. I'll pay for my passage, of course, and I've already signed a dozen waivers relieving everybody of responsibility for me." She nudged her seabag with the side of her foot. "I've got a gallon of sunscreen and my own food and everything else I'll need right here. I just want to hitch a ride. Sort of like Darwin."

"Darwin."

"On the *Beagle*."

"Darwin was invited to go along on that trip."

"Oh, let her come along, Walton." This was the man in the tropical suit, who stood leaning against one of his worrisome crates. He had sand-colored hair and a good profile, and he looked amused. He stepped forward and introduced himself as John Moen. He gave her a conspiratorial wink and said to Walton, "She doesn't look like she'll take up much space at all. Let her come."

Encouraged, she said, "I can even make myself useful if you need me to be. Swab the bo'sun, squeegee the fo'c'sle, whatever."

"A comedienne," Walton growled. "My insurance doesn't cover passengers who try to be helpful—or funny." He had no sooner spoken these words than he realized that he had ceased to scowl. He tried not to look abashed as he said, "But if you'll promise to behave yourself, come on, stow your gear below."

She stepped past him. Moen turned in place to watch as she went by, then gave Walton a look of astonished delight. Wicket looked at her and then turned quickly away as she passed.

"It'll be nice," Moen said to Walton, "to have someone to talk to on this scow of yours." He inclined his head ever so slightly to indicate Wicket. "For a change."

"I should've asked her if she had a note from her mother."

"Oh, I dunno," Moen said easily, "that jilleroo is older than she looks."

The frown began to reassert itself on Walton's face. "If I were you," he snapped, "I'd make damn sure she's of legal age." He turned away from Moen and told Wicket to finish securing the cargo and called out for the lines to be cast off. Then he went to the wheel, and with a thrum of diesels the boat moved smoothly out of the bay and away from the ship. Without, the view disappointed. The peneplained land appeared only as an off-white band separating the sea from the sky; the single emphatic note was provided by bright orange buoys marking a navigable channel among the delta's myriad braided courses. The Navy ship had stood well offshore to avoid the risk of running aground, for there was no abyssal ocean deep here, but inundated continental interior, with a gradient so slight that the land seemed simply to slip beneath the edge of the water like one sheet of paper under another.

Michelle Kelly came back on deck and found herself a place to sit among some crates. A camera hung suspended on a strap encircling her neck, and from time to time she raised it, peered through the viewfinder, and snapped the shutter.

Moen appeared beside her and held out a bottle of water beaded with condensation. She hesitated, then accepted it and thanked him. She rolled the cool plastic across her forehead before she drank. "I could've stayed in Stinktown and been this hot and sticky. May I ask how far upriver you're going, Mister Moen?"

"Please call me John. We'll reach my camp tomorrow. We make better time once we're out of this swamp." He regarded her with frank curiosity. "You can't just be rattling around loose here."

"I'm not. What do you do, John?"

Her using his first name evidently made up for her evasiveness, for he smiled at her and said, "I'm a geologist."

She nodded toward the great yellow truck lashed to the deck. "So that's yours?"

"Yes. Fair being fair, tell me what you're doing here."

"I'm working, too. Seeing as much of this world as I can, while I can."

"Who's your sponsor?"

"I'm privately funded."

"So'm I."

"I'm here because my father has the money and my Uncle Ivan has the clout. Ivan Kelly?"

Moen shook his head.

"Before your time, I guess. He was the first man to go through the hole. And my dad's a Hollywood screenwriter, so the pressure was really on me to make something of my life. So here I am."

"Here you are."

"Once I leave, I'll never get to come back. You don't get to come back unless some multinational's footing the bill. You, for instance, will get to come back all you like. You're looking for oil."

He was taken aback but recovered quickly. "Yes, I'm looking for oil."

She nodded gravely. "What else would you be doing? I've seen aircraft flying around everywhere towing those little gliders with the magnetometers. And that—" she nodded at the truck again "—is a vibrator truck."

He looked at the truck as though it had suddenly materialized from thin air. "Why, so it is. And that salesman swore it was a rec vehicle."

She made a visible effort not to smile. "You jack it up on a central pedestal and make it vibrate, and then you use the sound waves in rock to make subsurface maps."

"You don't say."

Now she did smile, excellently.

The boat entered the mouth of the channel. The brown, turbid water was choked with broad algal mats, some of them more than a yard across. Built of delicate interlaced filaments, they looked more solid than they were; they disintegrated into their constituent strands as the boat eased through them. Here and there low muddy islets supported other algal growth. The air was heavy with a stench of decomposition.

"A pomander would be handy right about now," she said.

Moen nodded. "Or nose plugs. But it smells ten times worse when the tide's out. The mud here's of such fine consistency that it feels like oil when you rub it between your fingertips. You'd sink right into it, over your head. The particles in it are all that's left of a mountain range. It's all been worn away and dumped here in a geosyncline. And it's full of decaying stuff."

"Charles Darwin said a wide expanse of muddy water has neither grandeur nor beauty."

"Smart old Charlie."

They saw a large, honey-colored arthropod, with bristly black grasping appendages outstretched, that had pulled itself onto an islet. It lay perfectly still among intorted tendrils of foliage and might have been looking around or listening or simply basking. Moen observed unnecessarily that there was little for it to see and nothing for it to hear. He opined that the creature's eyes probably did not work very well, and he expressed doubt that it even possessed ears.

She asked, "Are you an expert on sea scorpions?"

He shook his head. "No, not really. I was just repeating what some paleontologist said. I know my forams and conodonts—those are the index fossils I use in my work—but I don't know all that much about other Paleozoic life-forms and don't have much interest in them, frankly."

"Just in oil."

"Oil's fascinating. It's a product of a chain of improbable occurrences."

Michelle crossed her arms, leaned against the rail with her hip, and faced him. "I don't understand," she said, "how you propose to get the oil back even if you do find it. You can't pump it through the hole, and taking it out by the barrel would be prohibitively expensive."

He shrugged. "I'm sure there're people trying to figure that out. My job is just to find it. So. Can't we be friends in spite of everything?"

She gave him an appraising look. "I'm not sure I could be friends with anybody who thinks the way you do."

He laughed pleasantly. "Well, you're young, and I work for a big old evil multinational. We're supposed to have extremely definite opinions. But wait till we get to my camp and you meet Dews. You'll love Dews. Dews," and he laughed again, "is pure unreconstructed slash-and-burn, suck-it-dry, throw-it-away."

"Can't wait," she murmured.

Walton glumly watched Moen and the young woman from the pilot house. He noted how Moen had moved closer to her without appearing to realize that he was doing so. For a moment, both of them stood leaning on the rail, arms folded, elbows almost touching. Then Michelle casually turned away and incidentally increased the distance between Moen and herself without appearing to realize that she had done so. It struck Walton that Moen almost succeeded at covering his disappointment.

The two people at the rail were quiet for a time. The unchanging landscape glided past. Then Michelle asked where the facilities were, and Moen directed her belowdecks.

When she returned, she indicated the pilot house and its occupant with a nod and said, "Give me your extremely definite opinion of Walton and Wicket. There's more to them than meets the eye."

"You might better ask Walton about Walton. I've known him a while now. I've spent maybe eight years here, if you add up my field time, and in all that time I don't think I've ever seen or heard of him venturing more than a quarter-mile from water. He's got the boatman's view of the world—a navigable body of water bounded on one to three sides by terra incognita. There're probably sea scorpions with drier feet than Walton's."

"What about Wicket?"

"I've never been able to decide if he's not all there or if he just tunes me out. Or some combination of the two. He may be mentally handicapped or something. I'm surprised he got past screening."

"Interesting library they've got on this tub."

"Mm?"

"Books. Voltaire. *The Wind in the Willows.* Someone on this barge reads books."

"Well, what else is there for someone to do on a barge?"

Behind them, the big gray ship shrank to an insignificant speck on the landscape and was finally lost to view. Ahead, the highest visible point was a particular patch of orange rising slightly above the succession of swampy mounds. The patch resolved itself into the roof of a small prefabricated storage building at the base camp. Moored amid the islets, the base camp itself was a floating platform supporting the storage shed and smaller structures. A small motorboat tied up at a low pier sat motionless in the water, and there was no movement on or around the platform until Walton brought *Karen* close. Then the motorboat bobbed in the backwash, and a tall, thin, sun-darkened woman stepped out of the operations shack and stood watching and waiting until the barge was secured.

Moen gave Michelle a grin and gestured expansively. "Our home away from home! And there's our charming and lovely hostess, the Dame Paleontologist herself."

Walton, carrying a handful of mail, stepped onto the platform, with Michelle and Moen right behind. Walton gruffly introduced Michelle to Merry Grenon, who regarded her with undisguised amazement. After a moment, the older woman said, "What brings you this way?"

"I hope to get a book of photos out of this."

"Well, I hope you don't break a nail or anything."

Michelle's smile never wavered. "Would you mind if I took pictures and asked questions?"

"Not at all."

Close by, Moen favored the two women with a smile, and to the older he said, "Be careful what you say to her, Merry, she's got a sociopolitical agenda."

Merry Grenon said to Michelle, "Come on, I'll show you around," and then, by some means the young woman did not quite understand but had to admire, effortlessly detached her from Moen and, preceded by Walton, steered her toward a shed used as both laboratory and operations center. Moen obviously wanted to follow, but then he noticed that Wicket had begun unloading supplies onto the platform, and he quickly reboarded *Karen* to watch over his crates like a mother hen.

On one side within the shed sat radio equipment, and a small cabinet in a corner held cooking utensils. Two dented but clean-looking refrigerators stood in opposite corners; the door of one bore an emphatically hand-lettered sign, NO FOOD!!! and an excellent reproduction of Georges Seurat's *A Sunday Afternoon on the Island of La Grande Jatte*; the door of the other bore an equally emphatic sign, FOOD ONLY!!!, and an equally good reproduction of a van Gogh, *The Potato Eaters*. The rest of the cramped space was given over to a long work bench and racks of specimen trays.

Walton asked, "Where're the others?"

"Helen's ashore. Pete took the other boat upriver to try and catch himself some sharks."

Surprise and alarm struggled for supremacy in Walton's expression. "There are sharks here?"

Grenon plainly savored the moment. "Spiny freshwater sharks."

"Well, I wish to hell somebody'd told me. I've been known to dangle my feet in this river."

Merry Grenon offered him a pitying look. "We didn't know there're sharks here until about an hour ago. There're tons of things we don't know about this place, Bud. That's why we're here. Anyway, Pete found a decomposing spiny shark washed up on the bank, and now he's all excited. Here, I'll show you." She went to the refrigerator marked NO FOOD!!!, opened it, withdrew a metal tray. There was a thick odor of decomposition and preservative. In the tray lay a desiccated fish carcass about six inches long, blunt-headed, with ganoid scales and paired rows of spike-like fins along its belly.

"What's this," Walton demanded, "the chihuahua of the shark family?"

"It's Climatius," Grenon said proudly, "or a first cousin. The order Climatiiformes, in any case. Not really sharks at all, but the earliest vertebrates with jaws that we know about."

"Well, I'll be go to hell," Walton drawled. He looked askance at the mouth, frozen in a fierce toothy miniature grimace. "What does it eat?"

"Invertebrates and maybe small jawless fish. Sea scorpions probably consider it a delicacy."

A thickset middle-aged woman entered, set down her collecting case, removed a sun hat. Michelle was introduced to Helen Wheeler, who greeted her warmly and said, "It's always a pleasure to see a new face."

"I've just been admiring your sharklet," Michelle said, "and the art collection. Is this the Paleozoic version of the Louvre?"

"I'm afraid so. There're more in the bunkhouse. Merry and I wouldn't let Pete put up girlie pictures in there, so we got him a Modigliani nude instead. Now he claims he's in love." Wheeler gestured at the Seurat picture and said, "I saw the original once. It's stunning. You know about pointillism? Up close, it's just all these individual points of color that seem unconnected with one another. Step back, and you notice two things. First you notice that all those dots become a whole greater than its parts. Then you notice that each figure, each group of figures seems to have its own light source. You think, It shouldn't work, and yet somehow it does work." She turned and indicated *The Potato Eaters* and gave a soft little laugh. "And that's my idea of a religious print. I first came to the Paleozoic when I was a grad student, probably not much older than you. I kept coming back, and then one time I found God here. I mean God the source, the everywhere-spirit. I'm not talking about Jesus and religion. Some people turn to holy books and fairy stories—I don't know how else to put it. I don't care if Jesus walked on water or rose from the dead. Even if I did care, I still wouldn't believe it. I don't need to hear about miracles like those. The real miracles are life and spacetime and art. I can feel God's presence in art. Literature, too, sometimes. And music."

"Oh, yes," Michelle managed to say; she had been unprepared for the turn Helen Wheeler's monologue had taken. While she tried to think of something to say, she peered at the picture as though seeking out hidden meaning. Then memory came to her rescue. "My mother told me once she'd always thought Bach and Mozart must've felt the presence of God."

The other woman nodded. "Absolutely. But I'm partial to painters. God spoke through the great painters, at least into the twentieth century."

"My guess would be that God lost interest after Cubism."

"Maybe. But, oh, the Impressionists."

"Van Gogh," Michelle murmured, "was very disturbed, of course, but how could God's presence not be disturbing?"

Wheeler shook her head. "No. God's presence brings peace and joy. Poor van Gogh was mentally ill."

"Can't mentally ill people know God?"

"I believe anybody can know God. But looking at it realistically, I've got to admit that it seems easier for some people than for others."

Michelle and Walton returned to the barge. As *Karen* pulled away from the platform, Michelle, standing next to the pilot house, exchanged waves with the two women on the platform, then turned to Walton and asked, "Is Helen Wheeler always like that? Kind of, you know—"

"Goofy and mystical?" Walton snorted with amusement. "Helen's a case."

Michelle frowned slightly. "I liked her, but—"

"I like her, too, but she's still a case."

"Does she always start talking about God with people she's just met?"

"Well, it's not like she's decided that it's her personal mission in life to lead all her hellbent colleagues to Jesus Christ. She isn't trying to convert anybody. I think God is just one of the really interesting things in her life, like bugs and plants." Walton shrugged. "God's presence is disturbing. You said so yourself."

Gradually, as they entered the estuary's upper reaches, the character of the vegetation changed. The delta's winding channels converged, separated, and reconverged, at last merging into a single broad channel, brown and sluggish, with low banks overgrown in tangles of creeping, curlicued greenery, some with stems topped with button-like sporangia. The sun was descending behind them toward the now-unseen sea when they made their first stop upriver from the base camp. Walton brought the barge in close to the bank, and Wicket ran out a gangplank and maneuvered a heavily loaded dolly ashore. There was no one there to greet him and no sign of a camp, only a neat stack of specimen crates. Michelle looked questioningly at Moen, who told her, "Couple of scientists are off back there scraping lichens from rocks or some such. Baxter and Sterling. Husband-and-wife team. They can lug their own supplies into camp when they get back. Walton'll pick up their crates on the way back downriver."

"It's okay to leave stuff sitting there on the bank like that?"

"Who is there to steal it? Nothing's going to come along and eat it."

Vegetation on the floodplain gradually retreated from the land to the splash zones along either bank, exposing barren flatlands that stretched away to the horizon. The silvery phantom pools shimmering out on the baking white surfaces looked more inviting than the muddy water at hand. Wicket occasionally replaced Walton in the pilot house for substantial lengths of time, during which Walton might disappear below or needlessly inspect the cargo or simply watch the land as it rolled by. Whenever he passed near Moen or Michelle, which was as rarely as possible, he acknowledged their presence with a nod and tried not to make eye contact and to hurry on without seeming to hurry. Once, however, when he did inadvertently meet Moen's look, he was certain that he saw a glint of smugness in it, and he felt his eyebrows draw together. The reaction puzzled and annoyed him. What the hell does it matter to me, he thought fiercely, what these two get themselves into? Don't approve of shipboard romances or workplace romances, and here it's practically the same thing. He retreated quickly to the pilot house and sent Wicket to do busy-work.

He put the boat in close to shore for the evening. When the diesel engines were shut off, the silence was almost stunning. Wicket busied himself in the galley, filling the tiny space from side to side and front to back; he seemed to have room only for his hands, which worked expertly at transforming dried vegetables and meat bar into stew.

"You are welcome to join us for dinner," Walton said to Michelle, so stiffly that she visibly recoiled.

"We're having Walton's speciality," said Moen. "Meat bar in fusal oil."

"Thank you," she said, "but I brought my own food."

Moen grinned. "Coward."

She seemed to relax. "But if I can bring my veggie bars, I'd be delighted to sit with you."

There was little conversation at table, though. After dinner, the three of them paused on deck amid the quietude and watched the great cold moon's stately emergence from a vast bank of clouds. No mosquitoes vexed them. There were no insect noises, no frog choruses, no sounds at all but that of the backwash. There was not a breath of air. Wicket sat quietly by himself on a stack of pallets, reading a book by the light of a lantern.

Walton said, "Will you please read to me, Wicket?" The mate ducked his head sheepishly. "Please? No?" Walton gave Michelle an apologetic glance. "I like him to read to me before I turn in at night, but—in front of company . . . ."

Before he retired, Walton showed Michelle where she could string a hammock. Moen, a frequent passenger, had a bunk belowdecks as well; he was still on deck with her, however, and the two of them were listening to music from a chip pack when Walton made to go below. He paused and listened and decided that it was one of Brahms' overtures, the *Festival* or the *Tragic*—it had been some time since he had heard either, and they always had tended to run together in his mind. The music was punctuated by laughter. Michelle Kelly had a rich, uninhibited laugh, but it had the effect of making Walton go to his bed muttering about foolish young women. But he suddenly knew, and was not surprised to know, that the real problem was jealousy, pure and simple, and both the knowledge and its unsurprising nature only made him angrier. Dammit, he told himself, I refuse to feel jealousy over some little thing who's half my age, if that. Before he fell asleep, however, he heard Moen come below—alone—and turn in—alone—and, strangely gratified, he thought, Well, at least she's not a pushover.

The following morning, everyone on the barge was awake and had eaten breakfast by the time the violet sky began to lighten. Even as they watched, that quadrant faded to a deep-sea blue, streaks of rust-colored clouds appeared low above a backlit irregular line of highlands far to the east, and then the filmiest hint of pink suffused the sky behind the clouds. But for that glimpse of distant hills it would have been impossible to say that the land was rising before them, and as the sun continued its swift ascent the highlands faded and blended into the indefinite demarcation of earth and sky.

As they moved upriver, Michelle pointed out a small fish swimming at the surface. "Spiny shark," she said.

Moen peered over the side. "There're sharks here?"

"That seems to be the standard reaction. These are freshwater spiny sharks. Merry Grenon showed me a dead one at the base camp yesterday. She told me the scientific name, but I don't think I can pronounce it right."

They reached the oil geologists' camp before noon. It consisted of a few tents and an area marked off as a heli-pad, and total present population evidently comprised three more or less sunburnt men. Two were dressed in old clothes; the third, wearing only boxer shorts and boots, darted into a tent when he saw Michelle and promptly re-emerged wearing a more nearly complete ensemble. Moen displayed his previous particularity about his crates, and this time Wicket appeared to heed his instructions during the unloading. Then, laughing, boyishly happy, Moen personally drove the vibrator truck onto the bank, leaving deep tracks in the loose, crumbly marl. He invited Walton and Michelle to stay for dinner, and they accepted. Wicket's exclusion seemed to Michelle to be taken as a given.

Moen was clearly in charge and in his element. The camp's working day ended when he said so. This, as it turned out, was an hour before sundown, which gave the junior member of the geology team, a sweating red-faced man named Bloodworth, little time to wash up and prepare some kind of meal—"for up to a dozen people," Moen explained, "depending on whether the helicopter's brought some in or taken some out"—and seemed to leave Moen himself and his guests barely enough time to wash up and have drinks in hand when the edge of the sun dipped behind the far edge of the world. They sat with the other two members of Moen's crew, Dews and McCampbell, at a long camp table in the mess tent; the tent flaps were turned back so that they could watch the sun set.

"All I want out of life," Moen said as the harried Bloodworth placed a steaming tureen on the table, "is to be able to sip good whiskey and watch spectacular sunsets. No, actually, I want a good deal else. I want this team to produce the results I want to take back to my bosses. I want to be ten times richer than I am and ten years younger than I am, and to weigh ten pounds less than I do. I want to have back all the hair I've lost." He paused as Bloodworth set dinner before him. "I want a decent meal." He regarded the food. "Meat bar in fusal oil," he said, "my favorite," and laughed.

Bloodworth looked apologetic and backed away. Dinner was eaten with a minimum of talk, most of it having to do with the arcana of oil geology. Michelle dutifully chewed overcooked reconstituted vegetables and made no attempt to join in the conversation, nor did Moen's men make any attempt to draw her into it. It was obvious to Walton that she was conscious of the appraising looks they gave her whenever they thought she was not looking. Moen seemed thoroughly amused by the effect she was having on them.

My responsibility ends at the gangplank, Walton thought, and forced his attention to his food. He ate with such resolute single-mindedness that a second or two elapsed before he realized that the conversation had suddenly and unexpectedly taken a combative turn, that Dews had said something to which Michelle objected; he looked up and saw her regarding Dews piercingly, saw Dews return it with one of happy belligerence, heard Moen say blandly, "Dews, I don't think our young guest approves of any of this—do you, Miz Kelly?"

"I don't. Call me an eco-maniac, but I don't like the idea of raiding the past to keep the present going. A lot of people don't."

Dews leaned back in his chair and knitted his blunt red fingers over his midsection; Michelle did not flinch from his gaze. "The quantum-mechanics boys," he drawled, "say we haven't traveled into our own Earth's prehistoric past at all. They say there must be duplicate Earths, parallel Earths—each more or less different from our own. So nothing we do here can make any difference in our own timeline."

"It's certainly a convenient theory. But there's nothing here that contradicts anything we already knew for certain about mid-Paleozoic times. We knew about maybe two percent of the whole story from what we found in the fossil record. Now we can at least glimpse the other ninety-eight percent, and it's roughly what we imagined it would be. Even if the physicists're right, even if this isn't our own Earth, it might as well be. What about this planet's future? Even if it's only a duplicate Earth, what if, four hundred million years from now, humans arise but can't invent technological civilization all over again because the resources needed to do so aren't there?"

"There's no guarantee," Dews said, "that humans necessarily arise on Earth-type planets. Maybe humans don't make it here. Maybe the dinosaurs never go extinct, no big meteor crash, and the mammals never get their shot at greatness. Maybe there never are even dinosaurs here, just bugs and shellfish until the sun expands and the planet fries. We can't see into the future of this world and find out if it's a good thing or a bad thing to exploit its resources. Meanwhile, we need the oil."

"What we need is a replacement for the internal-combustion engine."

"You may not believe me, but I agree. I've been waiting all my life for one of those hydrogen-powered buckets. And you, Bud," Dews said to Walton, "how much'd that tub of yours save you if you didn't have to use diesel fuel?"

Walton did not look up from his dinner; he said, without enthusiasm, "A bundle."

"Right!" Dews returned his attention to Michelle. "But the fact of the matter is, we don't have a replacement, and—meanwhile—the internal-combustion engines we do have need the oil!"

Michelle said nothing but shook her head emphatically.

Dews rolled his eyes. "Eco-maniacs give me a highly localized pain. Because people like me know how to take what the earth has to offer, everybody, including you, lives better and longer than any people in history. But people like you don't want us to hurt their precious goddamn salamanders and bugs."

"Time out," Moen interjected, "for a sunset," and everybody relaxed as one and turned as one to watch the sun go down.

Conversation, slow to resume, restricted itself to requests for condiments, then died altogether. After the silence had stretched out across half an eternity Michelle suddenly said, "Well, everybody, how about some music?" and took her chip pack from her shirt pocket.

Simultaneously, Dews said, "What?" and Moen exclaimed, "Excellent idea!"

"I've got Mozart and the three Bees," she said, "plus bop, pop, hop, drop, and truckstop."

"Lady's a poet," said McCampbell, and Bloodworth asked, "You got the Shiners?"

She gave him a regretful look. "Sorry, fresh out. Oh, I know." She did something with the chip pack. "What I'm about to inflict on you is an actual top-ten country-and-western hit back in the twenty-first century," and at the touch a button there came a twangy guitar introduction, and then a woman sang, in a nasal but good-humored voice,

"*Baby, come on back with me,*
let's skinny-dip in the Tethys Sea.
Let's pack a bag and leave today
four hundred million years away,
and marvel at exotic fauna
living in or near Gondwana—
trilobites and placoderms
and seven thousand kinds of worms."

During an instrumental interlude, McCampbell said, "Sure's hell don't write songs like they used to."

"That's for damn sure," Dews said.

Moen laughed. "It's wonderful, boys. A top-ten hit, she says. I bet it's playing at truck stops all over America."

"We'll pitch a tent, and through the door
we'll watch those creatures flop ashore
and bet on how well each one waddles—
we'll be excellent role models,
we'll leave our tracks along the shore
and demonstrate what feet are for.
We'll brew some psilophytic tea
and make love by the Tethys Sea."

Moen laughed again as the song ended. "I bet there's not a trucker or a waitress in a hundred who knows what the hell it's even about."

"Course they will," McCampbell said. "It's about having sex in the great outdoors."

Michelle gestured with the chip pack. "Want to hear it in some other style?"

"Once is enough," Dews muttered.

Moen gave Michelle a sidelong look and asked, "What other delights've you got in that little box of yours?"

Walton flushed and frowned, and though he looked at Moen when he spoke, he clearly meant his words for Michelle. "I don't want to be a party-pooper, but I have to get an early start tomorrow. We're—I'm on a tight schedule."

Michelle leaned back in her seat, looked first at Walton, then at Moen. She slipped the chip pack back into her shirt pocket. She looked around the table and said, "It's been nice meeting you fellows."

"Come back any time," McCampbell ventured jocosely, "and bring your girl friends."

"Listen to you," Michelle said as she stood up. "Wouldn't it be more fun if you had some women geologists here all the time?"

"Yep," McCampbell conceded, "even if they were tree-huggers. Maybe especially if they were tree-huggers."

Michelle gave him a look of politest inquiry.

McCampbell said, "Gal who'll hug a tree'll hug anything," and laughed uproariously. After a moment. Dews followed his lead. Bloodworth joined in, but half-heartedly. Moen smiled thinly.

Walton rose and nodded to Moen, whose smile was suddenly replaced by a disappointed and slightly desperate expression;

the geologist almost overturned his own chair as he pushed to his feet. Walton cast a final look around the table, let his gaze rest for a moment on the grinning McCampbell, and murmured, "Gentlemen." As he turned away, he heard Moen utter Michelle's name, but without waiting to see if she would follow he began walking toward the river. He felt embarrassed and angry and vaguely unclean.

He did not look back until he had reboarded the barge, and he had no sooner done so than he saw her emerge from darkness into the light of *Karen's* lamps, looking as cool and casual as though she had been for a stroll around the block. Moen trailed one or two paces behind her with the air of someone trying to salvage an unexpectedly and rapidly deteriorating situation. She turned at the gangplank and told him gaily, "Thank you for a perfectly lovely evening," and came on board, and as she passed Walton she called out, "Perhaps we'll have time to visit again on the way back downriver."

Moen wilted on the bank. He did not set his foot on the gangplank. "Well," he said. "I guess I should say good night."

"Good night," she said, and Walton seconded her. The geologist smiled wanly and went back to his camp.

"I thought you might be thinking of spending the night ashore," Walton told Michelle in an even tone, without quite looking at her.

"So did he. In fact, I believe he had his whole weekend planned out. Straight-ahead romantic plunge on a boat, followed by hours of grunting and bucking. I guess setting me and Dews on each other was his idea of foreplay." She had plainly meant for him to laugh or at least smile.

Walton did not respond; he still would not look at her. "If you don't mind my asking, what're your plans for when we get back to the base camp? All I do is come upriver and go downriver. Occasionally, I hug the coast to Wegener Point and back, but not anytime soon."

The edge in his voice was matched in hers. "I might try to hitch a ride to someplace else. Or I could just walk."

"Walk? Walk where?"

Her tone became defiant. "Wegener Point's only about a hundred klicks north of the base camp, right? Stinktown's another few hundred."

THE DESPOBLADO ● STEVEN UTLEY

"But walk?"

She raised a foot and waggled it for a moment. "I may've grown up in car culture, but I know what these things on the end of my legs are for. If hiking through hills and canyons in southern California didn't prepare me—"

"It's mostly evaporite flats between here and Wegener Point. Truly grisly places. You can't possible carry enough food to last you till you reached the point."

"I wouldn't have to carry it. I can always find it lying around."

Walton shook his head—admiringly, in spite of himself, for though her cocksure attitude grated, he found himself liking her adventurousness and apparent fearlessness. He suppressed his irritation and said, "Nature girl."

"Why don't you let me make dinner tomorrow and see for yourself?" He looked dubious. "I promise not to poison you. I'd like you to try some of my food."

"Exactly what do you eat?" Walton said warily.

"Whatever there is. My Uncle Ivan was one of the first scientists to study Paleozoic life-forms and ecosystems in the Paleozoic. He told me what I'd be able to eat here and what not to eat. Um, Wicket is invited, of course."

Walton shook his head emphatically. "It'd just disturb him." Neither of them spoke for a good part of a minute. Then: "I mean, set something aside for him if you want, and I'll give it to him, but—everything considered, he's done quite well these past few days. He's doing the best he can. He can't do any better than he does."

Presently, from the direction of the camp came the sound of a diesel engine cranking up.

Michelle gazed off into the darkness. "Boys with toys," she said.

At last they left the floodplain astern, and the river changed its character, ceasing its languid meandering, becoming a great broad current coursing with seeming purpose. The landscape changed as well. The undulations of the peneplain had gradually become perceptible as such, next as low mounds of marl studded with broken rock, and then the land abruptly crumpled itself into a succession of barren knolls. The banks rose until it was usually impossible to see what lay beyond them. The rocks above the splash zone were spotted with lichens; below it, they glistened with slimy greenery. *Karen* made another stop at midday to leave a cache of dried foodstuffs and mail. Michelle went ashore to take pictures and, as she told Walton, collect some specimens of her own.

That evening, in the cramped cubicle that served as *Karen*'s formal mess area, Michelle set before Walton a serving of what seemed to be snap beans and brown rice. There was also a small mound of what could have been black beans or caviar. He said, "Is it a good idea to ask what this stuff is before I put it in my mouth?"

"Probably not, if you have irrational food prejudices."

He thought of her collecting sortie. "Then don't tell me afterward, either, okay?" He slipped his fork into the black beans or caviar and put three or four of them into his mouth. They were neither black beans nor caviar, but he allowed after chewing them a couple of times that they tasted pretty good. She beamed at him and dug into her own food.

When they had finished eating, he sat back and told her, "Michelle Kelly, I salute you. In you are met all the best of French and Irish."

"German, too. The name's just the legacy of my ethnically bewildered parents. I'm only very attenuated anything."

Walton started to gather up his tableware.

"No," she said, rising, "don't get up, I'll take care of the dishes."

He watched her putter in the tiny galley for a minute. Then he said, seriously, "Tomorrow we go on as far as we can. The last outpost this side of Gondwana. I'll appreciate your staying on the boat then. I can't be sure how he'll take to you being there." He thought, but did not say, *I don't want you getting into anything with him the way you almost did with Dews.*

Kelly glanced over her shoulder at him. "How who'll take what?"

"How the hermit'll take to you being there. The old man of the mountain, as I call him."

"Who is he, and what's his story?"

"He's part of the paleoclimate survey. Mans the radio station out here."

"What's his story? Nobody just becomes a hermit."

"No? Most people know or feel—even if they don't know they know it, or don't know they feel this—for most people, selfhood exists not in isolation from other people but in relationships to other people. But there're always some men who want solitude. In pioneer days, they were the ones who pulled up stakes and moved on because they felt crowded by their closest neighbors, five miles away."

Michelle dried the last dish and put it away. She turned, leaned against the tiny sink, began carefully drying her fingers. Without looking at Walton, she said, "Is that how it is with you?"

"God, no. I'm gregarious as hell."

Now she did look at him. "You know, Mister Walton, I believe there's a good deal more to you than meets the eye. You're not just some old river rat."

"No," he said slowly, "I guess I'm not."

"What's your story? Or don't you have one either?"

"I have a degree from the U.C.L.A. School of Philosophy. It's true. In another life, another time. On another world. I was the complete philosophy wonk. Even to having a tall, fair, Nordic girl friend who liked to dress in black. She did look fine in a leotard, too. The stuff of being and meaning was our breakfast conversation and our pillow talk. She was doing her thesis on Kirkegaard, which may explain why she was about as lively in bed as a Norwegian cheese. Well, here's the best part of her story—her name was Joy! So. I had my degree in hand, I was all set to start teaching the next generation of philosophy wonks everything I'd just been taught about ethical formalism and intuitionism and what all, when the news came out about the spacetime anomaly. Time-travel, expeditions to prehistoric times! Then and there, in an instant, my life turned itself inside out. I told myself, told my girl friend, Dammit, I want to go on one of those expeditions! Of course, as far as the National Science Foundation was concerned, a degree in philosophy wasn't all that relevant to Paleozoic research. So I hooked up with an uncle who plied the intercoastal Waterway out of Mobile and learned how to handle a boat. Hired out to one of the private companies. Now I'm a private enterprise in my own right, with my own damn government contract. Ferrying supplies and delivering mail. Never regretted it for a second."

"And Wicket?"

"My sister Karen's boy. I became his legal guardian after she died. He's terminally shy, in case you haven't noticed, but he's quite intelligent, never forgets anything, whiz at math. So I made him the company accountant. When they said I couldn't bring him along in my capacity as an equal-opportunity employer helping somebody overcome a handicap, I made him my business partner. And some people went to bat for me. Kevin Barnet, for one." Walton paused, then said carefully, "By the way, do you know Kevo well?"

"Well enough to know he's a character."

"He's hardly what you'd call an unimpeachable character reference."

"I think this was in the way of one character recommending another. I distinctly heard him call you colorful."

"You should take everything that man says with a five-pound block of salt. He's a drunken old bum and a lecher. I really don't care much for the man. But I owe him on Wicket's account. Anyway, I believe Wicket's happy here. He likes being on the boat, likes his work. He doesn't have to deal with anyone but me and the occasional lower life-form."

"Such as me."

"You know perfectly well what I mean."

The next morning as they went upriver, Walton called to her, and she saw him point to starboard. Well back from the bank the land was puckered into a line of rough hills, and set at intervals along the ridgeline were the improbable spindly forms of windmills. "Powers his generator. The old man of the mountain's. You'll see him around the next bend in the river."

"I don't even see the mountain."

"It's a metaphorical mountain. And he's a metaphorical old man." He tugged on the whistle cord, and *Karen* let out a piercing shriek. "That'll let him know to expect us. I don't want to scare him into the underbrush by just showing up. Metaphorical underbrush, you understand."

They rounded the bend, and Walton brought the barge in close to the bank. The radio station consisted of a shed fashioned of corrugated metal sheets, dominated by a dish antennae. A smaller shed with one open side housed the generator. The three people on the water waited. Nothing moved on the land.

"What do we do," Michelle said, "just toss everything onto the shore like before and leave?"

Walton shook his head. "I always like to see him. They always ask me when I get back, How'd he look? And I have to tell 'em. He'll show himself. He knows I won't leave until he does."

"How does he look, usually?"

"Like a Neanderthal who's down on his luck."

Wicket ran out the gangplank, took up a gigantic armload of cartons, and went ashore. Walton followed carrying a carton under each arm. After a moment's hesitation, Michelle picked up a carton and followed as well.

Walton glared back at her. "Asked you to stay on the barge."

"I think your hermit's off hiding someplace."

Wicket deposited his armload of cartons by the door to the shed and immediately turned back toward the barge. The door was ajar. Michelle set the carton on the ground, then, overcome with curiosity and helpless to do otherwise, stepped to the doorway and peered within. Her nose was crinkled in anticipation of squalor served up, perhaps, with the thick, sickening smell of dirty socks and foodstuffs gone bad; instead she found only an inconsistent sort of untidiness—a cluttered table, a disheveled cot, and radio equipment that looked well maintained and clean. A rude shelf mounted at eye level on the near wall contained not tapes or chips but old-fashioned books. She was not certain what she would have expected to find in the cabin of a hermit—*Robinson Crusoe*, perhaps, or *Heart of Darkness*—but it disappointed her to that the only titles she could read were those of electronics maintenance manuals.

She suddenly sensed someone behind herself and turned.

The old man of the mountain wore cut-off jeans, a tee-shirt, and a baseball cap—all frayed and rather dirty—and a pair of sandals that appeared to have been repaired with insulated electrical wire. His long, matted hair covered his head like the hood of a parka, and his beard grew up his face almost to the lower eyelids, yet the face in the midst of this unkempt hyperpilosity was that of a man in his mid-thirties. His eyes, clear blue, alert, nervous, never quite met hers. He gave the impression of an animal that found itself cut off from its burrow.

Walton hove into view behind and to one side of the man and said, "Hello." The hermit shot him a startled glance, and Michelle took the opportunity to step aside, out of the doorway. She made an apologetic sound as the man pushed by, trailing a sour smell. He stopped just inside the door, turned, stood there blinking and fidgeting as Walton continued speaking. "You remember Wicket, don't you?" he said, gesturing over his shoulder at the big man standing stock still on the path. "Of course you do. This—" indicating Michelle "—is our new friend Miz Kelly. Say hello."

"Hello," said Michelle.

The man looked as though he were about to speak but settled for nodding.

"We've put everything here by the door for you," Walton said.

"Good. Good. That's good." The man spoke as though it amazed him to discover that he still possessed a voice, and he seemed to repeat words as though to make certain they sounded right when he spoke them. "Thank you. That's good. Good."

"We'll be going now. Till next time. Michelle."

Michelle hurried to rejoin Walton, and then the hermit practically herded them back to the boat and watched until Walton had backed the barge away from the bank, brought it about, pointed its blunt bow downriver. Then he disappeared into his shed and did not show himself again. She imagined a couple of times that she glimpsed his face at the window, but could not be certain of it. The boat followed the bend of the river, and the radio station passed from view.

For some time after they had left the hermit's camp, Walton, in his pilot house with the windows opened to create the impression of a breeze moving through the confined space, watched Michelle as she moved restlessly about the deck. Occasionally she paused at the rail to peer at something unapparent to him. Finally, though, heat and glare drove her into such shade as the superstructure had to offer. He heard her back thump against the pilot house as she sat down by it, but he saw and heard nothing more of her for several minutes. Then, above the rhythm of the diesels, there came music. He recognized it after a moment as the emotive second movement of Bach's Violin Concerto in A Minor. It was followed in short order by "Pas d'action," from *Swan Lake*. Ah, Christ, he thought unhappily, we're going to be awash with melancholy all the way back downriver. She surprised him, however, by next playing the

"Dance of the Swans," and Walton could not help smiling, could not resist picturing for a moment a row of sprightly tutu-clad young women prancing and whirling along the stony bank.

After dinner, they sat looking up at the dark purple sky. Walton stretched, crossed his arms tightly across his chest, and made a contented sound. She looked around at him and said, "How'd he get past screening? The old man of the mountain."

Walton shrugged. "I guess he was well enough to get through screening. Living in the Paleozoic brought out the craziness in him. It's some kind of progressive disorder."

"What happens to him if everybody else here just folds up and goes home?"

"Well, that's not very likely to happen, is it? Listen, he's not the only one. There're several more just like him, living off in the badlands with just a radio set and some crates of canned goods and a case of whiskey. That one we visited today, he told me once that man is the ape that lives like a cockroach."

"I guess he's the living proof of that."

"He meant that we tend to pack ourselves together in confined spaces and live in our own dirt, and we eat anything and breed like crazy."

"That man needs professional help."

Walton shrugged again. "Nobody can help him."

"Not here they can't."

"Not back in the twenty-first century, either. Where could he go there, what could he do, to find the kind of isolation and seclusion he wants? Here, at least, he's happy, or content, or whatever the hell he is. You can't get much more secluded and isolated than four hundred million years in the past and way off in the hinterlands."

"He looked at me like I was—like I was I don't know what."

"Like you were just another member of the whole damned human race he came here to get away from. It's nothing personal. There's nothing personal about any of it. I'm not sure he really thinks of himself as a member of our species any more. Somebody who needs isolation that bad must've been born without the ape gene for gregariousness. I'm not sure what he thinks at all, to tell the truth. We may be just symbiots to him. We bring him food and whiskey, he transmits data to us. It's about the same kind of relationship you have with the bacteria in your guts."

"It sounds sociopathic."

"Maybe. It's anti-social at the very least. But maybe sociopaths are really mutants adapted for life off by themselves. Preadapted for life in the unknown places. It's always the loners who're the trailblazers, the first ones to go out into the unknown. Probably wherever the human race goes, out in space to other worlds, back in time, there'll always be some seriously unsocialized character way out ahead on the edge of everything. Maybe men like that are our ace in the hole. Maybe they guarantee the survival of our species."

"Not if they are all men and don't take along girl friends."

"There're women hermits, too."

"Out here?"

Walton shrugged. "Who knows?"

They said no more for several minutes. Then Michelle made an amused sound. "What do you suppose courtship between a male and female hermit is like?"

"Maybe like scorpions mating. Hell, I don't know. Maybe hermits aren't our ace in the hole. It's just a hypothesis."

"Well, I've had it up to here with hypotheses. Can a person buy something to drink on this beamy scow?"

"If it's scotch, and if a person doesn't call this beautiful and versatile craft of mine a beamy scow." He glanced at her sharply. "And I should probably ask to see some identification."

"I turned twenty-five in November."

"Moen was right. You are older than you look."

Walton fetched a bottle and two glasses, and he and Michelle settled into a comfortable silence. After a minute or two, however, he realized that he was unaccountably quite happy, and then after a moment more that he was perhaps not quite so happy after all, that he wanted to say to her and, moreover, that he probably would never dare to say to her, I think I shall miss you terribly when you've gone. He was grateful when Wicket, who had been sitting on a stack of palettes at the bow, reading a book, suddenly got up and came and stood about six feet from Walton and Michelle. Walton looked at him in frank astonishment and murmured, "Well, well." Wicket looked from Walton to a point in space near Michelle and then back at Walton, who told Michelle, "Looks like you've finally been sort of kind of accepted."

She made a visible effort not to look directly at the big man. "I thought he was never going to make up his mind about me."

"Moen distracted him for a bit. He's not crazy about Moen."

"Imagine that."

Walton gave Wicket an expectant look and said, "Will you please read from your book now?"

The big man softly cleared his throat and began to read aloud. He had a surprisingly sweet voice; he read with passable enunciation and made a respectable attempt at inflection. "'Fanny had the pleasure of seeing Edmund continue at the window with her, in spite of the expected glee, and of having his eyes soon turned like hers toward the scene without, where all that was solemn and soothing, and lovely, appeared in the brilliancy of an unclouded night, and the deep shade of the woods. 'Here's harmony!' said she. 'Here's repose! Here's what may leave all painting and all music behind, and what poetry can only attempt to describe. Here's what may tranquilize every care, and lift the heart to rapture! When I look out on such a night as this, I feel as if there could be neither wickedness nor sorrow in the world; and there certainly would be less of both if the sublimity of Nature were more attended to, and people were carried more out of themselves by contemplating such a scene.'"

Michelle laughed her good laugh and said, "Whoa!"

Walton regarded him with wonder. "What are you reading from?" Wicket shyly held the book out to him. "*Mansfield Park.* Jane Austen. Jesus Christ. You are such a romantic."

The barge moved with the current and put in at each of the camps previously visited to take on crates of specimens. The landscape smoothed itself out, and the river slowed and began to meander. In the amber light of a late afternoon, they approached the oil geologists' camp and saw gouged and furrowed marl along the bank. Its yellow sides caked with mud, the vibrator truck sat dormant amid a crazy pattern of treadmarks. There was no sign of the men. Walton reached for the whistle cord, then withdrew his hand. To Michelle, who stood leaning against the pilot house, he said, "Might be taking their naps."

"Looks like they've been cutting doughnuts."

"What else is there for them to do for fun around here?"

"Maybe they've been celebrating. Maybe they've found what they were looking for. Are we going ashore now?"

Walton shook his head. "Not unless you want to."

"I don't want to."

"Then not till we have to."

THE WAVE-FUNCTION COLLAPSE

All he can do at first is stare dully through the window at the barren Paleozoic landscape. Then focus sharpens, his mind begins to work again, disbelief increases in inverse proportion to subsiding shock, and soon his thoughts seem to outrace the helicopter's shadow below. He constructs his first hypothesis: Somebody's made a terrible mistake. By the time the machine swoops in low over the bay and circles to land on the ship's flight deck, the hypothesis has mutated into a suspicion: Somebody's playing a terrible practical joke. As he steps down from the cabin, he is almost angry enough to punch somebody, anybody—even the civilian liaison, who emerges from a group of Navy men, but whose solemn expression disarms him.

The liaison shakes his hand and guides him down into the ship, talking all the while. "We'll expedite your return, of course, you'll be home before noon, someone is going to be there to pick you up and, ah, take you wherever you need to go, damn, I'm *so* sorry."

Expedite, he thinks. Return. Home.

He gropes for the meanings of the words, cannot quite get hold of them, gives up the effort, consoles himself with the savage thought, Yeah, well, if this *is* a monstrous prank, somebody's sure as hell gonna catch seven kinds of hell for it. One doesn't with impunity throw the jump station off its holy schedule for the sake of a laugh. One doesn't get away with saying something about a man's wife that's neither true nor funny. He is amused by the latter qualification. A laugh or a sob escapes. *Especially* if it's not funny.

Despite the general sense of urgency, he does not go immediately to the head of the line at the jump station and, so, through and straight home to the 21st Century of the Common Era. He does not even go to the jump station to wait, but to sick bay. It takes time to make the station's tight schedule flex enough to accommodate him, and he has certain preparations to make in the meantime. One does not simply fling oneself through a hole in spacetime or whatever it is. He really wants, would give anything (he tells himself), for a good stiff drink or even a bad limp one, but what he gets instead is a quick physical examination and an emetic. "It's never a good idea to make the jump on a full stomach," the Navy doctor reminds him. "Dramamine is ineffective in the prevention or treatment of time-travel sickness."

While the liaison and the Navy doctor confer in a corner, he cools his heels and the minutes drag on and doubt eats away at his disbelief and the likelihood that this is a joke recedes. A lump of sorrow is forming in the center of his chest. It cannot be, he thinks, no it cannot be cannot cannot.

From a pocket of his patched work shirt (still permeated with the grime of inland proto-North America) he removes an old-fashioned paper envelope on which his name has been inscribed with a calligraphy pen, and from the envelope he takes several folded sheets of old-fashioned stationery, smoothes them across his thigh, and reads, "There's something very 19th-century—at least, something very romantic-novel-heroine-ish (whether fainting from the vapors category or ripped bodice/heaving bosom kind)—about writing letters and sending them floating off into the unknown after you. I suspect I'm going to spend a *fortune* on postage while you're gone. I've already sent one letter your way this week, but I won't say I hope it's caught up with you 'by now.' Even traveling by slow boat to wherever you 'are,' it must have reached you before the end of the Paleozoic age. Now I've made my head hurt.

Einstein notwithstanding, these revved-up ape brains of ours cling tenaciously to Newtonian notions of absolute time. We live in the now, trailing, to be sure, a few seconds of the past as we press ahead into the future, but it's always *now* wherever (whenever) we go. What's happening in the Andromeda galaxy this instant? Yes, of course, we can know only what happened there a million years ago, yet I exist in this instant, and the universe, too, and that includes Andromeda. And existence requires that something be happening. (I detest metaphysics. The universe exists even when we aren't looking at it or thinking about it.) And what about 400 million years? You are supposed to have a synchronous anchor embedded in your proper matrix, which is here (with *moi*) (sigh)— so say the physicists, anyhow. But doesn't that fly in the face of relativity? Isn't it too too Newtonian? Too too tootsie. Old song, I think. I've been too long without sleep. And, already, too long without you."

He holds the pages close to his face and inhales a subtle scent of her, and this helps him to decide on a course of action.

At length he is transferred to a little room adjoining the jump station. When the senior jump-station technician pops in to say that there will be an open slot in the schedule in about forty-five minutes, he clutches at her sleeve and demands that she refresh his memory on a couple of points.

"Explain," he says, "this business about the synchronous link."

He tightens his grip as she tries to pull away. She shoots a look at the doctor, who shoots one back. Its meaning is clear: Please just humor him, he's suffered a terrible blow.

"The link," she says, "it's sort of like a brake or anchor."

"Brake, anchor, what does it *do?*"

"It's, well, unless you can follow the math—"

"The hell with the math, tell me what it *does.*"

She jerks her sleeve free and glares first at him, then at the doctor, then back at him. Somehow jump-station techs have got the strange notion into their heads that they are an elite and therefore not quite answerable to just anyone. She would be perfectly within what she regards as her rights were she to tell him to take a flying leap at the moon. Nevertheless, possibly because the Navy doctor is present and Navy officers count for more than, say, someone who has obviously been off in the primeval hinterlands studying weird bugs and pond scum, she says, snappishly, "The link does what a link does. It connects. It synchronizes this spacetime matrix with the one on the, uh, other side."

"So an hour passes here as it passes there."

"Right."

"An hour or a day or a year."

"Right" (testily).

"So if you leave there on a Friday night and spend a weekend here and then go back, it's Monday when you get there."

"Basically that's it, yes."

"You can't twiddle with some knobs, shave off a day or two? So I'd leave here on Monday but get there on Saturday afternoon, say?"

Incredulity and contempt commingle in her expression. "This isn't some damn sci-fi show."

"But—"

"Nobody is messing with the link, period."

Damn, he thinks, scratch one plan of attack. "Then what about the many-worlds thing? Tell me about that."

The senior jump-station tech grimaces, looks imploringly at the doctor. "I got a schedule to keep, y'know."

"Please," says the doctor. "It won't take but a moment."

"The idea is," says the tech, grinding the words between her back teeth, "every possible universe is created at the instant it becomes possible. Like if it's possible for you to jump to either side, to the left or the right, you jump to the left in one universe and to the right in another. And you don't jump at all in still another universe."

"How do you know which universe you're in?"

"You split and get duplicated along with everything else when the universe splits and duplicates itself. You're always in the universe you're supposed to be in."

"No." He shakes his head. "I'm not. Not yet. Listen. I have a plan."

The tech glances anxiously at her watch. "And *I* have a schedule, and I'm *off* it. Sorry."

She withdraws toward her ozone-reeking sanctum and has just got through the door when he moves to follow. Just before the door swings shut behind her, he sees her see him coming and hears her yelp for help and feels her not inconsiderable weight thrown against the door. The doctor tries to pull him away, but he is a big man hardened by field work and efficiently stiff-arms the man while pushing the woman on the opposite side of the door steadily backward. Suddenly, she stops resisting. He tumbles through the door, and a couple of junior techs grab him.

They do not grip him quite firmly enough. He sends one of them spinning against their boss and as those two go down together in a noisy heap he simply brushes away the other, who lacks not only the grip but the reach as well. Reinforcements are on the way, however. He bolts. He disappears further into the depths of the ship. By the time the public-address system barks out a "Now hear this!" he has found himself a cubby-hole and a heavy wrench with which to discourage anything as unsubtle as a frontal assault. Thus entrenched, he ponders the puzzle he knows he must solve if he is to save his wife's life.

The Navy officers and enlisted personnel are not fools, they know their ship, and in short order they have located the man. Getting him out of his hiding place without hurting him or being hurt by him is another matter. Duly summoned, the liaison arrives with the doctor in tow and without preamble says, "We know you're upset, you have our deepest sympathy, but we're here to help you, so just come out of there right now, okay?"

Dangling his wrench negligently, the man answers, "First tell me about the cat in the box."

Nonplussed, the liaison looks at the doctor and the Navy officer and is met with blank stares.

"I know you're distraught," says the liaison, "but," and is cut short with, "What I am is *desperate*. I've been thinking in here, and I believe I may have the solution to my problem. But I've got to be sure I'm remembering stuff correctly. I need to know about the cat in the box."

Nearby, though out of the man's line of sight, the doctor abruptly turns and vanishes down a corridor.

"I don't think I understand," says the liaison. "What cat in what box? Look, can't we discuss this back at the jump station? That slot in the schedule won't be there much longer, you know.

The chief tech says she can't promise there'll be another one before next shift."

"The slot can wait until I'm sure of my plan."

"What plan? Look, why don't you just come out of there? We're *here* for you."

"I appreciate that. I appreciate everybody's concern. Thank you, everybody, for your sympathy and condolences. But I'm hoping to obviate the need for sympathy and condolences, and what I really need is your understanding and your cooperation."

"You have them, you know that!"

"Don't patronize me. Hear me out. Whatzisname, the physicist, says we're not actually in Paleozoic time, but some alternate dimension, universe, whatever. I never thought much about it before today. Now it's what *I have to believe*."

The doctor returns, practically dragging along the senior tech by her hand. The liaison heaves a sigh of relief and says, "Here's someone who should be able to tell you what you want to know," and he separates her from the doctor and draws her into the man's line of sight.

Clearly unhappy with this treatment, the chief tech swats the liaison's hands away. "Okay," she says, "I'm here."

"Please refresh my memory," says the man. "I've been trying to remember the experiment with Whatzisname's cat. The one inside the box."

"Schroedinger's cat."

"That's the one. Schroedinger locked a cat in a box with a radioactive substance and a Geiger counter."

"Actually, it was a *thought* experiment. He didn't really—"

"Whatever. The point is, the cat's in the box, and—and what?"

"There's one chance in two that within a certain length of time the radioactive substance will emit an electron that'll make the Geiger counter click. If the Geiger counter clicks, it activates some device that kills the cat."

"Yeah. And there's no way to tell if the cat's alive or dead unless and until you look inside the box."

"Yeah."

"Until you do look inside, the cat is neither alive nor dead."

"Um, well, it actually has to be one or the other, of course."

"Dead *or* alive."

"Yeah."

"There's no way it can be neither of those things or a little of each?"

"Uh, well," the chief tech says uneasily, "of course it can't."

"But *in principle* the cat is neither alive nor dead so far as it matters in the world outside the box."

"Uh, yeah, sort of. In principle."

"And there's something called the, uh, wave—wave fraction?"

"Wave-function."

"The wave-function, yes. So tell me about this wave-function."

"The whole experiment, the box and the cat and the rest, they're a system, and the so-called wave-function gives probabilities, nothing more, on how the system will work. It's equally probable that the cat is dead or alive. When you open the box and observe which state the cat is actually in, dead or alive, the wave-function is said to collapse."

"The wave-function ceases to be a wave-function *only* as soon as you try to observe it?"

"Yeah."

The man grins triumphantly. "Thank you," he tells the tech, "thank you, thank you, thank you," and to the liaison he says, "My course is clear."

"It is?"

"You can't send me through just yet. Not for a while, in fact. Maybe not for a long while."

"Why not?"

"It's her only chance."

"*Whose?*" During this brief exchange, the liaison's color has undergone dramatic variations.

"My wife's. The only way to keep her alive until I figure out my next move. Listen. Until I actually go through, what you say has happened hasn't happened. There's a chance it hasn't, anyway. She's like the cat in the box. Not alive, maybe, but not dead, either."

"You're pinning too much on an abstraction," says the liaison, turning to the chief tech halfway through uttering the sentence, "on a mathematical fiction, right?"

She nods. "The wave-function's just an expression. You can say a particle has both position and velocity, but if you try to fix the exact position, the particle doesn't have any velocity, and if you try to measure the velocity, the particle is in motion and isn't anywhere in particular. The wave-function's an expression of the probabilities of a particle assuming each possible state at the instant you measure it. Until that instant, all possible states exist in a potential sense."

"I understand enough. The wave-function goes from an indefinite state to a definite one only when you measure it. And whenever a collapse occurs, reality splits into as many parallel realities as are needed to accommodate each possible outcome of measurement. I mean to find the right reality. The one where my wife hasn't died. I mean to interfere with this wave-function and put off the collapse."

The liaison steps toward him, then away as he gestures with the wrench. "I realize that this must be very painful for you, but you have to face up to reality, you know."

"I reject the reality I'm being offered. I want— I *mean* to find a different reality. Get these techs to twiddle some knobs, cross some wires, so I get sent to a slightly different universe."

"'Twiddle some knobs, cross some wires!'" The chief tech looks as though she has heard blasphemous or perhaps only imbecile utterances. "What you're asking is impossible."

"No. This terrible thing that's happened, that everybody *tells* me has happened, that's what's impossible. I'm talking about a possibility. A possible universe."

"Okay, let me put it this way. Even if it was possible for us to do what you want us to do—and it *isn't*—the result you're hoping for's so *improbable*—"

"But not impossible."

"But so *very* improbable. Look, suppose we did twiddle some knobs and cross some wires for you—not that we're going to, but just suppose we did, and you got, ah, there—and nothing was different?"

"Then I'd talk your twin into shooting me through again, and if necessary, *her* twin, and then *hers*. Until I got where I wanted to go. Maybe if you gave me a note I could show to your twin—"

The liaison interrupts to ask, "Will you excuse me for a moment while I discuss something with the Navy?"

"Go ahead."

The liaison motions the Navy officer into a corridor, out of sight and out of earshot, and asks, "Can't you get him out of there?"

"He's a big strong guy, and he's found himself a big heavy wrench, and at the moment he's not in his right mind. I understand he's torn up about his wife. But I don't want any of my people getting hurt. They have wives and husbands, too."

"Isn't there another way into that compartment?"

"Yes, but he's got the door dogged good and tight."

"Well, how about pumping in sleep gas or something?"

The officer does not have to answer this question, so eloquent is his expression just at the moment.

"Well," says the liaison, "we can't just let him stay in there."

"Why not? Let him stay in there for a while. He can't hurt anything, just bang on the bulkhead a bit. He'll come out peacefully once he calms down."

The liaison glances at his wristwatch. "If we don't get him to the jump station in the next eleven minutes, it'll be tomorrow or next Tuesday before we can get him home. The family needs him there to help with, you know, arrangements."

"Then promise him whatever he wants, and he'll come out right now," and the officer motions to the doctor and the chief tech to join them.

"But," the liaison sputters, and gets no farther, because there is a glint of steel in the officer's eye.

"*Promise* him whatever he wants."

"Ah," says the liaison.

"Of course," says the doctor.

"Whatever," says the chief tech.

On receipt of the promise, the man drops the wrench with a clang and emerges from his cubby-hole, at which point several carefully selected bluejackets, each much stronger of grip and longer of reach than a jump-station tech, move in and restrain him until the doctor has stuck a hypodermic needle into him with the comment, "Just a mild sedative." The next thing he knows is the sinus-burning tang of ozone. The next thing he knows after that is where he is. The jump-station techs are at their places, he is strapped to a gurney. The liaison and the doctor move into his field of vision, and he strains against the straps and manages to croak, "You're killing her! You're taking away the only chance she has."

"Ah, my friend," and the liaison's voice, like his face, is full of solicitude, "I'm sorry, but she's already dead."

"Provisionally," he gasps, "she's only dead *provisionally!*"

The mild sedative, however, is having the effect of a strong one, and sleep comes before it can be recognized for what it is. Bulkheads become permeable membranes through which Dreamland oozes and ebbs like an impatient sea wooed by a jealous moon. Then he feels himself hurtling away from the world, toward some other.

"Poor bastard," says the liaison.

"Yeah," says the Navy doctor. "It'd be nice if he actually could slip into the universe he wants."

The chief jump-station tech shakes her head. "Nobody gets to pick the universe they're in. If they could, nobody'd hang around in the universes where there's death and sickness—"

"His *wife*," the liaison tells her severely, "died in a car crash. He just heard the news this morning."

She looks scornfully at the two men. "Well, it's a shame, but it only goes to show. I still say he must've seen too many sci-fi shows. Those goddamn things give people such unrealistic expectations."

"Nevertheless," the doctor begins, "I hope he," but the chief tech suddenly pushes past him and the liaison to glare and bawl at her people, "Let's *scramble*, boys and girls, we're on a goddamn *schedule* here!" and her people do scramble.

"Nevertheless," the liaison tells the doctor as they turn to go, "I hope so, too."

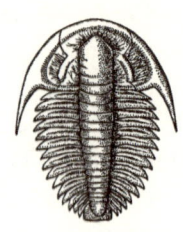

TREADING THE MAZE

"Cutsinger," he says breathlessly. "You're an awfully hard man to get to see."

Obviously not hard enough, but you don't say so. You don't say anything. The initial shock and surprise have somewhat abated, the impulse to fruitless recrimination has been suppressed, though when this is over you intend to find out why you've been paying good money for a security system if any lunatic off the street can invade your home, your very sanctum sanctorum. Your anger is evanescent, but not your fear. You have begun to consider the situation in which you find yourself with, well, not clinical detachment, but at least a certain clear-mindedness, enough so that the question of how he got in, what his antecedents may be, even, who he is, are all a good deal less important to you right now than, What does he intend to do next? You can't imagine the answer, or, rather, you can but you don't especially like to. All the clear-mindedness in the world doesn't change the fact that this disheveled intruder is armed with a pistol which he keeps pointed in your direction.

Moreover, though he has your undivided attention, he seems uncertain about how to proceed with whatever he does have in mind. Robbery? Not likely, given his patent lack of interest in his surroundings, and, anyway, what among the furnishings and contents of your study would be worth anything to anybody but you? He knows who you are, so it's something either personal or professional, but you're positive you've never seen this individual before, there are to the best of your knowledge no exploited or otherwise injured parties cluttering up your past, no cuckolded husbands, no colleagues whom you stabbed in the back. And, actually, he seems a little embarrassed to find himself here, invading your space, violating your privacy and your person. He looks not at you but at a point in the air one or two inches to the left of your head. When you move your head to put your face in his line of sight, he blinks, drops his gaze to the carpet for a moment before fixing it on a point in the air to the right of your head. You imagine that, were you to grab him by the ears and put your face in his, he might simply roll his eyes back in their sockets until you gave up and let him go. Not that you are about to grab him by the ears or any other body part. He might instead simply shoot you. The pistol makes the distance separating you from him—two meters, perhaps—stretch to infinity. Anyway, you are not and never have been a man of action. Physics, in your opinion, isn't a hands-on science, and physical courage and strength aren't its prerequisites.

At last the intruder says, "You don't look quite like your pictures," and you wonder frantically why that should be significant enough to rate mention. Perhaps he doesn't know you after all, perhaps he is indeed some lunatic off the street who has just happened to fasten on you. "I remember," he says, "the first time I ever saw you, years ago, when you first announced your big discovery. You talked about the possibilities it opened up. Scientific teams would go through your wormhole, to the world of hundreds of millions of years ago. Before there were even dinosaurs. Before there was much of anything except ooze and bugs and slime. And everyone bought it. I bought it."

Your tongue bestirs itself with effort in the arid cave of your mouth. Your lips seem fused together, unwilling to part. You say, hoarsely, very carefully, "I never claimed it was the world of four hundred million years ago. I went out of my way, again and again, to explain that it was a world *like* our world hundreds of millions of years ago."

The man nods. "Oh, I see that *now*. You weren't selling us time travel at all, but travel to another universe. *Then*, well, I was like everybody else, we all heard what we wanted to hear."

"I-I wasn't selling anything at all. I just stated the facts. Time travel is impossible. The existence of infinite multiple universes is assumed in quantum physics. As you admit, no one could be bothered to listen."

"Well, isn't that some fine comment on human imagination? We jumped at time travel, but we couldn't be bothered with a whole other universe! And yet it's—I read your book, you know. Man, did I ever read your book. 'Events Leading to the Infinite Regress.' You said that in a limitless series of universes that aren't exactly alike, the perceptible differences, the ones that aren't all at the subatomic level—the perceptible differences are going to range from, well, just barely perceptible to truly, thoroughly strange. Mirror universes, anti-matter universes, universes where cause doesn't precede effect. Where time runs backward or in some other direction altogether. You made plain old time travel sound not just impossible but pretty damn tame, really."

"What," you ask, gesturing at the pistol, "has that to do with infinite multiple universes?"

He appears not to hear the question. "But it's those universes that aren't very different from this one that really began to disturb me—*after* I'd already gone through. Oh, not at first. At first I was just like everybody else. And being there was mostly like field work anywhere. I lived in a tent, ate bad food, and worked like a mule from sunrise to sunset. And of course I took a million pictures. Now I find them very disappointing. It doesn't look so much prehistoric back there as just empty. It's really about as exciting to look at as intravenous feeding. But, oh, to *be* there—I loved every second of it right up until the moment—I was out in the middle of goddamn nowhere, you see. Every so often a supply barge would come through, drop off supplies, take out crates of specimens. And one day I got a letter. From my wife."

He reaches into the pocket of his coat and pulls out several badly wrinkled sheets of paper covered with fine script.

"Handwritten," he says, "on actual paper. An old-fashioned girl, my wife. But when you think about it, this—" the pages flutter as he waves them at you "—is vastly better than a chip. Much more personal. She touched the pages, shaped the words with her own hand. And what words! Listen to this," and he begins to read.

"'Greetings from the beach! I needed a trip. I immersed myself in work and exercised more furiously than ever after you were gone. But work refused to expand the amount of time I could allot to it, and we're both going to have to accept the fact that my stomach is as flat as it's ever going to be again. Anyway, I caught myself thinking and doing some very strange things. Such as, I couldn't remember the scent and taste of you. I put my head inside your closet and inhaled deeply. For a moment I thought I smelled you on your clothes. Then I realized what a picture I must present, standing there with my head in a closet. I'd be ruined in my profession if my colleagues knew, probably committed if my relatives knew. And all I smelled was cotton shirts and shoe leather. Not that those are bad smells, they just weren't the entirety of your scent. This whole episode would've been funny if it hadn't been pathetic. At least I didn't go to your underwear drawer. Anyway, here I am. I've brought work along, of course, and between that and exploring—which is just exercise with scenery—I ought to be able to stay busy while I'm here.'"

He looks up from the page and grins and asks, "Has anyone ever been that crazy in love with you?"

You say nothing. You have decided that you are indeed at the mercy of an insane person.

"Further down the page," he says, "she wrote, 'I do miss you terribly. It isn't as though you've gone to Antarctica or the moon or Mars. I can find Antarctica on a map. I can see the moon and Mars in the sky. Those are *places*. But the world of four hundred million years ago is buried so deep in the earth and so deep in time that it has no meaning. I try to make it exist for myself. I need to feel that you still inhabit a plane of being, that you are *somewhere*. I came here to the seashore, I think, to try to synthesize a sense of its reality with what's at hand, the texture of beach sand, the gleam of shells, the smell of salt water, the sound of the surf, the way the sky looks when sunlight suffuses a thinning overcast. I need this sensory input to try to flesh out the ancient world in your photos so that I can mentally experience it—imagine smelling, hearing, touching it as well as seeing it. I'm able to hold parts of it in my mind for a little while at a time. For example, I can see the broken limestone cliffs gleaming like naked vertebrae above your camp. But I can't make it all exist all at one time.'"

He stuffs the pages back into his pocket. "Well. Now the strangest day of my life gets into high gear. I'm still reading the letter when I hear a helicopter coming my way. When it circles overhead and begins to descend, I'm thinking, What the hell, this is wrong, I don't rate a helicopter. But it lands, and someone from the base camp hops out and tells me, 'I have some bad news.' It seems that, four hundred million years away, back here, now, in the twenty-first century—my wife is dead."

You scrape your dry tongue over your dry lips, wonder what to say, how best to respond. "I'm sorry. You have my deepest sympathy."

He shrugs and says, with a sardonic smile, "I guess I should feel guilty because she wasn't on my mind oftener. I guess she was pretty special. But I didn't come here for your sympathy. Let me tell you the rest of my story. They practically drag me aboard the helicopter, they take me back to the base camp, back to the ship and the jump station, and the whole time I'm trying to tell them there's been a mistake. I guess they thought I was crazy with grief. I wondered if I was crazy, too. Well, nobody's qualified to decide if he's crazy. So I started wondering instead about what you've been saying all along, that all those other universes exist, that, given infinity, all possibilities are probabilities, all probabilities are certainties. Just as we went into that prehistoric world from this one, mucked around, collected our specimens—over in the universes that aren't very different from ours, other clever physicists all named Cutsinger—or not—discovered their own wormholes, and other people like me went through. All thinking we're from the same place, of course. All thinking we're in the same place, too. All thinking we'll just naturally return to the same place we came from. Remember the old saying, wherever you go, there you are? Well, maybe people from this universe ended up someplace else. Maybe people from someplace else ended up in this universe." The man laughs harshly; when the laughter fades, a rictus remains on his face. "I mean, what guarantee do we have that we get back to the universe we start from?"

An expectant look forms around the rictus; whatever game he has now decided to play, he wants you to participate. "The synchronous link," you begin, but immediately he shakes his head and jabs the air with the pistol.

"Ah. We come to the crux of the matter. You asked what this—" he turns the pistol slightly, so that you can see a gleam of light along the barrel "—has to do with infinite multiple universes. It's simple. In each of two very similar universes, I finish telling you my story, and then I ask you a question, and you answer. In one of those universes, I don't like your answer, I think you're lying, so I shoot you. In the other, I think you're telling the truth, and I go and take my craziness with me and leave you in peace. Never bother you again. Word of honor. Anyway, what would you gain from turning me in to the police? I mean, besides peace of mind?"

He has essayed a real smile. It serves chiefly to make him look even more haggard. Now he steps backward; when his legs meet the edge of a chair, he sits down heavily. It is as though nervous tension alone has kept him on his feet this long; with its release, he can only sag in his badly wrinkled clothes.

"If I may please have something to drink," he says, and gestures carelessly with the pistol at a small sideboard.

"I'm not much of a drinker," you say, though the truth is that you suddenly find yourself wanting a drink probably as much as or even more than he does. "There isn't much of a selection."

"Just let me have whatever you've got. Brandy, whiskey, anything. I don't care."

You reach for a decanter, but before your hand touches it he stops you with another, more careful wave of the pistol.

"In the picture on your book," he says, "you're writing with your other hand. In all the pictures I've seen of you, you use your other hand."

A long, pregnant pause ensues. The distance between your outstretched hand and the decanter begins to stretch toward infinity.

"If I shot you in this side of your chest," he says, "would the bullet hit your heart? Or would it miss because your heart's on the wrong side?"

You make your hand cross the distance to the decanter and close around its neck. "Which side is the wrong side? Look at the titles of those books on the shelf there. Can you read them? If so, doesn't that strongly suggest to you that you're not in a mirror universe? You haven't been annihilated by contact with that chair, nor, for that matter, with the very air around you. Doesn't *that* suggest that you're not in the anti-matter universe? Pull down that volume of history, read for yourself how Germany did not win the world wars, how Benjamin Franklin did not invent the internal combustion engine in seventeen seventy-nine. As to anything subtler—" You present your back to him so that you can pour without letting him see how your hand shakes. You turn holding two glasses and offer one to him. "What difference does anything subtler really make? This is where we are and where we're going to be from now on. Regardless."

After another long, horrible moment, he lets the pistol droop toward the floor and accepts the glass. "Yes," he says as he raises it to his lips, "regardless." He drinks, smiles, nods. "Still. About the famous synchronous link. You showed off a machine and a lot of math to prove to everybody there's a synchronous link. But maybe it was all just painted cardboard and blinking lights and scribbles. It could all have been mumbo jumbo. Now here's the big question. Was it?"

Seated, with a drink in his hand and the pistol not aimed at you, he seems less threatening, enough so that you manage to feel defiant. "Are you," you ask, "a physicist?"

He hesitates. "No."

"Then it was all mumbo jumbo. Unless you can follow the math—" You can see a hardening glint in his eye. He doesn't want to hear about math. Time to change tack. "You seem to overlook the fact that I, too, went through the anomaly. I don't even like to go outdoors, yet I went there. Unlike so many of you, I had no particular interest in that other world, no particular desire or reason to go there except that I felt a consuming curiosity to experience a plunge into a spacetime anomaly."

"So you could write about it in your book."

"Whatever my reasons for doing it—" you find yourself saying this proudly; even a notorious homebody, and you are that and more, a recluse, an agoraphobe, can have done a physically adventurous thing in his time "—if I'd had any doubts whatever about the link—"

The intruder shakes his head in disbelief. "Never? No doubts at all, ever? Never the least shred of doubt, in the darkest hour of the night, that the great Cutsinger, Nobel winner and idol of geeks everywhere, might be, could possibly be, dare I say it, *wrong?*"

"No. None." You see him tighten his grip on the pistol. Pride, like anger, is evanescent. "Once," you admit. "One time. Just briefly."

That clearly pleases him. He relaxes again. "And?" He has the most searching expression you have ever seen on a human face. "I want to know all about it. I want you to tell me everything."

"There is not much to tell. I had a bad dream. It was just a dream, but it disturbed me so much, I moaned so loudly that I woke myself up. I was in my cabin on the ship, I could see a rim of light around the partly closed porthole cover. The clock and the sun go their own ways back there, the one lags behind the other, but both agreed then that it was time for me to get up. But all I could do was lie there gasping for breath. My body was rigid, my hands were clutching the frame of my bunk. I seemed to relax one muscle at a time. My fingers were stiff. They ached by the time I'd loosened my grip on the frame."

"Tell me about the *dream*."

"I—I dreamed I was lost in a maze. I couldn't go back the way I had come. I couldn't even look behind me, because the thing about this maze was that it closed up behind me as I walked through it. I could only see directly ahead of me, not even to the sides, and I could only go forward. I kept coming to places that were like the place I'd started from, but I was never sure, so I kept moving. Hoping I'd come to the place that looked right. The place that felt right."

He nods along in time with the rhythms of your speech. Then: "How did it end? Did you finally get out?"

"I woke up."

"And that was it? Just that one little hairline crack in your confidence in a theory?"

"Why would there have been anything more? It was only a dream. I was safe in my bed. I was able to assure myself by the evidence of my senses that the material, the natural world indeed remained material and natural. It was the same when I returned through the anomaly." You spread your arms, taking in the room and more than the room. "Here is reality. If you'd read my book more carefully, you'd understand that the infinite replication

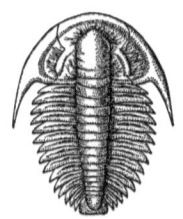

of universes has nothing to do with spacetime anomalies. The anomaly is just a path between two universes. How do I know? Here are my books, my home, and here am I, exactly where we're supposed to be."

"And here *I* am. Let me finish my drink, and then I'll finish my story." He gulps down the liquor, holds the glass loosely on one hand, the gun not so loosely in the other. "Back *there*, I get a love letter from my wife, and then I get the news that she's dead. And then I get back here and my wife's not only not dead, she's divorcing my ass." He raises the pistol and sights carefully along the barrel at your midsection. "And you know what the hell of it is, Cutsinger?"

He waits for a response; you can barely get the word out. "No."

"The hell of it is, I've never even been married."

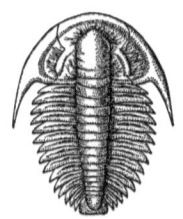

DILUVIUM

The Paleozoic sun rose with its usual suddenness, and Jack started awake when light touched his face. Sarah had left the flap turned back when she went out. Through the open end, he looked down a long, stony slope, onto a broad streambed. The rocks glistened from the previous evening's rain. The difference of a few meters of altitude and the absence of any plant life taller than a few centimeters allowed him, by the mere lifting of his head, to see far downstream, where the ancient eroded terrain, surrendering all pretense, became a hazy peneplain. The river threaded its languid way across the flatland to the limit of his vision. He watched the sky lighten to gray-blue. He could hear Sarah moving around outside.

Jack got up and washed his face with tepid water from the basin on the camp table. The aroma of coffee hung in the still air. He said, "Good morning," and kissed Sarah on the cheek.

"Enjoy the sunshine while it lasts," she said as she poured coffee into a tin mug and handed it over. "The weather station says we're in for more rain. More and then some. A line of thunderstorms coming in."

"Wouldn't know it to look at the sky."

"Check out that dark line along the horizon."

"Well, hell."

"Our mysterious visitor's still over there." Sarah nodded toward the opposite wall of the valley. The previous evening, they had been preparing to turn in when they saw the flicker of a flashlight in the distance.

"Where're the binoculars?"

"There behind you."

Jack peered through the binoculars but saw nothing.

"It's just one person," Sarah said, "I'm pretty sure. He's right by the streambed." She pointed. "See it?"

"Your eyesight's better than mine. Now who else could be here?"

"I thought at first it might be one of Van Thorp's people. They're supposed to be somewhere just north of here."

"They would've called or come on over."

Sarah nodded. "I gave him a buzz already, and he says all of his people are present and accounted for."

"Whoever it is should've come over and said hello."

"Would you try to cross that streambed at night?"

"Good point. I'll ask the frau überdirektor at base camp."

"Satellite should be overhead."

Jack picked up the phone, punched buttons, and said, "Ruth," and after a moment the voice at the other end said, "Why, Jack! What can I do for you?"

"We seem to have a stray person in our valley. Van Thorp says it's not one of his people. Any idea who it could be?"

"Let me check. Call you back in a second."

The second dragged into minutes. Finally, Jack shrugged and put the phone down and got to work; for several days he and Sarah had been collecting fossils along the ridge, a beautiful Cambrian outcrop. The morning passed. It was noon before Ruth called back.

"If it isn't some maverick of Van Thorp's," she told Jack, "I don't know who it can possibly be. There's not supposed to be anybody else in your area."

"Well, whoever it is," Jack said, glancing at the gathering overcast, "is going to get washed all the way downriver to you when this storm breaks. He's dumped his kit right on the bank of the stream, well below the highwater mark."

"Can you signal him?"

"We haven't caught so much as a glimpse of him. Guess I'd better wander over and save the idiot's life. Besides, I always like to know who my neighbors are. 'Bye, Ruth."

"Keep me posted, Jack. 'Bye."

Sarah stood looking up at the gathering overcast. "Sky's definitely getting darker. You don't have very much time."

"Let's make sure we're still all lashed down. Then I'll go check out our neighbor."

"You'd better step on it, then. In fact, why don't you go on over now? I can take care of everything here. That storm's coming fast."

"All right."

"Maybe you should take the first-aid kit." He looked at her; she shrugged. "Just in case."

Jack put the first-aid kit into his knapsack and, without preamble, set off down the slope. As he approached it, the streambed began to take on the appearance of a stretch of very bad two-lane blacktop. Water-borne sand and pebbles had eroded away softer rock, creating a network of narrow, sinuous channels, some as much as a meter wide and a meter deep. Dark turbid water gurgled in the hollows; Jack could see it as well as hear it as he stepped carefully from one stony rim to the next. The footing, treacherous enough by day, would have been impossible during the night.

He gained the opposite slope and called out loudly. A rolled-up sleeping bag and a backpack lay at the base of a pile of broken rock. He heard a weak cry, "Over here," and walked around the rocks and saw a long, lean man sitting on the ground, his back supported against a boulder. The man wore a khaki safari suit, now much the worse for wear. He had removed one boot; Jack could see for himself that the ankle was swollen. The man gave him a tired grin and said, "My prayers are answered."

"Is your ankle broken?" Jack said, dropping his pack.

The man shook his head. "Twisted it in the dark."

"Have you been lying here all this time?" Jack asked as he knelt and examined the ankle. "We saw your light last night. We're camped up on the opposite ridge."

"I didn't know anybody was around."

"Still." Jack dug the first-aid kid out of his knapsack. "You could've used your phone. Anyone in range would've answered your distress signal."

"Phone's on the blink. I don't know what the problem is. By the way, my name's Farlough. Jim Farlough."

Jack introduced himself, adding, "I'm with the P.R.I. team."

"Eh?" Farlough winced as Jack began to wrap his ankle.

"The Paleontological Research Institute. Cornell." Jack suddenly sat back on his heels. "Farlough? James Farlough? *The* Doctor Farlough? Advocates for Biblical Creation?"

Farlough grinned. "My reputation precedes me."

Before Jack could reply, his earphone filled with static, then Sarah said, "Just checking with you. Find our stranger?"

He touched his ear to show the other man that he had a call. "Yes. It's Doctor Farlough himself. From the A.B.C.s."

"What?"

"Doctor James Farlough. As in the A.B.C.s. You know."

Sarah did not respond immediately. Then: "Jack, you're kidding me."

"'Fraid not."

"*The* Farlough? *The* A.B.C.s?"

"'Fraid so."

"What's he doing here?"

"For starters, he's sprained his ankle."

"But how'd he get here? And—"

"Ask Ruth. I'll call you back, Sarah." Jack lowered his hand. To Farlough he said, "Did you come upriver on the supply barge?"

"No, over the ridge."

"Just you, by yourself?"

"Of course not. My group's camped two, three days' journey from here. Off thataway," and Farlough jerked a thumb over his shoulder.

"The only thing off 'thataway' is an evaporite basin the size of California. If your people aren't equipped any better than you, they're all going to die out there."

"Give us some credit, please. I thought this region looked promising."

The dark clouds had moved in quickly while they talked, and enormous raindrops began to spatter the dust around them. One struck Jack on the cheek with stinging force.

"Jack," Sarah said in his ear, "talk to me."

"I'm here."

"I couldn't raise Ruth."

"Take care of yourself, I'll be okay. I've got to stick with Doctor Farlough for the time being." He broke the connection and told Farlough, "I'm not going to try to lug you across the streambed. We'd fall in a pothole for sure. We've got to get to higher ground on this side, and right away. I've seen this stream in flood." He stepped back and surveyed the prospects, then pointed to a jumble of large boulders. "We should be able to stay out of the worst of it up there."

Jack gathered Farlough's meager equipment, stooped and got the man's arm over his shoulder, and drew him up.

"This is going to be sort of like running a three-legged sack race," he said, "with an anvil tied around my neck."

They crept slowly and painfully up the slope, with frequent pauses for rest. Raindrops smacked them with increasing force, until the bottom seemed simply to drop out of the sky. They were soaked and half-blinded when, at last, they found a sheltered space among the boulders that barely accommodated them. The howling wind defeated speech. Jack dropped the gear and lowered Farlough as gently as possible. Then he removed a heatpot from Farlough's equipment and got it going and stuffed the rest of the equipment into a dry crevice. The heatpot put out just enough light to cast their shadows on the enclosing rocks and just enough warmth to make them uncomfortable in their sodden clothing. Jack poured water from his canteen into a coffee pack and set that on the heatpot, waited half a minute, then decanted half of the pack's contents into a metal cup which he offered to Farlough. Farlough nodded thanks. They sat and sipped, Jack holding the steaming pack between his hands, and watched the storm. There was nothing else to do. Lightning flashes illuminated a black, endlessly writhing torrent at the bottom of the slope. Jack did not worry about Sarah but wished that he were snuggling with her in their sleeping bag. He was not sure afterward, but he thought he dozed off.

After what seemed like a long time, the wind abruptly fell off and the rain began to come down at a steeper angle. Jack could just hear himself when he asked Farlough, "Are you hungry? I always travel with a pocketful of crackers and a chocolate bar."

Farlough absently shook his head. He seemed entranced by the storm. After a couple of minutes, he said, "This doesn't look like it's going to let up any time soon."

"Are you comfortable there?"

"Yes. Thank you. Thank you for coming to my rescue. You know, it's exciting to think that we are, this moment, within a few years of the end of the Noachian flood described in Genesis. In the aftermath of the deluge, of course, there must have been localized—"

Jack sat back and said, "Just why are you here in the Paleozoic?"

Farlough looked around at him now, and his mouth twisted drolly. "For the same reason everyone else is. To find out things for myself."

"Looking for Adam and Eve?"

"Not at all. Adam and Eve have already been dead for quite some time. We are, as I said, actually in the immediate aftermath of the great global inundation described in the Book of Genesis. Between the expulsion from the Garden of Eden and the confusion of tongues."

"Do you really believe that?"

"No less completely and absolutely than you believe life just started from chemicals combining at random."

"Chemicals don't combine at random. They combine in very particular and predictable ways. Two atoms of hydrogen plus one atom of oxygen always equal water. And so on."

"We are here—my colleagues and I—to prove the truth of diluvial geology, which states that the fossil record and almost all modern landforms were created by the waters of the Noachian deluge."

"You thinking of interviewing Noah himself?"

"Noah's story has already been written. Unfortunately, it doesn't include visitors from the future."

"Do you suppose he's still floating around in the Ark, or is he already stuck on that mountaintop?"

"Our hope is that the repopulation of the world has already begun. It would be fascinating to observe the rise of the civilization that built the Tower of Babel. But all we need to prove our case is to find just one kind of creature that the conservative scientific establishment says shouldn't be here in the so-called Paleozoic age."

"You mean besides us anomalous humans."

"Anything that doesn't belong. You call this age the Paleozoic, your physicists prattle about spacetime anomalies and uncertainty principles and the infinite replication of worlds. *We* believe that God created the so-called anomaly so that we could at long last—but once and for all—prove the fallacy of the uniformitarian and evolutionist doctrines so dear to the scientific establishment. That establishment did everything it could to keep us from coming here. It took the combined efforts of right-minded public officials and private citizens to finally get us here. Private citizens raised the money, too."

"Well, if we establishment types start turning up anomalous artifacts, we'll know who to blame. I've never known a creationist who was above faking evidence."

"What sort of fake evidence do you have in mind, and—" Farlough held his elongate arms out to the sides "—where do you suppose I have secreted it on my person?" He lowered his arms and crossed his hands over his belly. "Not that there haven't been some fraudulent claims made in the name of diluvial geology, of course. Those so-called man tracks in that dinosaur trackway in Texas haunt us just as you establishment scientists are haunted by—" he gave Jack a cheerfully malicious smile "—Piltdown man."

Jack shrugged. "That crack hasn't drawn blood in a long time. Like all scientific frauds, Piltdown was eventually found out—by scientists."

"Nevertheless, the incidence of fraud among creationists is nothing like as great as among establishment scientists. Your whole system is a fraud, because of what you omit from it. Even when evidence of intelligent design literally crawls in front of you. I refer of course to one of the most enduring arguments against the theory of evolution—the bombardier beetle!"

Jack laughed out loud. "Ah, yes! Our old friend, the bombardier beetle! You know, when I was a kid, I saw the animated feature version of that allegedly beloved children's classic, 'Bomby the Bombardier Beetle.'"

"Clearly you didn't profit from the viewing."

"On the contrary. I learned an awful lot from it. I learned the beetle's ability to fart fire is certain proof of a creator. I learned bombardier beetles are cute, talk in squeaky voices, and somehow are cognizant of the Bible and its import—though it wasn't clear why they should be, since they don't have souls."

Farlough smirked. "You think I'm a narrow-minded, ill-read boob or even an illiterate, don't you? I am in fact an omnivorous, voracious reader. I read 'Bomby' at the appropriate age. I have since read Tolstoy, Kafka, and much else—even Darwin. Know thy enemy. I see by your expression you don't believe me. Very well, let's take Hazel May Rue's book, since you brought it up. The scientific establishment has always dismissed 'Bomby' as mere anti-Darwin propaganda."

"You can hardly blame us. It *was* published by the old Institute for Creation Research."

"Yet it addresses the same issues that concern Kafka—arguably the most twentieth-century of writers—in his famous 'Metamorphosis.' Gregor Samsa awakes one morning to find himself transformed—evolved or more accurately devolved, though Kafka doesn't use either term—into a gigantic insect. Gregor finds his new body ill-suited to the demands of survival, perishes miserably, and is swept out in the garbage. 'Bomby' embodies the creationist idea that everything *is* as it was created, thus, there can be no change—no evolution. But 'Bomby' also presents the idea that the agent of this creation, unlike the unidentified agent of change in Kafka's tale, is beneficent and knows best for all its—*his*, God's—creatures. Gregor Samsa necessarily fails to survive because his change is unnatural, literally ungodly, whereas Bomby, as his elders explain to him, will survive because God has given him survival traits."

Jack, who had listened open-mouthed throughout this monologue, shook his head and said in a dumbfounded and yet grudgingly admiring tone of voice, "Now I've heard goddamn everything." He leaned against the most comfortable portion of rock behind him. "Not that I'm conceding a thing, but I'm not going to argue flood geology with you any more. I'm going to take a nap."

"I'm just trying to pass the time."

"Try passing it in silent communion with the elements. I'd argue with you some more if we were back home and you were trying to convince the school board to put 'Bomby' on the required reading list. But we're here in Paleozoic time, hundreds of millions of years from home—"

"A few thousands," Farlough said good-naturedly.

"Whatever. Anyway, the sound of rain activates the sleep center in my brain. Part of my inheritance from some tiny insectivore."

Jack closed his eyes. Eventually, he did fall asleep.

The rain had subsided to a drizzle when he snapped back into wakefulness. Across from him, Farlough slept with his chin on his breast. Jack tried to call Sarah and got only a painful earful of static. He put the phone away and fumed for a while and then slept again. He awoke the second time to find the clouds had parted to either side of a bright full moon that poured down milky light. The phone still was not working, and the stream was still a roiling, hissing barrier. Across from him, Farlough awoke with a shudder. He stretched and looked out the mouth of their shelter and said, "What a big beautiful moon."

"I wish it was a new moon and the stars were out," Jack growled. "Then you could point out the north star to me."

Farlough regarded him with suspicion. "I'm not an astronomer."

"Oh, come on. Everybody over the age of six knows where the north star's supposed to be." Farlough did not rise to the challenge. "Y'know, there's this old sci-fi story—there's a planet with more than one sun, where night falls only once every few thousand years. When it does and all the stars come out, everybody goes crazy at the sight of them, and civilization collapses."

"Ah." Farlough nodded. "And you think the sight of the strange Paleozoic night sky should make me go crazy as well?"

"No, I think you're already crazy. But at least admit the sky here is strange. Notice how much bigger the moon looks? That's because it's closer to the earth than it will be in Cenozoic time."

"No, it looks bigger simply because it looks bigger. The deluge worked profound changes on the world. The atmosphere creates optical distortions, and—"

"I give up."

He tried several more times to call Sarah. Finally, he gave that up, too, and prepared a meal for Farlough and himself. They spoke little. The moon passed, and the sound of the racing stream lulled Jack back to sleep.

He was stiff and slightly chilled when he awoke for the third time. Sunlight slanted through gaps in his shelter. The heatpot was missing. So was Farlough.

Jack pushed himself up and stepped into the steaming morning. Almost at once the phone beeped.

"Jack," Sarah said. "Thank goodness. Are you okay?"

"I'm fine. But *he's* missing, and so's all his stuff."

"I haven't seen him, and I've been watching your side ever since the sun came up."

"Then where'd he go?"

"Where *could* he go?"

"Nowhere far away. Not with that ankle of his. I'm stuck on this side until the water goes down, so I may as well look for him. Any word yet from Ruth?"

"No. Still can't get through. Maybe the storm fried something down there."

"Keep trying. If you do get through, ask about a guy named Farlough and a creationist expedition. I'm going to look for our stray."

By that afternoon, Jack was able to cross the stream, picking his way carefully from the rim of one channel to the next. He trudged up the slope to the camp. He was tired and muddy, but Sarah embraced him tightly. She had coffee and hot food waiting, too. He dropped his knapsack, sat down wearily, and said, "No place like home."

"No sign of him?"

"None. Nothing. Not a trace."

"It gets weirder. I managed to raise the base a little while ago. Ruth says there's nobody here by the name of Farlough, and there's certainly no creationist expedition."

Jack looked at her solemnly. "This is starting to creep me out. You can't sneak so much as a paper clip through the anomaly. Never mind a creationist. Never mind a whole pack of creationists."

Sarah returned his look. "Are we imagining this?"

"No. Of course not." He dug the first-aid kit out of his knapsack and snapped it open. "I wrapped his ankle for him. The bandage is gone. He's gone. All his stuff is gone. *Where?*"

"What're you going to tell Ruth? You know she'll want to follow through on this."

"I haven't the faintest idea. I really don't."

Later, they gazed up at the night sky from their sleeping bag, and after some time had passed without words, Sarah, with her head against Jack's and her arm draped across his chest, said, "Maybe he was from some other place."

"What other place could he be from?"

"One of those alternate universes. Maybe the spacetime anomaly isn't just the interface between our own time and this prehistoric age. Maybe there really are infinite multiple universes like the physicists talk about. Each slightly different or a whole lot different from all the others. And maybe this man you met slipped through from one of them."

"We can't give Ruth a story like that. She'd have us sent home in straitjackets."

"What else can we give her? He was here, and now he's gone. So maybe he slipped back into some other universe. His own universe. And it's everything the creationists say this one is. It's cozy and confined and only six thousand years old, and there's no evolution, and the sun goes around the earth. Laws of physics there are apt to be suspended without warning. In our own universe, all Farlough and other creationists can do is fume about the physical laws governing it. But the unpredictable physical laws in that other universe let this other Farlough come through our universe for a little while."

Jack shivered in spite of himself. He said, "It sounds like a really terrifying place to live."

They lay at the base of the beautiful Cambrian outcrop and looked up at the moon and the stars, and the moon and the stars looked down at them, and at last one of them murmured to the other, "Well, I'm glad we're right where we are."

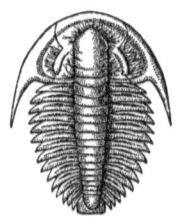

SIDESTEP

I don't understand. The doctor tells me not to worry, that the important thing now is for me to get better, the rest can wait. "You are making excellent progress," he assures me, "and once you get your strength back, then will be the time to answer all your questions. Let's not be in too much of a hurry to get back on our feet, okay? You've been through quite an ordeal, you know, you can thank your iron constitution for having come through." No, I think, I should thank God for having brought me through, for letting me survive what so clearly ought to have been unsurvivable.

Taking stock of my situation is about all I can manage at the moment. I feel terribly weak. When the doctor asked me how I am feeling this morning, I intended to gesture as though to say, "So-so," but my arm refused to move, my hand and fingers merely twitched, and when I made to speak, my tongue stirred reluctantly, clumsily, like a sleepy great beast at the back of a cave. The sound I uttered could have meant anything, everything, or nothing. Whichever it was, the doctor pretended to be pleased and did not press me to comment further.

So I lie here, taking on and giving off fluids through plastic tubes, drifting into and out of consciousness, aware of but not too concerned with the comings and goings of the doctor, the orderlies, possible others. Gradually I begin to make out and retain details and put them into meaningful relationships with one another. The doctor is a Navy officer, and I am in sick bay aboard a Navy ship; I know it must be a ship because I see pipes in the overhead, and I hear a faint but constant thrum of machinery that seems to emanate all around me. I find it somehow comforting. Then I realize that it is so because this must be the same Navy ship at which I, my companions and I, arrived via so-called spacetime anomaly and from which we departed into the wilderness, determined to seek out the first cities of men in the immediate aftermath of the Deluge.

Jim Farlough and Harold Dopp and I were founding members in excellent standing of Advocates for Biblical Creationism, the organization founded by Jim's father, the late, senior James Farlough. Originally we concerned ourselves with using our legal training in an effort to stem the tide of secular humanism, as exemplified by the Darwinian theory of evolution, in the public school system, but we soon expanded our activities into fund raising for candidates whose positions on various issues mirrored our own. Then had come the announcement about the discovery of the spacetime anomaly, allegedly permitting access to the world of millions of years ago.

I admit that I was disheartened at first. So many of these breakthroughs seemed to reinforce our adversaries' fallacious positions. But Jim said, "Remember, it's all a matter of finding the right evidence and correctly interpreting it. We must go through this anomaly and bring back our own evidence, which will finally and forever establish the truth of the Book of Genesis."

"They'll never let us go through."

"We have powerful allies," Jim said, "friends and sympathizers in high places. It is time we called in all our favors. The way is going to be difficult, God hasn't made it easy for us—but our triumph will be all the sweeter for the hardships and setbacks we shall have endured. I believe absolutely that this is our greatest opportunity to prevail against the conservative scientific establishment. From descriptions of the world on the other side of the anomaly, I am convinced that it is our world as it existed in the aftermath of the Noachian Flood."

Jim had produced maps and volumes of calculations, based on scrupulous reading of the scriptures, to show how the scientists had erred in identifying the barren postdiluvian lands of the ancient world as Laurentia, supposedly the ancestral North American continent that lay close to the equator during the Silurian Period.

"My own studies," Jim told us, "have led me to the conclusion that so-called Laurentia actually adjoins the mountainous region of Ararat—modern-day Armenia—from which the children of Noah dispersed to repopulate the world. In this past world, the waters have just barely receded. The landmasses are unfamiliar and have yet to be abundantly repopulated. I am sure it will be a very strange place to us—but God intends that we should go!" And he cited Genesis:

> And it came to pass in the six hundredth and first year, in the first month, the first day of the month, the waters were dried up from off the earth: and Noah removed the coverings of the ark, and looked, and behold, the face of the ground was dry.
>
> And in the second month, on the seven and twentieth day of the month, was the earth dried.

"I believe," Jim went on, "that the Lord has provided a doorway to the world as it existed from the time of Nimrod, 'a mighty one in the earth' and 'mighty hunter before the Lord,' through the time of the Tower of Babel. This was the time of the founding of mankind's first postdiluvian cities, Babel, Accad, and Calneh in the land of Shinar, out of which went forth Asshur and builded Nineveh, Rehoboth, Calah, and Resen. The whole earth was of one language and of one speech. Soon enough, of course, sinful man tried to go against divine rule by creating a world state, and raised up the Tower of Babel, leading to the confusion of tongues. We need only bring back simple proofs of these events to demolish forever the false and pernicious claims of the secular humanist scientists."

He made it sound so straightforward and easy, but anybody who had ever watched that tall, lean figure deliver a lecture or seen that hawk-like profile and those flashing eyes on television knew the power of his personality. I couldn't doubt for a moment that he knew whereof he spoke. Not then, anyway.

As I mend my interest in my surroundings naturally increases. My bed sits in a corner screened off from the rest of sick bay. I hear little but murmurings as people move above in other parts of the room; presumably there are other patients present, but they do not disturb me. No one disturbs me. Through a gap in the screen around my bed I have glimpsed an impassive, immobile young man wearing a white hat, a khaki shirt, blue trousers with a red stripe running along the seam—and a gun belt. The Navy has posted a Marine to stand guard over me. Who is being protected from whom is unclear.

But so it has been all along. The reception accorded us by the jump-station technicians on both sides of the spacetime anomaly (assuming it can be said to possess anything as prosaic as *sides*) could not have been more professional—or much cooler. In the 21st Century C.E. we experienced the anticipated delays as unsympathetic people pored over our paperwork, seeking any excuse to deny us access to the anomaly. But our paperwork was in order, down to the last dotted i and the least crossed t, just another instance of Jim's talent for meticulous planning and execution. We had to go to the trouble, he knew, because we could expect a lot of resistance all along the way.

Of course, it didn't hurt that several influential members of Congress had got behind this venture and helped to push it through. But if any one person may be said to have brought our hopes and plans to fruition, it was Jim Farlough.

Jim, Harold, and I went through the jump station without suffering any of the notorious side-effects. We then experienced more delays as different people, no less unsympathetic than those before them, re-examined our paperwork. Again, they could only pass us through. The civilian liaison, at least, was a consummate professional who never let on that he might not approve of our presence in his precious Paleozoic Era; he moved things along, got us and our equipment and supplies stowed aboard a Navy launch, got us landed at last upon the shore of the ancient world, and at that point was probably very glad to be rid of us.

We got our first look at the "Silurian Period" from the launch that took us ashore at Camp Number Two—the scientific expedition's base camp, consisting of neatly sited Quonset huts and tents. We had seen photographs and watched videos, of course, but knew that what is left out of a picture is often more telling than what is left in. We were determined to miss nothing. The camp nestled at the base of a long stony ridge, the nearer of two headlands bracketing a broad, smelly delta cut with braided streams. The river feeding these streams wound inland for many miles; it would be our road to Nineveh and Babel.

Landed, the three of us stood on the dock, savoring the moment, and then Harold said, "Let us give thanks unto the Lord."

It was one of the most heartfelt prayers I had ever uttered.

We assembled our gear and pored excitedly over Jim's map. The maps published by the scientific establishment had amused us tremendously—they depicted Laurentia as a chain of islands, the future sites of New York State and the Great Lakes region.

"It goes to show," said Jim, "that they see what they want to see, in light of their theories about continental drift and the world's being very old and so forth."

His own map, prepared after meticulous study of the scientists' charts and rigorously interpreted according to the scriptures, depicted a similar though not identical chain of islands emerging from the sea, but superimposed upon the outlines of the Middle East, with the locations of ancient (though hardly prehistoric!) settlements indicated.

"According to this," Jim said, "traveling upriver by boat will bring us to within an easy trek's distance of some of the earliest and most fabulous cities of the postdiluvian age." He looked around at the base camp and shook his head sadly. "They have come all this way, spent fortunes, to investigate snails and slime, while the real discoveries, the revolutionary discoveries, have been within their reach all the time!"

"If only," Harold put in, "we had one of their helicopters! Think of the entrance we could make at Nineveh or Babel—the *impression* we'd make!"

"Unfortunately," said Jim, "there is nothing in Genesis about three visitors descending from the sky in a flying machine. We're going to have to go in on foot."

We had got ashore in the late afternoon, and night fell sooner than we anticipated (the official explanation being that the Silurian days are shorter than those to which we are accustomed). No one wanted us here, but we weren't denied the use of the Navy mess tent or the sleeping quarters reserved for new arrivals.

INVISIBLE KINGDOMS: SILURIAN TALES VOLUME 2

Harold was tired and wanted to turn in immediately after supper, but Jim was too excited for sleep and wanted to look around a bit. We decided to take a turn about the camp.

This was when we received our first not altogether pleasant surprise.

We had been walking unhurriedly and Jim was talking of his father's lifelong struggle in defense of Biblical truth, when he raised his eyes to the heavens and suddenly stopped in place. His mouth worked, but no sound issued forth. I looked up and immediately saw why.

These were not the stars we had expected to see, laid out in the familiar constellations that mankind had known throughout history. We couldn't locate any that we knew, not even the North Star.

"How can it be?" I wondered aloud.

A long moment ensued, and then Jim cleared his throat and said, "It's some optical effect."

"Optical effect?"

"Refraction of light or something like that. So soon after the Flood, atmospheric conditions must still be greatly disturbed. I can't account for it any other way. The whole sky is a mirage of overlaid images of the heavens. Of course, this will make navigating rather more difficult once we set out overland, but we can manage with charts and compass. Still, that we should see such a sight as this!"

Neither Harold nor I could make any reply.

The day arrives when I am able to croak actual words in response to the doctor's heretofore largely rhetorical questions. My voice sounds as though it has been scoured with sand, my throat feels raw, my whole physical being feels desiccated, yet from somewhere within myself I squeeze out a tear of gratitude. It wells up in the corner of my eye, pools there, wets my lashes when I blink, and I automatically offer thanks to God.

"You've given us some anxious moments," the doctor tells me with a professional smile, "but it looks like you're going to be with us for some time to come."

"Where . . .?"

"Interesting how that's always the very first thing somebody wants to know when they wake up here. You're in sick bay at Number Two Camp. Aboard the ship, actually."

So I was right about that.

"How did . . . ?"

"Time enough for where, when, why, and how later on. Right now I'm going to run a few tests. Can you tell me your name?"

My name. Have I thought even once of my name since I awoke here? It comes to me after a moment, of course, but its connection to me seems tenuous, almost ghostly, as though it belonged to another person who lived a long time ago. The man who bore it burned away almost to nothing in the saltlands, leaving only a husk. His *name* seems irrelevant.

Nevertheless, I say the name for him, and he repeats it, though it clearly means as little to him as it does to me. He proceeds with his tests and keeps up a monologue the whole while, occasionally ending a statement on a questioning note to encourage me to make some sort of reply. My vocabulary of monosyllables expands. He goes away at last, and I fall asleep, into a dream or a memory.

The cargo barge boasted only the most basic conveniences, but we had not come expecting a pleasure cruise up river. The barge captain—not Navy, but a private contractor—appeared skeptical at first when Jim explained that we wanted to go as far inland as the craft could take us. "That's the backside of nowhere," the captain said, "past the last outpost. There's nobody around to come to your rescue in a hurry if you get into a jam."

"What kind of trouble could we possibly get into?" Jim asked him with the hint of a smile. "Dinosaurs? Savage peoples?"

The captain regarded him strangely. "It's very rough country, all rock and sand and not a green growing thing anywhere in sight. The rains here are torrential. The river swells and breaks its banks, washes away everything because there's nothing to hold it in place. I've seen whole hills erode away to nothing in a very short time."

His misgivings were understandable. Of the three of us only Jim, with his hook nose and intense expression, appeared capable of meeting danger and hardship. I am wiry but slight, with what I'm told is a perpetually mild expression. Harold, with his baby-blue eyes, his double chins, his flesh-colored hair, looked as though he belonged nowhere but in a brokerage office. Yet appearances can deceive.

"All three of us," Jim explained, "are experienced outdoors men, hikers, rock climbers. You needn't concern yourself on that account. We know enough not to pitch camp, for instance, in a river bed."

The captain wasn't giving up so easily. "Beyond the divide you descend into the saltlands. One of our scientists calls it The Grisly Place. Some bay or vast lagoon has been cut off from the open sea and left to bake in the sun. Imagine a salt flat the size of Illinois. It makes Death Valley look like a vacation spot."

"Then we'll have to go around it," Jim said, "to get where we're going."

"Around it? Beyond the saltlands there's inland sea stretching to the future site of Las Vegas."

"I'm sure you're mistaken. My research indicates—"

"I had better take another look at your papers," said the captain impatiently, and he did so. But he yielded at length before our perfect and thereby irresistible paperwork, and to the allure of our money—figuring, no doubt, that crazy people's money is as good as anybody else's—and we boarded the barge, to find places for ourselves among crates of equipment and supplies destined for various groups of scientists camped at intervals along the river. We left the base camp early in the morning and watched as the sun burned off the mist lying upon the estuary. It seemed a promising sign for three men on a mission from God.

At one point Harold suddenly called our attention to something floating or swimming in the water parallel to the barge. We saw a honey-colored hemispherical object adorned with two bulbous blank eyes and with a long segmented body wriggling behind, and even as we watched it crawled up onto a muddy islet to sun itself, or perhaps to proclaim itself master of all it surveyed, or simply to avoid the barge—possibly it perceived the vessel as a larger edition of itself. It was like some hideous hybrid of lobster and centipede. The thing walked on four or five sets of jointed legs; the forwardmost and largest of these terminated in claws like pruning hooks with serrated edges; and the whole creature must have been longer from its head to its spike-tipped tail than I am tall.

The three of us stared at it until the barge had left the islet behind, and then I said, "You don't suppose Noah had *that* with him aboard the ark, do you?"

Harold laughed nervously, and Jim whistled, clearly impressed. "Probably not," he said, "obviously it lives in the water—but what an *ugly* creature! It's almost enough to make you think Satan must have had a hand in the design of creation."

"Well," I said, "I'd hate to meet up with it sometime when I'm cooling my feet in a brook."

"That thing," said Jim, "was one of the famous so-called sea scorpions. Its presence here suggests we may see other animals the scientists suppose to have gone extinct before mankind walked the earth. Anything from dawn horses to mastodons. Perhaps we'll even see a dinosaur!"

"And what if," Harold asked, "we do see one? We have no weapons apart from our camp knives."

"Let us pray that any dinosaur we may see will be one of the peaceful herbivorous ones. I shouldn't worry too much, though. Given the denuded state of the landscape, the absence of land animals larger than scorpions—" he had shaken one out of his shoe in camp that morning and, after careful examination, pronounced it identical to those he was familiar with back home "—we have arrived soon after the recession of the waters, before the repopulation of the earth has gotten very far. And large animals like dinosaurs would breed very slowly anyway. So what are the odds? Anyhow, I *don't* think God is going to let his servants get eaten by dinosaurs before they fulfill their mission here."

"*After* they fulfill their mission," Harold said, "is okay?"

Late that first afternoon on the river, Harold came to Jim and me and said, "Something is wrong with our compass. The sun came up behind us, north should be to our right. Now the sun is going down directly ahead of us, and the compass needle points *south*, to our left."

"Let me see that," said Jim, and the three of us crowded together to examine the instrument. It was as Harold had said.

"Can it have been affected by all that electrical equipment in the jump station?"

"Possibly." Jim took the compass. "I'll go compare it with the one in the pilot house."

He returned after several minutes and handed the compass back to Harold. "I don't know whether to be puzzled or relieved. The captain's compass needle points south, too. *He* says it's because the polarity of Earth's magnetic field has reversed during this period of the planet's history. North is south, and vice versa. He also says everyone here is aware of the flip and makes allowances accordingly. Myself, I think Harold's right, I think it's the jump station's fault. Or something to do with the anomaly, anyway. However many compasses there may be in this time period, if they all had to come through and if they all point in the *same* wrong direction . . . ." He sighed. "I had better go recheck all my calculations in light of this development."

He retired to his charts and figures, and Harold and I leaned on the gunwale and watched the barren landscape slip past. After a time, Harold said, "Well, this morning, at least, it looked like we were finally in for some clear sailing. Just goes to show, it's always something. The Lord isn't making this any too easy for us."

I nodded agreement. "Still. Jim's right. We're going to accomplish a great thing for the glory of God. Our reward later on will be commensurate with our difficulties now."

"Amen."

The cargo barge's stops at camps along the river followed a pattern. While the hulking, silent mate manhandled crates off the barge, the captain conferred ashore with the scientists; it was obvious from his gestures and glances that we were the hot topic of gossip. His listeners might respond by staring at us where we stood lined up along the gunwale, or scratching their heads. Once, we heard derisive laughter. When the barge was in motion, we mainly stayed out of the captain's way as well as we could.

Keeping track of time under the present circumstances is difficult, but within a day or two, or perhaps three, the Navy doctor arrives with a visitor in tow, a Doctor Heflin, who asks how I am doing and if I would mind answering a few questions.

"My vital signs are good," I tell him. "This is my first attempt at being witty since I awoke in sick bay."

Heflin smiles and nods at the Navy doctor. "So Doctor Lane tells me. You're making a splendid recovery. You'll be up and about in no time."

"I must finish my rounds," Doctor Lane says, "so I'll leave you two alone."

"Thank you," says Heflin, and he and I regard each other curiously while Lane removes himself. Then, "Shall we begin?" and he takes out a pen and a small notebook.

"Are you a psychiatrist?"

"Hardly. I'm one of the expedition's resident physicists."

"And, what, you're writing me up for the camp newspaper?" This is my second attempt at wit in less than five minutes. I must be better!

"Let's say," Heflin answers, "that your case has ended up on my desk because no one else has a clue. So. Let's start with the basics. What is your full name?"

I tell him, and he writes in his notebook.

"Date and place of birth?"

I tell him when and where, and more, where I went to school, whom I married, how many children I have, whether or not I have ever been convicted of a felony. This last question makes my eyebrows go up and occasions a smile and a shrug on his part. "They insist that I ask that question," he explains. "Now." The grin fades. "Tell me in your own words how you came to be here. I mean, from before you left Holocene time, just before you entered the jump station back home. Tell me who you were with, what your plans were, everything you can remember."

"I was one of a party of three. The other two members were Jim—James Farlough and Harold Dopp. We had already sent our gear through. Jim, Harold, and I followed in that order. We arrived at the jump station here and were taken ashore, where we chartered a cargo barge captain to take us upriver."

"I see. What was the name of the barge captain?"

"Nelson."

"What happened next?"

"We rode the barge upriver as far as it was navigable and then struck out overland."

We left the cargo barge below the rapids and ascended through a country of tumbled boulders as big as houses, testament to the fury with which all the fountains of the great deep had been broken up and the windows of heaven opened. Here and there we noted the presence of small, delicate, feathery plants, but no animal life whatever. Harold wondered aloud if perhaps we had arrived so soon after the recession of the waters that not only had the creatures aboard Noah's ark not yet had the opportunity to repopulate the world, but "Noah could still be lying drunk and naked in his tent."

When we reached the crest of the divide three arduous days later, we paused to rest, restock our drinking water from cool, clear springs among the rocks, and give thanks to the Lord for having been brought so far. "From just such a height," Jim said, "Jesus and Satan in the wilderness must have looked upon the world."

From this vantage point we could look back upon the territory we had come through, down across the broken landscape to the glittering ribbon of the river that wound toward the haze-shrouded horizon. In the opposite direction lay more broken country, spreading in three directions as far as the eye could see. We could just make out a white band stretching along the horizon.

"That must be the saltlands," Jim said, reaching for the binoculars.

"It'll take us several days to get there," I said.

"At least," Jim said, "we'll be going *down*hill this time."

Heflin said, "Where did you think—where were you going?"

"Jim had spent years making maps and calculations he said would take us directly to the first cities built by men following the Deluge."

"The Deluge," Heflin says in an inflectionless voice. "As in the biblical Flood? Noah's Flood?"

"Yes."

"Ah. I see." There is a half-minute's silence during which Heflin writes furiously in his notebook and I think, Now comes the mockery. I have heard other people use that same flat voice when speaking the same or similar words.

Instead of mockery, however, Heflin looks up interestedly and says, "Even assuming that there were ancient city-building peoples for you to meet here, how did you propose to communicate with them?"

"Each of us had studied Hebrew, Greek, and Aramaic."

"But—"

"Moreover, we are in the time between the recession of the waters and the building of the Tower of Babel, when the earth was of one language and one speech. In other words, I don't know exactly how, but the Lord would see to it that we could communicate."

"I see," he says after a long pause. "Go on." He consults his notes. "You struck out overland."

"Yes."

"Using Jim's map?"

"Yes. And a compass, of course. We followed the river to its source and went over the divide. And . . . ."

"Yes? What then?"

"We came to the saltlands."

"The evaporite basin."

"Call it what you want." I know now that it was Hell.

We began our descent, following a small stream, and occasionally replenishing our canteens from it, until it petered out in a patch of slime. The temperature rose sharply as we went down through titanic jumbles of rock; the air was still, it was hot even in the shade of the boulders, and perspiration soaked us. That first night, we camped in a sort of natural amphitheatre.

Three days after we started down, we rounded a last cyclopean pile of stones and stood looking out over the bleak expanse of the saltlands. The flat, featureless, blindingly white plain stretched to the horizon. For the first time since we had set out on our quest my courage failed me. I had always believed in the Lord and drawn strength from that belief, but now, looking at the desolation before us, I was made weak, O God forgive me, I quailed at the prospect of venturing out into, onto, that baking wasteland. I glanced at my companions' faces. Harold's was sickly pale, and even Jim looked ashen. No one spoke for at least a full minute.

Then Harold said, simply, emphatically, "*No.*"

Jim and I looked at him.

"We'll *die* if we go out there."

Jim appeared to consider, then slowly shook his head. "The Lord would not have brought us this far only to dash our hopes by placing an impassable barrier in our path. This is a test. A last trial."

I wanted to accept what he said, as I had accepted everything he said till now, but something welled up from deep inside me, doubt, black doubt, pitiless black doubt. How could we, three people, carrying our equipment on our backs, carrying *only* what we *could* carry on our backs, hope to traverse this desolate place?

I said, "A test? Another test? Haven't we already proved our worthiness? Haven't we already demonstrated how dedicated we are to this task? Can God still not be sure of us?"

Jim paced, scowled, avoided meeting my gaze. Harold sat on a rock, glaring at the ground, his discontent almost palpable. Finally Jim said, "We'll just go around it."

Harold slowly raised his face; his expression was incredulous. "Go *around*? Jim, *look* at it. It stretches to north, south, and west as far as you can see."

"We'll skirt it to the north," said Jim.

"Why not to the south?" Harold demanded, and I said, "What difference will it make which direction we go?"

But Jim refused to let Harold's and my negative attitudes infect him. "We'll make camp here," he said, "and pray for guidance. We have been allowed to come this far, and we must go on. To turn back *now*, when we have come so far, to pass up this Heaven-sent opportunity, would be a *sin*."

We made camp. A sullen silence prevailed until after we had eaten our meal. Then Jim suddenly said, "Remember the story of Jesus walking on water."

Harold and I looked at him; I thought, mechanically, Matthew 14: 22-23, Mark 6: 45-52, and John 6: 16-21. I had excelled at this kind of thing ever since summer Bible camp.

"Following the miracle of the fishes and the loaves," Jim said, "Jesus went by himself up onto a mountain to pray, while the disciples put out in a boat. A storm arose, and the disciples were afraid. And Jesus came to them, walking upon the sea, and they thought him a ghost, and were still more afraid. But he said, Be of good cheer, it is I, be not afraid. And Peter said, If it be thou, Lord, bid me come unto thee on the water, and Jesus said, Come, and Peter—Peter, the adventurous and outspoken one among the disciples—got out of the boat and walked on the water."

Then he quoted directly from Matthew:

But when he saw the wind boisterous, he was afraid; and beginning to sink, he cried, saying, Lord, save me.

And immediately Jesus stretched forth his hand, and caught him, and said unto him, O thou of little faith, why didst thou doubt?

"Don't you see?" Jim asked. "A miracle brought us to this place, this time. Other miracles only wait to happen."

We didn't need a Sunday-school lesson to grasp Jim's point. Harold and I exchanged glances, and he shook his head.

"I'm not going out there," he said.

"O thou of little faith," Jim began, but Harold cut him off with an angry gesture.

"There must be another way to Nineveh. God wants us to complete our mission, Jim. He *doesn't* want us to commit suicide. And that's what we'll be doing if we go out there. No, thank you. I'm sorry, but, no."

"But we've come this far," Jim said.

"Well, we won't go much farther if we go out onto that salt flat. Just till we drop dead from heat and thirst. My mind's made up. You can go on if you want to, but you'll be going on without me."

"I'm very disappointed," Jim said, "but if that's your decision, Harold, well, there's no way I can force you to go." He turned to me. "What about you?"

"I've trusted your judgment this far. I guess I'll go with you."

Harold looked away quickly.

"What'll you do?" I asked him.

"Make my way back over the divide to that camp below the rapids. Try and make myself useful—or at least keep out of everyone's way—there until the next cargo barge comes by. I'll wait at the base camp to hear from you until the money runs out. Then I'll head home."

"Just as well," Jim said in clipped tones. "Where we're going is no place for the faint-hearted."

"You can't provoke me into changing my mind, Jim. God gave me good sense and expects me to use it."

"History will record that you were a coward!"

Harold shook his head. "No, because I'll be the one who writes the history. I'll be alive, and you'll be a dead fool." Jim looked at him in patent astonishment, and I could almost read his mind—

that bland-faced Harold should speak to him thus! Harold turned his attention to me. "You'll die, too, if you go with him."

"I have to go with him, Harold. He's brought us this far."

Harold sighed. "I'll give you my extra canteens and food. And my best wishes. And goodbye. I don't expect to ever see you again."

So Harold remained behind, and Jim and I set out together. When I looked back from a distance of less than a quarter of a mile, he waved and then turned his back on us and never looked our way again before he disappeared among the boulders.

Soon enough, the boulders began to wobble and blur in the heat and became an indistinct smudge. The divide itself became a dark, irregular band shimmering along the bottom edge of the sky; you could not quite fix your eye upon it.

Out on the salt flat, time soon ceased to have meaning. We had covered our heads to protect them from the sun, but the hot, still, thirsty air seemed to suck the moisture out of us; we could not be said to perspire. Every step we took raised a puff of salt and grit that found its way into our boots, our clothing, the very pores of our skin. Irrationally, I began to worry that, should I stumble and fall, I would never get up again, but shrivel on the salty ground like some hapless slug. Then my attention became centered upon Jim's brace of canteens as he trudged along ahead of me. Surely by now we were due for a drink of water. I consulted my watch and was dismayed to see that scarcely any time at all had passed since we parted company with Harold. I got a grip on myself and resolutely thought of nothing beyond the next step, and the next after that, and the next.

At irregular intervals Jim signaled a halt to take a compass reading, and finally I suggested that we drink. We sipped gratefully, carefully, and took stock. The heat-mist of morning had yielded to the full fierce glare of midday. A broad phantom lake, like a ghost of the sea that had perished here, shimmered ahead of us. We resumed our plodding advance, crunching the crusted grainy ground under our tired feet. Nothing else moved or made a sound.

At some point, as Jim paused for another compass check, I saw that the sun, now an oblate flaming ball, was sinking before us with a suddenness that took me completely by surprise. I turned in place and looked about. I could almost see Jim's and my shadow lengthen behind us, stretching toward the divide, which ran now like a row of gory fangs along the horizon. There was nothing else in the saltlands that could throw a shadow.

We pitched our light sleeping tent, washed down a frugal meal with a gulp of water, and turned in. We had not said a word to each other since our previous water break, a timeless interval earlier, but now Jim spoke. His voice sounded small in the deathlike stillness of dusk. He said, "Harold is simply wrong."

"It was his decision to make."

"It is a shortcoming of the twenty-first-century mind—the modern mind generally—that it does not readily believe in miracles or expect to encounter them in daily life. That is why they go unremarked. No one believes them to be miracles at all, but commonplaces of the secular scientific age. Yet here we are, returned by means of a great miracle to the age of miracles itself, when God never hesitated to intervene in the affairs of men. Today as we walked there came a moment of doubt. I almost turned back.

> *The sorrows of death compassed me, and the pains of Sheol got hold upon me; I found trouble and sorrow.*
> *Then called I upon the name of the Lord: O God, I beseech thee, deliver my soul.*

And then I felt the Lord at my side, and I took heart again. I could not have been more convinced of the Lord's presence if a pillar of fire had gone before us. He will not fail us. He will not let us fail."

We prayed together then, and I fell into an exhausted sleep. The saltlands did not become appreciably cooler during the night, and lay under the heat-mist when we put our heads out of the tent early the next morning. The sun showed as a baleful orange orb above the distant line of the divide.

We hurried through another sparse meal, took our first drink of water for the day, and after a compass check resumed our march. I had treated myself to a sort of morning bath, wetting a thumb and forefinger and running them over my eyelids to remove the previous day's grit. The relief was instantaneous and brief: the thin film of moisture evaporated almost at once. I began to recite, mentally, from the Psalms and found in probably the most hopeful and certainly the most famous verses a poignancy that would have moved me to tears had I been able to spare precious water for tears.

The Lord is my shepherd . . ..

At day's end, exhausted, parched, encrusted with salt and grime, we managed to pitch our tent and swallow our evening meal while barely speaking to each other. Only the evening's ration of water held any interest for either of us, unless you count our brief evening prayer, which even at the time struck me as more desperate than the previous evening's.

So passed the second day in the saltlands, and just so, a third, a fourth. All that fourth day my eyes burned and my vision grew blurred. That evening, I realized that I was going blind from the glare off the salt flat.

"When you were brought in," says Heflin, "no one could account for you. We're in touch by radio with the various scientific teams throughout Laurentia. Nobody had misplaced any personnel. So we took your fingerprints and a DNA sample and sent them with everything else we had on you—which was little enough—in a message-and-materials module. In due course we received the following information."

Heflin takes a folded sheet of paper from the side pocket of his jacket and opens it. He looks at me over the tops of his hornrimmed glasses. "Your fingerprints and DNA prove you are who you say you are. Yet you are *not* who you say you are. *That* person lives in Carrollton, Texas. It's a suburb of Dallas. You have the same fingerprints as this person, and the DNA is a perfect match. You share a name, you have a birthday and birthplace and parents in common, but not a lot else. He is a schoolteacher and a deacon in his church, and right now—which is to say, four hundred and eight million years from now, back in Holocene time—he is probably looking as perplexed as you do. Doubtless he's wondering why FBI agents are asking him when he was born, what he does for a living, and—" Heflin gives me an amused smile "—whether he's ever time-traveled."

"The FBI?" I am too stunned to think of anything else to say.

Heflin shrugs. "They were in the jurisdictional neighborhood, if you get my meaning. They've sent this other you on his way with a clean bill of health."

"I don't understand."

"Well, I can't blame you for that. The fact remains, you are not from around these parts, and when I say 'these parts' I mean Carrollton, Texas, in the Holocene, as well as Camp Number Two here in the Silurian. You came from someplace else close by—as close by as two universes *can* come to each other. You are perhaps familiar with the many-universes hypothesis in quantum physics?"

I make no reply, cannot even nod or shake my head, but Heflin proceeds as though I have answered in the negative.

"Essentially the hypothesis states that whenever two or more outcomes of an event are possible, the universe creates replicas of itself to accommodate each of those outcomes. Given the infinite number of events with more than one possible outcome, it follows that there must be an infinite number of universes different from one another in ways small or large. I came from the twenty-first-century Earth in one universe to this widely divergent mid-Paleozoic Earth. You, too, came from a twenty-first-century Earth—but not *mine*. Yours, if I may so, apparently has less stringent rules for people wishing to come through spacetime anomalies. We would never have let you come through. Nothing personal, but your lack of accreditation would have weighed against you. Anyway, you came from there to a widely divergent mid-Paleozoic Earth—but, again, not *this* one. That's why we have no record of you and your party. Then you went off and did whatever you did and somehow blundered onto this Earth."

"Impossible!"

"But true. When you went through the jump station with your Jim and Harold, you left your universe and possibly landed in the universe you were supposed to—but only temporarily. The transference must have happened *after* you were already in Silurian time, because, as I said, we have no record, none whatsoever, of you and your two friends coming through at this end. Somewhere between the time you came through and the time one of our 'copter pilots just happened to spot you lying on the salt flats, you crossed a boundary. You walked out of one world and into another almost but not exactly like it. *This* world."

"I don't believe it! I don't believe in your multiple universes any more than I believe in your theory of evolution or your Big Bang! This is some horrible trick!"

"Why should I try to trick you? Whether you believe in multiple universes or not, they exist," and he extends the unfolded sheet of paper toward me. A somewhat blurrily reproduced photograph fills one upper corner, and it could be my face that I see in it, yes, it could. "This isn't you," says Heflin, "it's your twin's driver's license mug shot."

"No. *No.*"

"What *I* don't understand," Heflin says, "is how three men— none of whom was a paleontologist, geologist, or archaeologist, all of whom were not just unqualified but untrained, underequipped, and in every other important respect unprepared—how you expected to overturn Darwin, Einstein, and everything in between."

"We were doing God's bidding. We trusted in God for the help we knew we'd need to get through the rough patches. Despite the obstacles in our path, our mission was really very simple. We had only to find one thing that didn't belong in your Silurian world. One thing, a single relic or artifact or specimen, that would be all it took to bring down your whole false edifice. Whether it was the Tower of Babel or only a fragment of pottery. Or some species that supposedly hasn't evolved yet. A bird, a cat. A human being."

"Instead, you found the salt flats."

"Yes. God was still testing us. That's what Jim said. God had chosen us as the instruments of divine will, but first we must demonstrate that we were worthy, men of unbreakable, unshakable faith. The saltlands would have daunted anybody whose faith was imperfect. I will confess that at first sight I was unnerved. I wavered. It seemed such a formidable hurdle to place in the path of men who wanted only to serve God. We had only the equipment and supplies we could carry on our backs. One look at that expanse of salt stretching to the horizon, and in a moment of weakness I knew beyond doubt that we would never make it across. We couldn't possibly have carried enough water even if we weren't carrying anything else."

"Yet you attempted to cross anyway."

"Jim said it was the last and greatest test we would face. God would not let us down, but would provide for us as the children of Israel had been provided for during their flight from Egypt."

"Manna drifting down from the sky," Heflin said, "and water

gushing forth from rocks on command. And you went along with this? You believed everything Jim told you?"

"We believed God had brought us this far for a purpose, and would carry us through to the end. Jim and I knelt there at the edge of the salt lands and prayed for guidance, for strength. God dispelled my doubts then. I knew that Jim was right. However hard the path, we were on it because God had chosen it for us and us for it."

"Do you want to hear what we know about your Jim Farlough? Oh, we checked on James Farlough, Junior, too. And Harold Dopp. Harold seems like a pretty decent sort, but as for Farlough, what a fine character you and he cast your lot with. Tax evasion, mail fraud, some other things even less savory."

I laugh harshly. "Perhaps those things are true of the Jim Farlough who inhabits your universe. Not that I believe he or it exists. The Jim Farlough I know is a man of God and a scholar. He has suffered persecution for his beliefs, but he has always held to those beliefs. Almost to the very end I would have trusted him with my life."

"Apparently. You trusted him with your life, and he led you out on a salt flat and left you there to die."

"I'm going blind from the glare," I told Jim through painfully cracked lips. "It's like snow blindness. Just hotter, is all."

"We must pray for the strength to prevail in this latest trial."

Something within me, already screwed tight, snapped.

"Not another test," I said. "Harold was right. We should have listened to him. I wish I had. We're going to die here."

"You can't mean that. Harold deserted us. He turned his back on the Lord, and he'll be punished for it."

"Can he possibly suffer as we're suffering right now?"

"Our travails will pass. But we must have faith. Why would God lead us out into this wasteland only to abandon us?"

"We *have* faith, Jim. Faith has brought us to this godforsaken place. *Misplaced* faith."

"Don't blaspheme against God."

"I don't think it was God who's led us into this hell. We thought it was God, we wanted it to be God, but all along we were being misled."

"By me?" he demanded in a startled tone.

"No, by the great deceiver himself."

"Do you think we wouldn't have recognized Satan?"

"We don't call him the great deceiver for nothing, Jim. It was Satan. He appealed to our sinful pride. We would be the final victors over secular science, remember? We would do it for the glory of God, of course, but there'd be enough glory left over for us. Satan baited the hook, and we swallowed it."

"No. What we heard was the voice of the Lord. What I'm hearing *now* is the voice of Satan. Defeatist talk!"

"Defeatist? I'm blind, we're exhausted, we're starting to run low on water, we're stranded in the middle of nowhere. How much worse does the situation have to become before you realize that this is hopeless?"

"I won't listen to you."

"You have no choice. We're not going anywhere. I intend to say what's on my mind. Jim, you can still see enough to read the compass. Let's turn back while we still have water and strength. I'll keep up with you if you'll lead the way. We'll go back and live to plan another expedition to find Babel."

"Go *back?*"

"It's our only chance, and maybe not much of a chance at that, but it's all we've got. We *can't* go on."

"No. We're *this close* to realizing our goal. I know it. I can feel it. I hear God's voice telling me, 'But a little farther, a little farther.'"

"That's not God, Jim. It's Satan. We've been led astray."

"No! Our faith, our will, they've been strong, they've never faltered till now." I heard Jim move away from me. "I'm not giving up," he said. "I'm putting my trust in the Lord. He will guide my steps, and if you'll take my hand, he'll guide your steps as well."

I groped for him but couldn't find him. "Are you crazy?"

"We'll die if we stay here."

"I don't want to stay here. I want to go back."

"I can't let your weakness keep me from accomplishing what I came here to do."

"Sin of pride, Jim."

"I *won't* give up. I'm willing to take you along with me, we can tie ourselves together, support each other, whatever, but I'm not giving up."

"Go on if you must. I'll make my peace with God right here. If I've failed the Lord by not going on with you, I'll ask his forgiveness."

"As well you should," he snapped, and sat down again at my side. He helped me with food and water but said little more to me, as little to me as was necessary. Our minds were made up. The next morning, the morning of the fifth day, he said, "Goodbye," and walked away, just like that. I listened to his retreating footsteps. I couldn't tell which direction he went. I was too weakened to care.

"There remains," says Heflin, "the matter of what to do with you."

"Why can't you just send me home through the jump station?"

"If only it were that simple. It's highly unlikely, however, that you could get home—that is, back to your proper universe— simply by going through from here. Probably you'd end up in the same world as your twin occupies. It would hardly be fair for us to spring a *doppelgänger* on him. I'm sure he already has enough to worry about, what with thinking the FBI is after him."

"You know what I think of your many-worlds theory. It's just an excuse to keep me prisoner here, isn't it?"

"Not at all. If we could get rid of you as easily as just shooting you through the anomaly, we would. Oh, I personally am delighted with you. You're the *tangible* evidence that other universes exist. But the fact remains, you're a king-size headache for us generally. We have no intention of keeping you prisoner, as you put it. But you must remain here as our guest until we figure out what to do."

"Guest or prisoner, whichever you call it, I am to be held here against my will."

"You'll have the run of the ship, or as much of it, anyway, as isn't off-limits to the rest of us civilians. Be warned that the captain isn't known for his sense of humor. In due course, you'll be allowed to go ashore. Meanwhile, we physicists and technicians will be trying to dope out a solution. You *got* here somehow, and it's perfectly reasonable to assume that you can get *back* somehow. Till then, we'll try to make you as comfortable as possible."

"When I do get back, I'll tell everybody how I've been treated here."

"Tell the world. Write a book. The title's ready-made. 'Prisoner of the Paleozoic.' Just be sure to include the part where you're rescued from the salt flats and nursed back to health and only then beaten with rubber hoses every other Tuesday." He gives me a wink. "We like our victims to be in tip-top condition before we persecute them."

So my captivity begins.

Heflin continues to interview me regularly, trying at first to elicit from me every detail of my visit from my arrival with Jim and Harold at the jump station to the last moments I remember out in the saltlands, and though I still don't believe any of this nonsense about multiple worlds I racked my brains trying to recall some incident that may have signaled the transition. But nothing came. So we have moved on to matters that interest him just as much. He continually pumps me for information about "my" world, and is continually disappointed that, as far as I know, I am the sole difference between mine and his. I have my own questions for him: Has there been any sign of Jim Farlough or Harold Dopp? "None," comes the reply. "Farlough must have wandered on until he dropped dead. As for Dopp, he may be lying dead among the boulders along the divide. *Or*—" Heflin stabs the air with a forefinger "—he may have got home." He smiles. "Even if he did have to walk all the way."

I also make the acquaintance of the ship's legal officer, and we confer fairly often. She is sympathetic up to a point—"When this is all over, you can sue everybody in sight. Wrongful incarceration, just for starters!"—but only up to a point. "Doctor Heflin is right about the need to proceed cautiously. We can't have you complicate life for your twin back home, who's an innocent party." As though I am a completely guilty party.

The ship's chaplain calls on me in sick bay regularly, brings me a Bible (Authorized King James Version), teaches me chess. He is a well-read, humorous individual, an easy conversationalist, and though he embraces the Darwinian and Einsteinian blasphemies I have come to enjoy his company and look forward to his visits. At least he accepts God as the source of all things, "even," he says with a smile and a gesture that somehow takes in everything beyond the confines of sick bay, "all this *very* strange quantum-physics stuff." When I am up and around, he promises, we'll go ashore together and take in the sights I merely glimpsed the first time I passed through.

At last I can leave my bed and hobble about. As promised, I am permitted reasonable freedom of movement aboard the ship. The jump station is on the list of proscribed areas, but I find myself lingering in its anteroom. One time the ship's chaplain happened upon me there; I had brought along the Bible he gave me, and when he asked what I was reading, I read the words aloud:

I am afflicted very much; revive me, O Lord, according to thy word.

Accept, I beseech thee, the freewill offerings of my mouth, O Lord, and teach me thine ordinances.

My soul is continually in my hand; yet I do not forget thy law.

The wicked have laid a snare for me; yet I erred not from thy precepts.

Thy testimonies have I taken as a heritage forever; for they are the rejoicing of my heart.

I have inclined my heart to perform thy statutes always, even unto the end.

The chaplain nodded. "Psalms. Loveliest of all the books of the Bible. Well, take heart. This too shall pass."

"I can't imagine how," I told him, "unless it's that I simply go ahead and die and relieve all of you of the burden of wondering what to do with me."

"Well, *don't* die on us. We'd still have to figure out what to do with your mortal remains. Couldn't just toss 'em into the estuary, you know."

The next evening, my dishonored king having suffered a fresh round of indignities at the hands of the enemy queen and her faithful rook, Heflin put in an appearance and invited me to go topside with him for a breath of fresh air. The hour was late, and activity had lessened throughout the ship, apart from the jump station, which never shut down. The ship's crew and the hundreds of scientists attached to the expedition made constant demands on the spacetime anomaly for everything from heavy earth-moving equipment to toothpaste.

Heflin led me to the helicopter deck, across which a pleasant night breeze blew. On the deck behind us two hulking helicopters, crouched like antediluvian monsters, were being readied by maintenance crews for the next day's missions. Before us, across the black surface of the bay, glittered the lights of Camp Number Two. It seemed forever since Jim and Harold and I had passed that way. I felt an acute stab of longing for my home and family, and wished that I might get word to them of my predicament, and said as much to Heflin.

"Would that we knew the address," he said. "I'm sure Farlough's and Dopp's people would like some word, too—on whatever world they may inhabit."

I felt a flash of irritation. "I wish everybody would stop with that. I'm never going to believe it."

"Well, you know, we could bring you and your *doppelgänger* face to face and thereby prove something to you, only I don't know *what* it would prove to you. Perhaps only that you've got a double somewhere. Or that we wicked secular humanist scientists are so desperate to make you believe in the existence of many universes that we'd hire somebody to pretend to be your double. Or—I don't know. There are illogical thought processes I'll never understand. For example, it would be fascinating to me, personally, to know how your Jim Farlough arrived at the notion that Paleozoic North America is really the ancient Middle East."

"I told you."

"Yes. Scrupulous examination of the scriptures. Well, it's just idle curiosity on my part, but it could easily become consuming curiosity if I let it. I'd also like to know why people go on believing in astrology and the Shroud of Turin, in the face of everything we know and can demonstrate about the falsity of those things." He looked at me intently. "I suspect some people just can't process new information and evolve these bizarre rationalizations to support old, cherished misinformation."

"One man's old, cherished misinformation is another man's absolute, eternal truths."

"Tell that to some of my hard-eyed colleagues here. Listen, we scientists collect evidence and draw conclusions from it. You can imagine—no, you of all people don't have to imagine scientists' opinion of anybody who reaches a conclusion and then gathers the evidence that supports that conclusion—excluding any that doesn't support it. It may not seem like much of a difference to you, but it's a crucial one to us."

I turned away from him and walked a few paces along the edge of the deck. "What can I say? I believe what I believe. So did Jim. And he could be extremely convincing."

"Evidently. You and your friends became obsessed with disproving a body of scientific thought you don't like, and what came of it? Two men missing, presumed dead. Body of scientific thought? Not a scratch on it."

"And as though that weren't enough for me to choke on, the Jim Farlough who lives in this universe—I mean, in your universe—isn't a very good person."

"It seems not."

"The Jim Farlough I know—knew—was honest and decent—headstrong at the last, and it killed him and almost killed me, but essentially he was a good man. I never heard a breath of scandal about him. Nothing. And yet, *here*, he's a tax evader and swindler and Heaven knows what else. Assuming there was anything to this many-worlds stuff—"

"Assuming."

"—how is it possible for a man, the same man, to earn salvation in one universe and be damned to an eternity in Hell in another?"

"He wouldn't really be the same man, would he? There'd be two versions of the same man, identical men with free will, the power to choose what sort of people they are."

I shook my head. "I can't make myself accept it. And yet. And yet. I don't know how to account for any of this. I think that's why I go to the jump station and sit waiting and watching for—I'm not sure what—for someone else to come through, perhaps, who has made that wrong turning, taken that small but crucial step to the side that takes him from everything he truly has, everything he truly belongs to. Your many worlds would seem to be the answer to everything, but I think it'd take a miracle to make me believe it."

"Well, don't rule it out," Heflin said. "It would just be a matter of learning to process new information. And as your Jim Farlough was wont to say, this *is* the age of miracles."

SLUG HELL

Silver, just returned from or soon to return to Slug Hell, avails himself of the base camp's facilities and its denizens' impersonal hospitality. He is just passing through, coming or going, and during the time he must spend here, resting up from or for his labors on the other side of the divide, he is conscious of being an interloper among insiders. It is, he thinks with wry amusement, the story of my professional life.

In common with nearly everyone else at the base camp, the three men whose tent he shares, Burleson, Martin, and Carstairs, work hard from sunup to sundown and consequently do not keep extravagantly late hours when they can avoid it. They have taken him in, but they have their own missions to accomplish and their own social arrangements to help them endure in this primeval wilderness. Silver therefore makes a particular effort to observe the niceties of camp life. There are no niceties where he either is going or else has just been, but he is naturally a quiet, even taciturn, individual and manages to be unobtrusive among other people without being standoffish toward them.

The camp itself, compared with Slug Hell, is the lap of luxury. He sleeps restfully on a comfortable cot and eats reasonably well-prepared food that does not grit between his molars. He soaks up water, color, sound, conversation. The camp members, both civilian and Navy, have their own recreations, so Silver has a chance to watch a softball game and listen to much recorded music, all kinds of music, and attends an informal exhibition put on by the expedition's Sunday painters. He is charmed by the paintings, which tend to depict not the muted Paleozoic vistas here but explosions of burgeoning Holocene flora. Everybody misses flowers.

He naps after these recreations, enjoying restful sleep of a sort impossible on the other side of the divide. Even deep in this restful sleep, however, he cannot remember whether he is either lying on a cot at the base camp dreaming of the saltlands, or lying in his bedroll out in the saltlands, dreaming of the base camp.

Somehow, now I am aboard the helicopter as it settles earthward. A swirling grayish whitish cloud raised by rotor blast expands outward from a point directly beneath the machine, loses momentum quickly in the thick hot translucent air, but takes its time diffusing.

The Navy aircrew and I, the lone civilian, peer out. The almost perfectly flat, almost perfectly white plain extends to the shimmering horizon in every direction. The pilot twists around in his seat to ask, loudly but still barely audibly above the dying whine of the generator and the slowing whir of the rotor, "Are you *sure* you want to get out here?"

I nod jerkily, probably resembling a bird dipping its head. The Navy people think all us scientists resemble birds, more or less.

The expression on the flight engineer's expression twists with consummate distaste. "Slug hell," she says.

I smile, admittedly a bit thinly, and check my gear a final time. I would be traveling light, carrying on my own back my entire camp, shelter, food, equipment, but for the all-important water tank which two bluejackets manhandle out of the helicopter. Unless you propose to drink brine, you bring your own liquid refreshment to this place.

I step out and down and separate myself from the machine and its crew. Brown, hard, gaunt, I already look desiccated, like an insect husk.

The helicopter lifts through a vortex of stinging dust, circles once, then heads west to complete its supply run to camps on the far rim of this basin. The crew will rest and service the helicopter, then pick me up on their way home to the base camp. I am on my own for the time being.

Of an evening, Silver accompanies his hosts, Burleson, Martin, and Carstairs, to the mess tent and returns with them to the tent. Silver and Carstairs sit or lie on cots opposite Burleson and Martin, and Carstairs reaches into his seabag for the treasured bottle of scotch, and everybody nurses a measure of liquor for a time and nobody speaks. Then the lamp is turned out, the men settle on their cots, sigh. Carstairs and Burleson and Martin somehow decide among themselves—tacitly, perhaps telepathically (Silver knows how it can be among people who work and live together, he has not always been a solitary field researcher)—whether to finish off the day with conversation or to settle for no conversation at all and just go to sleep.

When there is conversation, it usually pertains, such as it is, to that day's work, or to exciting news passed along from colleagues in camp—So-and-so has found a unique patch of lichen, or netted a strange new bony fish, or spent the afternoon sexing trilobites—but inevitably the talk (such as it is) turns to home and everything that home has that this world does not have. It is almost ritualized, and Silver welcomes the litany.

"After looking at psilophytes all day," Burleson says, "when I close my eyes, I see garden flowers, just a riot of them. Tea rose, columbine, zinnia, veronica, campanula, regal lily, Darwin and cottage tulips. Delphenium, gladiolus, peony, chrysanthemum. China aster, dahlia, snapdragon. Bearded and Japanese iris, pansy, trollius. Ah, ah!"

Ah, ah, indeed, thinks Silver.

"It's wildflowers for me," says Martin. "I was a hiker, not a gardener. I hiked all over North America. Slogged or canoed through the parts that weren't really conducive to hiking. Give me senna, wild iris, lotus, moccasin flower. Give me swamp milkweed and sneezeweed. Jacob's ladder, fringed gentian, pitcher plant. Lupine. Rose mallow."

"Ah," says Burleson, "*ah!*"

Ah, thinks Silver, *ah!*

"Lilies," says Martin, "I always loved the lilies. Tuberous water lily, yellow pond lily, meadow lily."

"Blackeyed Susan," says Burleson, "and bee balm and red trillium."

"Greater bindweed!"

"Butterfly weed!"

"And don't even get me started," says Martin, "on desert plants."

"Or flowering trees and shrubs."

I am in a place of silence.

The eardrum is an amphibian innovation, and amphibians themselves are an innovation whose time isn't due for many more millions of years. The only terrestrial vertebrates on earth (if this is earth; the physicists say no) are myself and my fellow human beings—all of whom are well out of earshot, over the divide, where rain falls and rivers run and things grow and thrive, and where my fellow human beings study rain, rivers, growing thriving things, and a good deal more besides. Can't blame them. *This*, however, is my chosen sphere of activity, and even I admit that it's an utterly hellish place. Evaporite basins always are. I've seen salt flats before, but this is the grandmamma of 'em all, stretching to the horizon and beyond in three directions. Somewhere far off is a sea that's being squeezed out of existence.

Let me make you a crude map of the world as it is now. Here, straddling the equator, is proto-North America, called Laurentia. Northeast lies Baltica, southeast lies Avalonia, both separated from Laurentia by the proto-Atlantic. Beyond Avalonia are the Rheic Ocean and a seafloor-spreading zone that's pushing Avalonia and Baltica into Laurentia. As these landmasses close, land levels rise, and the sea withdraws. It's a slow process, of course. The sea retreats by fits and starts, inches or fractions of inches at a time. Here a lagoon gets isolated and begins to evaporate. Along the seaward lip some water still spills into the lagoon, and that water, too, begins to evaporate, and the lagoon gradually fills and shrinks as chemicals in the seawater precipitate. Hydrated sulfate of calcium. Sodium chloride. Anhydrite. Potassium and

magnesium salts. The bones of the sea. As that Navy gal called
it: Slug Hell.

My specialty is extremophilic organisms. Apart from myself—
again, an interloper—prokaryotic extremophiles thriving in
these brine pools are the only living things in this hot silent
monochromatic hellhole. The majority is haloarchaea, but all are
extreme halophiles adapted to very high concentrations of salt;
amino acids on the surface of their cellular machinery permit
retention of water molecules. Indeed, they require a minimum of
ten times the salt content of ocean water to exist. For all their
adaptations, however, they are fragile organisms—place them in
distilled water, and they instantly lyse, burst and die from the
change in osmotic conditions. Their domains, marked by red
streaks due to carotenoid compounds in the cells, provide the only
real touch of color. They are, to me, the most remarkable life-
forms on earth.

Probably they were the first living things on earth and probably
they'll be the last. Eventually, terrestrial geologic processes will
stop, the atmosphere will thin, the seas evaporate entirely. By
the time the sun starts to die, the dominant lifeforms on earth,
the culmination of billions of years of biological evolution, will
be some orange and pink streaks in a brine pool. Not to worry,
however. Very similar organisms surely live in essentially the same
extreme conditions on other worlds circling other suns. All hail the
extremophiles!

But do it quietly.

I love the little buggers, but they are truly lousy conversationalists.

Carstairs laughs shortly. Carstairs' moment has arrived; his
contribution to the litany is contrapuntal, and Silver welcomes it.
He feels the greatest affinity for Carstairs.

"You have something to add?" asks Martin, as though he did
not know what the answer will be.

"You two are a panic. You carry on like botanizing young
ladies in Victorian England."

Burleson says, "Don't tell me you never look up from your pale
gray fungi and look around at this pale gray landscape and wish
there was a splash of color in it somewhere."

"Plenty of color splashed around here," Carstairs says.

"Earth colors," says Martin, "muted, washed out. Nothing *vivid*. Nothing the eye can really fasten on."

"Beg to differ. Sky here's so blue you can't look at it for very long at a time. And the swamp—all that vibrant chlorophyll green. Look out over the sea, it's velvety purple out beyond the headlands."

"But no *hot* colors," says Burleson.

Silver can almost hear Carstairs grin in the darkness. "Find yourself a volcano."

"No reds, I mean, no oranges."

"I just miss flowers, is all," Burleson says. "Psilophytes have their charms, but I'd just like to look at, oh, a magnolia blossom."

"Send for a picture of one from home."

"A *real* one."

"Then wait around here till the Cretaceous," Carstairs says. "Isn't that when magnolias first appear? Meanwhile, I rejoice in my fungi. They're already everywhere here in Paleozoic time. The most opportunistic multicellular lifeforms on Earth."

"Funny," says Martin, "I'd've said politicians."

Everybody laughs now and settles himself for the night, the evening's entertainment being concluded.

I love this work and am good at it, but this place even gets to me. I have dreamed that as I lay sleeping out here the very earth sucked every drop of moisture from my body. I have dreamed that things came out of the brine pools on moonless nights.

I dreamed of a man who came staggering across the saltlands. He was ragged and filthy. He had lost his equipment, his supplies. He had lost his way. He had lost his mind. I took him into my tent, though it was barely big enough to shelter me alone, and shared with him my meager food and water. Late that evening he began to babble of Biblical events, the Deluge, the Ark, the recession of waters. Somewhere behind this saltland, he said, were the fabled first cities of post-diluvial time. He was dead by the following morning, and I buried him in a grave scooped out by hand. "Better than embalming," I said, to no one in particular.

Poring over my specimens I suddenly overhear myself mouthing the words of a song popular back home,

SLUG HELL 🔆 STEVEN UTLEY

"She had different faces,
Different ones for different places
And every hour of every day,
And no one knew the whole array,"

and feel, suddenly, alone as I am, embarrassed.

Do I *miss* people?

Somewhat. Slightly. There are people back at the base camp whose company I enjoy. Anarchists, mostly, whose chief amusement, the thing from which they derive the most pleasure (apart of course from their work), is annoying the authoritarians. The authoritarians for their part regard the anarchists with disdain and suspicion, which is how it ought to be. The authoritarians, the true ones, are as few in number as the true anarchists, but the authoritarians have people, myrmidons, to do their bidding. Living and working in the midst of this amazing primeval world's myriad wonders, people with a distinctly small-town-in-the-midwest Junior-Chamber-of-Commerce view of everything. This is not to say that they, any more than members of the other two groups, are incompetent scientists, or, any more than the true authoritarians, incapable administrators, or, any more the anarchists, bad human beings. It's just that for people uninfected with boosterism, they are a royal pain in the ass.

These groups are capable of working together, for they are, all of them, highly trained professionals. Yet the struggle always rages between them, manifesting itself in matters as trivial, or as some people would put it, as *seemingly* trivial, as what to call the base camp. Its prosaic official designation is Number Two Camp; its real name, however, is Stinktown, because it's located at the mouth of an estuary, and at low tide it smells like the world's biggest *binjo* ditch. The first Paleozoic explorers necessarily established Number One Camp where the vagaries of the so-called spacetime anomaly put them, which happened to be approximately where I am right now, smack in the middle of a desolate evaporate basin. The camp was abandoned as soon as a relatively more hospitable site became accessible. Only a lunatic would come back here.

And here I am, again.

I could have brought along a chip player, of course, one small enough to fit right into my ear. I always tell myself this after I have actually arrived in Slug Hell. I think I prefer to hear music with my mind's ear as I work. For one thing, my brain has much greater storage capacity than any chip. For another, I have perhaps inherited my memory for music from my great-great-grandfather.

The evening's entertainment being concluded, Silver settles himself for the night, but sleep comes on him more gradually than for the other three men, affording ample time for reflection. He has an excellent, even an extraordinary memory, keeps his diary in his head, everything perfectly organized and accessible. He has only to reach in and pluck out the memories of similar evenings spent as a guest in similar tents, listening to similar litanies. One, in condensed form, goes: In the bay there are reddish placoderms with silvery bellies, and honey-colored sea scorpions and chocolate-brown ones and shiny black ones. The primitive land-living cousins look just like their descendants four hundred million years from now, just like the ones back in Texas, even to having exoskeletons that reflect ultraviolet rays from moonlight and other sources; in the darkness, they gleam eerily, fluorescent green and pink.

Another goes: Where most of you see only dull earth colors, I see a wonderful mosaic of white, gray, black, tan. Black basalt, gray granite. The beaches here are multicolored with flecks of brown feldspar, with quartz, clear, colorless, or tinted amber, peach, and pink.

And Silver thinks: There are vast stretches of beach white with coral and shell fragments that would unnerve me if not set off against the blue sea and sky. It is only the unrelieved whiteness of the saltlands, stretching to the horizon where the sea has evaporated, that disturb my sleep.

And Silver thinks of his great-great-grandfather, whose unpublished memoirs tell how, still in his teens, he escaped from Nazi Germany on foot during the late 1930s. (The rest of his family remained behind and was wiped out.) He walked the whole way to Marseille, where he booked passage or hired on as a deck hand (this much is rather unclear) to the United States. He was a great music lover, not a bad cellist in later life, and claims to have kept himself sane during his trek by playing out favorite Mozart and Brahms pieces in his head. He never whistled or hummed, he simply made the music happen in his head. Writing as an old man, he summed up his experience in this way: "Anywhere we find ourselves, we upright apes cannot do without beauty, even if we must carry it around inside our big ape heads." Throughout his journey across Europe, he had especially cherished the wrenching middle movements of Bach's Concerto in A Minor and Mozart's Piano Concerto No. 21.

And Silver thinks, in the moment just before he happily yields to sleep: I like those, too.

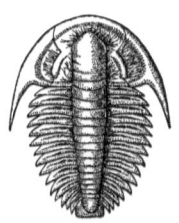

THERE AND THEN

The wind had shifted, and the night was full of land smells, estuarine smells, green slime, black mud, rotten eggs. The only sounds were ship and sea sounds; occasionally, there was also a murmur of conversation in the shadow beneath the eaves of the helicopter deck. Chamberlain's two assistants were back there somewhere, tending equipment, their voices muffled as if by layers of flannel. The moon had vanished into a vast, dense cloud bank. The fantail was so dark that I could see little of Chamberlain except his glowing red eye and, intermittently, red-tinged highlights of his face and hands. He looked devilish in those moments. He held the glowing eye sometimes between his fingers and sometimes between his lips. Every so often, its glow would expire, and he'd fumble with his pockets, there'd be a sputter of flame, the thick smells coming off the land would momentarily mix with that of burning tobacco. I wondered again how he had got his ancient and disagreeable vice past screening.

Chamberlain sat in his beat-up deck chair, surrounded by a mutant-toadstool growth of meteorological godknowswhat. I leaned against the rail. Hundreds of people lived and worked aboard, but late at night it was easy to get the feeling, and hard to get rid of it, that we were the only human beings in all the world. Actually, we represented a few tenths of a percent of present world population.

After a while, I said, "You should come."

"Too much work to do here."

"Oh, come on. We've both been cooped up here too long. We could both use some excitement."

"Hm." Hm was the sound Chamberlain made when he meant to laugh. "I hear they could use some excitement ashore, too. There's none of the tumult and squawk you just naturally associate with prehistoric times."

"You don't think a live sex act with trilobites will be exciting? Come on. A walk on the beach'll do you good."

"This the beach I smell? Ew."

"We'll be on a different beach. What you smell is blowing off the estuary. We'll be way around the coast from here."

"Still." The old deck chair squeaked unhappily as he shifted his weight. "I'm a meteorologist. Meteorologists aren't supposed to have to smell bad smells."

"Then don't smoke."

He called me a body-Nazi and ignited a new cigaret off the old. "Sure smells like the honey pot got kicked over."

"Gripe, gripe," I said. "You have it made. The weather never does anything here. The only forecast you ever make is, warm, east wind, possibility of showers. You sleep when you want, come out and play with your expensive toys when you want—"

"You've got no damn idea what my workload's like. Anybody has it made on this boat, it's you."

"—sit back and watch the sunset and drink till you nod off!"

He made a rumbling noise deep inside himself. "You know as well as I do that nothing enhances a sunset better'n a drink. And nothing enhances a drink better'n a nap." The glowing eye moved away from his face in the direction of his invisible assistants, Immelmanned, and went back to his face. When he spoke again, his voice was so quiet that I had to lean down into his nimbus of smoke to hear his words. "Those two wait till I'm asleep and then sneak away to fool around. If you know what I mean."

"How simply terribly shocking."

"It's true. Had my eye on 'em for a while." The eye brightened for a moment, fell away in his hand. "Definitely something going on between 'em."

"Well," I said, "what could be more romantic than holding hands under a prehistoric moon? Ooh woo, what a little moonlight can do."

"That from one of your damned old songs? Of course it is, got to be. I forgot, you're one of them. Listen, it's past the hand-holding stage with those two. They're up to the bucking-and-grunting stage."

I couldn't recall having seen either of Chamberlain's assistants in good light. Now, in my imagination, they appeared as shadows, rubbing against each other. I said, "Well, it's still most people's favorite way to pair-bond."

"Fat lot of good pair-bonding ever did you, Kev. None of your ex-wives has spoken to you in years."

"They've hardly been able to, under the circumstances."

"Anyway, you think I want a couple of disgruntled ex-lovers on my team?" He made a disgusted sound. "When they fall out, this boat won't be big enough for the two of 'em."

"Ship. This is a ship, not a boat."

"Ship, boat," he said dismissively.

"Rain, dew," I said, in the same tone. "If Captain Kelly ever hears you call his ship a boat, he'll keelhaul you, hang you from the yardarm, and make you walk the plank all in the same afternoon."

"He makes allowances for dotty scientists. Point is—"

"The point is, your young honeys are happy together right now. Maybe they'll stay happy together. There's always the possibility that things'll work out, you know."

"Hm. That what you told yourself along about the third time you got married?"

"Sure was."

"You are such a dog with women," he said, and extinguished his latest cigaret. A moment later, I heard a faint clink in the darkness. "Want another drink?"

"Sure."

He gave me another capful of brandy from his flask. Officially, it was a long walk from the Paleozoic to the nearest liquor store. In fact, there was probably enough booze on board to float us the thousands of kilometers to Caledonian Land—proto-Greenland,

Kalaallitt Nunaat-to-be. Old hands know that when a body needs a drink, only a drink will do. Pleasantly abuzz, I peered off into the darkness toward the shore. Its smells were palpable, but it wasn't even a glimmer in the night. The moon gave no sign of coming out of its cocoon of clouds. After a time, I realized that Chamberlain had fallen asleep. I left him snoring harshly in his deck chair, and his assistants to their alleged smooching, and went up to the helicopter deck.

The helicopters sat there like big metal sculptures of dragonflies lighted for Christmas. Mechanics tinkered with the motors while people wearing overalls loaded equipment and supplies. A shirtsleeved man stood by with the unmistakable air of a junior supervisor. He looked my way as I passed and seemed about to ask if I was authorized to be there, but then two of the mechanics said hello to me and I said hello back, and you could see the wheels turn behind the shirtsleeved man's face: maybe I wasn't a scruffy old stowaway, maybe I was somebody eccentric but important. I knew the mechanics and loaders but had no idea who he was. So many similar-looking people had arrived in the past few weeks that I didn't know who a tenth of them were.

The ship's engines throbbed suddenly as Captain Kelly got us under way. I put strangers out of my mind and strolled all the way forward and halfway back. Ours was in no way a lovely vessel. It had originally been designed and built during the Oughts to deliver Marines to beachheads and provide support with missiles and helicopter gunships. Not a lot had been done, or could have been done, to tone down its brooding militariness. The missile launchers were gone now, and the gun turret rebuilt to house one of the astronomy team's big telescopes, but the superstructure, helicopter deck, and boat bay had required no redesign. The forest of antennae, scanners, things, and stuff rising above the bridge looked formidably thorny. Except for human beings in helicopters, there wasn't an airborne creature on Earth, but still the dishes turned and cocked and listened, as intently as if swarms of kamikaze aircraft lurked over the horizon.

The task of renaming the vessel had fallen to a group of more or less prominent scientists, who duly voted to rechristen it *H. G. Wells*. Some nasty hustling little demagog in Congress scotched that on the grounds of Wells' having been, besides a lousy stinking Brit—this, of course, was well after the end of The Special Relationship between the countries—a communist or some closely related species of one-worlder. The story goes that, told to submit something "more patriotic and appropriate," most of the scientists next agreed that the vessel should be renamed after one or another of certain late-20th- and early-21st-century presidents, because the ship, too, would move boldly into the past. "This kind of reckless sarcasm," a dissenter warned, "will backfire on us," and, sure enough, it did. Most of us since neglected to call the ship anything except "here" when we were aboard and "the ship" when we weren't. And we did keep a big framed portrait of Bertie Wells hanging in the rec room, over his alleged epitaph: Dammit, I told you so!

The brandy and the stroll conspired to fill me with a luxurious sense of peace and belonging. When my pocketphone buzzed, I murmured absently into the mouthpiece.

"Kevo," said Ruth Lott, "you're up." Peace and belonging fled. Ruth had the mellifluous Georgia-accented voice I hated to hear. I said, "Ruth, all decent people are asleep at this hour."

"That's how I knew you'd be up."

"Okay, I'm up. I just hope you're calling about something really interesting, like maybe an out-of-clothes experience you personally have had."

The phone barely did her great sweet laugh justice. "I have a little job for you." She always had a little job for me. "Come see me, I'll tell you all about it."

I knew and she knew that she had me, but even a rabbit struggles in a lion's grip. I said, "It really is kind of late."

"Won't take but a minute." When I hesitated long enough to make her impatient, she said, "Oh, and before I forget—" her voice was as dulcet-toned as before, but I wasn't fooled "—note on your calendar, extension review next month."

"Now that's low!"

"Why, whatever do you mean?"

"It's blackmail!"

"No, actually, Kevo, it's extortion. Bye."

"Go ahead," I said into a suddenly dead phone, "hang up on me, see what it gets you."

Then, having no choice, I did as I was told.

Ruth was a Junoesque fiftyish woman with the world's sliest smile. She trained it on me when I appeared in her doorway. She said, "Are those the best clothes you have?"

"I was—I am going ashore when we get to Number Four camp."

"Please see if you can't make yourself just a teensy bit more presentable. I want you to meet a party at the jump station in a little while."

"Since when am I the official greeter? You break your legs off above the knee?"

"These are media types, they make documentaries, videos, something. They're supposed to be very good." I gestured, So? and she added, "So you're all media types. You should get along."

"There's got to be someone else on this bucket who's—what am I supposed to do? It's not like these people will arrive in any condition to listen to me give a welcome speech."

"All you have to do is say hello, show them around when they're up to it, whatever. I'm making them your responsibility."

"But why me?"

"Because you are not snowed under with work, you bum. How often do you actually touch your wordboard?"

I gave her my most pained look. "Writing isn't just a matter of touching a wordboard. You'd know that if you'd ever had specialized training in the putting together of subjects and verbs so that they agree. The real work's mental."

"You're mental," and she laughed her laugh again. "How is the book coming along? Think you'll have it finished by the Mesozoic? Listen to me, and believe me when I tell you this, I'm doing you a favor. Once we're privatized—don't give me that look, we both know it's a done deal—once we're privatized, the new bosses will be looking very carefully at their assets and liabilities here. These include," and she ticked them off on her fingers, "one converted assault ship with some el strange-o scientists embarked, and some hired help, and you. You've been hanging on here for too long. It's time you had visible means of support. You need to be seen earning your keep. This little job won't take too much of a bite out of your life. Just till these newcomers get acclimated. Just make sure they have a good time."

"What, find them women, young boys?"

"I'm serious. Northemico's sponsoring them."

That impressed me. Northemico figured prominently in the push for privatization.

"Think of this," Ruth went on, "as sort of an opportunity to do what a writer's supposed to do, make all of this, this—" She gestured helplessly, unable to find a word that took in everything from ship's routine to the reality of our surroundings and circumstances. I supplied it.

"Stuff," I said.

"Right. Make all of this stuff make sense to them." She eyed my attire again. "It really will help if you try not to look so much like a beachcomber."

"I *am* a beachcomber."

"Kevo, I put up with you because you make me laugh." She leaned toward me confidentially. "Even Captain Kelly puts up with you. He thinks of you as our resident artistic type and has the weird idea that you're brilliant. God knows why. The new bosses, when they get here, aren't going to put up with you unless you seem to be of use around here. They'll probably institute a dress code, too. Now go on, get to the jump station," and she urged me on my way with the kind of little wave women use to dry their fingernail polish.

The tang of ozone in the jump station was as sharp as an icepick up the nose. I tried out looks and gestures of welcome on Cullum and Summers, the two techs on duty. Summers appeared to think I was pretty funny. Cullum appeared to think I thought I was pretty funny. They did the synchronization countdown. The medical team showed up at the last minute, and the lot of us simply stood around the rail-enclosed sending-and-receiving platform and watched as its surface shimmered and grew bright.

First to arrive was a woman who was so shaken up by the experience that the medical team had to roll her away on a gurney. The man who followed her looked gray but insisted that he was okay, please take him topside. I couldn't talk him out of it. Cullum and Summers exchanged looks with me and quietly made a bet between themselves: I either would or would not get the fellow out of the jump station, through a short passageway, and onto the starboardside gangwalk before it was too late.

As it happened, I did, but just barely. The man made it the last couple of steps with both hands clapped over his mouth. He grabbed the rail, stood there uneasily for a moment, then leaned out over the dark sea, out into blackness, and retched at length. He didn't actually lose his lunch because he hadn't any lunch to lose. Only the first visitors to the Paleozoic hadn't known not to eat before making the jump. They had gone about suited as if for Mars—you weren't even supposed to breathe the air here, let alone cough up your socks. The past was supposed to be as brittle as a Ming vase—you didn't dare give it a cross look. It was a while before people got comfortable with the idea that if the past was resilient enough to accommodate an 8500-ton ship, it could probably accommodate the everyday stupidity of the species embarked.

I stood behind and slightly to one side of the newcomer. When he turned from the rail. I handed him a bottle of spring water and said, "This'll help." He took it, rinsed, spat over the side. When he tried to hand the bottle back, I declined as if I were doing him a favor. He pulled a handkerchief from the breast pocket of his jacket and wiped his mouth. He was in his late twenties or early thirties and well-built. He would have had, ordinarily, what I call friendly good looks. At the moment, in the light of the safety lamp, he had the color of oatmeal.

"If you want," he said, "you can say you told me so."

"That is our motto here."

He gingerly felt around the lower edge of his ribcage. His hands fell abruptly to his sides when he saw me watching him.

"I should introduce myself," I said, and did.

"Rick King," he said. I was grateful that he didn't offer to shake hands. "Can't those technicians do something to make it so you don't get rattled apart when you come through?"

"They've been working on it forever."

"You want more folks to come and visit you here, you're going to have to make the trip more pleasant." I didn't reply to that. The last thing I wanted was for more folks to come and visit me here. "They told me all those drugs I had to take would help."

"They did help. Without them, you'd be feeling really bad right about now."

"And this smell. Hits you right in the face."

"Uh huh. But we're moving away from it. Anyway, you get used to it."

He shook his head. "Can't imagine how."

"If you're up for it, a turn around the deck might be a good way to start."

I led him up a deck and forward. His color slightly improved after a couple of minutes, but heat and humidity were taking the last measure of starch out of him. I figured he was about ready to collapse, and I'd be able to hustle him off to quarters, then slip ashore before Ruth knew what was up.

"Except for the stink," King said, "I could be on a boat in the Caribbean or somewhere. With the stink, I guess I could be off the Texas coast. When I first heard about all this, I thought, wow, travel through time, see prehistoric monsters battling fang and claw, you bet!"

"Sorry, fang and claw haven't quite evolved yet."

"Well, so far, nothing's what I expected."

"Common observation." I had a niggling suspicion, founded on nothing more substantial than King's being some kind of film-maker, that all of his expectations had been shaped by the movies, that he had come prepared to see, besides primordial ferocity, jump-station technicians who were prematurely balding men dressed in white coats and carrying clipboards, not guys who could have been mistaken for air-conditioner repairmen and displayed much hairy butt-crack whenever they hunkered down to fix stuff. I wondered what King would make of the scientists ashore, who wore big khaki pants and canvas shoes that made them resemble ducks. Still, if he had to have crewcuts and creased slacks, there were always the people who attended to the actual running of the ship.

Suddenly, though not exactly unexpectedly, King made a sound like ah-rurr and pressed both hands against his abdomen. His expression was alarmed. "I think I better get to the restroom," he said.

"This way," I said, "to the head."

When he was finished in there, I showed him where he was to bunk down. Someone had thoughtfully brought his gear from the jump station and stowed it for him. King took out an object the size of a wallet, unfolded it with the thoughtless ease of long practice, and slipped it over his close-cropped skull—a headheld camera. A thin cable ran from the jawpiece to batteries and recordpack in his pocket; the spikemike stuck out like half of a set of insect antennae.

He looked my way, the headheld whirred faintly, and I pretended to become fascinated by the paint on the bulkhead. Headhelds disconcert me. I never know whether to make eye-contact with the wearer's natural eye or unnatural one.

"Be prepared is my motto," King said.

I looked at him in wonder. He was still a mess. I asked if he didn't really want to get some rest, and he said he was too excited. I sneaked a peek at my watch. The boat would be leaving soon, and I was bound and determined to be on it. I made my fateful decision and asked him, "Do you think you're up for a little boat ride and campout?"

"I'm up for anything."

I looked doubtful, and not just because I wanted to appear sincerely concerned about him. Then: "Okay, it's your funeral. I'll go get my things and meet you back here. We'll pop into sick bay to see how your friend's doing—" he had not once inquired about her in all this time "—and then we hit the beach."

"Great! D-day in the Devonian!"

Silurian, I thought as I turned away.

King's friend's name was Claire Duvall. Chance had treated him with kid gloves and smacked her upside the head: she had a mild concussion. King took the news well. I shouldn't have held that against him, because I was even more impatient than he to get to the boat bay, and with much better reason. Nevertheless, it rankled me.

The boat bay could have stood some redesign. The slap of waves against the hull reduced unamplified speech to so much mutter. You could ruin your voice working in this part of the ship. At night, you could ruin your eyes, too, and your shins if you weren't careful. Few lights showed. Captain Kelly, it was said, didn't like to excite the, understand, extremely limited imaginations of light-sensitive Paleozoic marine organisms. I could dimly see human figures working in and around a boat and called down, "How soon till we leave?"

"Kev!" someone called back. "Come on if you're coming."

Someone else bawled out, "Will somebody up there please throw some goddamn light down here?" There ensued a bit of rude jawing back and forth, and then a shaft of stark white light suddenly spotlighted the ramp of the boat bay as if it were a stage.

People froze like deer in traffic. I beheld the true object of my desire.

She looked like an ivory statuette from my vantage point. Up close and in good light, she had blue eyes and fair brown hair. She was wearing cut-offs and a tee-shirt, and at any distance and in any light she had the best legs in the Paleozoic. Vicki Harris had been haunting my thoughts for some time. All at once, I had seen her, though I'd been looking at her for weeks, months, who knew how long? Sometimes it happens that way.

The light was switched off. I remembered to breathe. King and I climbed down, and everybody found a place to sit amid the jumble of boxes in the boat. The motor coughed and gurgled as the pilot revved it. The sides of the bay loomed around us like immense black cliffs. As we eased out, the almost-full moon emerged from purple clouds, suffusing the air with milky light. Above the rhythmic prum-pum of the motor and the hiss of water parting before the prow, King said, "My God," and then, "Wow!"

"No kidding," said someone behind me.

I looked around and found that I could just make out the faces of my companions. Cardwell and Jank were aft with Hirsch, the pilot; Vicki Harris sat amidships. All of them except Hirsch gazed upward. I'd have done so, too, but for the warm pleasure I got from gazing at Vicki Harris. She noticed me staring at her and cocked an index finger moonward to redirect my attention.

"Seen it," I said.

She flashed a grin. "Me, too, but I never get over how it looks. It's like it's almost but not quite the same moon. Like the features I'm used to seeing don't exist yet."

"I asked Hill about that once. You know Sharon Hill? One of the astronomers. She told me it's the same moon, less some impact craters. The main difference is in rotational velocity or some such. We're seeing it sort of from behind and off to one side."

She directed a look past me. I heard a faint whirring and remembered King. I made introductions, and she reached around me to offer him a hand and said, "Mister King."

"Please," King said, "Rick," and held on to her a beat or two longer than I liked.

"Vick," she said.

"Vee for short," Jank said, behind her.

"Vee Vee," said Cardwell, "if you want to be really disarming."

"My delightful colleagues. Doctors Jankowski and Cardwell." Her tone of voice fell somewhere in the middle of affection, tolerance, and reproach. I'd learned from Jank—who'd affected not to find my sudden curiosity remarkable—that she hated her first name. I have few opinions about what parents should call their girl babies, though I know a trend when I see it: names ending with the letter *I* have become true artifacts; more and more young women are answering to monikers that end with O, Fujiko, Tamiko. Still, I had a lovely, sweet girl friend by the name of Vicki in high school and was ever afterwards kindly predisposed toward anyone who bore it. Not, of course, that I didn't find Vicki Vick Vee Vee Harris entirely attractive in her own right.

"It's Cardwell's performing trilobites," I said, "whose antics we hope to see."

"I should get some great stuff," said King. He talked past me, to her. "I make documentaries and things." Talk about disarming. Documentaries and things.

She said, "Really?"

Vick and Rick, I suddenly thought, oh no.

Jank evidently thought it was a bit much, too, for he said, "What other things," and paused, and added, "Rick?"

"Commercials," King said, "infotainment, that kind of thing." I could tell that he was slightly taken aback.

"So which is it this time," Jank demanded, "documentary or commercial?"

"Documentary, of course."

"Of course. And when do you start?"

King lightly touched the headheld. "I already have. You don't have any objection to being on television, do you?"

Now Jank was taken aback.

"We've been on television," Cardwell said. "Not lately, though. Been a while since we had a documentary crew through here." He had the same interested attitude he'd had the time he showed me my first prehistoric shellfish. He could have been joining in two colleagues' discussion of trilobites.

By the way Jank shifted in his seat, I could tell that he was buckling down for business. He said to King, "You seem a little undercrewed."

"My partner was badly shaken up by the jump. But what you mean, of course, is, why aren't I hauling around a lot of help? No one does that any more unless they're making big Hollywood product."

Jank wouldn't let up. "What's your background?"

"Media arts, of course."

"Of course. Aren't there any real scientists who can do documentaries any more?"

"I took the famous crash course in rocks, bugs, and stones before I came." King laughed. "Whoa, Mister Overqualified, huh?"

"Yeah," said Jank, "thank goodness you're not just some facile slime-sucking adman."

Everyone lapsed into silence. Vick and I exchanged embarrassed smiles. The wind sweetened. Hirsch turned the boat and expertly took it in, bringing us to rest without so much as a bump alongside a natural stone jetty. We all scrambled ashore carrying something and were greeted by several of the semi-permanent residents of Number Four camp. The jetty dipped into the beach's sandy slope at the high-tide mark; the camp sat above. The moon was down and the sky was turning gray by the time we had the boat unloaded. I somehow found myself at Vick's side as we lugged the last of the cargo along the jetty. King and Cardwell were right behind us. Jank was already out of sight among the tents.

"Let's do breakfast," I said to Vick.

"Sounds good to me," and then, probably—I told myself—because she wanted to make up for Jank's rudeness, she said over her shoulder, "Join us, Mister King?"

"You bet." He obviously was happy that she'd asked but sorry that she hadn't called him Rick.

We entered the camp, and Vick veered off. "Meet you at the mess tent," she said to no one of us in particular. I didn't care for how King watched her walk away.

I had Cardwell and Jank's standing invitation to share their tentspace; a geologist named Crumhorn agreed to take King in, though it was on short notice. Cardwell and I delivered him to Crumhorn's tent and were about to move on when he said, "I don't believe I've actually sucked any slime since grade school. I'm just a film-maker, Kevin." When he spoke my name, I felt a sudden, irrational, tremendous urge to rub myself all over with hot sand or maybe ground glass. "If I said or did something to set Doctor Jankoski off—"

"Jankowski," I said.

"Oh, Jank," Cardwell said, "Jank's just," and shrugged as if that explained everything. He had the dimensions but not the temperament of a bear.

"Breakfast," I told King, "is in the big tent over yonder," and set off to get mine and left him to get his as he would.

Vick had saved two places at the table. I settled into one of them and happily stirred my coffee. We listened to Rubenstein, a cartographer, who two days before had completed a trek overland from Stinktown, Number Two camp, on the estuary. "Only sign of life we saw the whole time," he said, "was one of our own 'copters, headed inland."

Crumhorn dropped into a chair across from me and scooped up a piece of toast. I asked where his houseguest was, and he said, "Conked out. Just like that. Hi, how do you do, snork, zzz."

"I was wondering when it'd catch up with him. He jumped in a few hours ago, and he'd been going like a chipmunk on an exercise wheel ever since."

"So," said De La Cerda, another geologist, "he's, what, a video producer or something?"

"Or something."

She shook her head. "These people just keep tricklin' in."

Rubenstein said, "You say that about everybody."

"I'm part-Indian," De La Cerda said, "and Indians know about people who keep trickling in. The Sioux had a word for white people, *wasichu*. It means, you can't get rid of them."

Rubenstein looked at her askance for a moment. Then: "You're not Sioux, you're mestizo or some goddamn something."

Hendryx, yet another geologist, said, "So sue her."

Amid the groans, Crumhorn observed that punning was a cry for help, and Westerman, the slight blonde botanist seated next to Hendryx, said, "I used to love this man. Now I'm for feeding him to the fishes."

Hendryx looked smug. "No fishes this time of the Paleozoic, right, Vick?"

"Just some armored ones that look like tadpoles wearing football padding."

"They always looked kind of art deco to me," said De La Cerda.

"Well," said Vick, "you have to go to Stinktown to find them, and then they're only about as big as your hand."

"Are they edible?" I said. One thing I did miss in the Silurian was catfish sandwiches.

Vick made a face. "They've got a taste sort of between salt and mud."

"Vick Harris," Rubenstein murmured over the rim of his coffee cup, "girl icthyologist and gourmet." He sipped and grimaced. "Talk about salt and mud. So where're all the big exciting fish? Where's old Dinowhatsit? You know the one, ten meters long, armored head. Mouth like a big ugly pinking shears."

"Dunkleosteus, alias Dinicthys."

"Yeah, that's the one, where's old Dunkywhatsit?"

"Not even a glimmer in his great-great-granddaddy's eye, I'm afraid."

"So," De La Cerda said to me, "what about this video guy?"

"Northemico sent him to make a documentary about you folks."

Both De La Cerda and Rubenstein gave me the same sharp look, and Westerman said, flatly, "Northemico."

In spite of myself, I spread my fingers in the air and said, "He's just a film-maker."

"You mean like you're just a writer, I'm just a botanist?" Westerman shook her head. "Nobody who's made the jump in the last month or so has been just anything. This film guy's just not as obscurely specialized as most of them."

"Wait a minute," Vick began, but Rubenstein cut her off.

"If he really is a film guy. Probably a spy."

"I don't think you're being fair," said Vick. "You can't go around automatically assuming someone's a spy just because—"

"Vick," said Rubenstein, "you gotta admit, Northemico and the rest of that pack've been slavering to get in here from day one. There's money waiting to be made here."

She appeared doubtful. "I don't see trilobites and seaweed as the basis for growth industries."

"Try oil." De La Cerda gave her a not-unkindly look. "Something's sure going on. On the ship—" she nodded vaguely in the direction of the sea "—we're suddenly cramped for space. Too many newcomers all at once. People I've never seen before are suddenly looking over my shoulder all the time. Suddenly it's harder to schedule use of a helicopter. Then it's just impossible, because they're all the time flying people and surveying equipment into the interior."

"And we all know," Westerman said, "that there's nothing in the interior to survey."

"Sure," said Hendryx, "not if you're a botanist!"

Westerman laughed along with him and then made a face at him. They must have been a riot in bed.

Crumhorn rested his elbows on the table and steepled his fingers. "No reason to think there's suddenly something mysterious or sinister going on," he said. "We've been surveying the interior ever since we got here."

"Think about what you just said," said De La Cerda. "We've been surveying. We've been doing this, that, every other thing. We, us, the members of this expedition. These other people belong to some whole other expedition. It's riding piggy-back on ours. Gradually, it's displacing ours."

"They want to know everything," Westerman said. "They don't want to tell you anything in return. Look, I don't mind answering questions about my work, I like talking about it. But these people ask all the wrong questions."

"What questions are those?" Hendryx demanded sharply.

"Tim," said Westerman. I looked at her in surprise. She was almost pleading with him. "We've talked about this."

"Bottom-line kind of questions," said De La Cerda. "Is there you-name-the-mineral here? Is there a lot of it? Things like that. And you can bet somebody's spent a lot of time calculating which natural resources might be safe to grab here and not have them missed four hundred million years from now."

Hendryx's wedge-like jaw jutted belligerently forward. "Nothing ever was missed, was it? So they can't have taken anything out. Or maybe they did, maybe you can take out whatever you want, because the past takes care of itself. It has so far."

Westerman folded her thin arms across her chest and gave him an angry look. "I can't believe I'm hearing this from you."

"You should get used to the idea that not everybody thinks exactly the way you do. From time to time, you might even try rethinking a position."

"Tim, you know if Northemico gets loose here, it'll make the Antarctic feeding frenzy look like a model of responsible conservation."

"That was different."

Several people demanded in chorus, "How?"

The beleaguered geologist glowered. "What have we missed from the Paleozoic? Maybe the stripmine scars are buried deep inside the earth. Maybe they've eroded completely away. Maybe they've been deformed beyond recognition and understanding."

"Lot of maybes," muttered Rubenstein.

"We know the landmasses are drawing together, and that the collision'll fold this whole region over on itself."

Everyone at the table was regarding Hendryx very seriously. Westerman said, "Are you saying anything people do here's okay as long as they hide the evidence under a mountain range?"

"Listen, the bills have to be paid, or we have to go home."

"This is home," De La Cerda said, "for some of us."

"You think so." Hendryx patted his lips with a napkin. "But you can't live here without supplies from the future, and the pipeline stays open only so long as somebody foots the bill to keep it open. If the government stops, then Northemico or somebody has to start, or that's all she wrote." He pushed his chair back, stood, surveyed the semicircle of mostly hostile faces before him. Vick hung back, and because she did, I hung back, too. "I want this expedition to continue as much as you do."

Westerman's mouth was set in a thin, straight line as she glared at his retreating back. An almost identical line creased her forehead. "I sometimes wonder," she said, "if good sex is worth all the aggravation."

After breakfast, Vick said she had to go with Cardwell to splash around in tide pools and collect specimens. I passed what passed for the cool part of the morning bringing whoever didn't have work to do up to date with the latest shipboard gossip and scurrilous rumor. It got definitely hottish toward midday, but then clouds scudded in at noon, dumped enough rain to cool things off reasonably, and, mission accomplished, scudded away. I took a long nap and was greatly improved for it. Rick King was up and around by late afternoon—days were shorter in the Silurian, and years consequently longer, by three dozen days—and looked rested, fit, and out of place in what I took to be the latest thing in 21st-century beachwear for men.

I had hoped simply to prowl the beach, poke at the occasional lump of cast-up sealife, and just enjoy being on land for a change. King, however, prevailed on me to steer him around and make such introductions as I didn't have to disturb anyone's work to make. Nearly everyone was polite, and De La Cerda, of all people, actually seemed charmed. Westerman couldn't keep suspicion out of her face, and King, to give him his due, received her chilly how-do-you-do and perfunctory handshake with admirable grace.

When we had run through the possible introductions, King studied the cliffs behind the camp. "What's up there?"

"More sand and rock."

"There a way up?"

I should have lied to him, but I didn't, so next I had to take him up the path to the top. He looked like Tarzan going up; I felt like Sisyphus. When we got up, he stood akimbo and gazed off at the low mountains in the distance while I sat on a rock and pretended that I wasn't panting for breath, that my heart wasn't rattling loosely in its mountings. It was getting into evening, and all of that bare jagged rock had begun to burn prettily.

Number Four camp was located on a stretch of coastline where erosion had cut away headlands to form slip-faulted cliffs. Detritus littered the narrow scalloped beach below. This was a rough bit of seafront, but wherever you made landfall, you found yourself on an inhospitable shore. The one-day North American west was a volcano range; one-day Appalachia was a chain of islands; between the two stretched an unbroken shallow sea. Just so your sense of direction would be utterly skewed, the equator bisected this sea from the future site of San Diego to that of Iceland. Equatorial North America was geologically part of the great northern landmass, Laurasia, whose southern counterpart was Gondwanaland, comprising South America, Africa, India, Australia, Antarctica. In all the unsubmerged regions of the world there was very little soil, and that, thin, poor, and as vulnerable as life on land itself. Actual greenery existed only beside the waterways. It didn't measure up to the popular idea of a coal-forest, with fern trees, dragonflies as big as crows, salamanders as big as sofas. None of the flora was more than waist-high; most were much shorter. Carpeting the lowest and moistest patches of the immense badlands was Cooksonia, a rootless, leafless plant, no more, really, than a forked stem, towering a mighty five centimeters above the ground. The giant sequoias of the day were lycophytes, club mosses, growing to dizzying heights of one meter. They were comparatively sophisticated—stems with forked branches bearing clusters of small leaflets—but still fell short of what you'd call rank jungle growth. They didn't soften the land's serrate outline so much as make it look furry and itchy. Munching happily through all this green salad were millipedes, some of them big enough to provoke a shudder but all of them perfectly harmless. Munching happily through the millipedes were scorpions that looked and carried on as scorpions were always going to look and carry on. There were some book-gilled arthropods that rated the adjective "amphibious." There were no terrestrial vertebrates, excepting human beings. On the list of things yet to be were lungs, flowers, wings, thumbs, bark, milk, and penes. I was happier here than I'd ever been anywhere else.

King broke a long silence by saying, "This is good stuff." He patted the pocket containing the recordpack. "Long slow pan from the primordial ocean to the desert of barren rock and drifted sand." He fiddled with the headheld for another couple of seconds. "This world's one big still-life, though."

"Take it up with the folks who punched the hole in time. Maybe they can open up a more action-packed era for you. The Mesozoic, or World War Two."

"What do they do for excitement around here?"

I took my cue from his choice of pronouns. He excluded me from his subjects, to remind me, I supposed, that we were both media types, cousin—if not brother—professionals. I said, "That depends on who you talk to. For Cardwell, it's trilobites. For Westerman, it's club mosses."

"What is it for you?"

"Being here."

He brushed that away. "Being here isn't the be-all and end-all of your existence. You're a writer, writing a book."

I had come ostensibly to write a book about life on and around a research vessel embedded in mid-Paleozoic time. The book still wasn't finished, but, any more, it was beside the point. I had lost all sense of urgency about finishing it. I didn't need the money. I didn't need anything to do with writing a book, except as an excuse to stay.

I said, "I'm here because this is my home."

"Is it now?" He shook his head. "One day, this place will be home. People won't just work and live here, they'll be born and die here. That's what makes a place home. Right now, this is summer camp. People come here, do the equivalent of making baskets and looking for arrowheads, and when the time comes, they go home."

"Hardly anyone goes ho—back. Not if they can help it. They just have to keep passing their extension reviews. It's less trouble to maintain us here than to replace us."

"Still—"

I slid off the rock. "It'll be dark soon. I'm not going to negotiate that path in the dark. Wouldn't advise you to try it, either."

I started down without waiting to see if he would follow. Later, in the mess tent, I saw him schmoozing with Hendryx and thought, Kindred spirits. Then I took it back. Hendryx was one of us. King, I swore, would never belong.

Everyone scattered into the dusk after supper, most of them claiming to have work that absolutely had to be done before Cardwell's show started. I changed to my least-ratty attire and went down to the high-tide mark ahead of everyone else to find the best seat. My chip player was in my pocket. I took it out and pressed the go button, and merely ancient music floated out over the prehistoric sea. It was "Stardust," recorded by Artie Shaw and His Orchestra in A.D. 1941. I stood swaying in time, enthralled as always by Billy Butterfield's incandescent trumpet. Jack Jenney's smoky trombone, Shaw's own soaring clarinet. Then, as I waited for the next track to begin, I heard somebody behind me and put my thumb on the stop button. Vick paused a short distance away. She said, "I heard music."

"Yes, you did," I said, and then, even more inanely, "I don't have earphones, I hate earphones," and before I could stop myself, "If God'd intended for us to listen to music on earphones . . . ." Babbling.

Fortunately, I relaxed my finger on the button, and Shaw's rendition of "I Surrender, Dear" throbbed out of the player and enveloped us like a smoky blue cloud. I was gratified to note that she listened almost all the way through the track before she said anything.

"What is this music?"

"Jazz. Swing. Music."

"It's," and she waited two whole seconds before finishing the sentence, "lovely." She waited again, listened some more. "Lovely and old."

"Barely pre-World War Two," I said, trying not to sound defensive.

"God, my grandmother wasn't even born then."

"Mine was a teenage girl in Indiana. She used to scrape up thirty-five cents somehow and go see Glenn Miller at the local theater. In those days, thirty-five cents was a lot of money for a teenage girl to scrape up."

"This is Glenn Miller?"

"A contemporary. Artie Shaw."

She looked like someone trying to decide if a name she'd never heard before meant anything to her. Then she admitted that it-didn't.

"No need to apologize," I said. "I'd be fairly astonished if you had heard of him. Pop music before Elvis Presley, before rock and roll, was like the Precambrian to members of my own generation."

"I have heard of Elvis Presley."

I decided from the way she said it that she probably didn't have him confused with some other, subsequent Elvis—Costello, Hitler, Christ, one of those. We listened to "Moonglow," "Begin the Beguine," and "Summit Ridge Drive." The chip contained dozens of other tracks that I'd personally selected from Shaw's body of work, but I didn't want to be a mere tune jockey. I thumbed the stop button twice after "Summit Ridge Drive" to switch off the player.

"Certainly does grow on you," she said.

"Uh huh. I have Goodman and Ellington, too. Cab Calloway, Billie Holliday, dozens of—I think American pop music peaked sometime between nineteen thirty-five and nineteen fifty." I looked at her closely. "I wrote a book about it once. Am I getting carried away here?"

She showed me a small gap between her thumb and forefinger. "Only a little. I know people who'd make me listen to the whole Flucks catalog." My utter ignorance of even a portion of the Flucks catalog must have been obvious. "Flucks does a lot of sub- and ultrasonic pieces. Some of them are said to make listeners lose, ah, muscular control."

"Gosh, why couldn't Artie Shaw have recorded songs like that?"

She laughed. "Well, I don't see the fun in it, either."

Other people had been drifting down from the camp all this while. They made themselves comfortable, talked, drank, or simply stared out to sea and waited. Jank showed up with a bottle of brandy, and the three of us passed it around and heckled Cardwell to get the show started. The level of brandy in the bottle got lower and lower. Lulled by a murmur of waves and voices, I nodded off. When I awoke, with a start, the moon was out, the tide was in, and it had become as chilly on the beach as it ever got. Next to me, Jank was gently shaking Vick awake. Everyone else was heading back to camp.

"Rise up, Lazarus," Jank said, "and walk."

I said, incredulously, "I missed the show? You let me miss the show?"

"Wasn't any show." He nodded seaward, at Cardwell, who stood in the foam at the water's edge, a master of ceremonies whose star act had let him down. "Tomorrow night, maybe."

"Doesn't he know?"

"When they get here, they'll be here." Jank helped Vick to her feet, and I made a point of helping. "Tomorrow night, the night after—some night this week, anyway."

Between us, Vick nodded agreement, sleepily. "Moon's full. This is the season."

"How can even the trilobites know when it's time? There's only ever the one season."

"If it'll ease the pain of this disappointment," Vick said, "why not come snorkeling with us tomorrow?"

"Love to."

Jank and I saw her to her tent flap like gentlemen. I started softly whistling "Embraceable You" as we moved on, and then King bounced up out of the darkness and announced that he had wangled us invitations to a poker game in Rubenstein's tent. He was disheveled and dirty. His shoes looked to be a total write-off, and his beachwear wasn't in much better shape. I couldn't decide whether that ought to raise or lower him in my estimation—the one because he didn't care that he had ruined his expensive outfit, the other because I imagined he could afford not to care. He was thoroughly pleased with himself. Through the simple expedient of spending a night on a beach, he had begun to prove me wrong and become one of the guys. I had never been so disappointed with the people at Number Four camp.

"In all this time," Jank said, "I never knew I had to have an invitation to play poker with Rubenstein." He looked at me. "How about you?"

I was dead tired, but something made me answer, "Oh, why not?"

"Sure," said Jank, "why not?"

Rubenstein poured each of us a drink and dealt us in. The drink was heavenly, the cards were trash. I looked across the table at him and demanded, "These all you have?" He asked how many I wanted and peeled them off. I looked at them and thought, Worse and worse.

"Yow," said Jank. "No cards."

"Yow indeed," said De La Cerda. "You're much too happy with your hand."

"Aah, he's bluffing," I said. "Jank always bluffs."

De La Cerda threw her cards down. "He wants you to think he's bluffing. I fold." The rest of us played out the hand, to our regret. De La Cerda looked smug as Jank raked in chips. "Told you so."

The deal passed to Jank. As he shuffled, he said, without quite looking at King, "How'd you get this assignment?"

After a second, King realized that he was the person being addressed. "Applied for it, how else?"

"Applied to Northemico?"

"Yes." A pause. "Much as you applied to the government."

Jank snapped a card down on the table in front of King. "I applied through the University of Texas."

"Play cards," Rubenstein growled.

We played. Jank won the hand again. The deal passed to me. As I shuffled, King said to Jank, "You talk like you think the government's one thing and Northemico's another. Like they're separate, and one's good and one's not." He shrugged. "Or one's bad and one's worse."

Jank stared determinedly at his cards. "Aren't they? Separate, I mean."

"Public government, what you think of as the government— its job is just to keep the citizenry in line, make sure they don't make trouble for the real government. Real government is private government. Its job is helping rich people to become more so."

We stared at him, all but gaped, in fact. Jank finally said, "If that's so, why the whole big show of keeping the corporations out of the Paleozoic all this time?"

"Takes a while to agree on how to cut up a pie so that everybody's happy."

De La Cerda nodded slowly, as if agreeing against her will. "Like carving up old gangland cities. It's just good practice to keep your trouble away from your money."

Rubenstein said, "Does anybody here want to play poker, for chrissake?"

"Just a sec." King shut his fan of cards and closed his hands around it. He looked straight at Jank. "You've got some grudge against Northemico, so, because I'm here making a documentary for Northemico, you've got a grudge against me. Lots of people get mad at the government. I get mad at it. Doesn't mean I'm mad at you or anyone at this table or anyone in this camp. I'm here to do my job, same as you."

"Remember the ad campaign," Jank said to nobody particularly, "when Antarctica finally got opened up?" I could tell from King's expression that he'd never imagined any connection between himself and Antarctica. "Yesterday's land of perpetual ice and snow, today's treasure chest of mineral wealth. My favorite was, what good is it to the penguins? Succinct. Punchy." He looked around at all our faces. "I'm willing to bet there's this bright entrepreneur somewhere who's seen pictures of the Silurian sea, how beautiful and serene it looks. He has a brainstorm. A luxury hotel in the prehistoric past! The Silurian Arms! Next thing you know, there's this whole big ad campaign pitched to assholes with money they don't know how to spend. The ads say crap like, come back, come home, to a quiet and unspoiled world. Dine at Chez Paleozoic, gourmet cuisine from then to now."

King had sat back in his seat and folded his arms while Jank talked. Now he said, "You may have missed your true calling."

He grinned to show that he really was trying to be a sport. "You'd have been an ace adman."

"No, I was born with a soul," and Jank grinned, too, like a carnivore. "About this luxury hotel. Hotels mean earth-moving equipment, mean draining all those smelly bayous. There'd have to be golf courses, too. Rich assholes can't live without golf. Golf courses mean landscaping Paleozoic Appalachia to resemble Palm Beach. There'd have to be colored people to work as caddies and groundskeepers and do all the crap jobs, and poor neighborhoods for them to go home to at night. And golf courses mean effluent runoff, and particularly they mean grass, which as Westerman will tell you is a flowering plant, not due to appear until half past the Cenozoic. Someone decides club mosses are boring and a few palm trees wouldn't hurt. So-called sportsmen won't get much of a kick out of little jawless fish, hey, this is prehistory, let's liven it up. Bio-concoct some big placoderms like Dunkleosteus, maybe even some plesiosaurs. Or just import bass. Earth history's going to get really twisted when all the little improvements take hold here."

King raised a shoulder in a half-shrug. "Sounds pretty farfetched to me. This is what's real. On the other side of the hole is an exhausted planet with nine billion people on it. On this side is a whole untouched planet."

"It's the same planet," Jank said. "Let Northemico go mine the moon instead, it's already dead."

"Too dead," said King, "and too far away. The Paleozoic's alive, and it's here. Are you going to sit there and tell me we should let our whole civilization run down so a few thousand folks here can go on admiring the place's natural splendors? Face facts. The thing's inevitable. When a thing's inevitable, the best you can do is accept it and try to find the good in it."

"Yeah." Jank pushed back his chair and got to his feet. "Just look where accepting the inevitable has got us so far."

I stood up, too. The buzz the first drink had given me was long gone; a second drink hadn't brought it back. Rubenstein, who had sat fuming with his cards fanned in his hand throughout Jank and King's set-to, cursed and flung down a full house.

Jank and I wove our way among the tents and down to the beach. I was past being ready for bed but felt he needed me to stay with him. "Well," I said, "he's right about one thing. The Silurian Arms does sound pretty farfetched."

"Like twenty-first-century America would have to De La Cerda's damn Indians? They never expected to get overtaken by events. People never do, and yet they always are. All of us here are going to be overtaken by events any day now. Any moment. We can't outrun them, can't duck them."

"Then what do we do?"

"Then we face a choice between, I guess, becoming some sort of revolutionaries or goddamn acquiescing in another Antarctica. Put that in your book, Kev."

"I guess," I said, "we'll all just acquiesce. What else could we do, really?"

"Toss certain parties through the hole and then wreck the jump station."

I looked at him unhappily. We weren't just talking about golf courses in the Paleozoic now. "They'd just open up another hole."

"You don't just open up another hole. You have to find one and widen it. They could look for a long, long time. Even if they found one they could use, the odds're against it, billions, trillions to one, that it'd bring them right back here. Even if they didn't miss by much, they could miss by five or ten million years."

"Which means," I said, "they don't play golf in the Silurian, they play it in the Ordovician or the Devonian."

"At least they couldn't mess up the Silurian. You can't save everything, you save what you can."

"Jank, the whole crew on the ship is Navy. They'd never throw in with mutineers. And you know mutiny *is* what you're talking about."

He was quiet for a moment. Then: "Yeah, hell, I know."

"Plus, the ship's not self-sustaining, and what is there to eat here? Trilobites, seaweed, bony fish Vick says taste like salt and mud. At least at your luxury hotel we could get a decent meal and a drink besides."

He seemed unable to decide how much of what I said was serious and how much was meant to be funny. After a moment, he gave me a comradely punch on the arm and said, "Meet you on the jetty tomorrow a.m." He walked away, and I quickly lost sight of him in the gloom.

In the morning, it took a handful of aspirin to ease my aching head and three cups of burnt-tasting black coffee to get my eyes ungummed. The one other late-breakfaster was Rubenstein, who pointedly passed my table to sit at another one and hissed, by way of saying good morning, "A full house!"

I found Jank and Vick on the jetty, and King, too, all of them with masks and flippers in their hands. I hesitated when I saw King. He was an annoyance to Jank, but for me he was definitely shaping up as a rival. I was wearing faded cut-offs and suddenly became very conscious of the contrast provided by his sculpted thighs and calves and my scrawny knobby old-man's sticks. Vick, however, didn't recoil in horror when she looked at me, and I was further emboldened when she gave me a smile and a come-on shake of the head that a plaster saint couldn't have resisted. There is no way, I told myself, I'm not going into the water if King does.

Still, as Jank was getting me equipped, I said in an undertone, "What's he doing here?"

Jank shrugged helplessly. "He found out somehow and asked Vick if he could come along."

"You want to drown him?"

"Maybe something will eat him."

The four of us waded out until we had to swim, then swam out to where the water was six or seven meters deep. Sea and sky were warm, calm, and very clear. It was another perfect day in a ten-million-year summer.

The bottom reminded me of a NatGeo holo. Reef life only looks disorganized. I wasn't a complete dub on the subject, being able to read a book and watch a documentary as well as anybody. Elsewhere in the world, coral polyps may already have been great, slow, patient architects, building barrier reefs the size of California; here, they were putting up lumpish, honeycombed bungalows. We passed over successive crescent-shaped zones dominated by gastropods, scalloped brachiopods, pink flower-like crinoids. In each zone, particular types of straight-shelled and slim tusk-shaped nautiloids jetted about above the bottom, looking like octopi in party hats. At their passing, particular types of elongate burrower disappeared under the sand with a minimum of fuss, and one or another variety of pillbug-shaped trilobite stopped grazing and dodged among the seaweed. The trilobites ranged in size from the fingernail- to the cracker-sized. There were prickly echinoderms, vase-shaped sponges, and limy stands of worm tubes. The first time I had ever seen any of these creatures, in clear, calf-deep water at low tide, with Cardwell standing beside me and pointing them out, I'd been disappointed. There's nothing strange about them, I'd thought, they're just these inoffensive little marine animals going about their business. In spite of myself, I had, like King after me, expected more in the way of red-mawed ferocity, or of glandular imbalance, at the very least. None of these creatures was longer than my forearm. Most were smaller than my fingers.

This wasn't a scary sea by later standards. Most of the marine life that was equipped to bite hugged the bottom, where the food was and, consequently, where the eating occurred. On dives you stayed off the bottom and always scrupulously observed the rule against touching anything unfamiliar unless Jank or one of the other marine specialists handed it to you. We glided as huge, remote, and inaccessible as planets above the world of burrowers and scurriers. Only a few of the nautiloids seemed to notice, and all they did was track us as we passed overhead. Halfway through the Paleozoic Era, there was already that unnerving gleam of intelligence in cephalopod eyes. I glanced over my shoulder to see how my companions were doing and saw King watching, not the sea bottom, but Vick's. The headheld—I hadn't seen him without it since he donned it aboard the ship—made him look as if he were wearing an echinoderm for a cap.

Directly below us, the free-swimmers suddenly executed hard turns and rocketed away with their delicate pale tentacles fluttering behind. That spooked the more alert bottom-dwellers, and the nimbler of these made for cover among the corals. An instant later, something moved angularly across the feeding ground. It had many variously-sized and -shaped appendages sticking out from under its streamlined headpiece, which was adorned with two blister-like eyes as purposeful-looking as radar housings on fighter aircraft. One set of long appendages resembled nothing so much as vise-grips, another looked like sculls, and several short bristly pairs between the two were expressly for locomotion. The flattened body behind the head was divided into a dozen segments; the tail ended in an awl-like spike. The animal tore straight into a hapless trilobite. The vice-grips went to work, raising a swirl of mud and wreaking fearful havoc—the trilobite flew apart at the joins.

All of us remembered at the same moment that we occasionally had to bob up for air. We broke the surface together, and King spat out his mouthpiece and yelled, "What the hell is it?"

"Eurypterid!" Jank told him.

"Sea scorpion!" I put in.

We went back under. Below our waving flippers, the eurypterid swept bits of butchered trilobite under the front edge of its head. The victim's survivors had quit the area as fast as their zillions of tiny legs could carry them, or had wedged themselves into crevices in the coral. Only some cephalopods warily hovered close by, tasting blood.

The eurypterid ate as if it didn't have a care in the world. Maybe it really didn't. It was the biggest animal I had seen in all the time I'd sojourned here, and even I knew a thing or two about its tribe. Eurypterids—the term "sea scorpion" was misleading; the animals' closest relatives were horseshoe crabs—were the biggest arthropods of all time. The biggest ever found, Pterygotus, was two meters long, almost three with its main claws outstretched. The one before us measured only about half that, but we maintained our distance, and I personally would've preferred the view from a strong glass-bottomed boat.

The thing finished its repast and half-scuttered, half-swam into a dark space beneath a coral shelf. Jank signaled to King and me to stay where we were, and then he and Vick went down to where they could peer under the shelf. I was relieved when they kicked away and rose, and grateful, too. I was becoming fatigued. We swam until we could wade, then splashed toward the jetty. I noticed that I was going in faster than I had gone out, impelled, no doubt, by that silly fear some people have of getting a leg laid open by a flick of a marine monster's spiky tail. Unmindful of me, Jank and Vick were talking breathlessly of eurypterid body parts, the chelicerae and the telson, the prosoma this, the ophisthosoma that. King kept abreast of them, not so much listening to what they said as simply watching them say it. That damned headheld.

We flopped panting onto the rocks, and Jank grinned at me and said, "I spent a whole year at Stinktown trying to study big live eurypterids close-up. Came away with almost nothing to show for it except a scar this long." He held up forefinger and thumb to show me how long.

"How do you mean," said King, "close-up?"

Jank's grin shrank to a smile, but he was too excited, he couldn't keep himself from answering, he'd have answered a blood enemy's questions about his specialty right then. "I tried nets and lobster pots. The varmints busted the lobster pots to pieces with their tails. I got this smallish one in a nylon net, almost a baby to the one we just saw, and had it half over the gunwale when it became annoyed and started taking the boat apart. It sideswiped me on its way back into the water."

"So, what, you just dived and looked at them?"

Jank shook his head. "Not at Stinktown. The water's too muddy. It would've been like diving in chocolate milk. With the possibility of blundering into a power saw thrown in."

"Well, I take it back," King said happily, "I really thought this place was empty," and he got up and strolled away.

"Empty," Jank breathed, "Jesus." I tried to gauge Vick's reaction, but she was busy with her mask and flippers and didn't look up.

We were celebrities at suppertime. As happens with marine life that gets away, the eurypterid grew larger and more fearsome with each telling, until I capped matters by describing it as having been big enough to gut an orca and likening it to a lawn mower as it ripped through mats of hapless bottom-feeders. Spirits remained high as everyone collected on the beach afterward. Cardwell was having to put up with a lot of heckling and did so calmly, like Leonardo's man who knows the truth and doesn't have to shout. King kept circling him. Arty shot, I thought, and sort of happened upon Vick among the rocks at the base of the jetty. Before I could say a word to her, however, somebody on the beach shouted, "They're here!"

A foaming wave cast up a dozen glistening shoe-sized lumps almost at my feet. The next wave brought another dozen, and the one after that, scores, hundreds. I heard Cardwell give a whoop— it was more of a bellow, actually—and my first thought was that the sound would scare away the creatures we had gathered to watch. Then I remembered that eardrums, too, were on the list of the yet-to-be. Cardwell rose to his full height and spread his arms in welcome, and from around him came applause and a ragged chorus of male and female voices, "Ta dah!" and one lone smart-aleck's demand, "Yeah, but what's your *next* trick going to be?" Everybody stood up and began moving noisily back and forth along the tide line. Almost at once I found King tagging along with Vick and me, but for at least a little while I didn't care. It was showtime.

Within twenty minutes, there were thousands of trilobites on the beach, females with males in tow. The females half-buried themselves in wet sand and dumped their eggs while the males released sperm. It doesn't sound like anything you'd want to lose your head about, but trilobite males were as eager as males of any species—some females had three or four suitors tagging after them—and there were hazards such as never spiced up human procreation.

Sometimes a trilobite was overturned. It would kick a bit with its legs, then contract the muscles running along its back, roll itself into a ball, and let the next wave draw it into deeper water—where it was at considerable risk from cephalopods and other predators. The press of bodies behind pushed some overturned trilobites too far onto land for waves to pull them back. Vick picked up one of these and showed me the paired, jointed legs. King leaned in between us to capture the moment for posterity. Vick turned and lightly chucked the animal back into the water, and then several more after it. Otherwise, they'd have still been on the beach, dying, when the sun rose. King stayed with us and managed to stay with her in particular. I was thinking about chucking him into the water when he asked her, "Why do you throw them back in? What about natural selection and all that?"

"What about it?" she said. "It's getting on toward the Devonian Period. Trilobites are on their way out anyway."

"Then why . . . ?"

I stooped, picked up a stranded animal, made an underhand toss seaward. After a moment, King did the same. Vick looked pleased with both of us, which of course only half-pleased me. I wondered how to get him to go be in somebody else's face for a while. God sent somebody—who, I didn't see and didn't care—to snag him by the arm and direct his attention to an especially frenzied or imaginative expression of arthropod passion. I offered up a prayer of thanks, motioned Vick to come with me, offered up more thanks when she did. We strolled for a bit, saying nothing, then climbed onto the jetty. The chip player was in my pocket, loaded with a sampler program. We looked at the moon and the sea and listened first to a Tommy Dorsey rendition of "Moonlight in Vermont" and next to a "Moonglow" by one of Benny Goodman's combos. She sighed. What a little moonlight can do.

At length, she said, "Can you dance to this music?"

My heart raced. I had picked out these tracks myself, with serious kootchiness in mind. June moon spoon. I said, "Millions did."

"No, can you dance to it?"

"I do what people've always done. I fake it. If all you want to do is hold on to somebody and move in time with the music, it's easy." I opened my arms. After a moment, she came into them. "Okay, now put your left hand on my shoulder. I hold you lightly at the waist. Now put the edge of your right foot against the inside of my left foot, and the inside of your left foot against the outside of my right foot."

"This is already starting to get complicated," but she leaned away from me and looked down to position her feet. "Tab A into slot A. Tab B into slot B. Got it."

"Don't press your feet against mine so tightly. Maintain the contact lightly. Relax, stay loose."

She shifted on her feet and leaned back in against me. I was happier for that.

"Now just glide with me when I move," I said. "I'm going to lead with my right foot and follow with my left. We take one step this way." We took the step that way, stiffly, like automatons. "Then another. Then I angle off a bit and take one step back. I learned how to do this in junior high school. It's served me well for over fifty years."

I could have kicked myself for reminding her how old I was.

The jetty lay like a titan's vertebrae half-buried in the sand, pitted and uneven and altogether not an ideal surface for what we were about. Nevertheless, she began to get the hang of moving with me, began to loosen up, and I held her close and as tightly as I dared and got dizzy on her scent. After a minute or so of that, I said, "Song's almost over." It was "Sleepy Lagoon." "We're going to end with a dip."

"What's *aieep!*"

"See?"

She was laughing and lost track of her feet and almost fell. I steadied her and didn't give her a chance to slip out of my arms, or to think about doing it. I'd picked these tracks and known what I was about when I picked them. Billie Holliday started singing "You're My Thrill," a performance that could raise goose pimples on a corpse. Vick made a sound like ooh. Then came an instrumental version of "Where or When" by Duke Ellington and His Orchestra; Paul Gonsalves' vaporous saxophone enfolded us. Behind us, somebody said, "Yo. Fred and Ginger. Want a drink?"

It was Cardwell, feet planted wide, face beatific in the moonlight. He held up a silver flask and offered us the screw-on cup. It looked like a thimble among his thick fingers. We gave him a smart little bit of applause, and I said, "Bravo, Doctor Cardwell!"

Vick asked him, "Who're Fred and Ginger?"

"Don't mind him," I said, "he's living in the past."

Cardwell, who was almost my age, snorted like a happy bull. "We're all living in the past."

We sat down on the end of the jetty and proceeded to get pretty silly together. She was between us, and at some point she slipped her arms around our necks and gave us a squeeze. We talked about trilobites and about nothing in particular, or didn't talk at all but listened to "Happiness is a Thing Called Joe" and "Blue Flame" by Woody Herman, "Body and Soul" by Benny Goodman, "Lover Man" by Holliday. We took turns dozing. It finally worked out, just at dawn, that Cardwell was dozing and Vick and I were watching the sea lighten and the night retreat to the west. She looked sleepy and content, past being drunk but still short of hungover. There was a small dab of mud on her neck. I brushed it away and said, "Doctor Harris."

She said, "Mister Barnett."

"How come both of us've been here as long as we have, and I've only recently realized what a swell person you are?"

A smile spread across her face. "You're slow."

Kiss her, moron, I told myself.

And at that very moment King came scrambling up the side of the jetty like the evil monkey he was and dropped into a squat before us. I heard the headheld's faint whir and saw its eye seek Vick's face. I couldn't tell from her expression whether she, too, was conscious of having been interrupted at a crucial moment. "All I can say," he said, "is, wow!" Mister Articulate. Someone on the beach hallooed and called him to breakfast by name. Somehow, he was still one of the guys. It eluded me.

Not everyone had stayed up drinking for nights running, or was old, so not everyone at breakfast felt entirely as washed out as I did. I wanted to hang around, to head King off at the pass if the need arose, but started to nod and almost face-dived into my food. I bade Vick as gallant a farewell as I was able without being a total clown and hobbled achingly off to my cot. The snoring hillock on the next cot was Cardwell; he had almost the same beatific look on his face. Jank, in skivvies, sat in a camp chair and scratched his pectorals. He nodded at a scrap of paper on my cot. "That came in from Sparks a couple minutes ago."

I carefully sat down on the cot. "You wouldn't have any hair of the dog, would you?"

He looked around blearily. "Is it after noon yet?"

I looked at the writing on the paper. *Call me. Ruth.* "Later," I said, and became unconscious.

Which was a mistake, because by the time I regained consciousness, Ruth, who was not someone who liked to be kept waiting, had had time to put a fine vindictive edge on her plans for me. Another mistake was concluding my account of King's impromptu beach holiday by telling her that he seemed well on the way to carving out a secure niche for himself in the camp and I therefore ought to be relieved of all responsibility for him. She agreed. Then, in as sweet-Southern-sexy a voice as though she were telling me to go ahead, pick something out of the Kama Sutra, she added, "This will allow you to devote your time to your other guest, Ms. Duvall, when you get back to the ship tonight." I sputtered, protested, tried to argue. She wouldn't argue. "Just make sure you're with Hirsch when she comes back," she said, "bye, hon," and signed off.

I spent some time complaining to anybody who would listen, but hardly anybody could listen. Everyone had work to do. Toward sundown, however—by which time I was well past disbelief and outrage and clear to the sullen cranks—Jank showed up at the tent to watch me toss my meager gear into my threadbare seabag and listen to me damn Ruth. When I had exhausted her as a subject, I started in on King, whom I likened, in swift succession, to a burr under my saddle, a thorn in my side, and sand in my undershorts. Jank burst out laughing.

My surprise and pain at his unsympathetic reaction showed. He said, "Sorry. Don't mean to make light."

"Keep an eye on Mister Smarm while I'm off the beach, okay? Don't let him work his bolt too much." I closed the bag and looked around. "Are you all the send-off I'm getting?"

"It's not like you're going back, Kev."

"I don't suppose you know where Vick's got to."

"Off checking specimens with Cardwell, where else?"

We didn't shake hands. It wasn't as though I were going back. We separated outside the tent, and I walked disconsolately through the camp. There were voices in Rubenstein's tent: the poker game was gearing up. At the end of the jetty, I found Hirsch fiddling around in the boat. We exchanged nods, and I was about to get in when I heard my name called. I turned to see three people coming along the jetty, Vick and Cardwell dressed in hideous Hawaiian shirts—his, with sufficient material in the one Vick wore for five or six dresses in her size—and King tagging along, duded up as usual. He hung back as they approached the boat. Vick hugged me warmly, gave me a quick kiss on the corner of the mouth, and said, "Sorry we didn't get to see much of you today."

"Well, you have a day job."

"I just wanted to make sure you knew I had a wonderful time last night."

"Cardwell supplied the trilobites and the booze."

Cardwell sighed like an old steam engine and said, "I just catered. You guys danced." He handed me some old-fashioned letters, written on paper, sealed in envelopes with names and addresses inscribed on them in ink. "Didn't get these into the mail pouch in time."

"No problemo."

I stepped away, stepped down into the boat. King had got it all with the headheld. The boat pulled away from the jetty. Luminous in the golden light of evening, Vick and Cardwell waved to me, and I to them, and as far as I was concerned at that moment the only way the scene could have been improved—short, of course, of a last-minute reprieve for me and the simultaneous annihilation by lightning of Rick King—would have been for Cardwell to strum on a ukelele and Vick in a grass skirt to call out *aloha oe* while Bing Crosby crooned, Soon I'll be sailing . . . .

Back on the ship, I pointedly did not report immediately to Ruth. I unpacked, showered to sluice off beach grit and thwarted hopes, stretched out on my bunk, with an anthology of essays plugged into the machine so I wouldn't look just like some old bum taking a nap, and took a nap. I was awakened by the ship's getting under way and lay staring up at the major decorative touch in my little compartment.

It was a framed reproduction, given to me as a birthday present by my third wife shortly before she called me a bastard and threw the cat at my head, of a map of mid-Paleozoic North America as it had been reconstructed by Charles Schuchert and other early-20th-century, pre-plate-tectonics paleogeographers. They had, among other things, rather seriously underestimated the extent of continental inundation and postulated persistent borderlands separated by seaways. I'd always been drawn to the region labeled *Llanoria (Mexia)*, comprising what I regarded as home territory, northeastern Mexico, southern and southeastern Texas, Louisiana, bits of Oklahoma and Arkansas. Disappointingly, where Schuchert had postulated land, later, better-equipped geologists had found evidence only of muddy sea bottom. Yet I remained charmed by Llanoria and the other strangely-shaped, exotically-named landmasses, *Laurentia (Canadia), Cordillera (Cascadia), Appalachia*, enclosing an inland sea studded with lesser lands, *Siouxia, Wisconsin Isle, Adirondack Island*. I think the reason for the enduring appeal of this outmoded representation was that Schuchert and his colleagues must have approached their task not simply with the idea in mind of mapping a prehistoric continent according to the data available, but also with something like the pleasure Frank Baum and Edgar Rice Burroughs derived from filling in their maps of Oz and Barsoom.

I went to the mess and glumly ate. Then I sat thinking that I really ought to go see Ruth. Then I sat thinking that I really ought to go visit Chamberlain on the fantail, and wondered what I should say to him about Vick and concluded that I didn't feel like being disapproved of by a solitary drunk who hadn't been involved with a woman since the Treaty of Ghent, who hadn't even been ashore in all the years he'd spent here. Then I went to see Ruth, who while waiting for me had thought up all sorts of little jobs for me to do.

The days dragged into a week. Claire Duvall got shakily back on her feet. I took her on brief tours, introduced her to various people, and disliked her a lot. She was attractive in her way, with eyes so blue they were almost violet and hair so black it was almost blue, like a comic-book character's, but I found her irritating company. All she could talk about was what a genius Rick was.

Ruth informed me that other newcomers, "important ones"— suits, in short—would soon be arriving, too, and maybe I should become the official greeter after all, since I was so good at it, and this was definitely the time to upgrade my wardrobe. I looked landward and burned with the torment of the damned. I couldn't even get a personal message to shore—Sparks regretfully informed me that radio traffic was at an all-time high, all day every day the air crackled with messages, either highly technical or else coded, from the interior. I was miserable enough to wonder if Ruth had somehow heard something about Vick and me, was keeping me on the ship and off the air out of spite, and more nonsense in that vein. The *wasichu*, those unsociable, obscurely specialized personnel who were taking over the expedition, continued to arrive and depart by helicopter, mysteriously, sinisterly. The suits didn't come and didn't come and didn't come.

On the afternoon of the eighth day, there was a knock, and Chamberlain appeared in the doorway, flask in hand. He said, "I got tired of waiting for you to come visit me." He gave me a closer look. "You sulking alone in here, or you want someone to get you good and drunk and listen to your tale of woe."

"I'm in no mood to be made fun of."

"Oh, come on." He was looking around for a place to sit. I moved a box of book chips, and he plopped himself down with a grunt. "Can I smoke?"

"I wish you wouldn't."

He heaved a sigh that was almost a whimper, fidgeted, remembered the flask. "Want a drink?"

I took a long swallow and handed the flask back to him. "I drink too much."

"Right now, you look like you can't drink enough."

"I'm about six minutes from going on a killing spree."

"Hm." He took a drink, stowed the flask, put his hands on his knees. "Our tail is tied in a knot today."

"You wouldn't understand."

"Welty, Eudora Welty, said that, whatever wonderful things we may do, fly to the moon, whatever—travel through time—we're driven by a small range of feelings. She said all our motives can still be counted on our fingers."

"You got that out of one of my books!"

"It matter where I got it if it's true?"

I regarded him sullenly.

"Man your age shouldn't pout," he said. He waited, heaved another sigh, slapped his thighs. "Well, I'm not going to try and pry it out of you. I'm your friend, schmuck. You need to talk, talk, I'll listen. You may find you're blowing whatever it is all out of proportion."

"I don't have a sense of proportion right now. Sorry, but there're just some things that're bigger than I am."

"Have it your way. I'm going back where I can smoke. Come join me when you feel better. You don't want to sweat out the storm of the Silurian in this little box."

"What? Storm?"

Halfway through the doorway, Chamberlain turned and gave me a big happy grin. "All signs meteorological point to a big 'un piling up in the east. They're evacuating the windward camps."

He almost didn't get through the doorway before I did.

When the boat arrived with the contingent from Number Four camp, I spotted Vick at once. A moment later, I spotted King as well. He had shucked his fancy beachwear in favor of cut-offs and a tee-shirt. He was sitting beside her in the boat. They were talking to each other. Whatever they were talking about, she looked as if she found it very interesting indeed. I told myself that it was only clinical interest, but even as I did, the sharp barb of jealousy sank into my aorta, I saw, realized, that she was holding his hand, there was a sick awful sinking feeling in the pit of my stomach, I knew he had novelty going for him, and sculpted muscles, and youth, and he'd surely let only me see him sick and whiny, and I hardly counted . . . .

Everything looked so ordinary. Everyone was tired and dirty. No one paid any attention to the new lovers, regarded them strangely or enviously or hatefully or any way at all, not even Jank, who sat at the bow looking gloomily preoccupied. What really drove home the idea that, somehow, incredibly, she was with King was her looking up, seeing me, smiling, waving, calling out a friendly greeting. She was radiant with guiltless happiness. I moved my hand at my side, the best I could do by way of waving back. Suddenly desperate to escape from the boat bay, I turned to go, and there stood Claire Duvall, staring down at the two people among all the people in the boat, with an expression of disbelief on her face that was only beginning to yield to hurt and anger. She looked the way I felt. I brushed past her and stumbled numbly through the ship. Someone touched my arm and said, "Hey, Kev, you okay?" and I made a noise, slipped past, kept walking until I was in my cabin, shut in.

I sat down. I exhaled emphatically, as if that would take care of matters, let me go on with my day, my life. Of course it didn't. I promptly found myself trying to pinpoint in memory the instant when the spark must have leaped between them. I shook those thoughts out of my skull only so I could wonder if she let him wear the headheld when they had sex, and if this wasn't strictly a short-term pheromone-propelled kind of relationship anyway. It seemed to me that world-view had to matter even between the sheets, but then I thought of Westerman and Hendryx's relationship, which had endured for years, and even prospered at times, in the face of major differences of opinion on every subject imaginable. I'd made so bold as to ask them about that, one time when we were sitting around ruining our livers, and received for an answer giggles from her and a dreamy grin from him. Pheromones.

I decided I needed some music and stuck Coleman Hawkins into the player, "I'm Through With Love," "What Is There to Say?" I could have gone with Cab Calloway or Fats Waller, who would've worked hard to cheer me up; at least I didn't choose Holliday and "Good Morning, Heartache." For all the difference it made. I went right on foundering in my tarpit of self-pity. I'd always loved women and the company of women. I'd had girl friends since I was in third grade, lovers since I was in my mid-teens, a lifetime of love's ups and downs, ins and outs. Yet I couldn't believe how awful I felt now. I felt every bit as awful now as when I'd been a high-school sophomore and Judy Biesemeyer had broken my heart. Nothing had a right, I told myself, to hurt me as much in my sixties as it had at fifteen, and yet why, I asked myself, would I ever have thought that it wouldn't? To which I could only answer, duh, dunno, just stupid, I guess. And at last it struck me, I hadn't just been passed over, I wasn't just stupid, I was ridiculous was what I was, a lover boy trapped in a flabby, loose-skinned, wrinkling, balding, shrinking, crumbling body, and the best I could hope for was that she hadn't noticed how ridiculous I was, that she had thought of me the whole time merely as a sweet old gent, not as—

I glared at my antique map of Llanoria, land that never was, and decided what I really needed was a drink. I stood up and sat right back down again. The deck was tilted. Then it was level. Then it was tilted again, but in the opposite direction. I stuck my head into the passageway and yelled at the first person I saw, "The ship's pitching!"

"Storm," he said, as if replying to a child, and unhurriedly went on about his business.

On the fantail, Chamberlain was sitting in his deck chair and peering out to sea while his assistants busied themselves among the gadgets. I could hear people yelling at one another up on the helicopter deck as they lashed down aircraft. The ship raced with the sea and before a cool, moisture-heavy wind. Far astern, spanning the horizon, seeming to reach clear into the ionosphere, were sheer cliffs of dark gray cloud.

"Sweet Jesus," I said, "where did that come from?"

"If that's not a number twelve on the Beaufort scale, I'll eat my barometer." Chamberlain spared me a glance along his shoulder. "You look worse now than you did before."

I barely heard him. I couldn't take my eyes off the clouds. Then my pocketphone buzzed, and the bane of my existence said, "Kevo, get down to the jump-station. Those vee-eye-pees are definitely on the way. You've got just enough time to change into some decent clothes."

"They're coming now?" I was holding on to the rail with one hand and needed two. "There's a big storm on the way, too."

"How're they supposed to know what they're jumping into? Twenty minutes, dear heart."

I screeched into the speaker and tossed the pocketphone overboard. Then I said, "Oh, hell, I shouldn't've done that. Some rockhound'll find it."

Chamberlain said, "We won't leave a trace."

"Can I have a drink? I'm having a bad day. First—and now suits jumping in."

He handed me the flask. "Cheer up. You're probably going to be treated to the sight of very self-important people puking like cats."

"Some treat."

He took a pack of cigarets from his shirt pocket, shook out one of the nasty things, braced himself against the rail with his back to the wind to light up. "Hurry on back here when you can. You don't want to miss this, it's going to be quite a blow. We can't outrun it, despite what the Navy may let on. May not even be able to ride it out on the lee shore."

I said, "You'd be a much happier person if you'd get yourself a girl friend," but the truth was, he looked happier at that moment than I'd ever seen him, as happy as Cardwell with his trilobites, Jank with his eurypterid—

—King with his icthyologist.

I suddenly felt so tired. This was the last time, I thought, I don't have another good love affair left in me, or even a bad one. I saw the rest of my life. I'd spend my time drinking and listening to people argue whether or not it was a good idea to use the Paleozoic to keep the 21st century clanking and sputtering along. Not that argument would stop it from happening. I'd hear Holliday sing another few hundred or thousand times of how she covered the waterfront, be dazzled anew at every playing of the Shaw or the Goodman "Moonglow," and hum along whenever the morning found me miles away with still a million things to say. The long, quiet Silurian summer would wear on, Laurasia and Gondwanaland would draw inexorably together, and the solar system would continue its circuit of the outer reaches of the Milky Way. I'd do whatever I had to do for Ruth to go on being a hanger-on here, and I wouldn't write, and if ever I found myself seeing anyone else whom I'm only been looking at before, I'd throw myself overboard . . . .

"Feel that wind," Chamberlain murmured. His long, thin hair whipped about his skull. "I've been thinking a lot about fetch today."

"Huh? Like with a dog?"

"Idiot. Fetch is the extent of open water a wind can blow across. Here we've got a northern hemisphere that's almost nothing but fetch. Wind, waves could travel right around the planet. Storm comes along, whips together a bunch of mid-ocean waves traveling at different speeds, piles 'em up into big waves. Big waves. Back in the nineteen thirties, a Navy ship in the Pacific sighted a wave over thirty-five meters high."

I was appalled. "You're hoping we break that record?"

"Hm. About time we had some excitement around here." He regarded me with approximately equal parts of amusement and tenderness. "See how quickly your priorities are getting straightened out?"

"Okay," I said, "so there're things that're bigger than the things that're bigger than me."

"Hm. Mm hm." For Chamberlain, that was a gale of laughter.

SILV'RY MOON

To the extreme and obvious annoyance of the civilian liaison, the man whom she had appointed to be the Canepis' guide failed to report to the jump station. She spent barely as much time greeting Dr. and Mrs. Canepi as courtesy dictated before stepping into the corridor to look for the errant guide—who, it immediately transpired, had been lurking there the whole time. The hiss, buzz, and crackle of the jump station duly yielded to a rising duet of recrimination and protests.

"Since when," they heard the man demand, "has this expedition been open to crackpots?"

The liaison's reply was muffled. Dr. Canepi, the shorter of the eavesdroppers, looked up at his wife and demanded, "What did she say?"

Mrs. Canepi explained, with regal calm, "She said, since we paid our own way and promised to behave."

"Ah. What—"

"Shh. Which is more, she said, than she can say for at least one person she knows. Presumably she means our reluctant guide."

There came a sharp cry. "I am not either a tourist!" It was clear from the man's tone of voice that he knew he might be overheard, and also that he did not care. "I have my work here like everyone else!"

"You're a hanger-on," the liaison said—Dr. Canepi had no trouble hearing her this time, for she now adopted an emphatic, no-nonsense tone laced with asperity; also, almost as though unconscious of the movement, he had edged slightly toward the door—"and it's high time we made some use of you. *Way* past high time."

"It's not like they're here to contribute to the body of data coming out of this expedition!"

"What do *you* contribute to it?"

"Color! Character! I'll have to watch him every minute, or he'll be picking fights with everybody!"

Dr. Canepi thrust his hands deep into the pockets of his safari jacket and rocked slightly on his feet and said, with exaggerated mildness, "We seem to have come at an awkward moment," and smirked, and added, "Those two ought to get married."

"Perhaps they already are."

"That'd certainly explain things."

"Look," they heard the liaison say, "this is a done deal, there's no point in arguing about it. The project's so strapped for money it's taking anyone who can scrape together the price of admission. They're here, it's their nickel, we are going to accommodate them!"

"Well, there's that, too, now that you bring it up—the whole matter of accommodation. They've got to be fed, transported, kept from hurting themselves, and the support force's resources are already stretched thin."

The woman fairly screeched in exasperation. "If that wasn't so lame, it would be pretty funny, coming from an old beach bum. Emphasis on bum. Listen to me and listen well. You are the only resource around here that's going to get stretched. You are going to take extra special good care of these people the whole time they're here. I don't want hear that they've been mobbed or gotten into a fistfight or anything."

The Canepis backed quickly away from the door a moment before the liaison burst through it with their guide in tow. She was a striking middle-aged woman, in high color but otherwise immaculate in a crisp tropical suit. At first glance, and at second, the guide inspired little confidence. He wore the unhappy expression of one who had lost a dishonest coin toss, and he did in fact look every inch an old beach bum, complete to faded Hawaiian shirt, ragged khaki shorts, and amateurishly repaired sandals. The reddish undertone of his loose and leathery skin suggested that he not only spent too much time in the sun but also drank immoderately. The half-open front of his shirt revealed a sinking chest and a slightly protruding belly covered with white hair. He gazed up at Mrs. Canepi and down at Dr. Canepi with exaggerated interest.

The liaison made introductions and told Dr. and Mrs. Canepi pointedly, "This gentleman is completely at your disposal. I must remind you that you are aboard a U.S. Navy ship and subject to its rules and customs while aboard. Ashore, you are subject to civilian authority. I hope your visit to Paleozoic time is an interesting one."

Mrs. Canepi smiled faintly and said, "How could it possibly be dull?"

As she turned to leave them, the liaison shot the guide an I-am-not-kidding glance from the cover of her professionally bright smile, and he made a face and said, "Well, let's have a nice round of applause for She-who-must-be-obeyed." Then he and his appointed charges submitted to prolonged and frank mutual scrutiny. Dr. Canepi bore a strong resemblance to an owl, even to the flyaway tuft of hair above each of his temples; Mrs. Canepi, a full head taller than he and apparently the better part of two decades younger, was slim and long-limbed and had gray eyes and metallic-red hair.

"If I *should* get into a fistfight," Dr. Canepi finally said, "*will* you pull me out, or just referee?"

"I think, Mister Canepi—"

"Doctor. I am entitled to the honorific."

"Sorry—Doctor." The guide's voice lacked conviction.

"I hold several degrees," Dr. Canepi said, and looked as though he expected the statement to be challenged.

"Well, to sort of answer your question, we're just going to keep you away from the geo-scientists. They're the main ones you don't want to piss off. The ones who work with their hands and sharp pointy things, and drink a lot after hours."

"I should think," Dr. Canepi said, almost as though in masochistic anticipation, "I'd have more to fear from the astronomers and physicists present."

The guide simply looked at him for a moment, then shook his head. "There aren't many astronomers and physicists present," he said, "and they never resort to common brawling."

"Just name-calling and back-biting."

"Be that as it may, what does the Institute for Extraterrestrialist Studies expect to accomplish in Paleozoic time?"

"Why, this strange prehistoric world offers something for any truly inquiring mind. Not long ago, in fact—that is, back home in the twenty-first century—I saw an interesting interview with a sociologist who was planning to come here. She made the comment that sociologists employ the same scientific methods that physicists, astronomers, and geologists do. 'We observe Brownian motion in our own ways.'"

"And your point is?"

"My point," Dr. Canepi said, with a mordant smirk, "is that just because you don't agree with somebody's theories doesn't mean you can dismiss their work as worthless."

"I think it depends on the theory. Racists have theories, terrorists have theories. Crackpots dote on theories."

"So do geniuses," Mrs. Canepi put in coolly, "and my husband is a genius."

The guide grinned. "Maybe a mad genius." The grin went away. "Emphasis on mad."

"Ah," said Dr. Canepi. "Hah. Droll. Very droll."

Mrs. Canepi, however, seemed unamused. She told the guide, "I shall be sure to mention your rudeness to that dear kind lady."

"What dear kind lady are you talking about?"

"I do not deal in wishful thinking," Dr. Canepi said, "but in truth. And the truth is, a great galactic civilization exists. Probably it is millions of years old. It may even be hundreds of millions of years old. It may have been old when life first appeared on earth. It may even be responsible for the appearance of life on earth."

"Which would make our world one big Petri dish. An ant farm, at best."

"Well, life on earth may be an experiment, but I believe these beings are essentially beneficent. They shared basic technology with ancient people in various parts of the world. I believe it possible that the extraterrestrials may be keeping tabs on this planet even now, in the Paleozoic era, because they see it as a likely place for the rise of intelligent life."

"Uh huh. So, the question still is, What the hell brings you to Paleozoic time?"

Dr. Canepi laughed. "Why, on top of everything else, this is just the greatest adventure of my life! Back in—back home, I've never been off planet."

"What," the guide said dryly, "never been taken for a ride in an alien spaceship?"

"Mock me if you will. During my career I've necessarily become inured to the sneers and supposed witticisms of the mundane-minded. Now could we please go have a look at the primordial scenery?"

"But of course. This way."

The guide led the two visitors from the jump station to a catwalk beneath the edge of the helicopter deck. The Canepis crowded to the rail and found themselves gazing across an expanse of brown water at rocky, denuded-looking headlands and green-tinged tidal flats that stretched away indefinitely under a patchy overlying stratum of mist.

Dr. Canepi made a face and said, "What a smell!"

Behind him, the guide said, "Well, this is what you asked to see—the primordial world in all its primordialness."

Dr. Canepi turned and said in a firm tone, "No, I came to see the radio telescope."

The guide's expression became dubious. "Have you got clearance for that?"

Dr. Canepi fished a folded sheet of paper from his pocket and handed it over. "We're entitled to everything on this list."

The guide grimaced as he examined the list. "One from column A, one from column B. Just how long do you plan to be here, anyway?"

"Oh, a few days."

"Only a few? Well, that's optimism for you. Scientists who spend a year here go back complaining they didn't have enough time, they barely scratched the surface. You are going to see everything there is to see in just a few days."

Canepi's smile broadened. "I know what I'm looking for. Anyway, it's our nickel. It's cost a fortune to get here, and not a penny of it came from the American taxpayer. I believe in what I'm about, and I'm willing to back it up with my own money."

The guide grimaced again. "Writing flying-saucer books must pay better than I thought."

"How soon can we go ashore?"

"Well, let's just go and find out."

He did not offer to help the Canepis with their luggage. They followed him to the boat bay and wedged themselves aboard a crate-laden sort of barge minutes before lines were cast off and it began to make for shore. Mrs. Canepi looked askance at the pile of material stowed amidships. "I do believe," she said to her husband, "this must be the same stuff we had to wait in line behind back home."

"The jump station schedule hurries up for no man," said the guide, "or woman."

"Since you have been appointed to escort us," Mrs. Canepi said, "I feel I'm perfectly within my rights to ask about your qualifications for the job. What do you do around here, when you aren't playing tour guide?"

The guide's expression became rueful. "I used to write." He nodded as though to reassure himself as well as his charges that he had used to write. "And then I was drunk, and then I died." He grinned at his two charges, who only stared back at him, and then frowned and said, "F. Scott Fitzgerald," in the patent expectation of its meaning something to them. When it patently meant nothing, he said, "Don't they teach anything in school any more?"

"As you were saying," Mrs. Canepi said smoothly. "First you were drunk, then you died."

"Oh. As I was saying. I went to work for one of the private corporations that came in. I'm a running-dog lackey of capitalists! But it's the only way I can stay here."

"What is there to stay for?"

"The scenery. The weather. The company. The stories! You want stories? Oh, the stories I've collected. They'd fill a book, if I felt like writing them down."

The Canepis looked around at the brown expanse of water, and Mrs. Canepi asked, "Do people scuba dive here?"

"Only when they have to."

"My husband and I love diving. We go diving off Belize every year."

Dr. Canepi said, "I'd like to get into the water here, splash about, you know, in the primeval sea."

The guide shook his head. "I wouldn't. The marine biologists tell me visibility's limited to just about the length of your arm. Their word's good enough for me. And you *don't* want to go bumping heads with a sea scorpion."

Dr. Canepi said, "I gather you've been here long enough to become friends with the scientists."

"Some."

"Do you believe everything they tell you?"

"Some."

"You take it on blind faith that they know what they're talking about?"

"Neither blind nor deaf. I'm a layman, I don't pretend to understand a tenth of what scientists say. I don't presume to understand the part I understand better than they do. Or even nearly as well. I know they're fallible human beings. I also know science is a self-correcting system. If the data say Jupiter has X number of moons and T. rex was an active predator, and then new data say Jupiter has Y number of moons and T. rex was a scavenger—well, science and scientists roll with the punch, so why shouldn't I?"

"What if," Canepi said, "the data suggest unequivocally that visitors from another planet raised human beings out of savagery and set them on the road to civilization?"

"Then I sure would want to know how you reached that conclusion when so many reputable scientists somehow managed to avoid it."

"Perhaps the answer is that most scientists are afraid to stake their reputations on radical re-interpretations of the data. There are real advantages to working outside the scientific mainstream."

"Doctor Canepi, something I do understand very well is words. A radical interpretation isn't the same thing as a persuasive one. I came away from the one book of yours I've read thinking you just don't know a whole lot about archeology, astronomy, or the price of beans."

As the guide led the Canepis through the neatly laid-out camp to the tent assigned them, numerous civilians and even some Navy personnel greeted him by name. One or two asked about his charges, and he answered simply, "Sightseers." To the Canepis he said, "I'm skipping formal introductions because it's way too hot for fisticuffs." Although it was not yet mid-morning, the warm air was gluey with humidity, and they streamed sweat as they walked. Dr. Canepi remained insistent about the radio telescope, however, and presently, after making inquiries, the guide brought them to a dirty, battered open van parked at the edge of the camp. He said with a sardonic grin, "Your carriage awaits."

Mrs. Canepi said, "Quite a limousine."

"Don't make fun of a veteran," the guide told her with mock severity. "This vehicle participated in opposed landings with the U.S. Marines."

"Not during this century, I'm sure."

The guide laughed, and Dr. Canepi offered his arm to his wife and said, "Come, my princess."

The only road in the world was steep, narrow, and unpaved. It had been blasted and bulldozed out of the great rocky slope behind the camp and described a series of long zigzags and sharp hairpin turns. The van lurched and jolted from rock to rut to pothole, slighting none in its way, for all the driver's efforts to keep the tires neatly between the parallel tracks of an earthmover that had gone up or come down earlier. With her entire being thus concentrated and the guide unequal to the task of providing interesting commentary, the passengers were left to their own devices, which consisted chiefly in appreciating the view afforded by the starboard windows of the precipitous drop.

After a particularly thrilling lurch to starboard, Mrs. Canepi serenely remarked that the tracks put her in mind of the footprints of some gigantic beast, perhaps Behemoth itself.

The guide decided not to let that pass. "You're anticipating developments by at least two hundred million years. There are no large terrestrial animals here, except for us humans. There are few enough terrestrial animals of any size here."

Mrs. Canepi gave the guide a superior smile. "I was merely exercising poetic license."

The guide essayed a superior smile of his own. "I *know* from poetic license."

The Canepis returned to absorption of the view. They could just make out the hazy opposite headland on the far edge of an estuarine expanse. At the bottom of the long slope lay the camp, and, beyond, the bay, brown and soupy with silt washed down from the interior highlands.

The van stopped at the top of the road, and the guide and his two charges stumbled forth, into the perfect sauna of the day, and stood plucking at the sweat-soaked fabric of their shirts. Then, suddenly unmindful of heat and humidity, Dr. Canepi darted forward, to the rim of a great gleaming concavity. Down in the bowl, two tiny human figures provided a sense of scale, albeit one skewed by the figures' mysteriously and disproportionately enormous feet. Other details began to register. Around the perimeter rose skeletal metal towers; cables strung from these supported a metal platform above the dish. Nearby was a rude hut of corrugated plastic; a woman with close-cropped gray hair stepped from within, and the guide introduced her as Dr. Hayes, head of the astronomy team. He did not mention the Institute for Extraterrestrialist Studies, and she did not seem to recognize Canepi's name.

Gazing raptly into the bowl, Dr. Canepi said, "Your Doctor Gabbert was wrong. It's *beautiful*."

Hayes fairly beamed. "It's essentially a working scale model of the Arecibo observatory in Puerto Rico. We call ours Junior."

"Doctor Gabbert didn't—he called it a piece of junk. To hear him tell it, he was going to have to use Jansky's original equipment—a few wires on a wooden frame."

Hayes said, "You knew Gab?"

"Well, no. But I knew *of* him. He had a reputation for, ah—well, not to put too fine a point on it, but some people thought he was a royal pain in the rump."

"He was all of that and more. He was a perfectionist. He believed in doing things right."

"I've heard that people at the N.S.F. used to take early retirement rather than keep appointments with him. I could be wrong, but I think that was meant as a joke."

"I'm sure it was."

"So? Do you agree with him? Which do you think it's turned out to be, a telescope or a piece of junk?"

Hayes, clearly warming to her subject, said, "Frankly, Gab would never have been entirely happy with anything less than his own very long base array. He originally proposed a line of dishes stretching across Baltica and Laurentia way into darkest Gondwana. He got just this one. I agreed with him about some things. This isn't the site I'd have chosen, either. I'd have gone farther inland, much farther. However, there was a large natural depression here on the ridgeback itself, earth-movers merely had to improve on it, and these headlands do break up storm winds that might otherwise play hell. There's enough solid rock between here and the camp to cut out radio interference. Not that there's more than a small fraction of one percent of the radio traffic here that we have to cope with in the twenty-first century. The dish is actually better than what we were originally going to get. Early on, there was a counter-proposal for a transit instrument on a simple mount. It would have been cheaper to build, but it wouldn't have been able to track. It would've simply used the earth's rotation to scan the sky. This was a compromise, really, and we still like to think it's a start. That steel platform supported by the cables strung from those towers holds the receiving equipment."

Mrs. Canepi asked, "What are those people doing down there?"

"Routine inspection. They wear special footgear to keep from damaging the dish. The dish itself is constructed of aluminum strips to let rainwater drain through. We get a lot of rain here. At Arecibo, local flora—ferns—were used to hold the ground together beneath the dish with their root systems. Here, now, root systems don't exist, soil barely exists, so we're having to make do with matting instead. The water's drained off and pumped out. There are plans for construction of another radio telescope in the southern hemisphere. That's still in the future. I don't think anyone's established a permanent camp in Gondwana yet. Not in the interior, anyway. But if it ever happens, with the two together we'll be able to map the entire Paleozoic sky."

Dr. Canepi grinned. "To say nothing of listening in at the waterhole."

"Um, well—"

The guide said, "The what?"

He went unanswered. Dr. Canepi looked gratified to have the astronomer regard him with new interest. She said, "You know about the waterhole." It was not a question.

"Well, I don't," said the guide, "so what is it?"

"The waterhole," said the astronomer, "is what we call the long-wavelength region near the hydrogen line. It's bounded at one end by H, the hydrogen atom, which is the most common and fundamental atom of the universe. It emits a natural radio signal with a wave-length of twenty-one centimeters. At the other end is the hydroxyl radical, the O-H molecule. It emits a signal with a wavelength of eighteen centimeters. And H plus O-H makes H-two-O, water, of course. Ergo, the waterhole."

"I'm afraid I still don't understand."

Hayes started to reply, but Dr. Canepi rushed in, "The thinking is that the hydrogen line is so obvious that any extraterrestrial civilization beaming signals to possible neighbors will use it." He smirked at the guide. "And I'm sure you thought this expedition was just about trilobites and things like that!"

The guide gave Hayes a dubious look. "Pam, do you actually expect to hear from an extraterrestrial civilization here in Paleozoic time? I mean, seriously?"

Hayes shook her head. "No more or less seriously than I'd expect to hear from one in Cenozoic time. I never said—"

"The Tau Cetians," said Dr. Canepi, "or the Polarians or whoever they are may have got a four-hundred-million-year jump on us, for all we know. And are you going to be sending out your own signals as well?"

Hayes shook her head again. "Sending signals is way low on our list of priorities. Even lower than listening for them."

Dr. Canepi frowned. "Why not? There's that old saying about what you're looking for, you tend to find."

"Except when it comes to extraterrestrial civilizations. Thus far, SETI hasn't got so much as a howdy-do from beyond. And here, the geoscientists can haul back trilobites by the ton, but any sort of paleo-SETI project faces even worse odds than back home."

"Still," Dr. Canepi said, "I *came* here because I believe the human race should avail itself of *every* opportunity to beam radio signals at the stars. Back in the twenty-first century, the shell of signals expanding outward from the earth has a diameter of not much more than a hundred light-years. My idea is that if we were to beam signals from this settlement in the Paleozoic era, they would have expanded *four hundred million* light-years outward by the twenty-first century. They would reach any technologically advanced civilization located anywhere within that immense sphere, and then all extraterrestrial radio astronomers would have to do is determine the point of origin."

Hayes regarded him very solemnly for some few seconds, and then, when she looked at the guide, he gave every appearance of trying not very hard to smother mirth. A red flush crept up her neck and across her cheeks, and she said, "Some goddamn practical joke!" To Dr. Canepi she said, "I don't have *time* for lunatics who watch too many sci-fi shows!" She turned and stalked into the hut and closed the door.

The guide's mirth had vaporized in the heat of the astronomer's accusation. He glared hard at Dr. Canepi, who seemed bewildered and deflated. Yet he managed to flash a defiant glance in the direction of the astronomer's hut. "Still," he said, "listening for signals might be worth a shot. Hope springs eternally."

The guide rolled his eyes. "Infernally, you mean. Come on, let's get back on the bus. I'm not welcome here any more, big thanks to you."

Dr. Canepi opened his mouth, then closed it as the guide jabbed a finger in his direction.

"You know, Doctor," he said, "every time I think I know just exactly how goddamn stupid and crazy some people can be, they go and prove I've wildly underestimated them."

On the way back down, Dr. Canepi sat slumped in his seat, staring out across the mudflats; his wife sat with her hands clasped in her lap and stared through the guide. As the van lurched to a stop at the bottom of the road, where the camp lay cocooned in heat and silence, the guide declared that as far as he was concerned he had discharged his official duties for the day and the Canepis could just fend for themselves until the following morning.

The Canepis plodded miserably to their tent. Mrs. Canepi said something about their peeling off sodden garments and using the communal showers, but her husband only sat slumped on a camp chair. With a resigned air, she sat next to him. The sky quickly darkened. Mrs. Canepi mopped her long, narrow face with a handkerchief and said, "I feel like I'm about to melt." Her husband did not look at her and did not say anything.

Then, from somewhere not too far away, came a masculine voice raised inexpertly but enthusiastically in song:

"By the light
of the silv'ry moon
I want to spoon—
to my honey
I'll croon love's tune!"

"Hazarding a guess," Mrs. Canepi said, "that is our guide, and he has a skinful."

Their guide appeared out of the dusk and came to an unsteady halt before them. He held up something in his hand and said, "Care to indulge?"

Dr. Canepi made a disconsolate sound but continued to stare at the ground; Mrs. Canepi said that she was allergic to alcohol.

"Well, then," said the guide. "She-who-must-be-obeyed says I'm to escort you to the mess tent."

"I believe we'll forego dinner," said Mrs. Canepi. "My husband is not feeling well."

The guide peered at Dr. Canepi. "No, madam, what your husband is," he said, "is *sulking.*"

"This is outrageous," said Mrs. Canepi, but she did not seem especially outraged; she sounded tired and washed-out and as though she were protesting merely for form's sake.

"You know something," the guide said, "your husband reminds me of me—when I was twelve years old. That's how old I was when I found a big tooth on a beach. It was maybe the size of my thumb, and I was absolutely convinced at the time that it was from a shark, or maybe even a whale. My dad merely glanced at it, then told me, No, son, it's a horse's tooth, or a cow's, or maybe a pig's. But I had my heart set on some immense and ferocious creature of the deep. I held on to the idea that it was a shark's tooth for as long as I could. I argued and argued about it. Finally, Dad showed me pictures of real shark and whale teeth, and forced me to admit, Okay, it's a horse's tooth. All the yearning and fervent belief in the world couldn't change it into something more interesting than a horse tooth. For the sake of dramatic closure, I wish I could say I traded the thing to another kid for something better, a real shark's tooth, perhaps, or a fossil. But I'm pretty sure I just tossed it out in the trash one day when my mother made me clean up my room."

After a moment, Mrs. Canepi turned her head just enough to make eye contact with the guide. "That was a kind of closure."

He shrugged. "Shall we go in to dinner?"

"Will you give us a moment, please?"

"Of course." The guide managed to turn himself around without falling and lurched away into the gloom. Presently they heard him singing again.

"Honey moon,
keep a-shinin' in June!
Your silv'ry beams
will bring love's dreams—
we'll be cuddlin' soon
by the silv'ry moon!"

Mrs. Canepi placed a hand on her husband's arm. "Dear?"

His lips trembled as he said, "It's a—such a *bitter* thing to be a scientific maverick. There are times when the examples of Galileo and Wegener are—almost not enough to sustain me."

"You mustn't lose heart, dear. Galileo and Wegener were eventually vindicated."

"It's the eventual part that's so disheartening. What does eventual vindication avail me *now?* I've spent my life and my fortune in the pursuit of an unpopular truth. And what have I got to show for it? Unpopularity and a reputation for untruthfulness in the scientific community as if I were a—flat-earther, creationist, animal psychic!"

"What is the regard of deluded so-called scientists," Mrs. Canepi asked, "compared to the reward the star people will give you? You've kept faith with them, and they'll keep faith with you. One day they'll take us away from our backward planet."

At that, Dr. Canepi mustered sufficient dignity to sit up straight and meet his wife's gaze. He raised her hand to his lips. "You always give me strength," he told her gratefully, "and hope."

"Because I believe in you, dear."

He stood and said, "Come, my princess," and offered her his arm, and she took it.

THE WORLD WITHOUT

Cutsinger's roommate lay upon his bed next to the curtained window, addressing himself to the mocha-colored ceiling. Cutsinger could not follow and did not want to follow the discourse, which was a variation on the day-after-visiting-day lament Cutsinger had been hearing ever since this particular roommate had been installed. It took the form of a mumbled, rambling editorial, by turns self-pitying and wrathful, about wretchedly ungrateful offspring and the certainty of their going straight to Hell, and Cutsinger understood from unhappy experience that this exercise would continue at least until dinnertime and possibly beyond. Sitting on his own side of the room with his back turned, with his knobby, pajama-clad knees clutched in his liver-spotted hands, he thought, I've already died and gone to Hell.

"Enough," he growled, "enough! Shut up!" He did not look around at his roommate, but his vehemence startled the other man into silence. Cutsinger wiped away a fleck of spittle with the back of his hand and waited, counting the seconds, knowing that it was hopeless, useless, pointless. Presently, his roommate began to speak again of treacherous children and the unerring vengeance of God.

"Listen to me," Cutsinger said. He did not raise his voice now; he spoke bitterly but quietly. "I don't give a goddamn about your children or if they never come to see you. If I was one of your children, I wouldn't come to see you either. All you ever do is whine and drool on yourself. They put you in this place because you belong here. I don't. I'm not supposed to be here. I just found myself here all of a sudden. Listen to me, let me tell you what happened," and he paused and listened for a moment to his roommate's unceasing, unchanging recitation of complaint and condemnation. "In quantum physics, we use a mathematical expression called the wave function to describe a particle or a system of particles and the way it changes in time. Are you listening to me? Did you get that? Particles? Systems of particles? Particles exist on the micro level, the subatomic level. You and I are systems of particles. We exist on the macro level. Am I making myself clear?"

The roommate went on with his own monologue. Cutsinger made a disgusted noise and began the long struggle to get to his feet. He was halfway out of the chair, gripping its arms and tremblingly supporting the weight of his upper body, when his field of vision contracted suddenly and turned gray around the edges. The world seemed to rise and tilt beneath his feet. He sat down hard and closed his eyes tightly and kept them closed until his head stopped spinning. He clutched his thin thighs and bowed his head and waited for his breathing to slow, his heart to quit racing. Dammit, he thought, I don't deserve this. The spells were coming more frequently all the time. He was afraid of what they might signify and afraid to find out what they signified. He had told no one about them.

He rested for several minutes while his roommate muttered and whined. Then, summoning his strength anew, Cutsinger began slowly and carefully to raise himself up again. This time, he got to his feet, opened the door, and made his shuffling escape.

Cutsinger's agoraphobia had grown worse over the years. The Venetian blinds in his room were never opened, nor the thick, heavy curtains. Days and nights were punctuated by meals, medication, bowel movements, lights out. The facility that was now his home occupied an H-shaped building with long glass windows at each point of the H; whenever circumstances conspired to have him approach, he did so with one hand raised before his face to block the sight of the world without. Occasionally he caught an inadvertent glimpse of it and was reminded that the seasons were color-coded, white winter, green spring, brown and red autumn, and that the building itself, built of brick and cinder block, was painted an unhappy yellow. His memories of the rest of that world, however, had long since become monochromatic and blurry.

Apart from the agoraphobia, he was desiccated and brittle, and various things variously hurt or did not function properly. But his mind seemed to him to be clear—certainly it was clearer than his roommate's, and he imagined that it was probably clearer than anyone else's in the entire facility. He flattered himself that he could still distinguish his moments of clarity, of acuity even, from his bad moments, and that he could still converse coherently and cogently whenever there was anyone willing to listen and make the effort to understand. But the doctors and attendants only humored him, and his fellow inmates were senile, a sad and saddening lot, individually either withdrawn and silent or else tending, with little or no prompting, to babble the most deranged or simply banal of religious sentiments. Most human interaction is talk; all the rest is incidental—so Cutsinger had come to believe. One spent one's life, up to a point, eating, fornicating, raising children, moving about, and, if one was lucky, thinking thoughts, so that one would have things to talk about when eating had become a chore, fornication an impossibility, and all the obligations pertaining to children were discharged. And in his own case, he had a gigantic need to tell someone about what had happened to him, what had become of him. Cutsinger had his own idea of what visiting day ought to be. He imagined that it would be diverting to be visited by some eager, intelligent, respectful person who wanted him to talk about himself. Perhaps this person would have seen him in an ancient documentary, or read about him in somebody's new book—Cutsinger assumed that somebody, somewhere, still wrote the occasional book. Perhaps this eager, intelligent, respectful visitor might even have read one or another of Cutsinger's own books. Although all of these were long out of print and he himself no longer possessed copies of any of them, he knew that he had indeed authored a number of books, both technical and popular, and that at least a couple of the latter type, *Events Leading to the Infinite Regress* and *The Great Wave-Function Collapse of '29*, had been best-sellers. But no such eager, intelligent, respectful person ever came to visit him. In fact, no one of any description ever visited him.

The main entrance in his wing opened into a room designated as The Chapel and used as a general reception area. Here were stuffed chairs, sofas, an organ, and an antiquated two-D color television set. Christmas was one week away. The Chapel accordingly had been decorated, sparsely and cheaply, with tinsel and paper Santas, angels, and stockings, and Cutsinger both hated the occasion and avoided the room on general principle. Now he had the ill luck to be standing in the corridor, outside his own door, when a white-uniformed press gang of attendants passed, herding a dozen or more of his fellow inmates; he found himself swept with them along the entire length of the corridor, into The Chapel. The curtains there had been closed, fortuitously preventing his seeing outside, but in one comer of the room, seven members of the local high-school band—six teenaged boys of assorted sizes, shapes, and complexions, and a tallish, pretty girl wearing plastic reindeer antlers upon her head—were arranging sheet music on metal stands. The girl, insufferably perky, announced that they would begin their program with "Come, All Ye Faithful." It was immediately clear to Cutsinger that while she and her companions meant well, they played badly, and he decided that he and his fellow inmates had been brought here in the capacity of human sacrifices, lest adolescent egos be bruised.

He made to rise; an attendant standing nearby unfolded his arms and cocked a questioning eyebrow, but Cutsinger said, just loudly enough to be heard above the racket, "Gotta use the can." The attendant nodded and refolded his arms, and Cutsinger pushed himself to his feet—too fast, because he suffered another attack of dizziness. It lasted only a second or two, and as he looked about, dazedly at first, then self-consciously, he saw that the attendants and his fellow inmates were watching the trombonists with varying degrees of interest. He essayed a step, then another, then another, and in this gradual manner moved past the attendant and back into the corridor. Behind him, "Come, All Ye Faithful" expired with a final strangled cry, and someone clapped desultorily.

"Thank you, we're glad you liked that," he heard the antlered girl say brightly. "The next number we're going to do is 'It Came Upon a Midnight Clear.'"

Cutsinger hastened on and decided to seek refuge in the men's restroom located halfway down the corridor. He closed the door behind himself and discovered that he was still unable not to hear the trombones. He promptly emerged and moved on, desperate to reach his room. Even his roommate's dreary babble was not as bad, he reflected, as a barrage of Christmas music.

At last he reached his room. The door was slightly ajar. As he laid his hand on the doorknob, his head spun and his ears rang again, deafeningly, and walls, floor, and ceiling whirled around him. He felt nauseous, and his head wobbled on his shoulders. "Oh, God," he said, and collapsed.

He lay quietly on the table while the physician on call dressed the large, tender bump in the middle of his forehead. When she stepped away from him, he carefully touched it and murmured, "Big as a plum."

"It's going to be the color of one, too," said the doctor. Her name was Judith Kraft; she was small and finely made, fortyish, with lustrous dark eyes—quite attractive, he had often thought, though he was long past all but the memory of sexual inclinations, let alone activity.

"I was trying to escape. From the Seven Trombonists of the Apocalypse."

That elicited a smile as she stood looking at his medical records on her computer screen. "Well, their hearts're in the right place, you've got to give them that. You're lucky bouncing your noggin off linoleum didn't break anything. But just to be on the safe side—"

"Is it serious enough for me to have to go into the hospital?"

"Hardly. But I am going to send you over to the clinic to have your skull x-rayed."

His heart sank, and he could not repress a shiver. He dreaded the prospect of being out of the building.

She picked up one of her instruments and peered into each of his ears. Up close, she was subtly, pleasantly fragrant. He momentarily felt the cool, tender touch of a fingertip on his temple. "What's the last thing you remember before you passed out?"

"Being dizzy."

"Like a reeling sensation?"

"Yes. And I wanted to throw up. My ears were ringing."

"Mm. Have long have you been having these episodes?"

"I haven't been having them," he said quickly, so quickly that he knew she could not believe him. He heaved a sigh. "I mean, I didn't have them until just lately. This month. Maybe part of last, too. No, just this month."

"Whenever it started, you ought to have told us about it right away."

He turned his head so that he would have to not meet her eyes, but he moved his hand to indicate that he accepted the reproach. "What is it? Have I had a stroke?"

"Nothing nearly as serious as that. Stroke isn't in your profile."

"I'm not ready to die."

"No, you're not, and we're not ready to let you, either." She put down the instrument and favored him with what was patently intended to be a reassuring smile. "As far as I can tell, all you have is an ear infection. It's causing a disturbance in one of the little semi-circular canals of your inner ear, which louses up your sense of balance. So you have a sudden attack of violent dizziness, ringing in the ear, vomiting. I'm going to put you on some antibiotics to take care of the infection. It's the bonk on the head that really concerns me."

"Do I have to go to the clinic?"

"Well, they can't roll that great big x-ray machine all the way over here."

"I can't go outside."

"It's just a short hop from here to there, and—"

"I can't go outside."

"Now, you won't be outside, you'll be safe inside the ambulance. You'll be just fine. I promise."

A great tear welled up on each side of his nose. He smeared them away with a thumb and forefinger and said, "This shouldn't be happening to me. This isn't my life."

He saw that she had not heard him. She was saying something about increasing one of his regular medications from ten to twenty milligrams. He extended his hand and laid it upon her bare forearm; obviously startled and slightly annoyed, she gently but firmly pulled away.

"I really don't belong in this place, Doctor. Nobody here has any idea who I am. Who I was. The most famous man in my field at one time."

She gave him a look of polite inquiry. "What field was that, Mister Cutsinger?"

"Doctor. I have a pee-aitch-dee. Physics."

She studied the computer screen. "Oh, yes, here it is. I see."

"No, you don't. I was tops in kew-em. Quantum mechanics. I became the leading expert on time travel."

The expression of polite inquiry became tinged with amusement and tolerance or with some such commingling of attitudes—he was not sure what they were, he knew only that he did not care for the look on her face, and he glared up at her.

"Time travel. Don't they teach people anything in school any more?"

"I remember hearing something about that, yes. Expeditions into the prehistoric past. That was quite a long time ago," and she smiled pleasantly at her own little joke.

"Do you understand," he said, "the concept of multiple realities? Do you remember the poem about the road not taken?"

"Don't you mean the road less traveled?"

"Whichever the hell road it was." He knew what he wanted to say to her, what he must tell her. I used to talk and write about these things so that anybody, idiots, politicians, could grasp the essentials. It all came back to him, the words were suddenly there for him as they once had been, all those years, all that time ago, but he was afraid that they would not wait long for him now unless he hurried, and so he began to speak urgently and breathlessly.

"In quantum physics, a particle or a system of particles and the way it changes in time are described by a mathematical fiction, an expression known as the wave function. Whenever a system is measured, the wave function gives the probabilities that certain variables will acquire certain values. The variables are such things as position, velocity, momentum, energy, spin, and when I say they acquire values I mean they can be measured. But by measuring the wave function, you reduce it to definite values, we say it collapses from an indefinite to a definite state. This leads to paradoxes unless you're willing to assume—"

He could that she was beginning to tune him out. He snapped, "I trust I'm not boring you."

"I'm sorry, I just have no idea what you're talking about."

He made an impatient gesture. "Then I'll cut to the chase. When wave functions collapse for whatever reason, reality branches. Continually. Countless times each second. The universe splits into copies, the copies split into copies. On and on, forever. For every possible outcome of every possible quantum interaction, a universe must exist to accommodate the difference, no matter how slight that difference may be. So there is an infinite number of physically disconnected and yet coexistent universes, all in more or less different states. Each copy is brought into being with its own space and time, its own material objects, everything. Its own human beings. You and me. We split just like everything else."

Doctor Kraft folded her arms; her expression told Cutsinger exactly what she was thinking. She was thinking. Now I've heard everything. She said, "I imagine I'd remember an experience like splitting."

"No. You don't notice the splitting because your sensory perception and memory don't operate at the quantum level. Only at the macroscopic level. Each copy of you is aware only of its own self and the universe it inhabits. Now, when you time-travel into the past, you don't literally travel backward in time. That's impossible. Instead you travel from one universe into another. From a present-day Earth to an Earth where conditions are as they were in prehistoric times. And then, of course, to get home, you have to travel from universe to universe again. And there—there's where everything went wrong. I—I didn't make it back."

Her eyebrows rose. After a moment, she said, "Obviously you did make it back. You're here, aren't you?"

"I'm not supposed to be here. This isn't the universe I was supposed to come back to. This isn't my world, and this isn't my life. This isn't how things were supposed to work out for me—shuffling around in slippers and a cheap robe, surrounded by drooling doddering crazy people—this isn't my life. My own life is in some other universe, on some other Earth, where I'm not in this awful place, forgotten, rotting away. Where I didn't lose everything somehow, my family and my friends, all my money. Where I'm doing what I'm supposed to be doing, living the way I ought to be living. Working on my memoirs, contemplating a life and a career full of accomplishments and honors."

He saw Doctor Kraft look up sharply as two men entered the room. One of them spoke her name, and she said to Cutsinger, "Here's Harry now to take you to the ambulance."

Harry, blond and immense in white, looked down at him and smiled. "Let's get you onto the gurney—easy does it."

"I can't do this," Cutsinger whimpered, "please—"

"You're going to be fine," said the doctor. "It's just a short hop over the clinic. They'll back the ambulance right up to the door and take you in, so you'll hardly be out in the open for more than five whole seconds, will he, Harry?"

"Three seconds tops," said Harry, "and you can keep your eyes closed the whole time."

Cutsinger suffered himself to be lifted off the examining table and onto the gurney, and then Harry and his companion maneuvered it out of the room. Their progress along the corridor was accompanied by the soft constant thrum of wheels on linoleum, the soft rhythmic padding of the white-clad men's feet, the soft intermittent murmuring of Cutsinger's fellow inmates as he passed their half-open doors. Cutsinger raised his head slightly and saw the corridor stretching before him to infinity. As the gurney approached it, infinity resolved itself into long glass windows, and he held his hand before his face to shut out the sight.

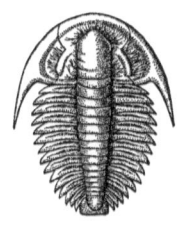

FIVE MILES FROM PAVEMENT

The Dame Paleontologist, that sun-blackened whipcord of a woman, sits down opposite me in the mess tent. We have not seen each other in several years—she has jumped in and out and in again, and for the past many months she's been collecting in the interior, somewhere far past Wegener Point. By way of greeting, however, she tells me, "You look like hell, and you deserve to."

"Why, thank you. And you're even pricklier than I remember."

"Your big tinker-toy's an eyesore. It looks like the bastard offspring of a drydock and an off-shore drilling rig. There used to be a lovely view of the bay."

We have been friends, or more or less friendly ex-lovers, or acquaintances, anyway, for decades, ever since our post-graduate days. Even if that were not the case, I'm too tired to be offended; though the sun will be rising soon, I'm already more than halfway through my work day. So, I let her crack about the structure pass, and she accepts my grunt as an appropriate response, contemplates the breakfast tray she has set on the table between us, shakes her head in obvious disbelief.

"When I came here the first time," she says, "the standard of living was lower than an opossum's. I'm not one of those boring old farts who never shuts up about how much rougher field work used to be, and how much tougher everyone had to be. Still—now—here's a perfect example of what I mean."

"Just what do you mean? It's an omelette."

"A Spanish omelette, for chrissake."

"The new cook's ambitious."

"What's next, quiche? Sidewalks? A beauty parlor and a sports bar?"

"I'll put those on the recommendation list."

But she digs in with real appetite—no doubt, off in the hinterlands, she subsisted on dried vegetables and meat bars, by comparison with which even reconstituted eggs must taste like gourmet fare. I used to call her The Girl Paleontologist when she worked out of the paleo-lab at the University of Texas in Austin. She always said she never minded roughing it, and I learned to believe her. In her line of work, she spent considerable time in the field, "five miles from pavement," as she was wont to put it, sleeping on rocks and shaking scorpions out of her shoes of a morning. One January, after a nearly complete plesiosaur skeleton had been discovered in a creek bed behind a subdivision, she was among those dispatched from the lab. It takes a while to excavate a thirty-foot-long prehistoric monster, so she and her colleagues had to take turns sticking around all night to make sure that curiosity-seekers or vandals didn't disturb the site. One horrendously cold night, I visited and found her and another paleontologist huddled shivering under the nearest shelter, a bridge. I had brought a Mason jar filled with brandy, and we partied like winos. They had to stay, however, after I went home to my warm bed and my warm wife.

The Dame Paleontologist eats her Spanish omelette, and my attention wanders; the background murmur is lulling. The mess tent is full of hungry construction workers, technicians, even a few scientists—some, like my companion, having breakfast, gearing up, others, like me, winding down.

Work proceeds around the clock, the "Paleozoic" (I insist upon the quotation marks) has become an age of steel and sparks, an industrial era, and the structure nears completion. Viewed from the shore after nightfall, the hard pinpoints of arc-welders' light flicker like supernovae against a softer background illumination of work lamps. The effect, if one exercises only a little imagination, is of a cubist sort of galaxy floating in darkness. I would not hesitate to set this artifact against the great cathedrals of Europe or the Egyptian pyramids, any of which would dwarf it but only in a purely physical sense. The pyramids are mounds of dead rock; this thing will hum with power. The cathedrals have stood for a few centuries, the pyramids for a few millennia; this structure will bridge four hundred million years. I have been intimately involved with it from the beginning, carried it from conception through fruition, and if memory serves (history, however, is not really my strong suit) it took lifetimes to build the cathedrals and at least some of the pharaohs lay unentombed while work continued on their final resting places.

Be those things as they may, I am not bragging too much when I say that no one has done more than I to make the human presence here possible. Not even Cutsinger. I have given my life to that end, built a career upon it, and this structure will be the culmination. In all modesty, it was due to my own foresight that this project has been undertaken. Early on, very early on, when the numbers of scientists visiting "Paleozoic" time were still in the single digits, I insisted that if this kind of thing was going to be done at all, we must do it big and do it right, impose order. Therefore, even as we attended to immediate problems, we would take the long view, plan extensively. Stabilization of the spacetime anomaly would have to be ensured, and as long as the anomaly did persist, the extent of our exploitation of it for purposes of research would only grow; we were talking not about anything as ephemeral as space stations, but about permanent bases and personnel numbering in the hundreds, perhaps even the thousands, because every branch of science, from microbiology to astronomy, would have something to gain from "Paleozoic" research. No résumé would be considered worth a second look if it did not mention "Paleozoic" field work or some activity related to a "Paleozoic" expedition. Early on, we physicists, chiefly Cutsinger, Morales, and I, solved the problem of spatial/temporal drift by inserting the equipment necessary to "fix" the anomaly at both "ends" and thereby establishing a synchronous link between the ancient "Paleozoic" and the immediate Cenozoic—what laypeople and lazy people stubbornly insist upon thinking of as The Past and The Present. This, however, was only a temporary measure, for not only would the number of scientists increase, but so, too, the duration of their visits and the scope of their explorations. We deemed it best that the "Paleozoic" "end" of the anomaly be "reconnected" to a vessel provided by, and crewed by officers and enlisted personnel of, the U.S. Navy. With its complement of auxiliary craft, this vessel, once having been inserted, would become the receiving/sending point in "Paleozoic" time in addition to serving in other capacities. But this, too, was a temporary measure. A ship, we noted, requires regular refits, and though routine maintenance "in the field" would be possible (some of the auxiliaries being specifically designed and equipped for this purpose), our vessel must perforce return to Cenozoic time for the sort of maintenance that can be performed only in a yard.

Thus, plans were drawn up and funds allocated for a large, permanent structure to house the stabilization devices so that the ship could be sent back as necessary and yet our synchronous link be maintained. It has been terribly expensive, but it will be worth every penny. Yes, there have been occasional setbacks. There have been accidents, too, more than expected, more than there should have been, and a few serious injuries among the workers, but no fatalities, fortunately. The majority of these can be traced to sheer exhaustion. I am not one to duck responsibility; I put the blame for this squarely on our having stuck to the twenty-four-hour clock in the face of the "Paleozoic" day's being less than twenty-three hours long. Work has to be completed on schedule, work shifts are necessarily rigid, but the human time-sense is fluid. Although we cope as best we can, the fact remains that our sleep cycles have been disrupted. A few concessions have been made—even the Navy finally allowed that, no matter the hour on the official clock, morning colors could wait until sunrise; there is hardly anything more dispirited than a flag-raising ceremony in the dead of night. It must be said that with very few exceptions Navy personnel of all ranks have comported themselves in a manner that is a credit to the uniform they wear and the flag they serve. All here are volunteers, and they are screened more rigorously than the civilian scientists. True, a few instances of substance abuse have been reported among the ratings, tempers have occasionally flared and landed disputants in the brig, but to the best of my knowledge there have been no instances to date of personnel going AWOL, if only because there's so little incentive to do so, no place to go that isn't exactly like every place one has already been. Tours of duty in war zones are traditionally described as long periods of utter boredom punctuated with moments of utter terror; a tour in "Paleozoic" time is long periods of intense activity punctuated with utter boredom. Obviously, morale is going to be affected even though the Navy has quite enough to do and everyone tries to stay busy. The Navy's here in a support capacity and is responsible for keeping between one and two thousand scientists safe, supplied, and in touch. The bulk of this population is concentrated along the Laurentian coast of the Iapetus Ocean (I'm stuck with these place names), but there are also camps deep in the interior and on some of the island arcs, and it could be, and has been, argued that the Navy is stretched thin. By the end of their tours the majority of officers and enlisted personnel are clearly good and ready to go home; the percentage of recidivists among them is low. Well, they are young, most of them, and whatever domestic touches they have been able to apply here are insufficient to distract their attention from the reality, the emptiness, the dullness, of the "Paleozoic" world; they yearn for the great wide wonderful world waiting on the other side of the spacetime anomaly, so busy. so noisy, so full of vivid color and things to do, and they don't care that the "jump" (as that wracking tumble is called) will rattle every bone in their bodies and put an unlucky few into sick bay with mild concussions or worse.

As for myself, I am locked firmly into Work/Sleep mode. My "days" and "nights" do not entirely correspond with actual days and nights, but they follow a pattern as surely as the sun and the moon trace regular courses across the sky. I am careful to make any really important decisions only early in the "day," when, like the morning sun and the evening moon, I am ascendant.

Now, however, in the mess tent, I am past zenith. The Dame Paleontologist continues to glare across the table at me while she chews and swallows her food. Then she says, "I've heard about the plan to build a power plant upriver."

"Well," I begin, "the generators here won't be capable of," and give it up, because she goes right on talking.

"Every time I get back here to Stinktown, I half-expect to see the first fast-food restaurant's opened for business. They don't even like you to call it Stinktown any more. There aren't just scientists and technicians here any more, now there're boosters. I hate to say it, old pal. but you've become one of them."

"I've always been one of them. Maybe the biggest one of all, too. Because I know that everywhere humans go, they stick. Some places are harder than others—Antarctica was, the moon is. Mars will be. But it's in our nature to try and keep trying until we do stick. My big tinker-toy as you call it will make it easier for us to stick."

"Every place we," and she twists her mouth as though she finds the word distasteful, "*stick*, we start importing our technology and our bad habits. It's no longer pristine here. I'm finding trash on the ground. The foot traffic here's been so heavy for so long that we've beaten paths into the bare ground. It no longer looks primeval. The best you can say for it is that it looks rustic. Boats and helicopters are pumping exhaust gases into the air, there're oil films on the water. You can see rainbows on the surface of the bay. And what's the latest estimate on the amount of stuff we've dropped *into* the bay?"

I accidentally overturn my cup; she watches with sour amusement as I block pseudopods of coffee with paper napkins. In only seconds the tabletop immediately before me is covered with steaming brown slush. As I scoop up the mess with still more napkins, she asks, "Did I finally hit a nerve?"

I long ago learned the proper response to this line of argument so well that it's become reflexive, I have rattled it off enough times, but, yes, she's touched on a matter which, irrationally, in spite of myself, I find worrisome: lost items. We've slung safety nets and catch pans underneath the structure during all phases of construction, and divers regularly scour the bottom. Such precautions are not one-hundred-percent effective, however, and these are murky waters. We're erecting this structure of ours at the mouth of an estuary. Every moment of every day, the turbid brown waters bring sand and silt from the interior badlands and deposit them as sediments. The bay's muddy bottom is the graveyard of uncountable billions of organisms ranging in size from microscopic to man-sized, and strewn among their remains in the general vicinity of the structure are hand tools, screws, bits of wire, who knows what else. I am a physicist, quantum mechanics is the only thing that accounts for the reality of our situation, and yet I would not be fully human if my head and my (for want of a more appropriate-seeming part of my anatomy) viscera were not sometimes at odds: this reality sometimes feels unreal. At some level of consciousness impregnable against calm, sound reasoning, I'm utterly unnerved every time I read an accident report (the rules are strict, a report must be filed if so much as one bolt goes overboard).

I begin, feebly, "There're guidelines," and once again I get no farther.

"Guidelines! We were so conscientious at first. We had to wear spacesuits, for chrissake."

"That was before Cutsinger proved—"

"Oh, never mind what Cutsinger proved or thought he proved. I never knew what he was talking about most of the time, and I bet he didn't know about half of the time. Especially when he said the hole's stable. Remember, once upon a time, long ago. he and you and every other physicist said the hole was impossible. It opened by itself. You didn't know what caused it, and you still haven't got a clue."

"That's not quite—"

"Oh, never mind your explanations, I couldn't understand them whatever they are. Maybe the hole'll close by itself, too."

"I doubt it very much. The anomaly's remained pretty stable all these years. We've almost ceased to think of it as an anomaly, in fact. And once we complete my tinker-toy, as you call it, we'll be able not only to maintain it indefinitely but to manipulate it as well. Excuse me," and I take a large wad of sodden napkins to the waste bin.

When I return to the table, she says, "Did you ever hear about that idiot who came up pregnant and wanted her baby to be born here? No, it's true, this really happened."

"I don't see how. It would've been in violation of the Navy's PWOP policy."

"Its what?"

"PWOP. Pregnant without permission."

She smiles; it's the first time I've seen her smile since—well, I'm not sure, it's been so long. "And all along," she says, "I thought the military lacked a sense of humor." The smile fades. "No, this was a civilian like us, a biologist or something. Somebody who should've known better. Somebody who was thinking like a colonist."

"Don't you think you're being just a bit hypocritical? How many times have you come through the anomaly? How many years of your life have you spent here in all?"

"I've loved it here, but I'm not a sentimentalist, and I've never had any patience with people who are—who profess what I consider to be too strong an attachment to this place. This world isn't ready for humans. It's not our home, we're not colonists, we're just visitors." She vehemently stabs the last bit of omelette with her fork, raises it halfway to her mouth, studies it for a moment, then returns it to the tray. "You're supposed to be on your best behavior when you visit a place, and not trash it."

"We're not trashing this place."

"You're making it over. The rest of us, we're only human, so we make stupid decisions, we get careless. We drop stuff. We lose things. We leave our footprints. We forget to clean up after ourselves. But you, you're deliberately trying to make it a fit place for humans to live."

"Look, I'm too tired to argue any more."

"Then don't argue, just listen. Let's say the hole closes by itself—as mysteriously as it opened—before you finish building your big machine. Or maybe you get it built but it breaks down. What happens then? When our supplies are cut off? Do we just starve then? Do we die out and turn to humus? Do we start eating invertebrates and nasty fish, raw? There isn't even wood for cooking or building here."

"We wouldn't be the first human beings who've had to figure out how to survive," and I get to my feet.

She rises, too, and we go out of the mess tent and into the new morning together.

"Walk me to my tent," she says. "We may not get another chance to say goodbye. It'll be the middle of the night for you when I make the jump."

Her tent is in the last row, behind which the ground slopes upward. She looks toward the heights and says, "Let's go up."

I make no attempt to stifle my groan. "I've got to get back to work." I say, and because I can see that that doesn't move her, I add, "I'm a tired old man."

"So? I'm a tired old woman. Come on, indulge me one last time. Let's go up just a little way."

I mutter an obscenity. Nevertheless, we climb, carefully picking our way up the stony slope. What, I wonder, does she have in mind in the way of saying goodbye? This isn't the first such slope we've climbed together. She was the bright protostar of the geology department at the University of Texas, as I was the physics department's, but the departments can be better described as compartments hermetically sealed off from each other. Thus, we met off campus, by accident, at a used-book store, in the "Science" section, a catch-all for works by and biographies of Hawking, Einstein, and Darwin, volumes on gardening and astrology, pet-care manuals, picture books of dinosaurs, creationist tracts, and more than half a century's worth of exposes of government conspiracies involving everything from extraterrestrial visitors to bioengineering projects gone horribly wrong. One or the other of us initiated an exchange of caustic and (so it seemed then) hilarious comments on this jumble of real, pseudo-, anti-, and simple non-science. An hour later, we were seated across from each other in a coffee shop, still entertaining ourselves with barbed witticisms. Within two weeks we became lovers. The affair wasn't serious; in fact, it was less an affair than a mere episode; it didn't end altogether amicably, but we got over it and went on to marry more compatible individuals, and to divorce them, and in the meantime never quite let go of each other. What really united us in an enduring, if often testy, relationship was our love of science and our contempt for superstition and irrational thinking. We were too different in other regards. I preferred the classroom, the laboratory, the library, order, quietude, a minimum of dirt. Her idea of fun was a weekend camping trip; she insisted, soon after our first tryst, that I accompany her to Enchanted Rock in Llano County. What, I asked—being a comparative newcomer to Texas—is Enchanted Rock? "An eerie and beautiful square mile of antiquity," she said, "a relic of the Precambrian, the second-biggest exposed batholith in the United States!" I affected disappointment: Only the *second*-biggest? "Don't mock the rock," she told me. "Idiots carved likenesses of Confederate generals on the biggest—that's Stone Mountain, in Georgia. *Our* rock is pristine. Actually, it's the merest nub on a planetoid-sized pluton underlying the whole region. To walk on it, touch it—" she sighed; she actually talked like this when she was in her twenties, before collecting seasons under hot suns smelted softness and whimsy out of her "—it gives you a sense of the alienness of Precambrian Earth. The Indians thought it was a magical place. So do I. So will you." And so I had, from the instant I saw it. The great bald dome of pink granite simply looked supernatural, unnatural, at any rate, like some titan's monstrous rock garden, palpably ancient. After dark, we crept out of our tent and coupled on the still-warm rock. I slipped my hands between it and her knees to cushion them, prevent their being bruised, as she bumped and bounced atop me. Then we lay spent and listened to the pop of cooling, cracking granite, and after a time I said. "So is this what you mean by field work?" And she laughed and kissed me deeply. At that moment, for just that moment, we may have been in love. A little later, she said, "I am going to do great things in my field." And I, I said, in mine, and waved at the sky, because I knew, then, believed, that humanity's destiny lay out there among the stars. It never occurred to me that my work would bring me closer to Precambrian time than to the nearest star.

Whatever she has in mind now, it surely isn't sex for old times' sake on a high rock. There's a limestone shelf big enough for both of us to sit upon and look across the camp and the bay to the open sea. Visible on the ridgeback above us is one of the towers supporting receiving equipment above the radio telescope's reflector dish; the dish itself sits in a natural hollow, screened from our view and from radio interference from the camp. The structure in the bay dominates the seaward view; the estuarine waterways seem to point to it. the bracketing headlands with their ellipses of sea stacks hold one's attention on it; even if one cared to go to the trouble to climb those distant slip-faulted cliff faces, the structure would still be the centerpiece, the sole *point* of bothering to take the view from the bare rain-pitted limestone up there. The sea beyond is only a sea, the landscape behind us is as barren as an empty parking lot. Moreover, the structure, though unfinished, already has a look of permanence, unlike the flimsy tents and Quonset huts in camp.

"Isn't it exquisite?" I murmur. "It's like the Taj Mahal."

She does not respond immediately, but after some seconds have elapsed, she says, "More like the Tower of Babel. A bad idea whose time has come."

She fingers a chert lump in the limestone as if she were touching old, familiar wallpaper, examines a weathered-out fossil shell, replaces it on the ground as carefully as if it were a cherished piece of bric-a-brac.

"I have to resist the impulse to collect any more souvenirs," she says. "We pried out a bargeload of specimens this time. Probably way too many." I know; the crates are aboard the ship, awaiting transfer to Cenozoic time. She's one of the handful of paleontologists who have worked in "Paleozoic" time as paleontologists. Most of her colleagues come to study living examples of, to confirm or disprove conclusions drawn from, the contents in their specimen drawers back home; she has always come, as she puts it, to get a 400-million-year jump on erosion, examining already ancient rocks that are already weathering away to grit and dust.

I ask, "Can you ever collect too many specimens?"

"I guess I'll find out when I go home and start pawing through what I've collected. I'll write my papers, lecture, and bask in the respectful regard of the scientific community. And in the less respectful but more affectionate regard of my family. I have young grandnephews and nieces I can terrify." She is brown and leathery, with piercing eyes and vertical creases in her face. "I'll be the ancient mummy woman, returned to life." Then she sighs and asks, "At what point does everybody else decide they're finished here? When do you go back through the hole and pull it in after yourself?"

"When have human beings ever left of a place once they've established themselves in it? People live in Antarctica now, and in space."

We sit side by side and say nothing for perhaps a minute before she says, "Do you know the history of the Viking colony in Greenland? Eric the Red founded it late in the tenth century. At that time, the climate along the southwestern coast wasn't any worse than what the settlers were used to in Iceland and Norway. Agriculture didn't amount to much, but fish and game were abundant, the settlers brought their domestic animals with them, and they lived fairly well. After a couple of hundred years, though, the climate began to deteriorate. It grew colder, the glaciers advanced southward, and finally the colony was hemmed in by ice and cut off from all contact with Europe. Centuries later, archeologists excavated the remains the last of the colonists. They were malnourished, stunted, deformed, diseased. They lived miserably and died out miserably."

"We have advantages those people didn't have."

"Such as?"

I laugh harshly. "Well, just for starters, equatorial Laurentia isn't about to ice up! We've got our knowledge and our technology—"

"And a supply line that's four hundred million years long. Everything we need has to come through the hole. Everything from fuel to food. Without fuel, all our machinery's just a lot of scrap iron. Without food, we wouldn't last long enough to see it go to rust. At most, this world could sustain about a hundred of us if we all lived far apart from one another and weren't too particular about what we ate."

"We could harvest the sea for food."

"With the Navy's help, no doubt. Well, what about the Navy? Remember, there wouldn't be any fuel for the ship or those auxiliary craft or the helicopters. How long do you suppose you could maintain a ten-thousand-ton ship even if it just sat there in the bay?"

"I'm tired of supposing highly unlikely things. Let's go back down."

"If we did somehow survive," she says, "we'd reproduce. If we reproduced here, in isolation, over time, we'd evolve. And what a gene pool we'd have to work with, too. Geeks and gobs. Do you know what quantum speciation is? It's the separation of populations of organisms that can interbreed into independent evolutionary units that can't interbreed. Each of these small populations in isolation—stuck on an oceanic island, let's say, or stuck four hundred million years in the past—becomes subject to the founder effect. That's what we call what happens when a new population is founded by individual organisms representing an extremely small sample of the genetic pool to which they formerly belonged—the ancestral population. Now, in all populations, there are always random fluctuations of gene frequencies. Genetic drift occurs. Mutation. The offspring's genes aren't perfectly representative of its parent's genes. Most mutations are fatal, and in a large population, those that do survive are swamped. But natural selection operating on small isolated populations quickly results in gene combinations unlike those found in the ancestral population. You end up with populations that're isolated not only geographically but reproductibly. You end up with entirely new species. The thing of it is, there's no evidence of that in the fossil record. Not the minutest hint of it, of us, of whatever we might become. That means one of two things must happen here. Either we leave, or we stay and die out and turn to humus."

"If we were actually time-travelers, it would probably only mean that paleontology's guessed right about that the odds against any particular *thing's* turning up in the fossil record. But we're not time-travelers. Nothing we do here can have any bearing on the future of our own world because this isn't our Earth as it was in Paleozoic times, but only one of an infinite multitude of Earths in the equivalents of Paleozoic time."

"What if it's a case of there being a unity in spite of infinite multitude, and an infinite multitude in spite of unity?"

"The universe is continually dividing, copying itself, as it jumps from state to state. The copies are infinite in number, they coexist in parallel with each other, and each is in a different state. That is, a separate reality exists for every possible outcome of every possible quantum interaction. And while most of the realities would be imperceptibly different on the macro level, given an infinite series of separate realities, there'd be gross differences as well."

The Dame Paleontologist grimaces. "I didn't really mean for you to answer me. If in fact that was an answer. All this multiple-universe stuff just makes my head swim. I flat don't believe it anyway. I never have."

I say, "I've got to get back to work."

We stand, dust off the seats of our pants, step away from the rock shelf.

"It is too beautiful," I insist, nodding at the structure in the bay. Even at this distance, human figures and the blue-white sparks of welding torches are visible.

She mimics my tone. "It does too look like a theme park on bad drugs."

"You have your fossils. I have that."

"I'm glad I won't be here to see whatever's going to happen."

"Whatever happens, I'll tell you all about it when I get back."

She shakes her head. "I don't think you will get back."

"I'm not going to be marooned here. Nobody is."

"What I mean is, you won't even consider coming back until that damn thing out there is up and running. Then the Jump'll probably kill you, or at least shake loose something inside you. Your brain, for example. You are an old man."

"I'm not exactly dragging around an oxygen bottle and pushing a walker in front of me."

"Not yet you aren't. Not yet." She looks away from me. Her voice becomes strained. "Just in case I never see you again—goodbye. Goodbye and good luck. You're probably going to need it."

"Don't worry so much. In the end—"

"Ah, God, darling," she says, turning toward me, *"in the end,"* and suddenly I hear a note of tenderness in her voice that has not been there in decades, not since that night on Enchanted Rock, and for the first time in I can't remember how long she touches me, on the hand, quickly, lightly, then lets her arm drop and stands disconsolately before me with tears sparkling on her eyelashes. I have misjudged her. For all these years, from the very first, I have cruelly misjudged her. "Who," she all but sobs, "can ever see the *end* of anything?"

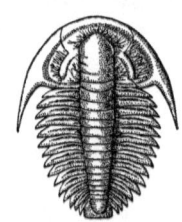

A PALEOZOIC PALIMPSEST

As aficionados of documentaries and attentive readers of Sunday supplements know, the Paleozoic expedition's main camp sits upon the verge of an estuarine marsh bracketed by barren headlands. Within the labyrinthine jumble of rocky debris along the base of the nearer ridge, a singular limestone slab stands as though balanced upon its edge in an area like a miniature arena. Unlike the camp's other points of interest, it is omitted from the official catalogue. Yet significant numbers of visitors to the Paleozoic eagerly negotiate the enclosing maze for the sake of inspecting it. Some few of these daring souls become lost, of course, and require extrication, occasionally by air (the camp maintains a helicopter for this purpose), while others wander through the maze and emerge without glimpsing that which they sought. (From time to time, guideposts and monitoring devices have been installed, but someone always removes or disables them. Attempts to identify and apprehend this vandal have failed.) Those who successfully penetrate the maze find themselves before an extrusion of vibrant red and orange, fluorescent yellow, metallic blue, shiny green: riotous, startling, illicit color—in marked contrast to the materially identical limestone masses ranged about it (indeed, to the drab

Paleozoic world in general). The finely grained stone typical of the region provides a suitable, albeit slightly undulating, surface for a variety of more or less indelible markers, including paint sticks, grease pencils, jet pens, charcoal, and chalk, as well as pocket knifes and other implements—according to one visitor, "You can scratch it with a paper clip, it's so soft."[1] Over the years, virtually the entire surface of the slab has been covered with markings, until "the rock is embedded in graffiti like the pit in a peach."[2] Much of the older graffiti has itself been deliberately obliterated, scrubbed off to make way for new graffiti or simply buried beneath fresh layers. Weathering and fading have also effaced many markings, moreover, at unequal rates, depending upon the graffiti's placement and the means used to inscribe it. In consequence, the beginnings of many inscriptions unconformably abut the middles of others and the endings of still others. "There can't be five unaltered independent clauses in the lot."[3] A geologist visiting the rock calls it "a perfect metaphor for geology. The old is obscured by the new, the new is partly erased, partly exposing the old."[4] No less proprietarily, an historian likens it to palimpsests, the parchments erased and reused by ancient and medieval scholars.

The rock is porous enough to retain traces of erased or obscured graffiti, which become observable under ultraviolet light; images obtained in this manner become legible with a minimum of electronic enhancement. This process is, of course, beyond the means and intent of the casual visitor, who therefore must be content with superficial inspection.[5]

The graffiti consist of the usual things which people throughout history have privately inscribed in public places: names, initials, dates, jokes, bon mots, cartoons, declarations of love enclosed in hearts, invitations to engage in a variety of improbable sexual acts, mostly unsought and mostly unsound advice, quotations, insults, non sequiturs, trivia, esoterica, outright arcana, and verse in various forms and of debatable merit. "The neighbor's sea scorpions are in the rosebushes again," begins one poem. "There was a young lady from Dallas," begins another. Perhaps

[1] Poz (pseud.), *The Positronic Express* (India Ink).
[2] *Ibid.*
[3] *Ibid.*
[4] V. Thorp, *A Life Among the Rocks* (Endocarp).
[5] B. King, *Earth to Earth* (University of Tennessee).

inevitably, the enormous body of verse has inspired an attendant body of literary criticism, itself ranging in form and quality from the brief and facile "If it doesn't rhyme/ don't waste my time" to a brambly critique of the works of 17th-century English poets John Donne, Richard Crashaw, George Herbert, and Abraham Cowley.[6]

An entire face of the slab is given over to a mass of graffiti consolidated under a heading painstakingly engraved by an unknown daredevil across the upper edge:

QUANTUM METAPHYSICS 101

A 21st-century humorist who had undertaken the "obligatory pilgrimage"[7] to the rock, noted in his own, farcical expedition memoir that the chief topic of the forum, if it may be said to possess such, was the interface of science and art or science and faith or science and something else. What you made of it depended on what you thought you knew about what other people had thought they knew and still other people had thought of what those first people thought. It was mathematics and metaphysics, morphology in both the biological and linguistic meanings of the word, metopes and modern art, Mozart and mo-pop, Mohammed and his mountain, Mann and *his* mountain, the "many-worlds" hypothesis (with monoversalists, multiversalists, and mimetoversalists biting at one another like cats, dogs, and fairly undiscriminating fleas), and ever so much more, all mashed into mush. If you looked away for an instant, if you so much as blinked, you lost your place and never could find it again.[8]

He discovers that disagreement over basic terms has prompted a graffitist to append "Essential and Other Pertinent Definitions," in the interest of promoting agreement on what we are talking *about*. Let us all concur that *quantum theory* "holds that energy is not

---

[6] K. Colt, ed., *Paleozolnk* (Necessary Impurity). Perhaps no less inevitably, several collections of this verse have been published, including *PaleoPens*, *PaleoPoets*, and the aforesaid *Paleozolnk*, all edited by Colt, as well as a selection of the criticism, *PaleoPoisonPens*, edited by D. Stepp and also published under the aegis of Necessary Impurity.

[7] L. D. Yerly, *My Silurian Sleep-Over* (Orcas Island Publishing), the basis of the interminably running *Paleozoic Pajama Party!*

[8] *Ibid.*

absorbed or radiated continuously but discontinuously, in definite units called *quanta*," while *metaphysics*, as used hereinafter, is intended to mean "the branch of philosophy that deals with first principles and seeks to explicate the nature of being or reality [here the viewer is advised by footnote to *see ontology*, further down the rock] and of the origin and structure of the world [*see cosmology*] and is closely associated with a theory of knowledge" [*see epistemology*].[9]

Although, remarkably (indeed, almost uniquely), the text enclosed within its rectangular border remains inviolate (save for the insertion of several competing systems of footnote symbols), vehement dispute over the offered definitions provokes extensive annotation.

I was inspired to admiration of the rock by my discovery upon it of an example of a literary form that surely dates back to Sumer and for all scientists can tell us even to the Paleolithic. Anyone who has ever entered a public restroom will recognize it. This example commenced, "S.Y.S. loves E. remipes" (S.Y.S. presumably being a paleontologist, E. remipes being an evidently popular species of sea scorpion), and proceeded as follows:

Better E. remipes than E. coli.

You know where you can put your E. coli!

Hey, watch it—my dog's a border coli!

It's pronounced kohl-i, not cah-lee.

Drink Coca-Coli.

I also have a pet vegetable from the coli family. Can you guess what it is?

Broccoli.

Coliflower?

May Coli smite you all, jaw and thighbone, ass and elbow.

If you ask me this whole discussion is pretty melancholi.

And did we ask you?

Well! I decided that if this was indicative of the material still awaiting my perusal, I could have it read in twenty minutes or half an hour at most. I confidently launched a frontal assault on that bastion of bewilderment titled "Quantum Metempsychosis" [*sic*] and promptly had to skirt an impenetrable line of fortifications comprising quotations from works of metaphysics (some of them in the original German, and at least a few of the shorter ones

[9] *Ibid.*

lettered in Gothic script, rendering them all the more impervious to understanding) only to find myself under a barrage of denigrations of abstract reasoning and the small-arms fire of dissertations on the relative incidences of "solitary vice" and general depravity among philosophers, paleontologists, and physicists. I came to a dead stop in a concertina-wire-like tangle of mathematical formulae, through which I could glimpse a patch of text on the far side, though I could make out only the terms "atemporality" and "aspatiality," the lines,

> Here I sit, broken-hearted,
> Tried to quit
> But can't get started,

and the desperate scrawl, "Help! I'm having a simultaneity breakdown!" Without understanding for an instant what that person was talking about, I believe I know exactly how he or she must have felt.[10]

Permitted, or compelled, to read only more or less at random, other visitors also mention the impossibility of syncretism, one going so far as to describe the graffiti as quaquaversal, a term in geology meaning "directed from a common center toward all points of the compass or turning and dipping in all directions."[11] Another observes that "these ostensibly serious exchanges inevitably degenerate into puerile nonsense," and reproduces as an example the following exchange:

Sirrah, you are a sorry sack of solipsism and a sciolistic one at that.

I micturate mightily on your meandering, monotonous, meaningless, and maximally moronic musings on mathematics.

Oh yeah?!

Yeah! Wanna make something of it?

Fight! FIGHT! ooops, I mean—sciamachy! sciamachy!

"To which," he says, "I confess I was sorely tempted to add *Quantum sufficit!* 'Enough already!'"[12] His collaborator springs to the defense:

---

[10] *Ibid.*
[11] Thorp.
[12] S. Nichols and O. Peabody, *Paleo Boys at Large* (Carlo).

The graffiti are not puerile. They are at least sophomoric, and I am coming around to the view that they do serve a useful function—provide the expedition's anarchists and jokers with an outlet for anti-social and anti-authoritarian sentiment, and so keep them from bloodily overthrowing local Officialdom. Therefore, I can only say to my esteemed colleague, whose pomposity, humorlessness, and priggishness fit him ideally for membership in Officialdom, *Fac ut vivas!* "Get a life!"[13]

The graffiti have not lacked for either champions or detractors among expedition members, and, perhaps contrary to expectation, opinion is not divided strictly along the demarcation between its civilian and military members. A Navy officer describes a rather touching incident which, unknown to him at the time, was to have an unpleasant denouement:

At midday, prickly heat engulfed the camp like amber, and people turned from the work or recreation that had occupied them throughout the morning and became, according to their natures, passive, lethargic, dormant, or perfectly inert. I was a newcomer, however, and this was my first time ashore, and I wanted to see everything. I put a pith helmet on my head, salt tablets in my pocket, and a canteen on my belt, and struck out into blinding sunlight and palpable humidity to seek such adventure as the Silurian age could provide. I did not feel like climbing the ridge in that heat, however. I had overheard someone on the ship say that there was "interesting stuff" to see among the rocks strewn along its base, so I decided to investigate.
　... The going was tricky, but it was shady in there, and cool. . . . As I penetrated deeper, however, the air grew still; if I had been perspiring freely before, now I was awash inside my slimy clothes. Then I stepped through a cleft and came unexpectedly upon a woman standing beside a graffiti-plastered slab of rock. She faced me but didn't see me because at that moment she had the front of her shirt pulled up so she could wipe sweat from her face, thereby affording

[13] *Ibid.*

me an excellent view of her bare bosom. I almost dislocated a number of joints trying to get myself turned around within the cleft's confines. I stuck fast for the moment and could only shut my eyes and stammer an apology.

"It's okay," I heard her say, "you can look now, I'm decent."

I risked a look and saw her regarding me with an expression of annoyance. I felt like one big hot blush, and that seemed to amuse her, for she abruptly cocked her hip and planted a fist on it, gave me an exaggerated wink, and said, "Hell-o, sailor!"

Then *she* suddenly blushed, and I realized after a moment that she had just then recognized my insignia. "Whoops," she said, "sorry, I didn't realize," and now I finally found my voice and told her no, *I* was sorry, *I* hadn't realized, and we went on like that for perhaps half a minute. She laughed nervously and said, "Can we please just start over? Pretend we just this instant laid eyes on each other for the first time? That I never disconcerted you by blatantly calling attention to my womanly charms?"

"I'm not disconcerted by womanly charms," I said, and immediately thought, That must be the most inane sentence to come out of my mouth in my adult life. I tried to recoup by adding, "You'd be surprised by what a Navy chaplain hears."

She laughed again. "Probably not as much as you'd be surprised by what an old gal knows."[14]

Apparently in consequence of this flustered beginning, the two dispense with further attempts at introduction.

I asked about the graffiti, and after a moment's hesitation, she led me on a brisk circuit of the slab. "Every other rock in Paleozoic time," she said, "is regarded as the scientific equivalent of a holy relic, untouchable by the uninitiated. But this one's been singled out for a different use—a profane use, if you will, but vital nevertheless. Here's where

---

[14] G. Madiel, *Infinite Worlds, Eternal God: A Navy Chaplain's Exploits Elsewhere* (U.S. Naval Academy).

expedition members come to satisfy the hardwired human need to make marks on things." Much of what I saw was the usual, by turns blasphemous, merely outrageous, or simply cretinous, but here and there was something clever, such as the protracted dialog between Maxwell's demon and Schrödinger's cat ("MD: You okay in there? SC: You go to hell!"[15]). I hadn't seen the word "consubstantial" in a graffito since divinity school. I would have stayed longer, but I became increasingly aware that she meant only to satisfy my curiosity and send me on my way as quickly as possible, so I thanked her and returned through the maze to camp.[16]

The following morning, the commander of the expedition's Navy contingent ordered a work party to the rock. That much is indisputable; accounts of what precipitated the order, what the order was, and what came of it do not simply vary but diverge to the point of flatly contradicting one another. The chaplain ever after denied that he had reported the existence of the graffiti ("clearly it was an open secret"[17]), admitting only that he had mentioned it in passing to fellow officers. He also claimed that Dr. Maven had somehow never got around to explaining that she was studying the graffiti ("She just said she'd been taking pictures of it"[18]), and that he had had no intention of making trouble for her or anyone else. A historian who accepts this, or at least does not reject it, writes:

> The definition of vandalism includes graffiti, so the commander was simply enforcing regulations—*or* (already our path forks!) perhaps he was acting out of personal pique, having taken umbrage at either a vicious caricature of himself rumored to adorn the rock, *or* ribald verse directed at a civilian expedition member with whom he was known

---

[15] J. Friel, however, in his *Pastimes and Past Tenses* (Matthewave), reports the demon's half of the dialog as, "Whatcha doing in the box, kitty?" while Kalen Gilligan, in *Meanwhile, Back in the Past* (DeForgeo), gives the cat's reply as, "Wouldn't you like to know!" and Yerly, as, "That's for me to know and you to find out!"

[16] Madiel.

[17] *Ibid.*

[18] Record of Proceedings. See footnote 21, below.

to be, *or* perhaps only rumored to have been, romantically involved, at some time, on some plane of being. *Or* not.[19]

In one instance, the offensive verse is given as

I have the hots for Professor Heather,
Whom I'd like to dress in leather
And tickle, with a peacock feather.

In a "sub-instance" of this development, the Navy commander denounces the "despicable doggerel" and acts the part of a protective lover; in a second sub-instance, he denies any romantic attachment with the Professor Heather in question but feels it incumbent upon himself to act on her behalf. But (ah ha!) the commander may just as well have been acting on the pique of one of his junior officers, who took umbrage at ribaldry directed at herself:

The jay-gee is a sonsy wench;
I'd lay her on a bunk or bench.
If she liked, I'd even spank her,
But I'm an enlisted wanker.

The work party hasn't even received its assignment, already we have half a dozen different versions of things, and we're still well shy of the commander's ultimately being dissuaded from having the rock (A) cleaned off, (B) pulverized, or (C) simply declared off limits to (1) all expedition personnel or (2) Navy personnel only. To complicate matters further, no one is really sure just *how* he was dissuaded and *by whom*.[20]

In the event, one person, at least, was sure that she knew how and by whom— or, more precisely, if the imperfections of the Record of Proceedings[21] can be said to allow for precision,

---

[19] King.

[20] *Ibid.*

[21] Unfortunately, the medium used for the Record of Proceedings (and much else of expedition members' quotidian experience) was the unstable JGoldman10™, eventually replaced by MemoryMat™. "Worse," King notes, "Madeleine™, Mnemosyne™, and similar 'enhancers' had not then lived

that she could certainly find out. (It is difficult to explain this record's having been overlooked by King, whose reputation for meticulous research must now be reconsidered.) According to the Proceedings, the work party was met at the site and deflected from its assignment by a female civilian named Maven who claimed the graffiti as the subject of her sociological research. By now, no one should be surprised to learn that conflicting accounts ensue. The petty officer in charge of the work party later admitted in proceedings that he had skeptically demanded to know what a sociologist might be doing in Paleozoic time, and claimed that the civilian had lost her temper and sharply informed him that she had work to do, that the interview was concluded, and that the Navy should mind "its own goddamn business, whatever the hell that might be."[22] She maintained in proceedings that while she may

down their association with the infamous Psychepick™ and regained the confidence of historians. Thus, any account of events that occurred (perhaps it is safer to write 'may have occurred') in the expedition's first decades must necessarily be an assemblage of bits gleaned from a single unreliable artificial source and even less reliable, and too often self-serving, human remembrance. Contradictions accrete to this day, long after most of the principals have passed on. . . . The seeker of truth must exercise due caution when turning to the recollections of former expedition members, many of them demonstrably untrustworthy (especially those who have passed on!). Glaring discrepancies exasperate even the most dedicated researchers and tempt them to give credence to the theories of a 21st-century physicist whose now-fading fame rested upon his intimate connection with The Spacetime Anomaly—as he preferred to call it in his alleged autobiography, a work that bears so little resemblance to contemporary accounts of his career that it might almost have been written (possibly ghostwritten) in one of the alternate universes which he so promiscuously postulated."

[22] Proceedings. "If she did say it," former Navy commander B. Greene writes in his *Eulogy for an Expedition* (U.S. Naval Academy), "it was gratuitous and unfair. All Navy personnel understood that scientific research was the expedition's *raison d'être*, that they were there purely in a support capacity. For their part, all civilians were supposed to understand that we were there to make their jobs easier." Reklen, in his *Rock of Eternity* (GA GL), expressed "no doubt that she was bipolar." This was unlikely, though not as unlikely as M. Raap makes out in *The Soul of the Silurian* (Darcy). "Bipolar people are generally diagnosed when they are still fairly young, and this was a woman in her late forties. Even if she had, somehow, not been previously diagnosed, she could not possibly have got past screening. You don't just show up at the jump station and say, 'Hello there, I'm a scientist, please send me to the Silurian Period.'" That she could not "possibly" have got past screening is arguable, given certain other individuals who did get past it. Raap suggests that she suffered an episode of something like stress-induced psychosis after

have indeed been curt with the petty officer,[23] she had answered his "impertinent" question comprehensively and concisely: "I'm doing what sociologists do anywhere there are humans living together in social groups."[24]

In her published memoir of the expedition, however, she amplified this answer to make it more comprehensive, albeit less concise, presumably in the way of dramatizing exposition to make it more palatable to a popular audience whose attention was not altogether biddable.[25] Now she goes on at length:

> "I'm doing what sociologists do anywhere there is human society, people living together in groups. The grist for my particular mill is here, *now*, where we have a relative handful of people isolated from the rest of their species—isolated by four hundred million years, according to one theory, isolated in a whole other universe, according to another. . . . "

When the petty officer shrugs this off (as well he might) and demands to know why his superior officer did not know the site was under her protection, she informs him, "I try to keep a low profile here," explaining,

> " . . . Back home, I can do oral-history interviews of former expedition members by the dozen and in broad daylight, but here I'm trying to minimize my presence because I don't want to make people self-conscious about what they write on the rock. I come here during the heat of the day or a

she passed through the anomaly and joined the expedition.

[23] "I was naturally alarmed by the sudden and unexpected arrival of sailors equipped with everything they needed, scrubbers, solvents, and orders, to wreck my project." Proceedings.

[24] S. Kate Maven, *The Community of the Rock: My Silurian Sojourn* (Carlo).

[25] Maven's *Community*, as Reklen notes in his vindictive *Rock of Eternity*, is an "aggressively self-dramatizing" work, though he lets his hatred of its author blind him to the fact that it is by no means the worst of its kind. That dubious distinction surely belongs to K. Barnet's *Silurian Tales* (Putnam Holt Rinehart Winston Harcourt Brace and Jovanovich or Their Heirs and Assigns), which concentrates (or tries to, through a fog of alcoholic self-pity) on sexual escapades and drinking bouts. His decline even from this abysmal level can be traced through the sequels he produced, *Devonian Dreams*, *Carboniferous Capers*, and *Jurassic Trailer Park Sluts* (also from Putnam et al).

little after sunrise or a little before sundown, take rubbings, photographs, do a complete three-sixty whenever it seems warranted, then clear out."[26]

Whatever really passed between protagonist and antagonist (her memoir leaves no room for doubt as to who is whom), the petty officer reported the incident to his superiors. A routine name check next failed to find Dr. Maven, which meant that her credentials could not be examined.[27] There was, of course, no question of her being in Paleozoic time under false pretenses. A jump-station technician volunteered the information that she had come through unaccompanied and carrying only a backpack. She had signed the register for use of the camp's communal facilities, but so little had been seen of her since then that no one could quite recall her or had a clear notion of what she might by doing in their midst. By the time her personal data were recovered, she and Reklen, the civilian liaison, had already fought the first skirmish in what was to unfold as a lifelong exchange of libel and slander, culminating in a lawsuit and a suicide. It began when he ("peremptorily"[28]) summoned her to account for herself, and received the reply that she was busy and he should go fuck himself. This, probably as much and possibly more than anything else, precipitated the formal inquiry to which in later years she referred as both a court-martial and a provost court. The terms are neither quite interchangeable in military usage nor applicable to what was really a most informal sort of formal inquiry— stressing "formal" as the operative word, as in "strictly for form's sake." "A half-dozen of us, evenly divided between Navy and civilians, sat in a sweltering Quonset hut and asked her and the p.o. a few questions. I had no beef with her, *unlike one of the civilians who instigated the whole thing*" [emphasis added].[29]

In the extant record, on being asked how long she thought the alleged vandalism had been going on, she answers, "Almost from

---

[26] In an letter found among the Reklen papers and dated years after former Petty Officer Eustt's retirement from the Navy, he insists that "all the bitch said to me was 'Shove off, sailor!'"

[27] It had not yet been realized that, despite usual safeguards, the humid, septic Paleozoic environment was inimical to JGoldman10™. ("JG10 had the attention span of a mayfly and the shelf life of a banana." Poz.)

[28] Maven.

[29] Greene. Undoubtedly he refers to Reklen.

the first!" and names several well-known scientists, previously in Paleozoic time, whose initials she claims to have found carved or written on the rock. "Most of the inscriptions are anonymous or at least pseudonymous—signed things like 'Old Dude' and 'Spangles' and so forth. Beyond doubt Navy personnel have contributed their share, just more discreetly than the civilians." This elicits expressions of doubt and denial from the Navy officers, though apparently not from the petty officer or other ratings that are or may be present (the record is unclear), and a stern reminder from the civilian liaison that, "As visitors to this pristine primeval world, we should not go around defiling it, trashing it, or marking it up."

"The absence of trash," she replies, "and the presence of art tell me that people respect the place very much."[30]

This prompts a rejoinder from the civilian liaison, that "to dignify graffiti by subjecting it to allegedly scientific scrutiny misrepresents scribblings and doodlings whose predominant characteristics are inanity, irreverence, and obscenity. Have human beings really come all this way, across hundreds of millions of years, just to snigger over smut?"[31]

A gap in the record occurs at this juncture. When the record resumes, visual exhibits have been brought forward, consisting of photographs of the limestone slab, taken from all sides at regular intervals. Careful examination of sequences of images reveals not only material of a pornographic or otherwise questionable nature, but also that all such graphic depictions of coitus and drawings of human genitalia, whether crudely or expertly executed, are soon effaced or, more frequently, revised into fabulous Paleozoic fauna or flora, e.g., "Trilobite me" and "Cocksonia." Scatological references and the like tend ("puckishly"[32]) to mutate into faux taxonomical terms. Even the English language's most familiar expression of insolent ill regard proves vulnerable to this sort of revision. The latter of a particular pair of "before and after" images reveals a cartoon of a beStetsoned gun-toting sea scorpion appended to an inscription amended to read "Fuckeurypterid andthehorseurydon"; another inscription has attracted the rejoinder, "You idiot, it's F-U-

[30] "She was as cool as Joan of Arc answering her inquisitors at Rouen." *Ibid.* In Proceedings, Reklen opines that she has "transposed the words *art* and *trash*."
[31] Proceedings.
[32] Maven, *Community*.

C-U-S," which segues directly into a brief technical description of an actual seaweed genus of that name.

The Navy commander then asks, "Does it not seem from this that even some of the graffitists are offended by pornographic material? That someone has appointed themselves [sic] censor?" and receives the answer, "Emendation isn't restricted to the pornography. Anything you inscribe on the rock is fair game for the next person who comes along." She declares in conclusion that "the human need for self-expression is part of our baggage wherever we go— in this case, *when*ever—and it always finds an outlet. *Voilà*. The rock, the outlet." The Navy commander, by now patently weary of the whole matter, says, "So be it," and summarily adjourns the proceedings over the civilian liaison's protests.[33]

In Maven's memoir, her succinct summation swells into a full-blown lecture:

> ... The rock is vital—indispensable—to the expedition's collective mental health in another way, too. It's a safety valve. It's not merely the major means, it's virtually the *only* means of genuine communication in your small, isolated, diverse, and segregated community.[34] When not actually required to interact—as now, for example—civilians and military personnel pretty much keep to themselves. When they do interact, they frequently confound one another. As now. Moreover, civilians and Navy personnel not only keep to themselves but to their hierarchical subgroups as well. These are defined by specialization or rank. Officers do not fraternize with ratings, of course. But, if they can help it, neither do field geologists and so-called black-box geologists fraternize. The astronomers and physicists look down—there is no other term to describe their attitude—look down on the geologists, who for their part emphatically do not look up to the astronomers and physicists. And everyone asks, as snidely as possible, what the hell a sociologist is doing here.[35]

---

[33] Proceedings.

[34] Note the use of the adjective "your," rather than "our." Maven pointedly ignores the existence of the official expedition newsource, inevitably christened *The Paleozoic Times*.

[35] Maven, *A Time Traveler's Tale of a Tempestuous, Truncated Trip* ("*T6*," original, unpublished version of *The Community of the Rock*), item

This final sentence was excised prior to the memoir's publication and appears only in the posthumously discovered version. But at last we seem to have arrived at the crux of the matter! Anger and paranoia roil just beneath the surface of the published version; they break through repeatedly in the original:

> The prospect of going in alone didn't daunt me. I liked working alone; the only times I ever engaged graduate students or other assistants was when there was a lot of pure donkey-work to be done.[36] I would have the use of communal facilities. I knew I would do excellent and valuable work if I could just scrape together the price of a damn time-machine ticket! In writing this memoir, I find I still am not quite capable of relating, in anything like an even-tempered (let alone even-handed) fashion, what I put up with, what I went through, to gain access to that strange other world. My grant requests elicited actual guffaws in certain quarters: "Sociology in the Silurian, bwah-hah!" "The Silurian Period is no place for the soft sciences, hee-yuk!" All these years later, those jackass brays of hilarity echo in my head.[37]

Her memoir's coda is laced with bitterness but concludes on what must be described as a strangely subdued note:

> The inquiry wrecked my project as completely as though I had just let the swabbies at the rock in the first place. I'd come to record and study and analyze, as unobtrusively as possible, remaining aloof from the mystagogic community of the rock while also respecting its unwritten, unspoken, yet unmistakable rules. How these had been formulated and disseminated, I could have discovered only by breaking the one against spying. I had to accept that the protocols existed. You did not litter the space enclosing the rock with empty beer cans, broken glass, cigarette butts, and used condoms. You could disagree and even revise or erase someone else's

SRCA1941 in DCMB collection.

[36] "The reason she worked alone because nobody could stand to work with her. She had no friends in her department and an unsavory reputation in her field." Reklen, *Rock of Eternity*.

[37] Maven, *T6*.

work, but you could not violate anyone's anonymity or cause it to be violated; you couldn't spy on people.

And it all went right down the toilet the instant the rock became a tourist attraction and I became a celebrity. After that, I couldn't go into the labyrinth and come out again without tripping over half a dozen idiots who wanted to gab and gawk and have their pictures taken at the rock. Within the week, I packed up and shipped out, leaving work undone, puzzles unsolved, mysteries unfathomed, secrets unlearned. I also left my own inscription on the rock.

. . . I am in no way ashamed of what I did manage to accomplish, which was the best work I could do under the circumstances; I only wish I had been permitted to carry through to the end. I told myself that when I got home, perhaps I would look around for another isolated—but less isolated—social group, perhaps at a research station in Antarctica, perhaps on a mission to Mars.[38]

She does not reveal what she inscribed, or even how she inscribed it, and it probably did not survive long, given the plastic nature of graffiti. This leaves the door opened wide for speculation. Her avowed enemy wastes few words: "Knowing her, it was probably 'Up yours!'"[39] One author[40] suggests, solely on the strength of its being written in pencil on the last page of her field notebook, a quotation from a work of fiction entitled "Lik", by Vladimir Nabokov (1899–1977): "Loneliness as a situation can be corrected, but as a state of mind it is an incurable illness." A more recent biography[41] makes a somewhat stronger case for an inscription visible in what seems to be her final image of the rock, a line which occurs again in *Community of the Rock*: "Sometimes what people don't say tells us more than what they do say." But as with so much else, we probably will never know.

---

[38] *Ibid.*
[39] Reklen.
[40] Colt, *PaleozoInk*.
[41] Raap.

ABOUT THE AUTHOR

Steven Utley is an internationally unknown short-story writer and minor Minor Poet. He resides in a small town in Tennessee, where the neighbors know him as "The Strange Old Man Who Lives at the End of the Block with Too Many Cats." In some alternate universe, he is rich and famous, but probably still has too many cats.

COVER

Nearly two billion years ago, volcanic activity was widespread, but the surface of the earth had cooled enough so that oceans could form. In this scene, life has not yet begun.

© The Field Museum #CK23T

Charles R. Knight (1874–1953) is internationally recognized as the preeminent artist of both prehistoric animals and contemporary wildlife, through his paintings, drawings and sculpture. Annually, millions of people are exposed to Knight's work in major museums and institutional collections.

EDITORS' NOTE

Steven Utley lost his short battle with cancer on 12 January 2013. He had approved the text of this volume and its predecessor, *The 400-Million-Year Itch*. Sadly he only ever saw the paperback edition of *The 400-Million-Year Itch*, but we hope he would have liked this volume, too.

—*Russell B. Farr & Liz Grzyb*

ACKNOWLEDGEMENTS

Copyright © 1996, 2000, 2001, 2002, 2003, 2004, 2005, 2006, 2008, 2013 by Steven Utley

"'Another Continuum Heard From!'" appeared online in *Revolution Science Fiction*.

"Babel" appeared in *Analog Science Fiction and Fact*.

"The Despoblado," "Five Miles From Pavement," and "The Real World" appeared online in *Sci Fiction*.

"Diluvium," "Invisible Kingdoms," "A Paleozoic Palimpsest," and "Silv'ry Moon" appeared in *The Magazine of Fantasy and Science Fiction*.

"Sidestep" is previously unpublished.

"Slug Hell," "There and Then," "Treading the Maze," "The Wave-Function Collapse," "The World Within the World," and "The World Without" appeared in *Asimov's Science Fiction*.

"Variant" appeared in *Postscripts*.

AVAILABLE FROM TICONDEROGA PUBLICATIONS

TICONDEROGA PUBLICATIONS LIMITED HARDCOVER EDITIONS

978-0-9586856-9-6	Love in Vain by Lewis Shiner
978-0-9803531-1-2	Belong ed Russell B. Farr
978-0-9803531-9-8	Basic Black by Terry Dowling
978-0-9806288-0-7	Make Believe by Terry Dowling
978-0-9806288-1-4	The Infernal by Kim Wilkins
978-0-9806288-5-2	Dead Sea Fruit by Kaaron Warren
978-0-9806288-7-6	The Girl With No Hands by Angela Slatter
978-0-9807813-0-4	Dead Red Heart ed Russell B. Farr
978-0-9807813-3-5	Heliotrope by Justina Robson
978-0-9807813-6-6	Matilda Told Such Dreadful Lies by Lucy Sussex
978-1-921857-00-3	Bluegrass Symphony by Lisa L. Hannett
978-1-921857-07-2	Bread and Circuses by Felicity Dowker
978-1-921857-16-4	The 400-Million-Year Itch by Steven Utley
978-1-921857-23-2	Wild Chrome by Greg Mellor
978-1-921857-27-0	Midnight and Moonshine by Lisa L. Hannett & Angela Slatter
978-1-921857-37-9	Prickle Moon by Juliet Marillier

TICONDEROGA PUBLICATIONS EBOOKS

978-0-9803531-5-0	Ghost Seas by Steven Utley
978-1-921857-93-5	The Girl With No Hands by Angela Slatter
978-1-921857-99-7	Dead Red Heart ed Russell B. Farr
978-1-921857-94-2	More Scary Kisses ed Liz Grzyb
978-0-9807813-5-9	Heliotrope by Justina Robson
978-1-921857-98-0	Year's Best Australian F&H eds Grzyb & Helene
978-1-921857-97-3	Bluegrass Symphony by Lisa L. Hannett

THE YEAR'S BEST AUSTRALIAN FANTASY & HORROR SERIES EDITED BY LIZ GRZYB & TALIE HELENE

978-0-9807813-8-0	Year's Best Australian Fantasy & Horror 2010 (hc)
978-0-9807813-9-7	Year's Best Australian Fantasy & Horror 2010 (tpb)
978-0-921057-13-3	Year's Best Australian Fantasy & Horror 2011 (hc)
978-0-921057-14-0	Year's Best Australian Fantasy & Horror 2011 (tpb)

WWW.TICONDEROGAPUBLICATIONS.COM

THANK YOU

The publisher would sincerely like to thank:

Elizabeth Grzyb, Steven Utley, Gardner Dozois, Barry N. Malzberg, Cat Sparks, Sean Williams, Kim Wilkins, Kate Forsyth, Jonathan Strahan, Peter McNamara, Ellen Datlow, Grant Stone, Jeremy G. Byrne, Garth Nix, David Cake, Simon Oxwell, Grant Watson, Sue Manning, Steven Utley, Bill Congreve, Jack Dann, Jenny Blackford, Simon Brown, Stephen Dedman, Sara Douglass, Felicity Dowker, Terry Dowling, Jason Fischer, Lisa L. Hannett, Pete Kempshall, Ian McHugh, Angela Rega, Angela Slatter, Lucy Sussex, Kaaron Warren, the Mt Lawley Mafia, the Nedlands Yakuza, Amanda Pillar, Shane Jiraiya Cummings, Angela Challis, Talie Helene, Donna Maree Hanson, Kate Williams, Kathryn Linge, Andrew Williams, Al Chan, Alisa and Tehani, Mel & Phil, Brian Clarke, Jennifer Sudbury, Paul Przytula, Kelly Parker, Hayley Lane, Georgina Walpole, everyone we've missed . . .
. . . and you.

IN MEMORY OF
Eve Johnson (1945–2011)
Sara Douglass (1957–2011)
Steven Utley (1948–2013)

www.ingramcontent.com/pod-product-compliance
Lightning Source LLC
Chambersburg PA
CBHW030236200626
46816CB00002BA/388